Witch You Would

A Novel

LIA AMADOR

AVON

An Imprint of HarperCollinsPublishers

Without limiting the exclusive rights of any author, contributor or the publisher of this publication, any unauthorized use of this publication to train generative artificial intelligence (AI) technologies is expressly prohibited. HarperCollins also exercise their rights under Article 4(3) of the Digital Single Market Directive 2019/790 and expressly reserve this publication from the text and data mining exception.

This is a work of fiction. Names, characters, places, and incidents are products of the author's imagination or are used fictitiously and are not to be construed as real. Any resemblance to actual events, locales, organizations, or persons, living or dead, is entirely coincidental.

WITCH YOU WOULD. Copyright © 2025 by Valerie Valdes. All rights reserved. Printed in the United States of America. No part of this book may be used or reproduced in any manner whatsoever without written permission except in the case of brief quotations embodied in critical articles and reviews. For information, address HarperCollins Publishers, 195 Broadway, New York, NY 10007. In Europe, HarperCollins Publishers, Macken House, 39/40 Mayor Street Upper, Dublin 1, D01 C9W8, Ireland.

HarperCollins books may be purchased for educational, business, or sales promotional use. For information, please email the Special Markets Department at SPsales@harpercollins.com.

hc.com

Avon, Avon & logo, and Avon Books & logo are registered trademarks of HarperCollins Publishers in the United States of America and other countries.

FIRST EDITION

Designed by Diahann Sturge-Campbell

Bubbling cauldron © Quarta/Stock.Adobe.com
Movie clapperboard © Taalvi/Stock.Adobe.com

Library of Congress Cataloging-in-Publication Data has been applied for.

ISBN 978-0-06-337754-7

25 26 27 28 29 LBC 5 4 3 2 1

Witch You Would

*For Jay, who is miraculous, simply the best
and
For Eric, pineapple*

CHAPTER 1

Penelope

The customer's blue ombré hair spell sparked like fireworks as he leaned across the counter, ranting about how I was the worst spell caster in Miami. I hid my nerves behind my best helpful-employee smile.

"Get your manager," he snapped. Literally, he snapped his fingers at me.

"I'm the only one here, sir." Just me and my pepper spray.

Espinosa's Spell Supplies was so small, I didn't have much room to move if he got violent. I'd have to run through a maze of shelves, knocking over bottles and tins and prayer candles, then dramatically throw myself through a floor-to-ceiling glass window to get outside, because the door opened inward. Bleeding to death on the sidewalk of a strip mall would suck. I could duck out the back door, through the workshop and storage room, but if I survived and anything was missing or messed up, my boss would kill me herself.

I needed to stop catastrophizing. It was super unhealthy.

"I have a very important interview! I can't go there with hair like this!"

I'd been having important interviews for months, and I'd somehow managed not to yell at random retail workers.

"Fix this! Now!" He banged on the counter. I almost pepper-sprayed my butt.

I could do what he asked, or I could tell him to leave. My brain threw together a montage of bad store reviews on Evoke, a lecture from my boss, my student loan payments, and the three-digit balance in my checking account.

"Do you have the spell recipe with you?" I asked. If I sounded more cheerful, I'd attract woodland creatures to help me clean and find a horny single prince.

He threw the instructions on the counter, clearly printed from a blog because they were covered in ads for weight-loss potions and "one weird tricks." Big sigh. Magic was like cooking: anyone could do it, and anyone could make up recipes, but that didn't mean you should trust random crap you found on the internet.

As soon as I saw one reagent on the list, I was pretty sure I knew what happened.

"Did you use a broken duskywing butterfly wing?" I asked.

His eyes narrowed. I bet myself a coffee he'd lie about it.

"No."

Mmm, coffee.

"They fall apart pretty easily, and the spell wouldn't work if it was broken," I said.

"Maybe you sold me a broken one."

Nice try. "We don't sell them, but if you recast the spell correctly—"

"I want this removed now!" A shower of sparks exploded from his hair.

I went over the recipe again. The infusion method used an essential oil, so soap should work for a counterspell, with lemon to balance the butterfly wing . . . no, orange blossom honey would have fewer side effects and better binding. I put the pepper spray in my back pocket and grabbed my notebook, sketching out a plan.

The customer grumbled. Checked his phone. Checked his fake designer watch. Checked his phone again.

"I think I have a solution," I said finally. "Our normal casting rate is twenty-five dollars an hour plus ingredients, but—"

"You expect me to pay to fix what you did to me?" he shouted.

Polite smile: slipping. "You cast the spell yourself, sir."

"Are you saying I can't cast a simple hair glamour? I've been doing this for longer than you've been alive! What are you, eighteen?"

I was twenty-six, and I'd started casting with my abuela Perla—my mom's mom—when I was old enough to stir a pot.

"You sold me the wrong ingredients!"

Not a chance. I always triple-checked everything. "Sir, I can do the casting for free, but I have to charge for reagents unless you bring your own. I—"

The door to the back opened behind me. I jumped sideways and tripped over a box of quartz crystals, landing hard on the non-pepper-spray pocket.

My boss, Ofelia Espinosa, loomed over me like a telenovela villain. Her bottle-blond hair and pore-free skin gleamed with glamour, and her navy wrap dress had a neckline so plunging, I would see her soul if she bent over.

"Is there a problem?" she asked, smiling at the customer.

"Yes!" he exclaimed. "Your assistant ruined my hair."

My official title was "spell technician."

"She's more of a salesgirl." Ofelia propped her boobs on her crossed arms, giving the guy a show. He bought front-row seats. "Why don't you tell me the whole story? Penny, take a break."

Whatever. I stood up, squeezed past her and headed for the front door.

Sunlight reflected off parked car windshields as I stomped down to the Castillo de las Frutas, an oasis of blaring salsa music and whirring blenders. The tables in front of the combination restaurant, juice bar, and café were always full. Old men played dominoes and complained about politics, people in suits cooled down with batidos, and delivery drivers loaded orders into spelled hot-cold bags. Pigeons puttered around, which meant the owl statue wards in the overhang needed to be replaced. The smells of fresh coffee and fried things reminded me that I'd forgotten to eat lunch. Again.

Life always seemed to happen around me, not to me.

Rosy waved through the counter window while she pushed and pulled and twisted things on the giant espresso machine. I didn't know how she kept her orange uniform shirt from getting stained— she swore no magic was involved. Her dark curls and skin weren't greasy or sweaty, either, while I needed a paper towel wipe-down in the store bathroom.

I banged my forehead on the ventana's counter. "Why am I such an asshole magnet?"

Rosy poured Cuban coffee into a foam cup, perfect espuma on top. "What do you mean? You haven't been on a date in six months."

Eight. "This comemierda says I messed up his reagent blend. His hair looks like New Year's Eve fireworks. Stop laughing!"

She did not stop. "Come on, that's hilarious." Rosy made an explosion noise. "It's like a Leandro Presto video."

I rolled my eyes. "That guy."

"Come on, he's funny."

Leandro Presto was funny like someone faceplanting into a cake. He recorded himself casting spells that always went wrong, then posted them on Jinxd for his billion followers . . . and Rosy was pulling out her phone to show me a new one.

"Is that Dolphin Mall?" I asked.

"Totally," Rosy said. "I can't believe they let him."

Me neither. Mall security rolled around on stand-up scooters, harassing you for breathing.

Leandro looked our age, with slicked-back dark hair, black-rimmed safety glasses, and a waxed mustache with curled ends. The nicest thing I could say about him was he explained what went wrong—after it happened. And he was kind of hot, aside from the mustache.

"That's way too much lady's mantle."

"Shh, don't ruin it," Rosy said.

He dropped a pinch of powdered carnelian into his cauldron, then dramatically threw his arms open and yelled, "Presto!" Nothing happened. He tilted his head like a confused puppy and peeked into the pot.

A massive cloud of foggy butterflies blew into his face. Leandro stumbled backward, coughing, his skin rainbow-stained. The creatures spread throughout the room, leaving bright smoky trails. Anything they touched looked blasted with colored chalk dust. Some people tried to catch them, and some ducked and dodged. It was a huge mess.

Rosy cackled. "How do his subscribers come up with this stuff?"

"Why does he do whatever they pay him to?"

"You do, too. At least he's having fun."

I put my head down on the counter again. She was right. My life was devoid of fun. A perfect example was waiting at the store.

"Sorry," Rosy said, putting away her phone. "I know there's stuff you can't do because of money. And time."

Fact. I'd been trying for years to translate and test the spells in my abuela's spellbook. It was the only thing of hers I'd wanted when she got sick and my relatives started claiming stuff, and thankfully, no one fought me over it. I hated confrontation. That was why I didn't do personal casting with store equipment—Ofelia would give me shit.

I had no good options, though, not for space or supplies or time. My efficiency's kitchenette was tiny; public library casting spaces and casting collectives got booked up fast; and coworking rentals were way out of my budget. Even if I got reagents at cost from our suppliers, I could only buy so much, because most of my pay went to rent, food, and bills. And I only had one day off every week, which I used for errands and chores before passing out watching TV or reading. So no side projects for me.

Why was this my life? All work, no play. But if I slowed down, flamed out, it would prove my parents right. Again. I would rather deal with a hundred shitty customers.

"Speaking of money and time . . ."

Oh no. Don't ask about the thing.

"Did you hear from the *Cast Judgment* people?"

She'd asked about the thing. "If I did, I couldn't tell you." I'd signed a nondisclosure agreement longer than a pharmacy receipt. I expected lawyers to jump out of the bushes like ninjas if I even thought about the show too hard. They probably would have put a geas on me to shut me up, if it weren't illegal.

Rosy mimed zipping her lips, then left to take someone's order. I stared at my warped reflection in the napkin dispenser. Did my internal freak-out show on my face?

Cast Judgment was a reality show, a spell-casting competition in its tenth season. Contestants were given themes and briefs, and they'd have one or two days to design and cast a spell for the judges. At the end of each round, one person was eliminated. The winner got a ginormous cash prize and a yearlong residency at the Desgraves Studio, a super-fancy magical arts center here in Miami.

Free workshop space, reagents, and equipment I could only drool over in catalogs . . . Yes, please. Even the losers got a boost—spin-off shows or spellbook deals or job offers. Competing on *Cast Judgment* was a total life changer.

And starting tomorrow, I was going to be on the show.

They were calling this season the Spellebrity Edition because every contestant would have a celebrity teammate. Two of the five had been announced, but I only cared about one: Charlotte Sharp.

Charlotte was the owner of Athame Arts, an artisanal spell company with stores in New York, Miami, Chicago, Los Angeles . . . She was rich, and famous, and talented, and she had started in a tiny shop, like me.

In my fantasies, after we won, she'd offer me a job. I'd humbly accept, and we'd jump into a fancy convertible spelled not to ruin our perfect hairstyles as we rode into the sunset. Though, technically, riding into the sunset in Miami meant driving into the Everglades to get eaten by gators . . . No! Bad Penelope. No catastrophizing. No gators, only good hair.

It had taken bribes, begging, and straight-up lying to get two weeks off work for filming and promo. Even if I lost in round one, I had to stay in a hotel with the other contestants until the whole thing was over, for NDA reasons or something. I wanted to tell Rosy so bad, but she lived on chisme; she'd never keep it to herself, and then the lawyer ninjas would attack.

The only person I trusted with the secret was my sister Emelia, who'd signed her own NDA. She was my emergency contact and alibi. Our cover story: spa retreat at a cabin on some Georgia mountain with no internet. Eme had also helped me forward my number to her phone somehow so she could cover for me, but that hadn't started yet.

My cell played a demonic growl, popping my thought bubbles. Someone had emailed the work account, which I'd set up on my phone with an alert because Ofelia wouldn't let me use the computer in her office.

I checked the preview and a cloud of glittery pink hearts floated around my head like foggy butterflies.

"I know that look," Rosy said. "You got a G-mail!"

"Maybe." Totally.

The "G" was Gil—Gilberto Contreras. He ran a blog called *Doctor Witch*, where he helped people with spell problems and shared recipes that actually worked. We'd been emailing for months. It started with him asking whether Espinosa's carried a specific beetle wing, but every store had run out, including ours. I called around and found some up in Lauderhill, and he was super grateful. Out of curiosity, I clicked the link in his auto-signature and read a few of his posts. Good stuff! Then I found his picture and my soul left my body. So, so hot.

When my soul returned, I noticed a mistake in one of his recipes: lemon balm instead of lemon verbena in a garden-enhancing spell. Because this was the internet and not an actual hot guy standing in front of me, I pointed out the oopsie, joked about how people would end up with mellow bees instead of perky flowers, and suggested he add a pinch of espresso—a trick of my abuela's. Then I spent hours obsessively checking for a reply, worried I'd been rude or weird.

But he tried my suggestion, and it worked, and he thanked me for saving everyone from an attack of pollen smugglers. We went from occasionally trading ideas to chatting multiple times a week about magical theory and personal stuff, and my smol insta-crush reached embarrassingly epic levels.

This email had a cute pinup-style picture of a witch, her skirt blown up by the wind, showing her legs. The caption: "Widdershins implies the existence of widderankles and widderknees." Under that he wrote, "Deasil are the jokes!" I snort-laughed.

"What's so funny?" Rosy asked. I showed her, and she shook her head. "I don't get it."

"It's a spell thing," I explained. "Widdershins is counterclockwise and deasil is clockwise."

"You two are such nerds." Rosy pointed a spoon at me. "One day I'm going to steal your phone and ask him out for you."

"You won't."

"I should, since you're a giant chicken."

She wasn't wrong. But at some point, I'd realized an important thing: I'd never actually introduced myself to Gil. I'd left the store auto-signature at the bottom of the email and kept hitting reply. For *months*.

I'd told him really personal stuff. Stories about brewing potions with my abuela when she picked me and my sister up from school, or my mom making me pull weeds for hours in the hot sun as punishment for mediocre grades, or my dad coaching my Little League team and putting me in the outfield because I couldn't catch. I hadn't told him my most painful memory, the one that still gave me nightmares and panic attacks, but I'd showed him a lot of my scars.

And the whole time, he'd thought I was my boss.

I was too embarrassed to say anything now. It would be so easy!

By the way, my name is Penelope and I'm not old enough to be your mom. But I couldn't do it.

Still, I kept the emails going. So what if I was only imagining he was flirting with me when he sent stuff like this witch pinup? I enjoyed my daydreams about him magically appearing at the store to ask me out.

It was never going to happen. He hadn't even hinted about meeting, unless you counted asking about places I liked to hang out. He didn't call the store or ask for my number. He probably had a girlfriend, or boyfriend, or nonbinary love of his life. And if he really was lusting after the picture of my boss posted on the website, I'd be a huge disappointment.

Rosy plopped a foam cup in front of me. "Do you need to get back to your asshole?"

I made a fart noise with my mouth and put away my phone.

"At least you're going on vacation." She wiped the counter. "I still can't believe the vieja podrida gave you two weeks off."

"Yeah, it's gonna be great!" And that didn't sound fakey at all. Wow.

I grabbed my cortadito and waved goodbye to Rosy. Daydreams over. Time to deal with reality.

THE DOOR CHIMES tinkled when I stepped into the store. Unless the customer was hiding behind a shelf, he'd left. Ofelia had either talked some sense into him, or caved and gave him exactly what he wanted. I wasn't going to bet myself anything this time; I wasn't a sucker.

"Is that you, Penny?" Ofelia called.

"Yes."

"Come to my office."

I put my cortadito on the counter, grabbed my notebook, and went to the back of the store.

Customers weren't allowed into this area. Too ugly. Bare concrete floors, good for drawing arcane circles with chalk. Ceilings: more concrete. Walls: believe it or not, also concrete. Basic bathroom to the right, cleaned by yours truly. Workshop and storage to the left, featuring a gas stove and oven, a scarred wooden table covered in spell-casting tools, shelves of reagents, and boxes of stuff I hadn't restocked in the front yet. Big roll-up door on the far wall, broken since always.

Happy memories of my abuela's kitchen ghosted through my mind. Watching the sun stream through the colored glass blocks of the door to the backyard. Sticking toothpicks into an avocado seed and resting it on the rim of a glass jar filled with a growth potion. Sitting at the table, kicking my feet under the flower-print plastic tablecloth while I ground herbs with a mortar and pestle. Climbing onto the counter to reach jars on high shelves. Feeling the rush of magic as I whispered an incantation and pushed my energy and will into the contents of a steaming cauldron. Turning the dial on her old-fashioned timer and watching it tick, tick, until it buzzed.

Ofelia had fooled me for a while, but I knew perfectly well now that she wasn't my abuela, and this place was nothing like that kitchen.

Past the bathroom, the door to Ofelia's office stood open. The room was just big enough to hold her desk, a chair, and a fancy antique cabinet full of impressive-looking magic stuff arranged like display candy at a movie theater. Her desk was covered in papers, which I was not allowed to touch, and which she loved to accuse me of touching.

Ofelia peered over the bright red glasses sitting on the end of her nose as she two-finger-typed something on her ancient computer. After a few minutes of letting me squirm and choke on her flowery perfume, she sighed real big and took off her glasses, glaring at me with watery blue eyes.

"Penny, Penny," she said. "What am I going to do with you?"

Did I mention I hated being called Penny?

"I need you to make the counterspell for that customer," she continued. "He'll pick it up as soon as it's finished."

"Okay," I said, opening my notebook. "I'm going to need—"

"Use whatever will work. But the cost will come out of your pay."

I put the notebook down and struggled to control my face. "I didn't mess up his hair. He cast his own spell, and he used a broken duskywing butterfly wing, which we didn't sell him. This isn't my fault."

Ofelia leaned forward, her leather chair creaking. "Can you look me in the eye and tell me you didn't give him the wrong blend of herbs?"

If she already thought I was a liar, why would eye contact matter? I looked directly at her pupils and said, "I didn't mess up his reagents. I always triple-check what I'm blending. I make sure nothing is stale or mislabeled. I measure twice so we don't give too much or too little. I'm extremely careful."

I didn't want anyone to get hurt because I'd made a mistake. Never again.

She stared at me, lips pressed together in a red line, then slid her glasses back on and returned her attention to the computer.

"Get to work on that counterspell," Ofelia said. "I left the original instructions out for you."

I stood up, clenching my notebook so hard, the spiral wire dug into my palm. I was halfway out the door when she stopped me.

"Before you go," she added, "I know you asked for time off, but under the circumstances, I think you'd better reschedule your little trip with your sister. Hmm?"

I did my best impression of a fish. "I can't. It's tomorrow."

"This job doesn't come with vacation time, and you've called in sick more than usual in the past few months. I was being generous because you've worked here for so long, but today's incident tells me you take this position for granted."

I worked at least ten hours a day, every single day except Mondays. I almost always came to work sick, and I hadn't taken vacation time in seven years—except for three *Cast Judgment* auditions and interviews that couldn't be scheduled on Mondays.

I didn't take the blame for the customer's problem, and now she was yanking my leash.

"We agreed on this weeks ago," I said. "I can't cancel the day before."

Ofelia looked at me over the top of her glasses. "If you're not here tomorrow, I may have to make some hard decisions. I hope we understand each other." She turned away, pretending I was already gone.

I leaned against the wooden table in the casting area. Was she threatening to fire me? Seriously? I ran this damn store while she had brunch mimosas with her friends. Tracking inventory, ordering stock, casting spells, helping people with technical questions, answering phones and emails . . . I had even started making extra money doing spell demonstrations at the library branch in the shopping center. The only thing Ofelia did was double-check the accounting stuff and make the bank deposits, because she was paranoid that I might steal money from her.

What if she wasn't bluffing, though? She had a bad temper. If I lost my job, my life would explode like hair fireworks. I had an associate's degree in magical theory, which meant I was competing with a bazillion other people for any entry-level position that didn't require a PhD and ten years of experience. Working at Espinosa's was as close as I would ever get to my dream job unless a miracle happened.

Cast Judgment might be that miracle.

If I won, I'd have $100,000 to live on, and I could work on my abuela's spellbook.

If I won. A big "if."

My parents and I almost never talked, but I could hear their voices in my head, especially my mom's: *Remember when we told you not to stay in Miami for college? Look how that turned out. Don't risk your job. Don't make the same mistake again, thinking you're better than you are.*

I was a spell technician-slash-salesgirl at a magic supply shop. End of story.

Unless it was just the beginning.

I'd made it on the show, hadn't I? Beaten thousands of people in the audition process? That had to mean something. Forget my parents: my abuela wouldn't want me to give up now.

I had to take this chance, or I'd regret it forever.

First, I had to make the counterspell for Sparkles. I put out the bell with the "Ring for Service" sign on the counter and made sure the anti-theft freezer charms were all in place on the shelves. Then I tied on an apron, put on my safety glasses, and started assembling and checking my reagents.

When I remembered to drink my coffee, it was already cold.

CHAPTER 2

Gil

When I first started making videos, my grandpa Fred told me, "Gil, you need a persona. A character. Someone you can leave onstage when you go home to your future wife. Rule number one: be someone else."

The trick to creating a memorable persona, he'd said, was to focus on a few specific, exaggerated details. People might not notice someone's hair or eye color, or the shape of their nose, but they'd remember a wacky hat and tie.

More importantly, when you took off the hat and tie, the odds of the same people recognizing you went way down.

That's why I sat in the passenger seat of my friend Sam's car wearing a tacky pink dress shirt covered in not just red and white flowers, but also tiny squares in a random pattern. I'd rolled up the sleeves almost to my elbows, and left the bottom untucked so it hung over my baggy jeans.

My Leandro Presto style: thrift shop bargains, two sizes two big.

Sam was a fashion icon by comparison. She wore a T-shirt that read, "Cinematographers do it from behind" and, in much smaller font underneath, "the lens." Her short hair was amethyst purple, while mine was slicked back with gel that tinted it a few shades darker. Eye makeup made her blue eyes pop; black-framed safety glasses made my dark eyes look smaller. My fake mustache was firmly attached, and thank god spirit gum was sweat-resistant, because it was hot as balls even with the AC blowing at my face. All practical, no illusion magic, also per Grandpa Fred's advice; illusions didn't always show up on video, I couldn't trust them not to go wrong at a bad time, and some people carried enchantments to see through them.

In the back seat, Ed messed with levels on the audio receiver, his dark head bent over the bag. He wore a pink shirt and glasses, too, but his polo actually fit, and he needed his glasses to see. Where Sam stood out, Ed tended to relax in the background. We'd been partners in *Mage You Look* for years, roommates and best friends for much longer.

Headlights streamed back and forth in the street as the last strip of orange sky faded to velvety blue. About fifteen people stood in the grass at the park outside, surrounded by a jogging trail and palm trees, a sand-filled playground nearby. Some teenagers giggled their way up a toddler-sized climbing wall and down a curved plastic slide. Pretty good for a last-minute announcement to my "live recording"–tier subscribers. The place had closed at sunset; we didn't have a permit for filming, but it wouldn't be the first time cops had kicked us out.

I unlocked my phone and tapped the email app. Nothing new.

"Waiting for *Cast Judgment* stuff, or did you email her again?" Sam stretched out "her" so it had three syllables.

I knew which "her" Sam meant: Penelope. I'd emailed her a little after lunch. Usually she wrote back faster, so she must have been busy. Unless the witch picture had crossed the line from flirty to gross?

"Aren't we really close to where she works?" Sam asked. "You could literally go over there now and ask her out."

"It's closed already." Not that I hadn't picked this park on the off chance that she might magically show up. Every time I'd decided I would call her, or surprise her at the store, I'd chickened out. I could make a fool of myself for thousands of strangers, but I couldn't talk to the girl I liked.

"You need to fortify and do the thing."

Ed passed me the wireless mic, and I clipped it to my shirt collar.

"She hasn't even told me her name." I got it from the friend who'd recommended her shop, who said the owner was never around and the cute tech answered all the emails.

"You know her favorite ice cream flavor and her shoe size, my dude."

And then some. "I don't want to assume she's interested."

"You're not assuming if you. Ask. Her." Sam punctuated each word with a flick to my forehead. Ow.

I rubbed the place she'd flicked. "It's not just that. It's the Leandro thing."

"You're not a superhero, Gil," Sam said. "Your rules are smart, but even with the Stalker Incident, you don't have to be this extreme about your secret identity."

Maybe that was true when I first started making these videos, but not anymore. And not only because of the Stalker Incident. Grandpa Fred warned me: the bigger you get, the more gravity you have, and the more people want to be sucked into your orbit. Anyway, I didn't want to argue about this again. Not when I was about to potentially get even more popular.

"You said you had something to talk about earlier?" I asked.

Sam tapped her fingers on the steering wheel, all serious now. "We've been thinking. Viewership and engagement metrics are good, we're getting more sponsor and ad requests . . ."

"Right." Where was this going?

"But we think you should skip the step-by-step demonstration videos."

What? "I have to do those. People are subscribed to that tier."

"Sixteen people. It's a waste of time we could be using to make more short content."

A waste of time I enjoyed. A lot. I liked coming up with spells and recording goofy videos and making people laugh, but I really loved explaining how it all worked. My grad school cohort had moved away, my thesis advisor had moved on, and none of my friends wanted to casually chat about intangible components, or Sina's correspondent distillation, or how applications of the law of participation could improve spell effectiveness. Sam and Ed cared about how the spells would look on camera and whether they'd go viral, but their eyes got that *I don't get it* look when I tried to get into the theory. My *Doctor Witch* blog scratched the itch a little, but otherwise, the only person I could really talk to about this stuff was Penelope.

So why didn't I go talk to her already? Ugh. Loser.

"Until we get rid of that tier, we have to do it," I said.

"So we get rid of it. Give refunds. It'll save us more money than we'll lose. Those videos get no traffic and no ad money, and they take Ed forever to finish."

"Not forever," Ed said. "But it's not an efficient use of our time or budget."

Sam stopped tapping and unlocked the doors. "I'm just saying, think about it. Especially if things change after this contest."

"I hear you." I didn't like it, but *Mage You Look* wasn't my show. We were a team. "When I get back in two weeks, we can decide."

"Fair enough."

I got out of the car and grabbed my box of supplies from the trunk. Sam and Ed joined me, each carrying their gear, and together we headed toward the crowd.

"Hey, everyone!" I said. "Just have to set up, and then we'll get started."

A few people cheered, and one asked, "What spell are you doing tonight?"

"A little something I like to call: 'U Jelly, Bro?'" I put the box on a picnic table and started taking things out.

Within minutes, I'd placed camping lanterns around where I would be performing, adding to the camera light and floodlights and nearly full moon. I slipped a bottle of water into my back pocket, then put my premixed plastic baggie of reagents and another baggie with the catalyst into a side pocket. Last was the mason jar where I'd combine the ingredients, a small hole punched in the lid to control the initial size of the emanation.

"Let me know when you're ready, Ed," Sam yelled, peeking over the monitor of her shoulder-mounted DSLR.

Ed dangled from the top of the nearby swing set, adjusting the wide-angle sport cam he'd clamped to the metal frame. He gave her a thumbs-up and climbed down, heading for another tripod-mounted DSLR off to the side.

My heart rate sped up like it always did before a performance. I let the stage fright have its moment. The spell would work because I'd practiced it three times and triple-checked my reagents. I went over my script in my head again: solid. I smoothed down my mustache with my thumb and forefinger.

A couple more people jumped out of a car in the parking lot, so I gave them time to join the audience. They were cute: a Black woman in an orange uniform polo and a tan brunette wearing a black T-shirt with the Frogtail logo on it. I had one just like it, since I bought a lot of their herbs. They had really nice customer reps. Mine was Greg. And I'd been staring at her chest for like ten solid seconds. Classy.

"Ready Freddy," I said.

Sam started recording, the camera light flashing into my eyes.

I spread my arms wide and faced the crowd. "Hello, mages!" I boomed. "Welcome to another unforgettable episode of . . ."

"*Mage You Look!*" everyone shouted in unison.

"Tonight's spell," I continued, "is a request from a subscriber who has a happy memory involving bioluminescent jellyfish. Remember, mages: don't try this at home."

I unscrewed the lid of the mason jar and wedged it under my arm, then pulled the bottle of water from my back pocket and poured it inside. The plastic baggie was next; I dumped the contents into the jar as I rattled off the quantities and how I'd prepared them. I must have gone too fast, because Ed used the *slow down* hand motion.

Frogtail Shirt whispered something to her friend. Three people shushed her.

I screwed the lid back on, plugged the hole with my palm, and shook the jar, murmuring an incantation under my breath as I infused the mixture with my intention. The water turned inky black; people oohed. I held up the jar to distract them while I slipped my hand into my pocket and palmed the next reagent.

"And now, the catalyst." With an exaggerated flick of the wrist, I made a dried shrimp appear in my hand. "This delicious crustacean helps jellyfish glow." I pretended to eat it, and everyone laughed.

Except Frogtail. She looked grossed out.

"When I add this shrimp and say the magic word, a cute little glowing jellyfish is going to fly out of the jar." I dangled the shrimp above the opening in the jar's lid, waggling my eyebrows as I looked across the crowd.

Frogtail said something again. Someone hissed at her.

I gathered my energy and intentions and pushed them into the shrimp, which I'd already infused with part of the spell. Magic rippled down my arms, prickling my skin and warming my hands. I dropped the shrimp into the jar, flung my free hand into the air, and yelled, "Presto!"

Everyone went quiet. The inky black water began to glow a pale blue, coalescing into a blob that drifted aimlessly. A tiny jellyfish popped through the hole in the lid, rose a few feet higher, and hovered in place.

"Isn't this little buddy adorable?" I asked. No one was impressed, of course, but that was the idea.

A few seconds later, my "little buddy" started growing. It went from the size of a marble to a lemon, then a mango, then a basketball, and kept going.

"Uh-oh," I said. "It's not supposed to do that."

The strands of its trailing tentacles dangled like shimmering fishing wire. From the center of its body hung arms like thick ribbons with scalloped edges. It was pretty accurate to life, if I said so myself. When it got as big as a giant beach umbrella, I stepped underneath the jellyfish and looked up. "I must have put in too much star anise."

The crowd chuckled. Time for phase two.

"Thankfully it's only a residual echo of the real thing, so it doesn't sting!" I ran my hands along the tentacles, which shifted like a beaded curtain, leaving glowing neon streaks on my skin.

And then they reached out and circled my wrists.

"Guess the echo remembers how to catch fish," I joked as more tentacles wound their way around my legs and chest. I pretended to struggle, shifting my expression from *haha* to *yikes*.

The central arms grabbed my shoulders and pulled the whole jellyfish body down, until I was wearing it like a hat. I yelped as the jellyfish sucked my head into its mouth.

The audience cracked up. For extra comedic effect, I wiggled and made a few more muffled sounds that could have been bad words. Once the laughs slowed down, I got one of my arms loose and tried to push the jellyfish off my head. It didn't work, of course—it wasn't supposed to—but the laughing came back. The tentacles got me again, and after a brief but mighty battle, I freed myself.

My whole body glowed in neon blues and purples, coated in a sheen of spectral residue. My mustache in particular probably looked ridiculous. I wiped the color off my glasses with my fingers and everyone lost it.

The jellyfish brightened, and I froze, hands and one leg up in a defensive pose. With a sound like a rushing wave, the creature dissolved into a cloud of glitter that spiraled up into the night. The laughter changed to *ooh*s and *aah*s. For a moment, it was like the whole Milky Way spread across the sky instead of just a few random stars and planets, and then it was gone.

I shouted, "Presto!" as everyone clapped. The show was over.

Sam and Ed stopped filming and I joined them for our post-spell routine. Ed climbed back up the swing set to get the sport cam. I picked up the lanterns, still covered in faintly glowing neon stripes. Sam started playing back her video, and we all hunched over the tiny screen. I was a little more stiff than usual, but it was good enough. With this, we had a solid buffer to last through my *Cast Judgment* time.

Some people left; others went back to the playground or stood around soaking up the vibes. Some hovered like they wanted to ask me questions but were too shy. I'd mingle in a minute, though I couldn't stay long. I had to check in at the hotel where I'd be staying during filming.

The replay finished. I said, "If Ed adds some silly sound effects and a few funny captions where my energy drops, I think it'll be okay."

"Are you nervous about the show?" Ed asked, adding quietly, "I know spending so much time in character is a lot for you."

It was, but this would be a good opportunity for *Mage You Look*. More exposure hopefully meant more subscribers and sponsors and ad revenue, which meant a bigger budget, which meant we could raise rates for everyone who worked for us. Might sell extra merch, too, if we were lucky.

Grandpa Fred thought I could get my own cable show out of this, but honestly, I had the feeling the producers had signed me up to be comic relief. I wasn't one of their stars or some fancy CEO; I was the latest Jinxd account to go viral on the regular. I was there to "capture the youth market," to paraphrase my agent.

Most importantly to me, though, I was competing for my grandpa's charity: Alan Kazam's Schools Are Magic. Funding for classes in anything beyond basic, boring rote-memorization casting kept getting cut from public elementary schools, along with art and music and anything else deemed insufficiently essential. AKSAM provided a free magic curriculum, appropriate to the grade level and with all necessary reagents included. And it was fun! I'd done some school visits as Leandro Presto, and guiding crowds of adorable, excited kids through the lessons was incredibly fulfilling.

More than these videos, if I was being honest with myself. Especially if we cut the explanations. Not that I'd tell Sam and Ed that.

Fundraising was tough in the best of times, especially when so many people were broke. AKSAM donations had dropped, and the charity was on the edge of shutting down if they couldn't get a cash infusion, fast. If I won *Cast Judgment*, the check for $100,000 would keep the lights on for a while longer and pay for a hell of a lot of magic classes. Even if I lost, they'd get $10,000, which would be a huge help.

I'd do my best, but I was up against industry pros way further along in their successful careers. It wouldn't surprise me if I lost in the first round and spent the rest of the shoot reading in my hotel room since we couldn't leave early because of our NDAs. But I was damned well going to try, for the kids and my grandpa.

Sam finished packing her cameras while Ed checked his phone. Frogtail walked back over to her friend in the crowd just as Sam nudged me to start mingling.

"How did you like the spell?" I asked them.

"It was awesome!" Orange Polo replied.

"Yeah, doing a spell like this at night was really nice," the guy across from her said.

"You could do it at the beach next time," someone added.

"Nah, the parking sucks," someone else said.

"What about you?" Sam asked, pointing at Frogtail, who was even cuter up close.

Before she could answer, one of the teenagers jumped in. "She wouldn't shut up about how he was doing it wrong," he said.

Oh. Ouch.

Frogtail looked down at her sneakers. "It was cool. Just, you know, the star anise."

"Too much," I agreed.

"Way too much. Half a seed would have been enough. Though if you had used more shrimp, you would have a bunch of small jellies instead of one big one?"

"Right, the size would be proportional to the ratio of the catalyst to the reactant."

Her eyes widened like I'd surprised her. Oops. Leandro Presto shouldn't be rattling off variations on the theory of compositional conformity. Grandpa Fred's rule number two: stay in character.

I gave her my best himbo grin. "That's what I read on the internet, anyway."

Her eye roll said she bought it.

"My friend's a spell tech," Orange Polo explained. "She helps people with magic stuff. You know, proofs their recipes, tells them if their ingredients will interact. Keeps them from making mistakes."

That explained the urge to correct me.

"If you ever need help with one of your spells, you should email her. Or call her."

Was she trying to wingman? Grandpa Fred's rule number five: hands off the fans. That rule was especially sacred since the Stalker Incident.

"It's okay," Frogtail said. "You don't need some rando telling you what to do." After a breath, she added, "You really should be more careful with your magic, though. What if those tentacles had gotten wrapped around your neck and choked you? Or the jellyfish suffocated you like a plastic bag?"

Neither of those things was physically possible with this spell, but she couldn't know that. What would Leandro say? "They didn't, so it's all good."

"It's not all good—you got lucky. One day someone's gonna get hurt."

"I always tell people not to try the spells at home."

Frogtail frowned. "That won't stop them. You need to be responsible with the content you put out there."

That's why I explained everything so carefully. In the videos no one watched, that Sam and Ed wanted to get rid of. "Don't worry. If anyone gets hurt, it'll be me, and that video will go super viral."

"Is getting likes seriously all you care about?"

"Nooo." I paused for effect. "Likes *and* subscribes."

Everyone laughed, and I hoped that would be the end of it. Instead, it got worse as other people started dunking on her.

"Can you make a spell to give yourself a sense of humor?"

"Or maybe one to take the stick out of your ass."

"Hey, whoa," I said. "Be nice."

Even if they heard me, they kept going, and Frogtail stood there and took it with this flat look on her face, like she'd heard worse. I had to stop it, but I couldn't figure out how Leandro would do it.

Suddenly I was a kid again, before the divorce, listening to my parents fight, past the point where I could defuse it with a joke. The shouting, the name-calling, the cold sarcasm . . . I wanted to hide in my room until it was over. My mouth refused to work, like all my words got stuck in my throat and wouldn't come out.

Finally someone asked, "Why do you hate fun?" and I could almost see the top of her head blow up like in a cartoon.

"I don't hate fun!" Frogtail clenched her hands into fists. "I just don't make an ass of myself on Jinxd. Some of us don't need to be told how cool we are all the time. Some of us fix spell problems instead of causing them. Some of us care more about helping people than being famous."

She didn't really know me, only Leandro Presto, but still. Every word hit like a punch.

"Hey," Sam said. "Cool your tits."

This was my fault. I should have known my fans—which Frogtail clearly wasn't—would want to defend me, and I shouldn't have let them take it so far. Why did I always lose the power of speech when stuff like this happened?

I mean, I knew why, but you would think all the therapy would help me deal better.

"S-sorry," Frogtail stuttered, her face red. "That was super shitty of me. Sorry. I'm so sorry." She practically ran away, toward the parking lot.

I started to follow her. I didn't know how, but I wanted to fix this. A car beeped, and Frogtail slid into the front passenger seat and slouched too low for me to see her.

I stopped at the edge of the sidewalk. Epic fail.

Orange Polo joined me, looking worried. "She isn't usually like this."

"It's my fault. I let it get out of hand."

"She had a super-bad day at work. I keep telling her to quit, but where's she gonna go? SpellMart?" Orange Polo shrugged. "That's why I was kinda pushing her on you. Sorry."

"It's okay. She seems really smart."

"She is. Super smart. And she works so hard. I just wish someone could appreciate it."

"I'm sure someone will," I said, but it sounded weaksauce even to me.

Orange Polo jingled her car keys. "I should go. She has to be up early, and I already kidnapped her so I wouldn't have to come here alone." She walked backward away from me. "It really was a great spell! Better than the one from Dolphin Mall. And you're even cuter in person." She grinned, then turned around and gave her hips a little extra shake.

Sam stepped up next to me. "Nice. Too bad about rule five. Hey, did I tell you the new bad pickup line I heard yesterday? 'You dropped something . . . my jaw.'"

"Not now, Samantha," I muttered.

"Oh snap, full-named." Her eyes got big. "You're really upset. What's up?"

"I wish I'd handled that better."

"Haters gonna hate. Don't stress about it."

More quietly, Ed said, "Leandro isn't you. He's just a character."

A character people didn't take seriously, which was the whole point. But it stung to have it rubbed in my face. As if it didn't take a lot of skill and hard work to be a clown.

I'd tried the usual path for someone with my degree, and it had gotten me nowhere. My parents still asked how my job hunt was going every time we talked. Had I applied to that listing they saw on NetWorkedIn at the University of Never Gonna Hire Me? What about that research position that required me to have started publishing papers when I was in diapers? Explaining that the economy didn't work how it had when they were my age was a waste of time. I was lucky to be an adjunct at a community college. Recording dozens of crappy video auditions was how I'd ended up creating Leandro Presto in the first place.

Orange Polo's headlights came on and the car backed out. I got a glimpse of Frogtail looking out the window, then they were gone.

"We'd better get home," Ed said, adjusting the shoulder strap of his bag. "You have a long day tomorrow."

A long couple of weeks, even. Tonight I'd be at a hotel in Edgewater, and tomorrow I'd be on a soundstage in Wynwood. I would meet the hosts and judges of *Cast Judgment*, I'd meet my fellow "Spellebrities"—ugh, what a ridiculous name—and I'd be assigned my casting partner. Hopefully they wouldn't be too disappointed to be stuck with a Jinxd joker.

My PhD had to count for something, though, right? Not that I could tell them I had one. People saw what they expected to see, and Leandro Presto was just a curly mustache, safety glasses, and tacky shirts. But even a fake guy had to do real work. My friends were counting on me to network, but more importantly, my grandpa's charity needed money.

Every kid deserved a little magic in their lives.

So did the grown-ups, no matter what Frogtail might think. I summoned up a smile and turned back toward the fans who hadn't left yet. "Anyone have questions before I head out? Or want a selfie?"

CHAPTER 3

Penelope

If I could travel back in time and kick Past Penelope for thinking today would be a triumphant montage to the tune of "Victory Is Sweet," my butt would already have a bruise.

I woke up before my alarm went off, worried I'd sleep through it. My curly hair refused to cooperate, so I pulled it back in a ponytail and prayed for professional stylist intervention. A button popped off my shirt, right under my boobs. All my other nice shirts were packed and I'd had to sit on the suitcase to close it; the only one I had left was a fake-silk peasant shirt in a once-trendy shade of yellow that would make people ask who wore it better, me or a rubber duck.

I had planned to make scrambled eggs and toast like a real adult, but the button debacle made me late, so I poured store-brand chocolate puffs from the bag directly into my mouth while driving. I splurged on an online coffee order, then spilled it in the parking lot because the lid was loose. Ahh!

The sun was perfectly positioned to stab my eyes for the longest hour and a half of my life, in bumper-to-bumper traffic from Kendall to Wynwood. By the time I got there, my head ached from lack of sleep and caffeine, and people honking at each other as if it would magically make rush hour go away. Magic had its limits.

Why didn't I go to the hotel the night before? Why did I think sleeping in my own bed would be better? Right, because I'm a co-memierda.

The long drive gave me plenty of time to think about Leandro Presto. I'd been such an asshole to him. I'd spent hours casting, then waiting for that shitty customer to pick up his counterspell, then Rosy had dragged me to the park . . . Leandro screwing up yet another spell was the sprinkles on my bad day sundae. But no matter how much he annoyed me, I shouldn't have let it turn me into an evil, cranky monster.

If I ever saw him again, I'd apologize better. Maybe I'd email him after the show finished filming? By then, he'd probably have forgotten I existed.

I was also definitely not going to think about how he was cuter in person, especially when he smiled. Nope. No me meto en eso. Rosy could stay president of the Bad Mustache Fan Club without me. I could look, though. Respectfully.

And what was that casual dropping of the theory of compositional conformity? He'd played it off, but I wasn't sure I bought his act.

There had to be more to Leandro Presto than it seemed. Sort of like how pro wrestling was fake, but the moves were real. Not that I'd ever find out, so why did I care?

To distract myself from my own bad brain, I called my sister. She should be driving to work now, too, and Atlanta traffic was almost as bad as Miami. Worse, according to her.

Emelia answered on the third ring. "What's up, Penelup?"

"The sky, Emeli," I replied. "On my way to the thing."

"On a scale of capybara to chihuahua in a thunderstorm, how nervous are you right now?"

"Three chihuahuas, and they all have to pee."

"Well, don't do that on camera. Unless you think it will help you win."

"Bold strat, but I'll pass. How are you?"

"Dealing with work stuff, as usual. Don't get me started. We are all about you right now, and how you're awesome."

Was I awesome? I didn't feel that way. Not after yesterday, and especially last night.

"Do I hate fun?" I blurted out.

Emelia paused. "Did someone tell you that? Give me a name and I'll call Javi."

Our cousin Javi was nine feet tall, with hands as big as stop signs. The thought of him picking up Leandro Presto by his weird shirt and growling in his face was kinda funny, but also not nice. He wasn't even the person who'd said it.

"No Javi. No bullying people for telling the truth."

"It's not the truth. But . . ."

"But?"

Emelia snickered. "You said 'butt.'"

"You said it first!"

"You can be fun," Emelia said. "Sometimes you're just a little . . . reply guy."

"What does that even mean?"

"Like, you hate it when people are wrong on the internet."

"Okay, but—"

"You said 'butt' again!"

"—I don't go around telling people they're wrong." Except for that time I literally emailed Gil to correct him—oh my GOD. I sighed and banged my forehead on the steering wheel. It gave a tiny surprised beep.

"You get salty. It's not healthy, that's all I'm saying."

"You're right. I know you're right."

"I'm always right. So listen to your extremely right big sister: Stop stressing about this. Stop overthinking. Normal amounts of thinking only for the next two weeks. Okay?"

"I'll try."

"They picked you for this show because they liked what they saw in auditions. Be that person and you'll be fine."

That person was the happy customer service personality I used at work every day, so that shouldn't be too hard. I hoped.

We shot the shit until I pulled up in front of a giant concrete warehouse that looked like every other warehouse around it, down to the spelled graffiti art shimmering and shifting along one wall. The parking lot and all the streets were packed with cars, a catering truck, and multiple trailers. A few people carrying plastic bins walked past me like they had places to be, others leaned against the wall or chatted, others were glued to their phones.

An earpiece-wearing, tablet-wielding man in a navy polo shirt with a hexafoil logo checked my ID and pronounced me allowed to be there, then a valet handed me a ticket and drove away in my ancient sedan, probably to another lot or garage somewhere. I realized I'd left my coffee cup in the car, so that was going to smell great in two weeks. Too late now.

Or not. I could still rush back to Espinosa's and pretend this was all a dream.

No! I'd made it this far, and I wouldn't give up. If I could just get partnered with Charlotte Sharp, even if we lost, I knew my whole life would change.

I got a grip on myself and my luggage and opened the door.

A weirdly normal office waiting room greeted me. Cream-colored walls with generic abstract artwork, chocolate-brown chairs, lighter brown carpet tiles on the floor. A reception desk in the corner with a fake orchid and a phone. Nothing else.

It was also freezing. I tried not to shiver.

A woman stepped through a door in the far wall. She also had a navy polo shirt, an earpiece, and a tablet. The corporate uniform, I guess?

"Penelope Delmar?" she asked.

"That's me," I replied, maximum cheerful.

"I'm Rachel, production manager." She tapped and swiped on the tablet. "Did you read today's schedule?"

Only like ten times. Twenty, max. "We're doing individual interviews, meeting the hosts and judges, then meeting our celebrity partners?"

"Correct. Pair interviews after that. Lunch should be around one, dinner around six, then we have a night shoot at another location before we wrap."

"Quadruple cafecito day, got it." I hesitated, then asked casually, "Do you know who we're being partnered with?"

"It's a surprise for you." Tap, tap, swipe, tap. "Remember, before we start filming, I'll be collecting everyone's cell phones, tablets, and computers. Per the terms of your NDA, you'll get your personal items back temporarily on day six, but under no circumstances are you permitted to share any information regarding the status of the competition. Emergency protocols are in your handbook. Your social media accounts are also being monitored, so don't try anything cute."

"Don't want the lawyer ninjas coming after me," I joked.

She flashed a fake smile as she spoke into a microphone clipped to her collar, presumably attached to the walkie-talkie on her hip. "Little Manny! Front desk."

Little Manny bounced in. He looked younger than me, with thick green glasses and short black hair. Instead of a polo, he wore a hoodie over a black T-shirt and jeans.

"Take Penelope to the greenroom," Rachel said. "The rest of the contestants should be coming from the hotel soon."

Little Manny held the door for me. We crossed a big, open area with one lonely cubicle that hadn't been ripped out. Along the walls were separate offices with empty nameplates on their doors, except one with an LED sign that was turned off.

"I should have brought a jacket," I said, rubbing my arms. "I didn't realize it would be so cold."

"Yeah, they keep it like sixty-five in here," Little Manny said.

The store was always seventy-eight degrees. I didn't have to worry about winning; I was going to die of hypothermia. I pictured myself blue-skinned and covered in icicles like the guy in that horror movie with the ghost hotel. And I was catastrophizing again.

"Is there a Big Manny?" I asked.

"Yeah," Little Manny replied. "And Just Manny."

"So many Mannys."

Little Manny pushed his glasses up. "That's why we have different names."

"Right. So Big Manny, Little Manny, and Manny?"

"Not Manny, 'Just Manny.'"

"Ah. Got it." I did not got it.

Little Manny led me to an office with a printed paper sign taped to the door: "Greenroom." Inside were a love seat, chairs, and a few side tables, plus a long table at one end covered in food and a minifridge full of drinks. Cozy-ish, in a college-meeting-room way.

"Snacks and drinks are for anyone," Little Manny said. "Hair and makeup should be ready for you soon."

"Cool, thanks."

When in doubt, stress-eat. A box of pastelitos de queso called my name, and I'd inhaled two before I realized I should leave some for other people. I slid sideways to the fruit and veggie platters, helping myself to a grape because the celery looked sus.

It was weirdly warm, for a grape. Hmm. I peeked under the serving dish; someone had tied the cooling charm backward. I pulled it out and started separating the strands of knotted yarn.

The door to the room opened and a woman who looked a little older than me walked in. I'd learned the word "statuesque" for a vocab quiz in high school, and wondered when I would ever use it. Well, here she was. Statuesque had to be six feet tall, with honey-blond hair that fell past her shoulders and a movie-star tan. Her pearly pink shirt belted at her waist, showing off her curves, and her black pants were so tight, I wondered how she was going to bend over while casting. A chunky purse hung from her bent arm, the expensive kind I'd only ever seen behind a counter guarded by women who wore too much perfume.

She sat in a chair and dug around inside her purse. Was she a celebrity? Another contestant? I'd ask when I finished with the charm.

I retied the knots, muttering the usual incantation and gently feeding energy and intention into the working. With a satisfying rush that made my arm hairs stand up, the spell settled and the charm got colder in my hand. I slipped it back under the platter, wiggling my fingers to get the post-magic tingles out.

Heeled boots clicked on the floor behind me. I slapped on my customer service smile, but she was looking at the food, not me.

"What are the ingredients in these?" she asked, gesturing at a box of croquetas. Her accent was more California than Miami, heavy on the vocal fry.

I checked the lid. Just the name of the bakery. "I don't know."

"Well, can you find out?"

"It might be on the bakery website, I guess." I pulled out my phone to check.

She glared at me like I'd insulted her mom. Talk about icy blue eyes. "People could have allergies, you know. Ingredient lists should be posted on all food items."

A light bulb appeared over my head and clicked on. "I'm not crew. I'm a contestant."

If she was embarrassed, she didn't show it. Her chin went up, her lips got pouty, and she stalked back to her seat without another word.

Wow. Rude.

The door opened again, and three people came in together. First was a tallish white guy, cute in a punk way, with a septum piercing and spiked-up hair between dirty blond and light brown. He wore jeans and a black T-shirt with three dinosaurs on it, in the colors of the trans pride flag.

Second was an Asian woman, shorter and heavier than me, with shoulder-length black hair dyed pink at the ends. She had cat-eye glasses in the same pink, and she wore an extremely adorable cottagecore dress covered in tiny flowers. Big kindergarten teacher vibes.

Last was a Black dude with nearly shaved black hair, thick and shorter than the white guy but taller than me. His short-sleeved green henley was tucked into his belted khakis, and he moved more slowly than the other two, like he knew how much time things took and he wasn't about to rush.

White Guy waved at Statuesque. "Hey, Felicia, there you are.

We thought you missed the van." His voice was mellow, his accent NPR with a twist.

"I got a ride with a PA," Felicia replied without looking up from her phone.

He saw me and lit up like a Christmas tree, grinning so big I couldn't help but grin back.

"You must be the missing contestant," he said. "I'm Quentin, and this is Amy and Dylan."

Amy smiled shyly, while Dylan stuck his chin out in greeting.

"I'm Penelope," I said. "Are you from out of town, or . . . ?"

"Oh, ya," Quentin replied. "I'm from Minneapolis, Amy's from Jersey, and Dylan is from Baltimore."

He didn't mention Felicia. Huh. "Nice. I'm from here. Miami, I mean."

"Do you live on the beach?" Quentin asked.

"No way, too expensive. I don't go to the beach unless I have to."

"You don't like the ocean?" Amy asked. Her voice was high and sweet.

"It's okay to look at," I said. "The sand, though, yuck. Gets all up in everywhere."

Felicia made a disgusted noise. Quentin laughed nervously, his cheeks turning pink, and I realized what I'd just implied. Ah! Subject change, go.

"Do you know who you're partnered with?" I asked.

"Nope," Quentin said.

"Isn't it a secret?" Amy added.

Dylan hmmed, then said, "I bet we don't find out until we're on camera." His voice sounded like it should come out of a subwoofer.

"I hope I get Jaya Kamath," Amy said, fiddling with a charm hanging from her necklace. "I love her show."

Before I could do a magical girl transformation into a Charlotte Sharp fangirl, Little Manny reappeared. "Penelope, hair and makeup time."

I shoved my suitcase and backpack against the wall, then followed him to another one of the offices. Hair and makeup consisted of folding tables, folding chairs, and floor-length mirrors propped against the wall. More mirrors sat on the tables, the kind that magnified your face so you could count your pores. Two people, mid-chisme, stopped and stared at me with identical, unreadable expressions.

"This is Fina and Bruno," Little Manny said.

Fina reminded me of my tía Maria: soft and curvy, with a cheek-pinching vibe. Her magenta hair was pulled back so tight it made my scalp hurt. Bruno was a young reincarnation of Walter Mercado, down to the blond hair and arched eyebrows.

"Mija, that shirt," Bruno said. "It's like a rubber duck."

"Increíble," Fina agreed.

I winced. "I have other shirts in my suitcase—"

"No, we can work with this," Fina said, tapping her bright red lips with one long acrylic fingernail. "If wardrobe hates it, they'll fix you."

"It will pop on camera," Bruno added.

It would also be partly hidden by one of my work aprons, thankfully.

"What is it you do, mija?" Fina asked.

"I work in a store. Like, a botánica? As a spell technician."

"Sounds nerdy." Bruno waved his hand in a circle at me. "Turn around and take down your hair."

I obeyed, shoving the hair tie in my pocket. Bruno and Fina sucked their teeth.

"When was the last time you cut it?" Bruno asked.

I had no idea. They muttered about split ends and hair products while I avoided looking at my reflection.

"Do the sloppy albóndigas," Fina said. "We'll go, cómo se dice, hipster."

Hipster? Oh no. And what did meatballs have to do with hair?

They combed, yanked, pinned, and sprayed my curls into submission. Makeup followed, airbrushed foundation and eyeliner and mascara and blush, plus eyeshadow and lipstick in colors way more exciting than I would have picked. The meatballs turned out to be a pair of messy buns perched near the top of my head.

"What do you think?" Fina asked.

"Awesome!" Not. I looked like an anime character, which wouldn't be a huge deal except that Charlotte Sharp would never take me seriously.

"Come back here if you need us to fix anything," Bruno said, flapping a hand at me.

"Good luck, mija," Fina added.

I would certainly need it. Between the cold and my nerves, I'd gone from three shaky, peeing chihuahuas to a whole kennel.

Rachel came to collect me this time, a finger pressed to her earpiece like she was half-listening to someone. "Liam is ready to mic you," she said, hauling me back to the greenroom. On the way, we passed Little Manny, Felicia, and Amy going in the other direction.

Liam turned out to be a smiling dude about nine feet tall with a pair of headphones around his neck. He looked at my shirt and sighed like he wasn't mad, just disappointed.

"Is that polyester?" he asked.

"Maybe?"

"Can you change?"

"Not without messing up my hair."

"How would you feel about wearing a big hat?"

Rachel cut the air with her hand. "Absolutely not."

They launched into an argument about clothing noise and mic placement. At some point Little Manny returned with Felicia, and Rachel sent Quentin and Dylan off with him. She and Liam kept going until Liam said something about a hollowed-out pen and I got an idea.

"Would this help?" I pulled an apron out of my backpack. Loosening the neck strap so I wouldn't mess up my hair, I carefully slid it over my head, tightened it, and tied it around my waist. My pencil and notebook went into a side pocket.

Liam stared at my chest with a puzzled half smile. Rachel raised her eyebrows.

Rosy bought me this apron for my birthday two years ago. It was a cute retro style, with red ruffled edges and nice big pockets. I loved the print: white fabric with orange and red llamas and flaming hearts. "Las llamas de mi amor" was stitched in white cursive font on the red heart-shaped chest pocket.

"Is that . . . inappropriate?" Rachel asked.

"No, it says 'the flames of my love,'" I explained. "It's a pun? The word for 'flames' is spelled the same as 'llamas,' but it's pronounced 'yamas'—"

"As long as it isn't bad. Liam, can you work with this?"

"I guess." Liam taped a tiny microphone to the top of my apron, then tucked a transmitter thingy inside the top pocket. "Don't touch it," he warned.

"I'll guard it with my life," I said solemnly.

He cracked a smile and moved on to Felicia, sitting stiffly on the couch, phone in hand. Another deep sigh escaped him as he muttered about silk being impossible. Eventually Amy came back, then Dylan and Quentin arrived together just as Liam finished with Amy.

"We're getting close to camera time," Rachel announced. "As soon as everyone is wired, I'll be around to collect your phones, tablets, laptops, and any other devices prohibited by the NDA. If you have any last messages to send, do it now."

I whipped out my phone so fast, I nearly dropped it. I'd put it on do-not-disturb mode, which meant I hadn't noticed a bunch of calls and texts coming in. Rosy, my sister, and . . . oh no.

The voicemail from my boss was surprisingly short. "Penny, this is Ofelia. Since you're not here, and you're not taking my calls, you've clearly made your choice. You can pick up your final paycheck when you return your keys. If anything goes missing, I'll tell the police you're responsible."

My mouth hung open in shock and disbelief. She'd actually done it. She'd fired me.

Seven years. For seven years, I busted my ass working for Ofelia, teaching myself everything I could to be a good spell technician, quitting college so I could be full-time. Seven years and she'd just . . . dumped me in the trash like a used tissue.

"Are you okay?" Amy asked. "You look sick."

What could I say? That my boss—former boss—was a spiteful jerk? That now I definitely had to win this show, or at least hope Charlotte Sharp gave me a job that started literally as soon as we stopped filming or I wouldn't be able to make rent next month?

"I'm fine," I lied.

CHAPTER 4

Penelope

Hands shaking, I texted Emelia while my stomach tried to escape through my belly button.

ME: I GOT FIRED OMFG

EME: NO SHE DIDNT

EME: what a raging come ping a

EME: comepinga, stfu autocorrect

ME: lolsob

EME: do you need money?

ME: not yet

EME: you can sleep in my bathtub

EME: like a sad mermaid

EME: I'll get you some shells for your boobs

ME: conch shells lol

EME: more like snail shells

I snort-laughed while continuing to freak out. I could multitask. Then a worse thought occurred to me: I couldn't drop off the store keys for two weeks because I was stuck here.

A movie played in my brain: Ofelia can't find some random item; Ofelia calls the cops and blames me; a SWAT team dramatically blows open a wall in the warehouse, rushes in, tackles me, and cuffs me while everyone screams; my mom cries on TV about how I'd always been a failure, especially compared to my sister, but she didn't know I was desperate enough to turn to a life of crime; Rosy tries to bring me an escape spell hidden inside a pastelito—

ME: ffffffffff

ME: I have to turn in my work keys but they're at my house

EME: I'll take care of it

ME: excuse me how

EME: I have my ways

> **ME:** you're going to ask Cari to break in
>
> **EME:** ding ding ding

Our cousin Carina had like twelve jobs, all side hustles. She was also our family fixer, always running around Miami to help someone out. Most importantly for this situation, she had a locksmith kit.

> **ME:** they're on a hook by the front door
>
> **ME:** make sure she locks up again after
>
> **EME:** duh not her first time
>
> **ME:** okay they're taking my phone in a minute gotta go

Eme sent me a GIF of a cartoon otter saying, "You got this!" and it made me feel a little better.

I tried to figure out what else I needed to do before I was cut off. Tell Rosy? No, she'd want to talk; I texted her a dancing girl emoji. Call Ofelia and beg for my job? That wouldn't work unless I did it in person, and if she said no, then I'd have no job and no *Cast Judgment* to win. Maybe if I explained where I was, I could convince her the show would be great free publicity for the store? Except she'd never be able to keep it a secret, and the lawyer ninjas would take me out.

Another thought smacked me. Gil. I needed to email him before Ofelia did.

Why hadn't I ever told him my actual name? Why hadn't I asked him out? I made a constipated hippo noise and tried to open the store email.

I was locked out.

Ofelia had once bricked her computer by downloading enough malware to destroy reality, but she'd managed to change the email password three seconds after firing me. How?

Rachel called, "Five minutes!" before vanishing again.

Five minutes? It took forever to mic me and Felicia. I guessed cotton shirts weren't abominations in the ears of the sound gods.

I opened my personal email and started a new one to Gil. Thankfully I remembered his email address. My brain slipped into some anxiety flow state as I typed faster than I ever had in my life. I barely even knew what I was saying. I think I told him I was going out of town and begged him to wait for me, like this was some period movie where I was going to war and he would be left behind, staring out the window as a single tear rolled down his cheek and sad violins played.

I hit send before I could edit. When would I get my phone back? What if my email went to spam and he never saw it?

Why did I care more about this than getting fired?

A reply appeared. No way. Too fast. I opened it and my stomach sank to my feet.

An auto-reply. Apparently Gil was actually going out of town instead of pretending like me, and he would only be checking emails periodically. I almost hit my forehead with my phone, except that would mess up my makeup, so I just shook it and growled.

I was fired, I would probably never talk to Gil again, and—

Stop it, Penelope! Breathe. I couldn't be distracted right now. We weren't starting the actual spell-casting until tomorrow, but I needed to make a good first impression on Charlotte Sharp. There was no way she'd think I was a cool, competent caster if I was twitching like I'd had a venti espresso.

"Time's up," Rachel announced. "Please place any phones, tablets, computers, and similar devices in the box."

Little Manny put a large metal bin on the floor, and we all surrendered our electronics. Rachel closed the lid, locked it, and muttered an incantation. Glowing blue sigils floated about an inch from the sides and top for a few seconds before sinking into the surface with a silent rush of energy and a whiff of sulfur.

No turning back now.

"Okay, we're good." Rachel tapped her tablet and gestured at the door. "Let's get you to the set."

We followed her like ducklings—or a rubber duck, in my case.

The warehouse part of the building somehow managed to be enormous and claustrophobic at the same time. Fluorescent lights hung from bare concrete ceilings twenty feet above me, outshone by an array of sun-bright LED panels on stands. A fancy camera mounted on a crane thing loomed to one side like a long-necked metal dinosaur. There were carts with mystery gadgets covered in dials and buttons and switches, cables snaking across the floor in every direction, and plastic bins and latched cases for equipment. It smelled like sawdust, paint, and a hint of body spray.

In the middle of the open space rose a giant room with high walls and double doors but no ceiling. Cables poked out of small holes in the insulated drywall, some leading to power strips and extension cords, others to a tower of blinking lights and TV screens in front of fancy ergonomic chairs. Unlike the quieter office area, here people rushed around, setting things up, moving them, muttering into walkie-talkies or collar mics. It felt like I'd stumbled into a beehive and I had to watch out or get stung.

Rachel led us through the double doors in the room-in-a-room, where we immediately hit another wall that branched into a hallway going left and right. We went left, turned a corner, and came to a stop.

In front of us, the *Cast Judgment* set waited in all its magic-making glory. The white walls were covered in stylized runes, sigils, mandalas, and other symbols that looked impressive but were magically inert. A giant silver pentacle gleamed on the floor, the prep stations arranged in two rows behind it, plus one in the back center. Stainless steel countertops and tables gleamed above brightly colored cabinets and shelves, one color per contestant—or in this case, per team. Each station also had its own wooden table, chalk-painted floor area, fridge with freezer, and fancy six-burner gas range with oven, way nicer than the one I used in the store.

Oh, right. I was fired. The delicate flower of my good mood withered.

"Amazing," Amy breathed.

"This is so . . . wow," Quentin said. "It's one thing to see it on TV, ya know?"

"For real," Dylan agreed.

Felicia looked bored.

Rachel walked to the other end of the room and muttered arguments into her collar mic that ended with her stabbing her tablet with her finger like it had offended her.

"Schedule change," Rachel told us. "We're doing solo and pair interviews after lunch, pairs first. Host and judge intros and partner assignments now. Camera guys are on their way to get everything set up, then Isaac and Tori will take over."

A bald bear of a man strolled in carrying a complicated-looking camera on his shoulder. He wiggled his fingers at us, put the camera down, and waited. Another camera person ducked behind a wheeled tripod thing near the entrance, and I think there was one more in the back of the room somewhere. Lights were turned on and off. The camera on the crane swung into position overhead.

Everything suddenly went quiet as a storm blew in. Isaac Knight, the showrunner. His brown hair was rumpled like he'd been running his hands through it, and his goatee was starting to take over the rest of his face and neck. Like most of the PAs, he wore jeans and a hoodie, but unlike them he'd paid extra for designer logos. He couldn't have been much taller than me, but his vibes filled the room as he looked around. Chisme online said some people called him Isaac Nightmare because he was hard to work with. I couldn't imagine he was much worse than Ofelia and some customers I'd had; maybe I needed to imagine harder. He focused on me and the rest of the contestants, and it was like looking into the black eyes of a shark.

"You five," he said, pointing in our direction. "Stand next to your stations so I can see how you look."

We hadn't been told which stations were ours, so none of us moved.

A lady in a black turtleneck and jeans with an asymmetrical brown bob spoke up. "Amy, you're red. Quentin, orange. Felicia, yellow. Dylan, green, and Penelope, blue."

We scrambled past each other, almost colliding. Then we all stared expectantly at Isaac.

Isaac frowned. At me. What did I do?

"Tori, why isn't she team yellow?" Isaac asked. "She's wearing yellow."

"She's also wearing red and orange," Tori of the turtleneck said slowly, picking each word like it was a melon at the grocery store. "Do you want wardrobe to—"

"No, just switch them around," Isaac said, flapping his hand. "Isn't her celebrity wearing yellow, too? It works. Matchy-matchy."

My pulse sped up. I tried to remember if I'd ever seen Charlotte wearing yellow.

"Okay," Tori said. "But Felicia is wearing pink."

"And her celebrity is wearing blue. Swap them."

Tori tapped something into her tablet as Felicia and I traded places. Now I was in the back left and she was center back. I swallowed spit and tried not to fidget.

"Everybody look eager and excited," Isaac said. "Nate, give me medium and close shots of each of them."

He turned and walked out. I kept swallowing. How was my mouth so dry? Look excited, he'd said. I put on my retail smile. The auditions had been stressful, but this was a whole other level.

And we hadn't even started spell-casting yet.

After a hundred years of staring past the camera at the entrance, then at camera guy Nate's shoulder, attempting to emit positive energy while the giant lights around us shifted miniscule amounts, Isaac came back and pronounced us ready.

"Get the talent in here," he told Tori, slurping a green smoothie through a giant straw.

The drink reminded me of Rosy, dancing as she made batidos, humming along with the restaurant music. I wouldn't get to see her as much now that I was fired, not unless I got another job in that shopping center. Maybe at the daycare? Or the gym? Or the Vaquita up the street?

It hit me that I had never really expected to win this competition. Sure, I'd daydreamed about money and time to work on my abuela's spellbook, about meeting famous people and impressing them enough that they'd hire me. But I'd never thought through how much my life might change, because I didn't really believe it would. Every step of the audition process, I waited to get the call or email telling me I was out. Every time I made it to the next stage, the only person I could celebrate with was Emelia, so none of it felt real.

But it was. It so was. And I could win, damn it. If I was good enough to be here, I was good enough to go all the way.

If only I could make myself believe that.

Rachel reappeared, followed by the host of *Cast Judgment*, Syd Hart. They were tall and thin, with pale skin and long black hair, and tiny crow's-feet around their blue eyes that told you they smiled a lot. They wore a leopard-print shirt under a black leather jacket, a look I could never pull off. On the show and in interviews, they were goofy and told a lot of jokes, but maybe they were more serious in real life?

"Syd will start with their usual thing," Isaac said. "Contestant intros, then judges, then we'll do the celebrity pairs. Any questions?"

"One question," Syd said. Isaac made a *get on with it* circular motion with his hand.

"What is a witch's favorite subject in school?" Syd asked.

Everyone stared at them. Nate snickered.

I raised my hand. "Spelling?"

"Correct!" Syd grinned and tossed something at me.

A lemon candy. I felt like I was in third grade again, getting a treat from the teacher. And suddenly, I wasn't as nervous anymore.

Isaac looked like that meme of the guy with the smiling mask over the angry crying face. "No more questions? Good, great. Tori, take over." He stalked out, and Syd winked at us.

"I can't believe he hasn't hexed my mouth shut," Syd said in a stage whisper.

Rachel vanished back into the hallway. Tori started issuing orders—I guess she was the director? Assistant director? I didn't understand all the show titles. Someone else brought in one of those things with an arm that clapped shut and made a loud noise, with digital numbers on the front.

"Remember," Tori said, a calm breeze compared to Isaac's thunderstorm. "One camera will be on you while Syd talks about you, but other cameras will always be rolling on everyone together. Don't stop looking at Syd, don't fidget, don't pick your nose. When the judges are introduced, wait for Syd to finish, then clap and get excited, but not too much. This isn't a concert or football game. When your celebrity is brought out, same deal. Big smiles; you're hyped to partner with them. Got it? Good. Let's roll."

The butterflies in my stomach caught fire. I wanted to work with Charlotte Sharp, but the other options were probably great. Just . . . not as great. I wished I'd practiced reacting in a mirror. I didn't want to look unhappy if I ended up with someone else.

The person with the clapper thingy stood in front of the camera on wheels and rattled off something fast, then opened the arm and snapped it shut. The noise was so loud I jumped.

Syd moved smoothly into the same spot the person had been standing in and looked straight into the camera for a count of five, then began.

"Some people cast spells for work," Syd said. "Others cast them for pleasure. These five competitors will be casting for the chance to win a yearlong residency at the Desgraves Studio and a hundred thousand dollars in cash. And our panel of experts will cast the most difficult thing of all." They paused dramatically. "They're going to cast judgment."

I knew from watching the show that it would cut to the title and play a little theme song now, but editing would add that stuff later.

Syd continued. "Our contestants have come from all over the country to beautiful Miami, Florida, for a very special season of *Cast Judgment*. Instead of competing alone, they'll each be partnered with a Spellebrity caster to push their creations to even greater magical heights. But before we introduce those special guests, let's meet our lucky five."

They turned around to face the camera at the back of the room while Nate walked slowly in front of us. "Amy Song is a studio musician from Jersey City who sells handmade charms online in her Mirage shop. Dylan Williams is a grocery store baker from Baltimore who experiments with magical pastries in his spare time. Quentin Adams is an auto mechanic from Minneapolis who tinkers with antique enchantments. Felicia Rivera is a real estate broker and interior designer from Los Angeles with a flair for fashion spells."

She definitely looked like she had strong clothing opinions.

I was, embarrassingly, "Last but not least, Penelope Delmar is a spell technician from right here in Miami. If you need help with your magic, just ask her." Syd grinned, and we all chuckled politely.

Syd gestured at a PA, who ran over and handed them a bottle of water. They took a quick swig, made some weird noises, then turned back around to the camera in front of us and stared silently at it for a few seconds before continuing.

"Now, let's bring out our judges," Syd said, launching into introductions that I already knew from watching the show.

Fabienne Desgraves, founder and owner of Desgraves Studio.

Dark brown skin and eyes, black hair almost shaved on the sides but longer on top. Coral jumpsuit cut like a suit jacket in front, a short cape draped over her bare arms. Deep red lips curled in a mysterious smile. Her comments usually focused on style, flair, and cool factor.

Doris Twist—not her real name—started in the 1980s with her show *Witching with a Twist*. Pale and as old as my abuela, hazel eyes watery but still sharp. Cream-and-purple dress with lavender sweater, gray hair pulled back in a tight bun. Very politician's wife–meets–church lady. Super nice; whenever she said something even a little critical, she sounded really sorry.

Hugh Burbank—surprisingly his real name—owner of Burbank's Boutique. Dark green shirt and gray slacks that matched his eyes and hair respectively. Fashionably tan skin like Felicia's. Permanently sneering. Also shorter than I expected; he seemed to loom over everyone on the show. Camera tricks, I guess. His compliment sandwiches were bunless shit burgers.

What if I messed up so badly that he hit me with a burn epic enough to turn me into a meme? Oh my god! Shut up, brain. Smile. Clap. Catastrophize later.

Syd took another quick water break, but this time they called Tori over and held a muttered meeting. At one point they both looked at me, which totally didn't make my anxiety worse, nope.

Eventually Syd nodded and faced us again.

"Now," Syd said, "it's time for our fabulous competitors to meet their celebrity partners."

"Stop," Tori called. "'Spellebrity,' Syd. You have to use the trademark."

Syd grinned sheepishly at us and repeated the phrase correctly. They continued. "First, we have Jaya Kamath, host of *Jaya's Charm-*

ing Charms and author of the *CIY Charms* spellbooks. Jaya will be paired with . . ." Dramatic pause. "Amy Song!"

We all clapped as Jaya walked over to Amy. She wasn't quite at Amy's level of cottagecore, but they looked like they shopped in the same store. Both seemed happy.

The other intros went the same way. Tanner Byrne, host of *Spell Rehab*, did reproductions and restorations of old enchantments. He was sent over to a delighted Quentin. Zeke Murphy owned a famous magical candy shop in the Strip District in Pittsburgh, Zeke's Sweets N'at, same name as his show. Dylan was his partner.

Just me and Felicia left. Oh my god. Was I sweating in this freezing warehouse? Had I put on deodorant this morning?

"Charlotte Sharp is the owner of Athame Arts—"

My blood thumped in my ears like bass at a club. Charlotte wore a pale blue knit top with navy pants. Her blond-highlighted hair was styled in a bun with loose strands framing her face that probably took her stylist forever to get perfect. Her honey-tan skin was—

Wait. Her sweater. Was blue. Not yellow.

"Charlotte will be working with . . . Felicia!"

I really hoped the camera wasn't pointed at me, because I had no clue what my face was doing. Hopefully still smiling. My cheeks definitely hurt. I forced myself to clap for Felicia, who didn't look as delighted as she should after stealing my partner.

Okay, she hadn't actually stolen my partner. I was still salty, though.

"We're especially excited to be able to pair our local competitor, Penelope, with another Miami caster."

What? Who? I stared at the hallway entrance.

"You may have seen his work on his popular Jinxd channel—"

No! No. No no no. Please no.

"—star of *Mage You Look*—"

Kill me.

"Leandro Presto!"

Leandro turned the corner, waving and grinning at nobody in particular. His safety glasses were on, hair slicked back, mustache waxed and curled, and he wore a vintage yellow shirt covered in drawings of, I kid you not, hamburgers and French fries. He froze the instant he saw me, and we stared at each other across the room like stunned telenovela characters.

"Stop!" Tori shouted. "Let's do that again. Penelope, Leandro, we need more enthusiasm, please."

Leandro turned around and marched back into the hallway, shoulders up to his ears. Felicia chuckled. I wanted to stab her with my pencil. Instead, I dug deep for excitement, some shred of satisfaction. All I could find was a sinkhole of despair.

With Leandro as my partner, I was totally fucked.

CHAPTER 5

Gil

I wore my goofy grin like a mask and tried to focus on Syd. They were explaining tonight's group activity, which I had already been briefed on since I was providing the entertainment. My brain kept sliding sideways to Penelope, who stood next to me in the greatest apron I'd ever seen. Las llamas de mi amor! Legendary pun.

When I'd gotten my partner's bio from Rachel earlier, I couldn't believe it. Not only would I be stuck in a hotel with my secret crush for two weeks, but we'd be working on spells together. I hadn't had to fake how excited I was when I walked out to meet her.

Except Penelope was the woman from the park who hated me.

Maybe "hated" was a strong word. But last night had been a huge mess, one I had to clean up if Penelope and I were going to win this competition.

Funny how quickly my pessimism had flipped to "maybe we have a chance." I knew what Penelope was capable of. Now I just had to convince her that I wasn't going to be a failboat captain.

"Our Spellebrities have a reputation to maintain, after all," Syd said, cutting through my thoughts. "Some more serious than others."

That was my cue. I went with mock confusion, looking around and mouthing, *Me?* while I pointed at my chest. Everyone chuckled.

Penelope's smile looked super fake, though. Ouch. This was going to be a mission.

Syd wrapped up the scripted stuff. The judges left, probably to their trailers. The contestants were separated from the celebrities, and we were led back to our greenroom, abandoned until it was our turn for confessionals or publicity shots.

The place looked like a fancy hotel bar: expensive couches and leather chairs, glass-topped coffee tables, a dining area, even a bookcase stocked with random hardcovers. Tiered platters full of tiny appetizers lured me over to the polished mahogany counter. College had taught me never to pass up free food. I filled a plate and inhaled egg sushi rolls, tiny quiches, prosciutto-wrapped dates, and pastelitos de guayaba that looked nothing like what I usually got from a Cuban bakery. The slits on top were in a flower shape, and they were covered in powdered sugar. I had two anyway.

Charlotte grabbed a sparkling water from the fridge and sat alone at a table. She might as well have wrapped herself in a bunch of do-not-cross tape; she'd made it clear earlier that she wasn't here to socialize with any of us.

Jaya and Zeke took up spots on the couches, trading recipes for cookies or something. Tanner joined them, his mellow voice and accent reminding me of old movies and NPR reporters, which fit his old-timey vest-wearing vibe. If I didn't know Zeke was from Pittsburgh, I probably would have ignorantly guessed Boston, though he sounded twangier. "Dey" instead of "they" kinda stuff. Jaya's British Indian accent seemed faded, like she'd lived in the US for a long time.

I wondered what I sounded like to them? Super Miami?

The conversation wandered away from food, and even though Jaya and Tanner and Zeke tried to include me, they started talking about mutuals and contract renewals and options and some party they went to at the Home Casting Network building a few months earlier. It reminded me of events with my parents before they split up, when I was old enough to get dragged out and shown off for their friends and business contacts, but not to actively participate in their conversations.

Like I had as a kid, I mostly zoned out, until it suddenly got relevant.

"Yinz guys heard about Doris Twist?" Zeke asked.

Yinz?

Tanner nodded stiffly. "Makes me a mite nervous, I don't mind telling you. She's had her difficulties, but I thought she was safe. If they can do this to her, they can do it to anyone."

"Is she okay?" I asked.

"She's retiring, after however many years on this show," Jaya said.

"Is that what they're calling it?" Zeke asked. "Retiring? From a show she started?"

"Making room for young blood." Tanner gestured at me. "You could be next on the roster."

"Maybe," I said. "Guess it depends on how this Spellebrity thing goes."

Zeke rubbed his bald head. "The number crunchers have their own magic math that only makes sense to them. Don't stress about it. That's your agent's job."

"This business is cutthroat," Jaya agreed. "Take care of yourself, because you never know when it will be your neck on the block."

"Win or lose," Tanner said, "just do your best."

Charlotte made a scoffing noise. I wasn't sure why.

"And do be nice to your partner," Tanner added. "Poor girl looked like she had the shock of her life seeing you walk in."

That made two of us. Before I could decide whether to confess that we'd met before, the UPM, Rachel, appeared.

"Mr. Presto, if you'd follow me, please?" she said.

"Lead the way, Rachel."

Rachel took me through an empty cubicle farm to a room with an LED sign on the door that read, "Recording." Liam, one of the sound guys, checked my mic and transmitter and pronounced me ready.

A makeup lady—Fina, I think?—was also there for touch-ups. She muttered something about my mustache; I hoped it hadn't moved. I'd used a new adhesive that was supposed to last longer than spirit gum and look more realistic for TV. It would be harder to get off, but that was better than having a fake facial hair malfunction.

The room was mostly dark, with a few soft lights, as if the people inside were meant to be floating in some astral plane where inner thoughts manifested externally. Creepy. Two chairs sat against the wall behind the door, one of them already occupied by Penelope. I gave her what I hoped was a reassuring smile; she gave me the same fake one from before. Great.

Camera guy Nate waved from the corner, and Tori closed the door behind me. I sat down and swallowed the stage fright making my egg sushi want to come back up.

"For this confessional," Tori said, "you've both just been told you're partners, and you're going to talk about each other a little. All compliments, you're happy and excited to work together, you're ready to win. Got it?"

We nodded.

"Penelope first," Tori said. "I'll count you down. Ready?"

Penelope inhaled sharply but nodded again.

"Nate, start rolling. Penelope, give me some hype in five,

four . . ." The rest of the countdown was done on her fingers silently, then she pointed at Penelope.

If I hadn't already known how she felt about me, the absolute mierda she talked about how fun my videos were and how much she'd loved my butterfly spell at Dolphin Mall would have tricked me into thinking she was a fan. She was fresca como una lechuga, as my dad would say. We were going to crush this.

"Leandro, your turn," Tori said.

Ah. Fuck. I'd spent the whole time staring at Penelope like a happy puppy. Sam would laugh her ass off if she saw me now.

I had to say nice things without accidentally letting anything slip that Leandro shouldn't know. What had her bio said? Stick to the basics, Gil. Rule two. Stay. In. Character.

"I'm really excited to work with a spell technician," I said. "She'll know everything about all the reagents and equipment we're going to be using. She has a lot of experience helping people solve problems and prep for casting. Maybe she can even stop me from making mistakes before they happen!" I grinned at the camera, then at Penelope. She was still fake smiling.

"Now, give us a battle cry," Tori said. "You're going to win, you've got this, whatever."

Penelope seemed stuck, so I stepped in. "Miami gotta represent! We're not here to play, we're here to win. No jokes, just game face." I made a fake-macho duck face for the camera, then looked at Penelope.

She laughed. A real one, I think, because it sounded surprised. I held up a hand for a high five, and she slapped it.

"Good, great." Tori tapped her tablet. "Now we need a few minutes with Leandro alone." She got up and opened the door. "Little Manny! Take Penelope back to the greenroom."

Penelope followed Little Manny out, forehead wrinkled, shoulders hunched. Maybe that laugh hadn't been real. The door closed, sounding loud in the small room.

"Tell us about your charity, Leandro," Tori said.

This was my chance to sell Alan Kazam's Schools Are Magic to anyone watching. Even if I didn't win, this might help bring in more donations.

I explained how Alan started his magic career because of what he learned as a kid in school, how his first performances were for elementary classes, and it led to him getting a local TV show that eventually went big. Almost everyone my age remembered watching him "putting the fun in magic fundamentals." Then I went into why he had founded the charity, and what the money was used for. With any luck, my whole speech would make it into the show, hopefully with some intercut video or pictures from the AKSAM archives.

I didn't mention that Alan Kazam was my grandpa Fred. Family secret.

Tori did more tablet things. "That was great, thanks so much. Since we moved the schedule around, you have publicity shots with our stills photographer now, then you'll have time to go back to the hotel to prep for tonight. Did you need anything, any reagents or gear?"

"I've got it."

"Great. Someone can take you out to the van when you're ready." Tori opened the door. "Rachel, I need Tanner and Quentin next, please."

Liam de-mic'd me and Rachel led me to the photographer's studio space. I posed in various goofy ways for about a half hour, then headed to the exit to wait for transport. Penelope was back in her greenroom, presumably, because she wasn't outside.

Tonight, I promised myself, I'd have a talk with her. I'd convince her we were a solid team even if I had to make a total fool of myself to do it.

I'D CHECKED THE prices for Casa Coquí online, and I would probably never stay at a place this nice again in my life, unless one of my parents paid or that legendary show deal manifested. When I got in last night, I'd barely noticed anything except how tired I was. Now I took a closer look around.

Cozy sofas and chairs covered in frog-print pillows were arranged around coffee tables, like this was someone's living room instead of a hotel lobby. Framed, enchanted moving pictures of ferns and palm fronds decorated the walls, along with more coquí pictures and mirrors in different sizes. There was even a guitar propped against a cabinet, like someone would be right back to pick it up.

The front desk was an actual desk, distressed wood painted white with a bubbly glass top. The woman behind it was named Alina, according to her name tag, and her clothes were more casual than corporate. Dark hair, bright red lipstick, and the kind of smile that probably made strangers talk to her at the store. I smiled back at her as I went for the elevators.

The third floor had sky-blue walls with rainforest pictures between doors, spelled with short loops of leaves moving or tiny frogs peeking from inside big bromeliads. Near the elevators, there was an ice maker and vending machines with bougie drinks, candy, and chips. Also, optimistically, condoms. My room was first on the left, next to the emergency stairs, which would be handy if I needed to make any secret escapes without my mustache. I swiped the key four times before it worked, then muscled my way in.

My room was bigger than the one in the apartment I shared with Sam and Ed, with a kitchenette, a queen-sized bed, and a balcony overlooking the street instead of the bay. The housekeeper had left tiny chocolate frogs on the pillow when I first got here, but I'd told Alina I didn't want daily service. One fewer person poking around my stuff.

I checked the reagents for the spell I'd be casting at the venue later. Maybe I should explain to Penelope what it was actually going to do. Tell her the secret—one of the secrets—about Leandro Presto: that my mistakes were intentional. Enough people already assumed my incompetence was an act, part of the show; she might trust me if she knew for sure.

No. The stakes for this were too high. Rule number two: I needed to stay in character, to protect my himbo persona. And her reactions when I goofed during the competition had to seem natural.

I couldn't risk it. I'd have to earn her trust some other way.

The bathroom was swank, with a multijet shower big enough to fit two people. A full-length mirror hung next to the bathroom door; I checked for mustache integrity. The new adhesive was holding. My skin would probably peel off after two weeks of this, though thankfully Sam had loaded me up with moisturizers to help with irritation. I pulled out the adhesive remover and brush, then started at one edge of the mustache and proceeded to slowly work it off.

Face cleansed, I had time for a quick nap before the evening event. I flopped down on top of the covers and stuck a pillow over my eyes to block out the sun peeking around the edges of the curtains. Before I could even start to worry about whether I'd be able to shut off my brain enough to fall asleep, I passed out.

A PA POUNDING on my door woke me up from a dead sleep. By the time I had my mustache back on, I'd missed dinner. A caterer in mid-cleanup took pity on me and made me a chicken sandwich, which I ate in the elevator.

Sunset peeked through high-rise condos on the other side of Biscayne. At the front of the hotel, a giant black party bus took up most of the two-lane Edgewater street. Tinted windows hid whatever sloppy-drunk sins people committed inside. Crew carried stuff on and off, Rachel furiously tapped her tablet, Liam walked around putting mics on people again, Tori argued with Nate and a massive dude about something, and the rest of us stood around roasting to death. Penelope stayed with her group, and I stayed with mine.

"Ever been in one of these before?" Tanner asked me.

"For a friend's bachelor party," I said. "This one's probably nicer."

Charlotte's eyes were hidden by giant sunglasses, but her lip curl told me she thought I'd said something funny. I had no idea what.

"Just do whatever Nate says, Big Manny," Tori finally snapped. Nate climbed into the bus with his camera, and the other guy, Big Manny, followed him.

To the rest of us, she said, "We're going to film you all getting on the bus now. I want excitement, the bus is really cool, oohs and aahs, okay?"

We all said it was okay. Well, Charlotte lowered her sunglasses, then slid them back up. Tori yelled at Nate to start rolling, and we slowly piled in.

Neon lights and black lights made everything look like a tacky futuristic video game. Black pleather couches lined the walls, with sunken tables between them for people to put their drinks. Just to the left of the entrance was the bar, stocked with enough booze to get us all wrecked real fast—not that any of us would be drinking, as far as I knew. The ceiling was mirrored, the floor was fake marble, and at the front, a giant TV played a loop of the *Cast Judgment* opening with no sound.

Nate and Big Manny smooshed together at the back like two football players in a golf cart. I tried not to feel bad for them while I pretended to be impressed and excited.

Everyone paired off with their partners, except for me. I ended up with Big Manny, across from Tanner, who sat with Quentin. Penelope grabbed a spot by Charlotte and the tall blonde, Felicia, near the front. The doors closed, the engine was running, but we didn't move.

"Where's Leandro?" Tori asked. "Get up here with Penelope."

Penelope winced. Maybe she hadn't ditched me on purpose, but now we definitely had to play nice. I grabbed my backpack and switched seats.

Syd popped open a bottle of champagne; through the power of TV magic, we were all given flutes of bubbly apple juice instead. A disco ball spun from the ceiling, and we pretended to drink and party for maybe five minutes, with the bus still parked.

"Good, that's enough for now," Tori said. "We'll have a couple more shots as we go." She pressed a button and sat down. The bus revved up and pulled away from the hotel.

I thought a couple of the contestants might want to keep partying, but all of them chilled out and started talking to their partners. Penelope wouldn't even look at me. She seemed to be trying to psych herself up for something.

"Hey, Charlotte," she said finally. "I just wanted to say, I'm a huge fan."

Oh. It was like that, huh.

Charlotte smiled, eyes still hidden behind her sunglasses. "Thank you. Were you the contestant who works in a store?" Her voice was smoky, New York but toned down.

I could almost see the hearts in Penelope's eyes. "Yes. I know you started in retail, too. You're such an inspiration."

"Everyone has to start somewhere. Thankfully I had enough talent and ambition that I wasn't stuck there for long."

Penelope flinched. I might not have noticed if I hadn't been staring at her.

"I started doing kid parties," I blurted out.

"I'm sure you did," Charlotte replied.

Grandpa Fred's rule number three: commit to the bit. "Kids can be hard to impress, but they love to tell you what to do. And when a spell blows up in your face, they laugh their little butts off."

"Sounds delightful." Charlotte rubbed her forehead like she had a headache and stared out the window.

Felicia wrinkled her nose and made a quiet huffing sound. A laugh? Penelope didn't speak again, just grabbed her knees like she was trying not to touch anything. Especially not me.

I read the room and shut up. Penelope had obviously wanted to be Charlotte's partner, not mine. Somehow I didn't think Ms. Fancypants CEO would have been nicer even if they were teamed up. I didn't know that, though. Neither did Penelope.

It didn't matter. We were stuck together, and we had to make the best of it. For the rest of the drive, I mentally rehearsed the script for my spell, trying not to feel worse than I already did.

CHAPTER 6

Gil

Miami traffic meant it took forever to get to the club in South Beach where we were filming. We stopped to pretend to party again on the Causeway, Star Island on one side and the cruise ships at the port on the other. On 5th Street, giant cranes towered over half-built concrete high-rises, with shiny new blue glass buildings competing to block each other's views of the water. Art deco stores and restaurants and hotels and condos were lit up like the inside of the bus, bright neon pinks and blues and teals and reds, selling the same kind of fake we were. People in bathing suits and flip-flops passed others in fancy dresses and ankle-breaking high heels. Half of them wore makeup or glamour—or both, taking the chance that their dates or potential hookups didn't have a spell to see through their illusions.

I never came out here if I could help it. There were less crowded beaches for when friends wanted to hang out and party, or we'd go to someone's pool and not have to deal with sand and strangers.

The bus stopped and Tori got out first, talked to someone outside, then came back in. "We're moving you through a small, controlled crowd into a VIP area. Energy up, big smiles, stay hyped."

Penelope got up; I pulled on my backpack and stood behind her. When Tori gave the signal, we left the party bus, cheering quietly.

Inside, the ceiling rose two stories, painted black with shiny chrome pipes and ducts crossing it. The left wall was a long, mirrored bar, bottles on shelves that went all the way up, lit by green and purple neon. To the right, an empty chest-high stage surrounded by rigging and speakers said this place hosted a lot of shows. No chairs or tables, just an empty dance floor with about a dozen people standing around.

The second camera crew stayed on us as we passed through the club, their lights shining at our faces, leaving bright spots everywhere I looked. Rachel waited for us upstairs in an area overlooking the stage inside, with another small bar plus an open circle of seating around a wooden table.

Still paired up, everyone sat except me. I had a spell to perform.

Tori positioned me with my back to the balcony, the second camera in front and Nate to my left with a view of the table. One mic and makeup check later, I started setting up my reagents and gear. While she'd avoided me before, now Penelope watched me like it was her job; everyone else drank mocktails and poked at bar snacks.

Deep breaths. Focus. Be funny.

"Ready Freddy," I told Tori.

She counted me down and gestured for me to go.

I grinned at the camera. "Welcome to *Mage You Look*, *Cast Judgment* edition! We're here to have a good time before we start the competition tomorrow."

Quentin cheered, and the others followed a few heartbeats after. I gave him two thumbs up before grabbing the deck of cards sitting on the table.

"I call this spell 'The Queen of Hearts, She Made Some Hearts.'" I cut and shuffled the deck in a fancy series of motions with one hand, then two, then I let the cards fly across the air between my hands in a wide arc. Manual dexterity could be as impressive as magic, if it looked cool enough.

"The queen of hearts, she made some tarts, all on a summer's day." I cut the deck and turned it around, showing the queen of hearts card. "The knave of hearts, he stole those tarts, and ran off and ate them and got a massive stomachache."

A few people chuckled. I revealed the jack of hearts, then shuffled the deck again.

"The king of hearts called for the tarts, and he was super salty when he found out they were gone." I showed the king of hearts, then put him back. "The queen hated to see him upset, so she had to make more." I stopped shuffling and spread the cards out in front of me on the table. "I need a volunteer for the next part."

Everyone looked at Penelope. She fake grinned and stood next to me.

"Pick a card, any card," I said. "But make sure it's the queen of hearts. We need her for the spell."

Penelope ran her hand over the cards like she could feel out the right one, then picked one at random. The surprise on her face was awesome. She turned the card around and showed it to everyone: the queen of hearts.

"Thank you, m'lady," I said, then flipped over all the cards with one hand, starting from the end. The rest were alternating versions of the king and jack of hearts.

"Oh!" Amy said, delighted. Quentin clapped, and Zeke made a gesture like, *can you believe this guy?*

"Now, we could make tarts appear, but that might get messy." I reached for my premixed reagents and dumped them in a glass mixing bowl. "So instead, our queen is going to make some candy conversation hearts. Here we have gelatin, powdered sugar, and salt."

Penelope peeked into the bowl, still holding the queen. I handed her a spoon.

"Could you stir while I pour?" I asked. She nodded. I slowly added a bottle of lemon-lime soda to the bowl, trying not to be distracted by how I could brush her shoulder if I moved. Once it was all blended together, I held up a small tin.

"This is a pre-spelled blend of honey, rosemary, and forget-me-nots, plus the ashes of the recipe for the hearts. Law of contagion for the win! Penelope, could you hold up that card?"

She did, and I dipped a paintbrush into the gooey mixture, then carefully painted it over the hearts on the playing card.

"And now, the raw materials." I used the same brush to add some of the lemony gelatin.

"When I say the magic word, the queen is going to make some hearts for her kingly husband, so he knows exactly how much she loves him." I looked down at Penelope, who stood so close to me, I thought my own heart was going to pop out of my chest.

She would hate the next part.

"Here, let me have the card, and you can catch the hearts when they come out," I said. Penelope nodded and held out her cupped hands. Then she turned her head so only I could see her and mouthed something at me: *stop control*, I think, which meant she had figured out the flaw in this casting. I pretended not to understand.

Murmuring the incantation I'd written, I focused on filling the card with my energy and intent. Tingles ran up and down my arms. As soon as I felt the magic link between the card and bowl solidify, I said, "Presto!" and gestured at the card.

The places I'd painted with goop glowed pink. A pair of perfectly shaped conversation hearts fell into Penelope's palms. Everyone gave a little cheer.

Then another pair fell out. Then another, every couple of seconds at first, then faster and faster until they were pouring out. Penelope tried to catch them, but they quickly overflowed her hands and clattered onto the table.

"Oh no," I said. "I forgot to add something to the spell to make it stop and start on command. Here, let me . . ." I handed the card to Penelope, who dropped all the hearts she was holding as more fountained out. I rummaged in my backpack, pulling out a rubber chicken, a rabbit plushie, a knotted handkerchief that kept going and going, and finally a bottle labeled "Salt" that I held up with a loud "Aha!"

I tried to pour some salt into my hand, and it quickly became clear the bottle was empty. I rubbed my neck and grinned at Penelope.

"Looks like we have to wait for the reagents in the bowl to run out." I gestured at Penelope. "Next time, I'll leave the heart-making to the queen."

They all laughed, even Penelope, though hers sounded forced. Hearts continued to pour from the card, piling into a small mountain that collapsed under its own weight, making her wince. With a sound like a bubble of chewing gum popping and the faint smell of burnt sugar, the rush finally stopped.

Tori clapped. "Great! That's it for Leandro. Anyone want to dance on the table?"

"I don't think my husband would approve," Quentin said dryly. Amy turned bright red, and no one else seemed interested, so Tori pivoted to having the bartender make some impressive-looking spelled shots.

Penelope put a hand on my arm. "Can I talk to you?"

I followed her to the elevator landing, my heart speeding up like a car at a yellow light. Before she started talking, I held a finger in front of my lips and motioned for her to turn around. She did, and I turned off the mic transmitter clipped to her pants, then gestured for her to do the same for me.

"Okay, now we're mostly private," I said. "What's up?"

She stared at the elevator door, her face scrunched up like she was thinking unhappy thoughts. Finally she said, "First of all, I'm sorry about last night. I had a really bad day, but that's no excuse for being a jerk."

"It's okay, it happens. People have said way worse stuff to me online." Her eyes got big, and I raised my hands. "Not that you're like those people! It's fine, we're good, don't worry about it."

"I just didn't want . . . you know, bad first impressions and stuff. We have to work together."

"We will. I know you were just saying nice things about me in the confessional, but I really do think we're going to be a great team."

Penelope flushed and smiled. "Thanks. But."

But?

"I get that you're probably here because you're cute, and funny, and your whole brand is messing up."

I thought so, too, but it hurt to hear from her. Wait, did she say "cute"?

"I don't know what you get out of this besides more likes and subscribes, but winning is really important to me."

What would Leandro say? "No worries. We're gonna be legendary. We should start planning our victory dance now." I did a quick salsa step and spin, landing with a cocky smile.

Penelope blinked. "Okay, that was surprisingly good."

"I've got some moves. I'm not going to do them on the table, though."

She paused like she was about to say something else, then sighed. "Look. I'll be honest. I got fired this morning."

"Oh, shit, I'm so sorry. Are you okay?" I stepped closer, almost touched her without thinking, but caught myself.

She shrugged, her eyes watery. "I'm not trying to get pity likes. If anyone else were my partner, I probably wouldn't have said anything."

Double ouch. "Because you would know they're taking this seriously."

"Yeah." Penelope's big brown eyes looked up into mine. "Please, can you just do your best? Your real best. Don't wreck our spells to be funny."

I couldn't promise not to be Leandro—rule number two—but there was room to maneuver if I was careful. And I was always careful.

"No spell wrecks," I said. "Not unless you count wrecking the competition."

The smile she gave me seemed worried. She didn't believe me. What did I expect? I had to earn her trust.

I gave her an elaborate bow and gestured at the table. "Shall we clean up my mess, m'lady?"

"Don't 'm'lady' me," Penelope said. "Do you even own a fedora?"

"Only a trilby," I joked. I think she muttered "oh my god" under her breath, but she started walking away.

I grabbed the back of her pants, and she spun around like I'd smacked her ass. "Our mics," I said, hands raised. "Sorry."

She relaxed and turned back around, and I flipped her mic on, then let her do mine. I glanced back at the other contestants and celebrities, and caught Tori staring at us with an expression I couldn't read. It made me nervous.

One more thing to be nervous about. Now it wasn't just my friends and my grandpa's charity counting on me to win, it was my unemployed partner. No pressure.

With a big, fake grin, I used the queen of hearts card to scoop candy into the salt bottle. If only real hearts could be dealt with so easily.

My mustache was hanging halfway off my face when my hotel room phone rang. I hadn't had a landline since high school, so it took me two more rings to figure out what the noise was and pick up.

"Hello?"

"Mr. Presto, this is Rachel, with Hexafilm."

Unit production manager. Okay, back into character.

"Hey, Rachel, what's up?"

"Isaac wants to meet with you and Penelope in the morning, before your scheduled call time. The van will pick you up at seven thirty."

Ugh, so early. "Sure, no problem."

"Thank you, Mr. Presto. Have a lovely rest of your evening."

It was almost midnight, but sure. "Thanks, you too."

I hung up and stared at the phone. What did Isaac Knight want with me and Penelope?

It was pointless to worry about it, even if I knew I couldn't help myself. I'd find out soon enough.

I finished de-mustaching, showered, and crawled into bed, dreaming of climbing a candy heart mountain and falling off a cliff.

TV SHOWRUNNERS APPARENTLY didn't slum it in boutique hotels in Edgewater; they stayed in a downtown high-rise condo where enchanted statues of Greek myths slowly transformed from humans to animals or plants in the entrance, and a dozen valet people wearing white gloves and silly hats leaped to open car doors before you even parked.

Penelope and I were met in the lobby by a tiny squirrel-cheeked lady who introduced herself, "Hi I'm Mary Isaac's assistant so nice to meet you Isaac is waiting for you upstairs come right this way," without taking a single breath, while power walking backward. I wasn't sure whether I was impressed or worried about her blood pressure.

A private elevator zoomed us up to the penthouse. The doors opened inside the room, showing off an incredible view of Brickell and the bay through floor-to-ceiling windows. White marble floors, white leather couches, clear acrylic chairs and tables . . . The only color came from the blue sky and water outside. I felt like I should wash my hands before touching anything.

Isaac sat in a fancy ergonomic chair behind a clear desk. Even from a few feet away, he smelled like he'd had whiskey for breakfast and tried to cover it up with mouthwash and expensive cologne. His beard said he was going full lumberjack or kept forgetting to shave. His clothes said someone, presumably Mary, was getting paid to iron his T-shirts. He grabbed an orange stress ball with a cussing face emoji on it and squeezed. It squeaked.

Tori stood behind him to the right, her face blanker than the

Greek statues downstairs. She wore a navy polo with the Hexafilm logo, her short brown hair smoothed into a faux-hawk.

What did they want to talk about that couldn't have waited until we were on set? I tried to relax my shoulders as I sat on one of the uncomfortable clear chairs next to Penelope.

"Here's the deal," Isaac said. "The two of you have chemistry potential." Squeak. "You're giving that popular-nerd-meets-anime-waifu thing, you're both putting out the vibe, and audiences eat that shit on gluten-free crackers." Squeak. "They watch *Cast Judgment* for the stories, the drama, the frisson of fappability that comes with finding a new RPF ship." Squeak. "We want you to lean into that." Squeak. "You get what I'm saying?"

I thought I did, but I also only understood half the words he'd just used.

"You want us to . . . pretend to be into each other?" Penelope asked. "Romantically?"

"Bingo bongo," Isaac said. Squeak. "We won't know how many more episodes you'll get, obviously, so this might be one and done." Squeak. "But there will still be promo, publicity shots, the whole shebang." Squeak squeak. "Keep it up long enough and you'll stay on the public radar for weeks."

Penelope seemed freaked out, and I didn't even know what I was.

Isaac looked behind us and swore. "Mary, that vulture is back. Handle it."

"Yes, sir!" Mary said.

She opened the door to the balcony, where a giant black bird perched on the wall. The smell of roadkill drifted inside. I gagged.

"Are either of you in a relationship?" Tori asked.

I forced my attention back to her. "I'm not."

"Me either," Penelope added.

"Good, good." Isaac scratched under his chin. "Not that it matters, but we want to be able to control the narrative on socials."

A thunk from the balcony was followed by a terrible hiss. "Go away! Shoo!"

Tori cleared her throat.

"Of course, I'm not gonna twist your arms," Isaac said. "You're not contractually obligated to . . ." He stared into space and spoke deliberately. "To engage in any behavior or activities that you deem morally objectionable or . . . inappropriate? I don't have the legalese handy." Squeak.

"We can provide the necessary contract language if you'd like," Tori said.

To cover their own butts, not ours. That's how these things worked, according to my lawyer dad.

"What would you want us to do, exactly?" I asked.

Squeak. "Nothing serious, you know, just a little wink wink, nudge nudge."

That was not exact.

"So act flirty?" Penelope asked. She sounded flat, like she'd stuffed her feelings into a hat so she could magically pull them out later.

"Right, yes." Squeak. "Make googly eyes at each other, smile a lot, maybe a little Latin love, know what I mean?" He shook his butt in the chair, biting his lower lip and running a hand down his chest, and I knew I'd never hear the phrase "Latin love" without seeing that in my nightmares.

"The goal is to create the illusion of increasing intimacy," Tori said. "Nothing excessive. Our editors just need something to work with, escalating over the course of the competition. Assuming you aren't eliminated today."

This was a lot to process, and I realized I'd already broken character by failing to play this off or crack jokes, but what the fuck.

"We need to talk about it," I said.

"Sure, go ahead." Isaac slouched down farther in his chair. Squeak.

"Me and Penelope, I mean. Alone."

"Ah, right, gotcha." He waved a hand at us. "Don't let me keep you, then. It'll be time for hair and makeup soon, then round one begins." For some reason, he followed that with a deep, evil villain laugh.

Tori's neutral face cracked to let an eye roll through.

Isaac stopped laughing suddenly. "No, but seriously, get out of here, we're done."

We got out. The last thing I saw as the elevator door closed was Mary swinging a broom at a spread-winged turkey vulture. Mood, buddy.

I FELT LIKE my head was going to explode, but I made myself walk the usual Leandro way to the van that had brought us here.

"After you, m'lady," I said, giving Penelope a sweeping bow.

Penelope climbed in, buckled up, and rubbed her face with both hands. I left a seat between us, close enough to talk but not to hover.

"So," I said. "That happened."

Her mouth twitched. I thought she was going to start crying, but instead she cracked up.

"Oh my god," she wheezed. "I can't even."

I grinned. "Has your ability to even been compromised?"

"What did he call us? Popular nerd meets what?"

"Anime waifu? Is that like . . . the body pillows?"

"I don't know. My cousin Daniella likes that stuff."

"Anime?"

"And swords. She does ren faires." Penelope gave a tiny snort and covered her mouth. "Do you think they put us together because they were hoping we would . . . what did he say?"

"Put out the vibe?"

She squealed and lost it again.

"Don't worry about what he said." I pointed at her. "You get to decide what you're comfortable with. We can be all business, no party."

"No party?"

Rule two, Gil. "Okay, not no party, but not that kind of party."

"Not a pants party?"

Yes! "No pants party. Normal levels of normal party."

Penelope sucked in a breath and blew it out. "I can't believe this is happening. We're supposed to get popular by pretending we have a thing, and then what?"

"We could fake a huge pretend breakup and make everyone pick sides. Go on a couples therapy show, get back together, break up again . . . We could probably get a solid few years out of this if we're creative."

"This shouldn't be funny," she said, "but it's too wild not to be. I came on this show hoping to get a better job, you know? By showing how awesome I am at casting and spell design? But instead, they want me to be your arm candy."

"Oye, 'scuse me, I'm clearly the arm candy here," I joked.

"Por favor."

"Okay, we can both be arm candy, but I get to be the gummy bear."

Penelope half smiled. "What am I, a chocolate bar?"

"Jelly bean. Cinnamon jelly bean."

"First of all, no way. I'll accept French vanilla or cream soda. Second of all, we have to figure out what to tell these people."

True facts. "What do you want to tell them?"

"I don't know." Penelope sucked her teeth at me. "And I'm being a total asshole, just worrying about myself. Sorry. Would this be a problem for you, for your show?"

Would it? Sam had a better sense of this stuff than I did, but I couldn't ask her. I smoothed down my mustache. "I don't think so?"

"It wouldn't, like, mess with your subscriber numbers or something?"

"I might actually get a few extra people hoping for early access to secret chisme."

Penelope scrunched her face up. Was she actually considering it? My brain hydroplaned.

On the one hand, this could be a huge mistake, and not for show reasons. I was emotionally invested, and Penelope had no idea. Whatever she had with me as Gil would probably expire like milk once she found out the truth, and I extremely didn't want that. Not before we'd had a chance to see where things could go with us.

On the other hand, maybe this *was* my chance. I'd waited months to ask Penelope out, and now she was right here. We were stuck together unless we flamed out. I could chill and have fun. Embrace the chaotic potential. Maximum flirt power. Fake it 'til you make it, even if I wouldn't really be faking.

Because honestly? Even though Grandpa Fred's rule number one was "be someone else," Leandro was still sort of me. He was the goofy parts I hid from teachers so they would praise me, and from my parents because I was supposed to be their brainy, serious, future professional son. Yes, I was the nerd who started the *Doctor*

Witch blog so I could help other magic nerds nerd out safely. But I was also the clown who wanted to make people laugh by shoving a pie into my own face. As tired as I was of never being taken seriously as Leandro, I'd only started pretending to be him because I was tired of getting nowhere as a brainy, serious professional.

If Penelope could like Leandro as much as she seemed to like me, wouldn't it be worth the risk?

Penelope nodded to herself as if she'd made her choice. I waited, trying to breathe normally.

"Let's try it," she said.

I exhaled slowly. "Are you sure?"

"As long as you're okay with it?"

"I am. Okay with it, I mean. If all we're doing is, uh, putting out a vibe, we could always deny anything happened later, right? Say it was people's imagination?"

"True, true. We just have to be careful."

Her stomach growled, and she grabbed it like that would stop it. "Did you skip breakfast? Because I did."

"No, but . . ." I waggled my eyebrows as I pulled a banana out of my pocket.

Penelope lost it again. "Are you . . . are you trying to . . . give me the banana in your pocket?"

"Maybe I'm just happy to see you."

She held out her hand. "Yes, fine, give me your warm pocket banana. I'm too hungry to care."

I was so going to prank her with another banana later. But for now, I watched her eat and wondered how we were going to pull this off.

CHAPTER 7

Penelope

𝒩ot only was I partnered with Leandro "Spell Disaster" Presto, I was supposed to flirt with him, too. How was this my life?

Before we'd met, the idea of faking feels for him would have been ridiculous. Even now, the whole situation gave me stress giggles and stomach acid. My brain was popping out catastrophes faster than his spell had made candy hearts. But talking with him had helped; the more I got to know him, the easier it would hopefully be.

Back at our hotel, I ran upstairs to get my backpack full of random stuff I might need: tools, change of clothes, hand sanitizer, breath mints, tissues . . . mom purse stuff. Today's work apron went inside, too.

Breakfast was served in the restaurant-slash-bar, which was rainforest chic like the rest of the hotel. Fake branches and palm fronds hung from the ceiling, with slowly spinning fans that felt decorative since the AC was doing all the work. A mirrored wall of bottles sat behind the bar counter—why did every bar do this?—and a dozen square tables full of people were crammed together, too close to be ADA compliant. Two long tables at the other end of the room held covered serving dishes, tiers of sliced fruit and pastelitos, rows of roll-sized Cuban bread, and a bunch of other stuff. Hurricane Film Crew had trashed most of it.

I shoved three pieces of cheese directly into my mouth, then wrapped a couple of pastelitos and bread in a napkin to take with me. Hopefully there would be more snacks in the greenroom.

Leandro wandered up. "The next van is coming in about ten minutes."

His shirt today was, as always, an experience. The lavender fabric looked silky, with a button-down front and collar, and long sleeves he'd rolled up to show off his surprisingly muscular forearms. Profiles of large yellow and black long-stemmed flowers were interspersed with swirls of smaller black leaves and floral patterns, plus random yellow buds and blossoms.

As soon as I saw it earlier, I'd known what apron I'd wear today. I could have gone out of my way not to coordinate, but that felt petty. We were a team. And we had a vibe to put out, apparently.

We sat in the lobby to wait. Leandro watched me stuff food in my face while fiddling with the zippers on his backpack. Zip, unzip. Zip, unzip. Was he nervous? I guess he wasn't used to being on a big TV show, either. Especially not a competition. Or maybe it was the flirting thing?

I wanted to say something comforting, but I had nothing. Nada. The more I ate, the sicker I felt.

Leandro left and came back with two travel cups of coffee, putting one on the table in front of me. He hadn't asked how I wanted it, and I didn't want to risk opening it to check. I smiled on the outside and armored up inside before taking a sip.

It was perfect. Milky and with enough sugar to give me instant cavities. What? How?

My face must have done something weird because Leandro asked, "Sorry, is it okay? I can—"

"It's good. Great. Thank you." Mm, sweet caffeine.

He relaxed and drank his own coffee. The silence got uncomfortable.

"Do you like sugar?" I asked, pointing at his cup.

"Nah, I got used to drinking it black in grad school."

The idea of Leandro Presto going to college would never have occurred to me in a million years. I'd assumed he was mostly self-taught, like me.

I yeeted my feelings of educational inadequacy into the sun. "Where did you go to school? What did you study?"

He cupped a hand around his mouth and whispered, "I could tell you, but then I'd have to curse you."

Paranoid much? "Sorry, I didn't know it was a secret."

"It's fine, I just try to keep stuff private."

"Don't want fangirls showing up at your house?"

Leandro winced and looked down at the table. "You'd be surprised how weird some people can get."

"Really?"

"The first time someone handed me her underwear, I dropped them like they were on fire."

"It's happened more than once?"

His mustache twitched as he made a stinky-smell face. "Three times. At least cookies I can share."

Poor little popular boy, such a hard life. Okay, I needed to stop having bitch-eating-crackers reactions to him. Positive Penelope mode, on!

"Don't worry," I said. "I promise I won't be weird. I mean, I'll be normal weird. Cool weird."

"Flaming-llama-hearts weird?"

"Exactly! Here, look." I pulled out today's apron. This one was purple, covered in cartoony black cats with yellow eyes doing cute magic things. Some peeked out of cauldrons, others played with wisps of magic, and some hung from the handles of broomsticks like the kitten in that inspirational poster. I'd worn a black shirt, figuring it was neutral enough to make wardrobe happy, so the apron wouldn't clash.

Leandro looked at his shirt, looked at my apron, and smiled at me like I'd given him a present. My face warmed up as I smiled back. I wasn't going to give him my underwear anytime soon, but I could admit he was cute. To myself. Privately.

"That is definitely cool weird." His smile faded, and he moved to sit next to me, lowering his voice. "Before we start today, should we, um, set boundaries? So we don't cross any lines and make each other uncomfortable."

"What are you thinking?"

"I'm not sure." He sipped his coffee. "No wedgies? No whipped cream fights? No sharing a plate of spaghetti and slurping up the same noodle?"

"Definitely none of those things," I said. "Honestly, what even is flirting? I'm trying to think of how it usually works in movies and TV shows, and my brain is empty."

"No real-life experience to use?" Leandro asked. "Not trying to be chismoso, just wondering."

"I don't really date." I stared down at my sneakers. "Sometimes I go out dancing with friends, or have a few drinks at karaoke night, but the rest of the time I'm working, or, um . . ." My face felt warm.

"'Um'?"

"Don't judge me. I read, mostly books on magic theory, whatever I can get at the library. I watch documentaries, and *Cast Judgment*, obviously." Did I want to tell him about my abuela's spellbook? Not yet. Too personal. "There's also this blog I like that gives spell advice and recipes, a local guy runs it. It's pretty cool."

Leandro choked on his coffee and started coughing. I put down my drink and slapped him on the back a few times, until he waved at me to stop.

"I'm good," he wheezed. "Went down the wrong way."

"That happens to me a lot." Also I sometimes missed my mouth and spilled water down my shirt. Like a boss.

"So you don't have mad flirt skills," he said finally. "Me either. Maybe we should practice?"

I'd known he was probably faking being a himbo, but every time he said something reasonable, it still surprised me.

"Practice is good," I said. "We need to get comfortable, like . . . looking flirty? Touching each other? Not inappropriately, just, you know, being in each other's personal space?" I was suddenly extremely aware of how close we were sitting, the smell of his . . . aftershave? Cologne? Deodorant? I had a good nose—helpful for a spell technician—and I could pick out apples and lavender and something woodsy.

"I can hit you with some extremely bad pickup lines?" he suggested. "My friend Sam collects them."

I could never. "Okay."

"Be warned, these are really bad." He gave me an exaggerated eyebrow wiggle. "Hey, girl, I lost my phone number. Can I have yours?"

I covered my mouth. "Oh my god. Bro."

"What about . . ." He narrowed his eyes, like he was trying for a smolder. "Are you from Tennessee? 'Cause you're the only ten I see."

"I do not believe a human being has ever said that unironically. No way."

"Damn, girl, you look like trash. Want me to take you out?"

I snort-laughed. "How does anyone come up with these? They're fake. Tell me they're fake."

"I don't know, but Sam has a million of them." Leandro grinned. "I should probably save some for later."

"Smart."

"Vans are back!" someone yelled from the doorway. "Let's get talent to the lobby!"

As I put my apron away, Leandro's smile faded again. He looked like a kid who'd dropped his ice cream and was trying to be a big boy about it. Thinking about fangirls? Worrying about the round, or how to be flirty?

Whatever it was, I sort of hated it. He always seemed cheerful, even when his spells went wrong. Like he knew he was a clown, that the joke was on him, but he liked to make people laugh and he could laugh at himself, too. Maybe this was Leandro when his mask slipped. He'd smiled at my apron, though, and his funny-awful pickup lines. I wanted to get that back.

"We need a secret handshake," I blurted out.

Leandro blinked at me like I'd slapped him with his rubber chicken. "A secret handshake?"

"Or not, I mean, if you don't want to—"

"No, I love it!" His face lit up again. "We could . . . Do you know how to dance? Salsa?"

"Yeah, for sure." Unlike my sister. I just didn't get out much because of work. And after last night, I already knew he had moves.

"How about this." He held out his right hand. I took it, then he put out his other hand above it without letting go. I grabbed that one, so our arms were crossed, one hand on top of the other. He brought my left arm up and over my head slowly as he turned me around so I was facing away from him, then raised my right arm and kept turning me until I faced him with our arms crossed again, but reversed from how we'd started. We stared at each other for a few seconds, and I wondered what he was thinking, because I was kinda wishing we could actually dance together. With music. And less stress.

Was he looking at my mouth? No way, not after that lecture about fangirls and underwear. Get it together, Penelope.

"Then what?" I asked.

"And then we can, hmm, blow it up?" He tossed my hands up and made an explosion sound while he wiggled his fingers in the air.

I laughed. "Okay, I think I can remember that."

"Let's try it faster?" he suggested. "To practice."

We did, and by the third time we had it down. A couple of PAs clapped and hooted at us, and I blushed while Leandro gave them an elaborate bow. Felicia, standing nearby, rolled her perfectly mascaraed eyes.

"So should we do that when we win a round, or when we do something cool, or what?" I asked.

Leandro shrugged. "Let's go with what feels right."

Of course he didn't want to plan it.

Before I could pin him down, Felicia sneered at us. "You two are ridiculous. You're not going to win. Everyone knows you're just here to make the rest of us look good."

Someone said, "Oooh," and loudly finger-slapped a few times like we were gonna scrap. Leandro froze, and my brain refused to come up with a snappy response. I'd said almost the same thing last night, hadn't I? Nicer, but barely. With an epic eye roll, Felicia walked out.

"What's that French thing?" I asked.

"French thing?" Leandro replied.

"You know, when you come up with a really sweet clapback way after the thing happens?"

"Esprit d'escalier?"

"Yeah." Himbo my ass. "I'm going to figure out the best insult ever for that witch in like two hours, while I'm watching a cauldron boil."

A smile twitched at the corner of his mouth. "Or in the shower? I always have good ideas in the shower."

"Hey, me too! I keep telling myself I need to buy bath crayons so I can write them down."

"Smart."

We stared at the door and sighed at the same time, then said, "We should go," in unison.

I cracked a smile, he smoothed his mustache, and together we headed out into the Miami morning sunshine.

LEANDRO AND I stood next to each other at our stations, wearing our matching clothes, trying not to look nervous as Syd did the usual opening banter. Bruno and Fina did my hair and makeup again, with the "sloppy albondigas" from yesterday—Amy said they were called space buns—and purple and gold eyeshadow to match my apron, which they loved. Was this anime waifu? Probably.

Syd finally cleared their throat and grinned, as if they knew we were all ready to explode from suspense. "Since we're in Miami, and this edition of *Cast Judgment* features truly amazing Spellebrities, we've decided the theme for this season will be: celebration!"

Celebration? Like, a party?

"Every spell you design and cast will be working toward a huge, final event, a party like this show has never experienced before."

Butts. I wasn't a party person. My cousin Gina worked for some extremely fancy event planning company, but we didn't hang out much. Not that it mattered, since I couldn't call her for help.

"For today's round, one of the most basic things every good celebration needs is . . ." Syd paused dramatically. ". . . light! As fun as it is to party in the dark, we want each of you to come up with a unique, interesting lighting method that doesn't involve anything flammable. No candles, no lanterns with open flames, no fireworks or sparklers. Got it?"

We all nodded. I glanced at Gil, who was smoothing his mustache again. He seemed to do it when he was nervous.

Syd raised their arm and gestured at a giant LED clock on the wall. It lit up with a number eight and a bunch of zeroes. "Your time begins . . . now!"

The timer switched to seven fifty-nine as the seconds began disappearing. I pulled my notebook and pencil out of my apron pocket. As soon as the empty page was open in front of me, my brain locked up like my car's brakes in the rain.

What were words? What was magic? Who was I? Seven fifty-eight and thirty-six seconds. Thirty-five. Thirty-four.

"Penelope?" Leandro peered into my eyes like he was checking for a concussion.

"I'm good," I said.

"Are you sure? Because you're choking that pencil to death."

"No, I'm not." My knuckles were white, and the wood creaked.

He grinned. "Knock, knock."

"Who's there?"

"Broken pencil."

Hah. "Broken pencil who?"

"Never mind, it's pointless."

I snort-laughed. "That was so bad. Hashtag dad jokes."

"Made you laugh."

"I wasn't laughing, I was choking on how terrible that joke was." I did feel better, though. He'd fixed my brakes, and now the car was moving again.

Was that flirting? I didn't know.

I wrote "LIGHT" at the top of the paper. "Okay, brainstorm time. Lighting methods, no fire. Has to be awesome."

"Don't worry about awesome yet," Leandro said. "For now, just ideas."

I could do that. Let's see . . . chandeliers, fairy lights with residual memory-echoes of cucuyos inside instead of bulbs, those glass ocean floats that lit up when they touched water . . . Leandro's jellyfish. Cool, even if the underlying spell was flawed. I didn't want to copy his work, though. Plus the glow hadn't been very bright; I could picture Hugh Burbank giving me his hard stare as he said something like, *Lighting should actually light up the area around it, Ms. Delmar.*

I shivered.

"Are you cold?" Leandro asked.

"Yes." Also catastrophizing. I wrote "jellyfish" and tapped the page with the pencil's eraser. "Thoughts?"

He smoothed his mustache. "Aurora borealis?"

Fun. I wrote it down. Still not bright enough, but maybe with stars . . . Oh god.

"Sparklehair," I said.

"Sparkle . . . hair?"

"I had a jerk customer the other day. He screwed up a hair spell and ended up with fireworks on his head."

Leandro's lip curled like his mustache. "How did he do that?"

"Broken duskywing butterfly wing."

"Ooh, those are fragile."

"Right? But he tried to play it like I messed up his reagents."

"You? No me diga." Leandro dramatically covered his mouth, then leaned against the counter on his elbows. "I bet you've never messed up a spell in your life."

"I wish." I'd learned to be careful the hard way.

"So, sparkly hair?" he asked. "Turn everyone into a walking light?"

"Has to be environmental. The sparkles, though . . ." I tapped the pencil against my mouth. What could we pair with sparkles like that?

A crack of thunder outside made me jump. Miami weather. If the storm hadn't hit us yet, it would soon.

Storm. Hmm. I wrote that down.

"Storm, like clouds?" Leandro asked. "What about party fog?"

Party fog! "If we could make that glow brightly, and add the sparkles to simulate lightning . . ." I started scribbling ingredients that might work for the spell.

Leandro read over my shoulder. "Do we want it to float overhead or stay at ground level?"

Ground would be easier. "Let's try to float it."

"Playing on hard mode," he said. "Nice. What's our delivery mechanism?"

What containers could trap a spell like this inside? "Bottle, like a genie? Balloon? Mason jar?"

"A teapot!"

"What?" I blinked at him.

"You know, like a tempest in a teapot?"

"Is that a pun?"

"It's a saying," he explained. "It's when a small thing gets blown up into a huge deal."

"So like . . . exagerada? Muy dramática?"

"Pretty much."

Well, he was the pun expert. Every spell for his show had a funny name.

"Tempest in a teapot it is," I said, writing it at the top of the paper with a flourish. I smiled at Leandro, who grinned back.

"Should we high-five now?" he asked.

I sort of wanted to, but Felicia's bitch ass popped up in my brain. "Not yet. Let's work up to it. We don't want to do it too much or it will get old."

"True, true." He looked at the list of reagents I'd started. "If we don't want the cloud to dissipate too fast, we're going to need something to make it persistent or regenerating, beyond the mineral oil."

"Spearmint?"

"Maybe zephyrlily . . ."

We debated how they would interact with each other and what activation mechanisms would work best. Hot or cold mist? How thick did we want it to be? How large did the teapot need to be to account for Boyle's principle of hydrostatic recursion? Which base incantation type did we want to use? I didn't notice the camera crew creeping up on us, with Syd in the lead, until they were right next to our station.

My customer service smile activated instinctually.

"Yellow team!" Syd said. "You're matching again. Adorable."

"We're on a wavelength," Leandro added, making a wave with his arms.

Thunder rumbled again, louder this time. Rain started pounding on the roof.

"Do you two have a plan yet?" Syd asked.

"Yes," we said at the same time. Leandro made a *go ahead* gesture at me.

"We're calling it 'Tempest in a Teapot,'" I said.

"Catchy!" Syd grinned. "Are you planning to bottle some of the bad weather we're having right now?"

Leandro and I laughed.

"Well, I'll let you get back to it. Check in soon!" Syd drifted away, toward Quentin's area.

Deep breath. That went fine. I glanced at the clock again. Seven twenty-five. Yikes.

"I'll get the reagents, and you prep the equipment," I told Leandro.

He nodded and started digging into the cabinets. That surprised me. For some reason I'd expected him to argue or clown around more. Maybe he really would take this seriously. I could only hope.

I raced to the supply area, which was through the exit and down the hall in the other direction. It was somewhere between the size of a dollar store and a grocery store, taking up the whole back part of the warehouse. Aisle after aisle of ingredients beckoned, with shelves high enough that I'd need the conveniently provided wheeled ladder to reach some things.

I grabbed a cart and went nuts. Every so often I saw something that looked like it might be worth adding to our spell and tossed it in, too. Dylan passed me at one point, and we shared distracted smiles. Amy paced frantically, and I asked her what was wrong.

"Have you seen any origami paper?" she asked. "I thought it would be near the inks, but . . ."

"Paper is by yarn and textiles," I said. "Don't ask me why, I don't make the rules."

Amy laughed, her eyes scrunching up behind her red glasses. "I bet you're the kind of person who gets asked for help in stores a lot."

She was right. "I also put stuff back where it goes when I find it on a random shelf."

"Well, thank you. I appreciate it."

Felicia avoided me like I was contagious. Whatever.

By the time I got back, Leandro had everything in place: bowls in rows by size, cast iron pot on the stove, vacuum pump assembled and waiting. Again, a surprise. I'd assumed he would be messier.

I unloaded the stuff I'd picked up, trying to keep our area as neat as he had. One by one, I made sure the prepacked reagents hadn't expired, then opened them to check that the insides matched the labels. Everything looked and smelled fine.

"You chop, I mash?" Leandro asked, peering at the herbs and flowers. "Unless you're not as good with a blade as I am." He twirled a knife like a fancy Japanese chef, grinning.

"Well, now I'm definitely doing it," I said. "With my luck, you'll drop that on my foot."

"I'm careful." Spin, spin.

"Give." I held out my hand, and he offered me the knife hilt-first with an elaborate bow.

I chopped. He used the mortar and pestle to grind what needed to be a paste. I started water boiling, glancing at the clock again. Six forty-nine. Ah! What next?

On and on we went, step by step, reagent by reagent, building our spell up. When it came time for the first cooling of the fluid components, I carefully poured the pot's contents into a heatproof bowl and covered it with plastic wrap. Leandro held the fridge door open, and I carried the bowl over, trying not to trip over my own feet. Inside it went, and when he closed the door, I sighed in relief.

"Handshake?" Leandro asked, waggling his eyebrows.

"Handshake," I agreed. We grabbed each other's hands, did our quick dance move, and made the appropriate explosion noise at the end. I turned around, smiling, to check my notes for the next part of the recipe.

Then thunder crashed right on top of us, so loud I jumped away from the table and backed into Leandro. Without a flicker of warning, the power went out.

CHAPTER 8

Penelope

The warehouse was pitch-black with the lights out since they'd boarded up all the windows. Outside the soundstage, people yelled, and random flashlight beams appeared and disappeared. Something rattled; glass shattered. Someone shouted a nasty phrase in Spanish that would have made my dad's eyes get big, and he cussed like it was his job.

Leandro wrapped his arms around me. Thunder cracked again, and I flinched, grabbing his forearms. He squeezed me tighter, his chest pressed against my back. He was definitely smuggling muscles under his loose shirt. Rosy would love that bit of cheese.

What I wouldn't tell her was how nice it felt, this emergency hug. Kind of . . . cozy? Safe? Which was weird, considering his entire career revolved around hecking up spells. Bro was spinning a knife around a minute ago like nothing. I should have been flipping out, but I wasn't. And his smell . . . Sweeter than most guys went for. I liked it.

Something brushed my hair. His nose? Was he sniffing me? No way. My brain was all like, you smelled him first! But one, shut up, and two, I was smelling the air, and it wasn't my fault he was in it.

The lights flickered on. Either the power was back, or this building had a generator.

"Check your spells, everyone," Syd said, their voice raised to be heard over Isaac shouting at the crew from the other side of the wall. Tori listened to something through her earpiece that must have pissed her off, because her face went through like fifty microexpressions before she stomped out.

I stayed where I was for a few more seconds, then squirmed. Leandro let go, but he moved his hands to my shoulders and turned me around.

"Okay?" he asked.

"Totally," I lied. I was shooketh. But that was a problem for future Penelope.

The fridge hadn't lost power long enough to affect our spell, but we peeked at it anyway. Yup, still there.

Around us, everyone else was dealing with their own issues. Dylan and Zeke had apparently been mid-incantation, and had to dismantle some of what they'd done and start over. Amy smiled sadly and threw something in the trash. Quentin and Tanner weren't around; maybe they got stuck in the supply room? The judges had stopped near their area, just across from us, waiting for them to come back. Doris Twist leaned in for a closer look at some mechanism they'd assembled, while Fabienne Desgraves checked her watch and Hugh Burbank, arms crossed, tapped a finger against his forearm.

Felicia nearly ran into Quentin as he came back through the hallway, carrying a big box. He said, "Ope!" and apologized, and she ignored him. I looked at Charlotte to see if she'd noticed, but she was busy pouring a casting circle with flour.

I had to do that, too. Except I needed salt. I grabbed the bag I'd brought from the supply room and checked the drawers for a funnel. Nope. I bent down to check the cabinets and found one in a basket in the back. When I pulled it out, I caught Quentin grinning at me from the other side of the aisle.

"What?" I asked.

"Nothing," Quentin replied innocently. "Just noticed someone enjoying the view."

I reached for the scissors and tried to figure out what Quentin was talking about. The view? What view? What was there to see while I was looking for a funnel? Bending over to check inside cabinets . . . oh my god.

Had Leandro been looking at my butt? I glanced at him, but he was reading the spell recipe.

Fake flirting, right. I should remember to check him out, too. Not that I could see his butt; his shirt was too long, and his pants were too loose. His forearms, though . . .

I cut open the corner of the bag, held the funnel so my thumb covered the narrow opening, then filled the top with salt. I plopped the bag back on the counter and moved to the chalk-painted floor area, carefully drawing the salt circle on it, then adding the sigils we'd agreed on in the appropriate places. What next? Leandro had the spell. All I had to do was ask for it. Instead, I tried to remember what I'd written down. Candles? No, one candle, and . . . a swift feather? Yes! Mierda, in which order did I need to place these reagents . . .

Why did Quentin have to tell me a thing that might not even be a thing but now I was making it a thing? This was ridiculous.

Leandro put the spell down and wandered off to crack jokes with Syd. I tried to look chill as I practically jumped over to grab the recipe before he came back.

Glass bowl of rainwater, then candle, then moonstone, then feather. Okay.

"Ms. Delmar," a deep voice said from my right.

I managed not to jump this time. The judges stood next to me, Nate and his camera behind them, checking out the sigils and reagents. If eyes could shoot lasers, Hugh Burbank would have burned a hole through my head. Customer service smile: on.

"Hey!" I said cheerfully.

"And what do you have for us today, Penelope?" Fabienne Desgraves asked.

Okay, I had to stop calling these people by their full names in my head. I was an adult. First names, go.

"This is our 'Tempest in a Teapot' spell," I explained.

"And what will it do?"

How much did they want me to say? "It should create a small cloud that glows, with sparkling effects inside, like lightning."

"That sounds absolutely charming," Doris said, smiling at me like everyone's favorite grandmother. She was always so nice.

"How bright do you expect it to be?" Fabienne asked.

"Basically, like, moonlight during a full moon. Bright enough to see, but not too bright to look at."

"How large an area should it fill?" Hugh asked.

I bit my lip as I did the math in my head. "A couple hundred square feet?"

"Seems a bit simplistic." He looked away from me. "Hmm."

Simplistic? Oh no. I had to figure out how to up our game.

Wait, what did "hmm" mean?

I turned my head just in time to catch Leandro dropping a lit match into a bowl. A column of flame burst upward like a blowtorch, at least four feet high, inches from his face.

Adrenaline hit me like a truck. I froze. My heart pounded, and my mouth tasted like I'd licked a nine-volt battery. As I watched this fire shrink and sputter out, memories burned through my mind. Billowing smoke, the shrill beeping of the alarm, the extinguisher sending a useless stream of liquid onto the floor, the smell of burnt skin, the sirens—

"Oops," Leandro said. "A little too much mineral oil." He sounded like he was far away, like I was trying to hear him over the sound of ocean waves crashing in my ears.

Breathe, I told myself. The fire is gone. Everything is okay. Inhale, count to four, exhale. Nothing was damaged, no one was hurt. Inhale, count to four, exhale. Where's the camera? Smile.

My lips wouldn't move.

"I hope the rest of your spell is more successful," Hugh said. Leandro grinned at him, and the judges moved on to Amy and Jaya's station.

Leandro came up next to me, still grinning. "Talk about las llamas de mi amor, huh?"

He could have . . . the fire could have . . . My ability to form coherent thoughts stayed wrecked. Everything tilted sideways, and I barely caught myself on the table as my legs tried to stop holding me up.

"Hey!" Leandro grabbed me, his face too close to mine. "Penelope, holy shit, you're shaking."

My jaw stayed clenched, but I managed to choke out, "Bathroom." He started to walk with me, until I got control of my body again and pushed him away. I didn't look back as I hugged the wall until I got to the exit, then managed to get lost even though there were two directions to pick from. A PA took pity on me and led me the rest of the way.

The contestant bathroom was a few steps up from basic, with framed mirrors and granite counters and even a chair and table in case I needed to, I don't know, wait for a stall? Hide and read a book like when I lived with my family? Ride out the tail end of my panic attack?

Yeah, that one. I sat down and put my head between my legs.

Don't think about the past, I told myself.

Me cago en la hora que tu naciste, Penelope!

It's over.

She could have died!

What happened can't be changed.

You think you're going to get a degree in this? No me diga!

Shut up, Mom! Shut up shut up shut up.

A quieter, calmer voice said: *You can't let one accident stop you from casting forever, mi vida. We all make mistakes. That's how we learn.*

Abuela always trusted me, believed in me. If she knew what I was doing now, she'd be so proud. Even if I didn't deserve it.

I'd make myself deserve it. For her.

The room didn't have a clock, so I had no idea how long I stayed there, remembering how to breathe. Eventually my anxiety about needing to finish the spell won the wrestling match with my low-grade PTSD. I checked my makeup for battle damage, swallowed the nasty-tasting pill of my feelings, and power walked back to the soundstage.

I expected to find either a mess at our station or everything exactly as I'd left it. Instead, the magic circle was ready to go, with each reagent in the appropriate location, and Leandro was quietly mixing something in a tall pot using precise clockwise motions.

What the hell was up with this guy? One minute he was all chill and competent and smart, and the next he was blowing stuff up. I thought about pro wrestling again, about fake drama and choreography mixed up with real skills, and wondered what ratio of PhD to fuckup I was dealing with here.

Did it even matter? Anger grabbed the steering wheel from anxiety and started driving me. If he was screwing up by accident, he needed to stop messing around and follow instructions. If he was doing it on purpose, he needed to warn me so I wouldn't freak out again.

Later. Focus. The wandering camera crew stood next to Dylan and Zeke, but I kept my fake smile on for any other cameras that might be watching.

I checked the recipe to see where we were in the steps. He must have been brewing the potion that would react with the stuff in the fridge when the command was given. That meant all we needed was to imbue the catalyst with our intent using the circle, then wait until the two potions were ready to combine in the teapot.

Except . . . Hugh said this was too simplistic. How could we take it to the next level? I should ask Leandro—he did have a good imagination—but I super didn't want to talk to him.

Storm things, go. I shook my brain and hoped something interesting would fall out.

We already had the spark lightning effects from the duskywing butterfly wing, but maybe quiet rumbling to go with it? That might get annoying, but the extra sensory angle would make the spell more complex. Scent? Maybe alternating layers of petrichor and something else. Salt water and jasmine? Yes, that would be nice. But this was a lighting spell, so the lighting needed to go all out.

Leandro had mentioned the aurora borealis earlier, and I had a sudden mental image of it raining down in streaks of color. Could work, but how to integrate it into the existing spell recipe?

"You're halfway there, everyone!" Syd yelled from the front of the room. "Four hours remaining!"

Ew. Barf.

Leandro walked up to me slowly, like he was worried I would spook. "You okay?"

I ignored the question. "What do you think about adding scent and a color effect to this?"

"Like what?"

I explained my ideas, and we both drifted into brain land to think them over. We reached for the pencil at the same time, our hands touching, then flinched back.

"Go ahead," he said.

Fine. I would. I did.

He didn't read over my shoulder this time; he waited until I was done, then asked, "May I?" and gestured at the paper.

I handed it to him and waited.

"Crystal and mirror array for the infusion, do you think?" he asked.

I nodded.

"Okay. We'll need a nine-point circle with at least four tangents—"

We fell back into our earlier discussion pattern, but the enthusiasm was gone. All business now, like two classmates assigned to a school project. A couple of times he wandered off to clown around—juggling plastic containers, joking with Doris Twist, sneaking up behind Syd with his rubber chicken—but otherwise the most ridiculous thing about him was his comemierda grin under his curly mustache.

He didn't touch me again. So much for flirting.

The clock on the wall ticked down, down, down. Crew rotated in and out on some arcane break schedule. Syd shouted again when we had an hour left, but I didn't jump. I was in the zone.

With about twenty minutes to go, Leandro and I carefully combined our separate reagents into one of the teapots I'd found in the supply area. It was plain white porcelain, to which I'd added some sigils that should give the spell an extra level of cool if they worked properly.

Big if. I hated that we didn't have the chance to test anything. It wasn't like baking cookies, where we could make a double batch for backup. Everything had to work correctly the first and only time we cast this.

"Fifteen minutes!" Syd yelled.

We were finished, though. I glanced around the room and thought about all the times I'd seen casters rushing around as Syd counted down from ten. No one seemed to be freaking out. Amy started to clean her area, but Tori barked at her to leave it. A messy counter was more dramatic, I guess. Maybe I should spill a few things on our table?

I thought of the fire and shivered. Nah.

The clock seemed to slow down as I stared at it. Leandro stood just outside my personal space bubble. I caught him looking sideways at me a few times, but he didn't say anything. Until he did.

"Do we want to do the secret handshake again when the time is up?" he asked quietly.

I thought about it. "Not at the end. They probably want us looking stressed and out of breath. If we win the round, let's do it."

"Okay."

No argument, no pressure, just "okay." Why did that make me angry?

Because of the fire. It had set me off, and now I wanted him to be more of an asshole. I had built up a Leandro in my head from his videos, someone I didn't like or respect, and I wanted the real guy to give me reasons to go back to feeling that way. I wanted a clear Leandro-is-a-giant-jerk moment so I could shit-talk him to Rosy and my sister afterward.

Maybe I wanted to be able to blame him if the spell went wrong, so I could tell myself I'd done my best, but I couldn't possibly win when I had a comemierda yelling, "Presto!" and wrecking stuff behind my back. If he listened to me, and respected me, and cast the spells correctly as we'd planned them, then if we failed it would be my fault, too.

Rosy would tell me I needed therapy, then we'd laugh about how we couldn't afford it.

Five minutes.

Two minutes.

"One minute left, casters!" Syd shouted gleefully.

Leandro jumped up like a rabbit and ran to the exit. What? Why?

He ran back holding . . . a flower? Oh god, had we forgotten something?

"Thirty seconds!"

Leandro slid to a stop next to me, catching his breath. He grinned like a naughty kid and handed me a gardenia.

"This isn't part of the spell," I whispered.

"Ten! Nine! Eight!"

"It's for you," Leandro said.

Ah. Flirting. Sweet. I smiled back, only half faking.

"And time's up!" Syd announced. "Step away from your stations and prepare to be judged."

I stepped back automatically, putting my hands up like I was being arrested. Not that I'd ever been arrested. Also, I was still holding the gardenia.

The judges stood around Syd, all looking suitably kind or serious. I could practically hear the theme music as we all tried to figure out what we should do now.

Tori clapped to get our attention. "We need a few reaction shots here. Give me nervous, confident, excited, whatever feels natural."

Natural? I covered my mouth because a hysterical laugh was trying to get loose and make me look unhinged. I ended up with the gardenia on my cheek. Was this Leandro's way of apologizing?

"Penny," Tori said.

It wasn't Ofelia, but I still flinched. Then I felt weird for flinching. It was just a nickname.

She didn't notice, or didn't care. "You and Leandro did some kind of handshake earlier. Let's see it again."

The cameras pointed right at us. Natural. Right. So much for not doing this unless we won the round. Leandro grinned at me like he always did, but I wondered if this time his smile was as fake as mine.

I stuck the gardenia in the front pocket of my apron. The smell drifted up, sweet and soothing. Leandro looked at it and his smile seemed to change. More real?

I held my hand out and he took it. By the time we'd finished our spin and explode, everyone was staring at us, not just the cameras. A few of the crew clapped, and someone whistled. I blushed.

"Great job, everyone!" Tori said. "We're going to break for food now, and we'll start the judging in an hour. Does anyone have any questions before we lock down the room?"

Quentin raised his hand. "When do we get our phones back?"

A few people laughed.

"Day six," Tori said. "If there's an emergency, we'll notify you or your contact as needed. Anything else?"

"Are we doing confessionals after judging?" Amy asked.

"Yes, first the Spellebrities, then the pairs, then solo contestants."

Why Spellebrities first? I wondered. Maybe Leandro would tell me.

Except he couldn't, because once again, we were taken to separate greenrooms. Catering had left us a tray of random sandwiches and croquetas and mini fried chicken drumsticks, like this was a Cuban birthday party. There was also a bowl of falafel with a tub of tzatziki next to it; Felicia and Amy went straight for that while Dylan and I hovered over the sandwiches and Quentin tried the chicken. I'd barely eaten all day, and now I was starving.

Eventually Quentin blurted out, "That blackout was something, wasn't it? I can't believe they didn't have an automatic backup."

"Did it mess with anyone else's spell?" Dylan asked.

"Yes," Amy replied. "I had to throw out a half-spelled paper component."

"We had just put some things in the fridge," I said. "I'm glad the power didn't stay out, or the potion might not have cooled down in time."

"Tanner and I were in the supply room," Quentin said. He rubbed the back of his neck. "I screamed. It was really dark!"

"Did Tanner say anything?" I asked.

"He said, 'Oh fudge!'"

Hah. Adorable.

"What about you, Felicia?" Dylan asked.

"My spell is excellent," Felicia said. "I'm sure the judges will agree."

So stuck up.

"You're not worried about getting cut this round?" Quentin asked.

"Don't be ridiculous," Felicia said. "There's no chance whatsoever that I'm going to lose." And then she straight-up turned around to eat without looking at us.

"Well, I'm worried," I said.

Amy swallowed a bite. "What did Leandro set on fire?"

"I don't know," I said. "I, um, had a bathroom emergency, and he fixed it by the time I got back."

"Knowing him, he probably messed up some essential step," Felicia said, still facing the wall. "I'm surprised he didn't set his mustache on fire."

Amy gave me a sympathetic look, and Dylan went back to the table for another sandwich.

Quentin patted my arm. "It's not your fault you got stuck with Leandro Presto."

"I flipped out when I saw him," Dylan said. "I was so glad I already had my partner."

Irrational urge to defend him: rising. "He's not that bad."

"He was totally checking you out, you know," Quentin said.

"And he gave you that flower," Amy added.

I couldn't tell them about the flirting thing. "He's just being a goof for the cameras."

Quentin sighed. "I miss my husband. We haven't been apart this long since before my top surgery."

Top . . . Oh! Right. Trans man.

"I don't have anyone back home but my mom," Dylan said. "I miss her cooking, though. These sandwiches are . . ." He picked out some wilted lettuce and curled his lip.

The conversation switched to wondering what the celebrities were eating, how fancy their greenroom was compared to ours, what other field trips we might be taking, what we would do with the rest of our hotel time if we lost . . . Felicia sat as far from us as she could and occasionally rolled her eyes, like she was annoyed at slumming with us common folk.

Finally the door opened, and Little Manny stuck his head inside. "Meal is over. Time to go—"

We all jumped up like our butts had springs in them.

"—to hair and makeup for touch-ups."

Quentin laughed, and it cracked ice we didn't know had frosted over us. The rest of us laughed, too, except Felicia, and we followed Little Manny to our doom.

CHAPTER 9

Gil

Why did I give Penelope that flower?

We stood at our stations, waiting for the judges to call us to the pentacle-floor demonstration area. An extra camera had been brought in, and both of the shoulder-mounted camera operators stood by, waiting for instructions. Everything had to be lit differently since we were all doing lighting spells, so the grip and electric crew had turned off the floodlights and ran new cables for the smaller spotlights they'd brought in. Isaac Knight squinted at everything like it had personally offended him, and barked orders at Tori until he finally stomped outside to his special showrunner's chair area. Chairea? Heh.

Random numbers had been assigned to us for presentation order; Penelope and I were going fourth. She fidgeted with something in a side pocket of her apron, probably a pencil. The gardenia was still in the front pocket, its white petals peeking out. Had she forgotten it was there, or left it on purpose?

I had made that particular plan last night, before Isaac dumped his flirting thing on us. Freak-out countdown runarounds were popular on the show, even if they had to be edited in after the fact. I figured it would be fun to surprise Penelope with something nice.

After how she reacted to the fire "accident," I should have yeeted my plan into the sun. I don't know what exactly set her off, but her skin had turned as white as the gardenia petals. She acted like she was in shock—not surprise-birthday-party shock, just-got-in-a-car-accident shock. Couldn't talk, dilated pupils, full wreck. Everything had been going well, and then she turned into a completely different person. Or herself, but with all the life sucked out.

I had to fix it. I didn't know how yet, though. And if we lost now, I'd never get the chance.

Charlotte checked her watch. Jaya hid a yawn. Zeke rubbed his head. Tanner had his eyes closed, like he was asleep standing up, or maybe meditating. Dylan just stood there looking chill, Amy kept blinking behind her glasses, and Quentin had wrapped his arms around himself in a nervous hug. Felicia had a smug smile. I did not like it.

And Penelope kept fidgeting with whatever was in her pocket. I wanted to grab her hand and hold it so she'd stop. Or maybe so she'd mess with my fingers instead.

That couple of minutes during the blackout when I'd hugged her . . . Okay, so I'm a nerd. In my nonexistent spare time, I read articles about the latest magical advancements, and books with titles like *Historical Studies of the Properties of Intangible Spell Components in Caribbean Cultures*—which I then reviewed on my *Doctor Witch* blog. I like comedies and action movies with badass fights. I don't watch romantic stuff on my own, but I'm down to cuddle with a period drama where everyone should fuck already but they never do. I'd pretty much stopped dating when Leandro Presto got big enough for strangers to start getting parasocially weird—I hadn't even told Penelope about the Stalker Incident, and I probably never would. I've had girlfriends. I've used the L-word and meant it. I'm twenty-eight years old, not sixteen, and this is not my first crush.

But hugging her was an Experience. It shouldn't have been! It wasn't even a real hug, just me trying to keep her from hurting herself. And then I sniffed her hair like a creeper. I'd spent months refusing to look Penelope up online out of some sense that I'd be invading her privacy, and the first chance I got, I was all up in her personal space being weird.

Something was wrong with my brain, and I didn't know whether it was stress from the competition, not getting laid enough, or months of accumulated feelings from emailing a smart, funny person suddenly leading to . . . this arroz con mango. Probably all of it.

Tori yelled, "Quiet!" and the command was repeated by various voices. A camera assistant stepped in front of the camera aimed at Syd and the judges, snapped the slate, and left.

Syd waited about a ten count, then smiled. "Welcome back to *Cast Judgment*. It's now time for our contestants to present their spells. They'll be judged based on how well they conform to the brief, how technically challenging their work is, and how creatively impressive and innovative the final product is."

There was a point system, but we wouldn't get our scores. That was for the judges and the lawyers making sure this contest wasn't rigged.

"Our first contestant and Spellebrity pairing is . . . Amy and Jaya!"

Together, Amy and Jaya carried their spell to a table placed in the center of the pentacle. It looked like a piano made of paper, one of the self-playing kinds with a rotating drum covered in musical notes. Beautiful calligraphy sigils covered the outside, mathematically precise in their distribution. Really cool stuff.

"Tell us about your spell," Syd said. Jaya gestured for Amy to go ahead.

Amy cleared her throat. "Our novel lighting method is a piano that activates when music is played."

"Let's see it," Syd said.

With a nervous smile at Jaya, Amy touched the middle key and stepped back. The spotlights dimmed so we stood in darkness almost as deep as when the power went out.

Music filled the room from unseen speakers, a simple classical tune. After a few seconds, the piano started to glow a soft white, with the light concentrated in the keys. Each note and chord lit up in a pale yellow, then drifted up and floated in the air, until a wide area was literally bright from the song. When the music ended, the piano stopped glowing, but the notes remained.

Shit, that was impressive. I recalculated our odds of winning and did not love them.

"Does this complete your spell?" Syd asked.

"Oh yes, sorry!" Amy said. "That's it. The notes will fade in about ten minutes unless the music starts again. Thank you."

We all clapped, and the judges stepped forward to examine the piano. They asked a lot of technical questions about the recipe, the methodologies used to create it, and so on. I hadn't expected them to be so rigorous—or at least, I had assumed Hugh might, and Fabienne, but even Doris had some observations that didn't fit her nice abuela persona.

Eventually they ran out of questions and Hugh said, "We're ready for recorded comments."

The two extra camera people took up their positions, and spotlights pointed at the judges so they'd be visible in the dim room.

Fabienne went first. "This is a lovely spell, Amy and Jaya. The flexibility that allows it to work with any played music is impressive. That said, the piano design itself could be more polished."

Doris smiled. "I think the entire thing is charming, quite sweet. Very easy to imagine it at a variety of parties, perhaps with different-colored light options to match the decor."

All of us held our breaths when it was Hugh's turn. I didn't understand why viewers liked his *I'm a giant asshole* approach. If I did that with students, I'd be fired.

"It's a decent concept," Hugh said. "Fairly marketable in theory. I think it's a bit too dim to be truly functional, and the base model is flimsy. Paper may hold the enchantment once, but you'd have to take extra steps to make it durable."

Ouch. Well, could have been worse.

"Thank you, judges," Jaya said, and Amy repeated the words. They carried their spell back to their station.

Next to me, Penelope leaned forward to give Amy a thumbs-up. Amy smiled back and looked away shyly.

Dylan and Zeke were up next. They brought out a tiered glass platter covered in a couple dozen disco balls, each as big as a softball. The one on top was larger, maybe soccer ball–size. They put the platter on the table and stepped away, both crossing their arms over broad chests.

"For our spell, we made individual disco lights for people to carry around," Dylan explained.

"How do they light up?" Fabienne asked.

"You gotta touch them or pick them up," Zeke said.

Hugh raised an eyebrow, stepped forward, and grabbed a disco ball. As promised, it started to glow, rainbow-colored lights shooting out in every direction. Fabienne and Doris each picked up one as well, and they glowed the same way.

"Is that it?" Hugh asked.

"Naw, that ain't it," Zeke said. "Take a bite."

Dylan grinned, a flash of white teeth in the dark.

Maintaining eye contact with Dylan, Hugh bit into the disco ball in his hand. The interior of the ball glowed neon in all the same colors. Hugh chewed, turning the ball to examine it from different angles. Fabienne and Doris took bites, too.

Hugh finished chewing first. "It's delicious. Is that lemon?"

"Limoncello and mascarpone," Dylan said.

"Truly excellent," Doris said. "The exterior is brittle like candy, but the cake inside is fresh and, dare I say, light?" She chuckled at her own joke.

Fabienne smiled and took another bite.

They handed their disco balls to a PA, wiped their hands with napkins, and then the round of questions started. Eventually the judges stepped back for final comments.

"Edible lighting is certainly novel," Fabienne said. "Making the pieces individual and portable is interesting, and this could easily be scaled up for a larger crowd. In this case, it's good they weren't too bright, or one would be blinded trying to eat them."

Doris smiled broadly. "These lights of yours are simply scrumptious. I'd happily serve them at my next party, especially if they could be ordered in different flavors."

"They were indisputably delicious," Hugh said. "However, if they only activate when picked up, that makes their utility as a lighting fixture somewhat limited. And once you've eaten them, the light is gone, and we're all left in the dark."

Bro wouldn't know fun if it bit him in the face.

"Thank you, judges," Dylan said. Zeke stuck out his chin. They started to carry the tray back to their area.

"Hey, what about us?" I asked.

Zeke grinned and tossed a ball at me. I caught it, and the light in my hands cast rainbows all over my shirt and our table. I took a bite. Holy shit, it was good.

"You wanna try it?" I asked Penelope, holding up the ball.

Penelope hesitated, then leaned in. I expected her to take it from me, but instead she ate it out of my hand. Her eyes got big like she was surprised, and she gave a throaty little moan that went straight to my cock.

Down, boy. "Awesome, right?"

"It's super good."

"Here." I handed it to her. "I'll steal another one."

She grinned. "Don't cry at me later if they run out."

Not a problem. Her smile was worth giving it up.

Now it was Felicia and Charlotte's turn. The spell was cool enough, I guess, a swirling mass of tiny crystals that moved up and down and around a central spoke. The casting circle must have been incredibly complicated to handle the motion path and the looping. It also made a rushing, tinkling sound, somewhere between a waterfall and a wind chime.

Honestly, I zoned out because I didn't give a shit about those two witches, and also I kept sneaking looks at Penelope while she ate the rest of the disco ball. She seemed to be having a religious experience. I hoped Liam wasn't hating all the chewing sounds coming from her mic. When she finished, she had a tiny dab of mascarpone on her nose; I indulged in a fantasy of licking it off, then kissing the flavor out of her mouth. Thank goodness I was wearing boxer briefs and loose pants.

Fabienne thought the light was good, Doris thought it was great, Hugh thought it was technically impressive but lacking creativity.

Seriously, did they plan that in advance, or did it come naturally to them?

No time to think about it now. It was our turn.

I let Penelope carry the teapot to the table. Our sigil decorations weren't as nice as Amy and Jaya's piano, but they were solid. Hopefully the spell itself would be impressive enough that we wouldn't get kicked in this round.

Syd gestured at the table. "Tell us about your spell, yellow team."

Penelope looked at me, and I stuck out my chin at her. Talk!

"We call it 'Tempest in a Teapot,'" she said.

"Leandro's idea, I presume?" Hugh asked.

"Only the name!" I grinned and wagged my head from side to side.

"It activates when you put on the lid and turn it." Penelope demonstrated, then stepped back. The lights went out and we waited.

A trickle of smoky light drifted out of the teapot's spout. It took longer than I expected to thicken into a cloud. Probably needed more time in the fridge. Smelled good, though, just like Penelope planned, a mix of that earthy scent after it rained, a fresh ocean breeze and a hint of night-blooming jasmine. Once it reached critical mass, covering the whole area inside the containment circle, the glow was nice and bright—like night during a full moon, but the clouds were doing all the shining. Then the sparks started, bursting inside the floating mass like tiny fireworks, lightning without thunder.

"Does this conclude your spell?" Syd asked.

"One more phase," Penelope said. "Then it loops."

I had just enough time to worry the next part wouldn't trigger, when finally it did. Streams of color shot down from the clouds, greens and pinks and violets that shimmered and shifted like thin shafts of vertical aurora borealis. When Penelope had described her idea to me, it sounded nice, but this was great. Like a magical laser show, but softer, more natural.

The cycle ended, and the colored lights stopped, then the sparkles, leaving just the glowing clouds. That was my cue.

"Presto!" I said, and took a bow. I gestured at Penelope, who fake smiled and curtseyed, fingers pinching her imaginary skirt.

The judges came for us now, checking out the spell from underneath, circling the teapot like sharks sniffing for blood. The questions started biting: What did we use to form the clouds? And the lightning effects? How were the scents added? How long would it persist before dissipation? What if it needed to be dissolved prematurely? Were any of the components toxic if inhaled or ingested? Was it flammable?

Penelope answered most of the questions, which I was totally good with. Leandro Presto was supposed to be a himbo; rule number two, stay in character.

Maybe more importantly, if Penelope was going to have a chance at getting hired after this, she had to prove she could hang. She couldn't do that if everyone thought I was coming up with the spell ideas or the techniques to implement them, himbo or not.

Eventually the questions stopped, the judges retreated for final comments, and the spotlights came back on. I wanted to grab Penelope's hand, but I settled for a quick arm bump and a smile. She smiled back, her usual fake one, barely hiding the face twitches trying to break through like lightning.

"This is an interesting variation on fog or smoke effects," Fabienne said. "The cycling works well to keep the spell from becoming static too quickly. Some minor sound element might have been a welcome addition, though it could easily annoy depending on what is chosen."

"I almost wanted to get out my umbrella and rain boots," Doris joked. "The color portion was just delightful, and the clouds themselves cast a lovely light. Quite soothing for a tempest."

Now Hugh. I sucked in my breath, and I think Penelope did, too.

"It's a bit unimpressive to me," Hugh said. "Most of this can be reproduced using mundane, mechanical means and a little creativity. It did emit enough light to see by, at least."

The air hissed out of me like I was a balloon deflating. Wow, that was rough.

"Thank you, judges," Penelope said. I repeated it, and this time I carried the teapot back to our station.

Shit. Double shit. That had not gone well.

Honestly, it would probably take a miracle to save us, given what the judges had said about the other spells. I hadn't joined the show expecting to win, but every episode I stayed on would be another chance to talk about Grandpa Fred's charity. I needed more time, more chances. And Penelope needed the money, because exposure wouldn't pay her bills. I glanced sideways at her; she seemed to be doing the same math. Her smile was slipping.

I grabbed a paper and pencil and scribbled a note: *Hang in there, kitten.* I slid it down the table toward her, tapping her arm so she'd see it.

She rolled her eyes at me and wrote back: *Motivational poster? Really?*

I thought it was purrfect for you.

Stop!

Meow :)

She tried to take the paper away, but I crumpled it up and palmed it, pretending to eat it. The corner of her mouth turned up like she was trying not to smile and couldn't help it. I glowed a little inside.

Quentin and Tanner had moved their spell to the table while we passed notes. From the back, it looked like some kind of doll holding a ball and a ladder. The doll wore an old-fashioned top hat and coat with baggy pants, somewhere between stage magician and vaudeville clown. Everything was either made of scraps of metal or painted to look like it—very antique shop vibe.

Quentin rubbed his hands together. "This spell is called 'Hanging the Moon,' and it's inspired by automatons Tanner and I have worked on back at home. Our separate homes, I mean."

I laughed.

"My husband always said he'd hang the moon for me," Quentin continued. "So I wanted to do it for him."

Penelope awwed. I think Amy did, too.

Quentin pressed a button on the back of the automaton and stepped away. The doll-man started to move, surprisingly smooth and realistic. It set up the ladder as if it were propped against something, even though it was only touching air. Then it climbed the ladder, still holding the ball. When it got to the top, it lifted the ball above its head with its tiny metal hand.

And then nothing happened. We all waited, but there was no light, no other movement.

"Is your spell complete?" Syd asked.

"No, it's not," Tanner said. He and Quentin moved toward it, not touching but looking from different angles.

The doll-man dropped the ball. It bounced on the table, then rolled off and hit the floor with a loud clank. The ladder fell, taking the doll with it. The whole thing collapsed, and a bunch of the component metal bits broke apart and scattered in all directions.

Holy shit. Massive fail. When I'd said it would take a miracle for us to stay in the competition, this was not the miracle I ordered.

Quentin's face fell to pieces just like the spell. Tanner shook his head, but he also seemed . . . confused?

"I assume that was not meant to happen," Hugh said.

"No," Quentin said sadly. "I don't know why it didn't work."

Syd stepped in then. "Unfortunately there are no second chances on *Cast Judgment*. You'll be judged based on the spell as it was presented. Judges, questions?"

I was pleasantly surprised that the judges didn't skip the question portion just because the spell went wrong. They asked the same kinds of things they had for the rest of us. I listened more carefully than I had to the others, wondering if I could figure out what might have happened. I had a lot of experience making spells fail on purpose, after all.

Penelope seemed to be doing the same. She got that squinty, poochy-lipped face she made when she was thinking hard.

The judges all said more or less the same thing in their own ways: "Nice idea; too bad it didn't work." And that was it for the round.

I thought we might get shoved back into our greenrooms, but instead we waited at our stations for the judges to finish scoring. They didn't leave, just moved to a corner of the room. Each of them seemed to be working separately, then they got together to figure out who would be the winner of the round, who would be bottom two, and who was leaving.

Nobody talked. Quentin looked like he was trying not to cry.

Tanner seemed resigned. Everyone else was somewhere between bored and relieved.

I twirled a pencil in my fingers and thought about trying to distract everyone with a trick. I read the room and closed that book fast.

Finally the judges finished and presented the results to Syd, who took them with a more serious face than usual. Tori started yelling orders. The camera people grabbed their gear, the main lights turned on overhead, and the rest of us came out of our collective dream-space and back to reality.

"Now it's time to reveal the results of round one of *Cast Judgment*," Syd intoned. They made eye contact with all of us, one by one. Very dramatic.

"First, it's my pleasure to announce the winners of this round," Syd continued. "Their spell was not only a novel lighting method, it was also, dare we say, light on the tongue? Dylan and Zeke, congratulations!"

Dylan and Zeke smiled and fist-bumped as we all clapped. I couldn't argue with the judges' choice; those disco balls were great.

"Now, unfortunately," Syd said, "I must announce our bottom two teams. One of them will be leaving us today, while the other will have a chance to redeem themselves in round two."

Penelope tensed next to me. She expected the same thing I did. And it still sucked when it happened.

"Penelope and Leandro, your lighting method was functional but relatively mundane compared to the others," Syd said.

I shrugged and grinned while Penelope nodded.

"Quentin and Tanner, your lighting method was interesting, but ultimately didn't function at all."

The pair wore nearly identical expressions, like they'd chewed on aspirin.

"The team that will not be moving forward to the next round is . . ." Syd paused for dramatic effect. "Quentin and Tanner. I'm sorry."

I wished I could be glad about it, but instead I just felt sad. Quentin accepted hugs from the other contestants, while Tanner shook hands. Syd finished their outro-slash-lead-in to the next episode, and that was it.

Tori clapped. "Okay, time for confessionals!"

Right. This wasn't over yet. In more ways than one. Penelope sighed, and I gave her shoulder a quick squeeze. It didn't seem to help. Grandpa Fred's rule number three came to me: commit to the bit. It was worth a try.

"Meow you doing, kitten?" I asked.

"Oh my god, do not," she said. "No more cat puns."

"I'm just kitten around."

Her lips struggled not to smile. "Stop!"

"With the right cattitude, anything is pawsible."

That one got a snort-laugh she covered with her hands. Mission accomplished.

For now, anyway. One round down, but how many more would we get?

CHAPTER 10

Penelope

I'd visited the Tropical Oasis Botanic Gardens all the time growing up, either on field trips with school or because my abuela was super into horticulture. Two years ago, a hurricane tore through and damaged a lot of the trees and plants. Fortunately enough rich people on charity boards jumped in to get things fixed by some botany mages, and the place felt just as magical as it had when I was younger.

Tall royal palm trees stood in rows on either side of the stone walkway leading to the entrance. Past the gift shop and offices, it was like the place existed somewhere outside Miami, far from where people lived. Thick ficus roots sprawled across the leaf-covered ground like the cables back in the studio. Dozens, maybe hundreds, of different kinds of palm trees were arranged in clusters, mixed with flowers in more colors than a paint store. Oaks, mangroves, gumbo-limbo, pines, mangos, avocados, mangosteen, tamarinds . . . cascading walls of purple orchids and bursts of bromeliads . . . plumbago and bougainvillea and gardenia and jasmine . . . The variety was incredible, some native plants and some transplants.

Hah, Leandro would probably like that pun.

We were here to see a special exhibit of magical glass sculptures by a super-famous artist, Everly Bale. Instead of being displayed in the gallery, each piece had been placed somewhere on the grounds, for people to find as they wandered. All of them felt as if they belonged in nature. A miniature tree sprouted from the ground, spread leaves and branches, then grew a single golden pear that dropped and shattered into glittering dust, from which another tree grew as the first one shrank and disappeared. A vibrant peacock opened and closed its incredibly realistic tail feathers. A tiny fairy with iridescent wings and a flower hat climbed a cluster of glowing pink oyster mushrooms.

The difference between this quality of enchanting and the stuff we'd done fast on a soundstage was enormous. I didn't have an artsy brain at this level, but in a way, this was the dream: winning that space at the Desgraves Studio to create for a whole year, to learn and grow. All reagents and gear provided, no other major responsibilities to deal with, and that big cash prize to cover expenses. I could translate and test all of my abuela's recipes, and if I managed to finish that early, I could figure out what my version of these kinds of experimental projects might be. I could play and have fun instead of only doing what people ordered.

But if we lost . . . I slammed the door on that thought, locked it, and fed the key to an alligator.

Camera crews trailed after us and our tour guide as we walked down shaded paths until we reached a long, covered corridor with limestone walls that overlooked a lake. Ducks swam, ibis and heron stepped in the shallows, and turtles sunned themselves on the rocky shore. A sculpture that looked like a beached jellyfish stretched its long tentacles into the water, the balloony part expanding and contracting like it was breathing.

It was weird being here and pretending everything was cool after what happened last night. We'd hung out on the pool deck when we got back to the hotel, trying to cheer up Quentin and Tanner, who were both still trapped in the hotel with us until filming was finished thanks to the power of those lawyer ninja NDAs. Quentin swore their spell shouldn't have gone wrong, that he thought someone might have messed with it. Felicia made an ugly comment about accepting responsibility for his failures and not wallowing. I snapped and asked her if there was an ice palace somewhere missing its princess, and she got all huffy and left.

Quentin thought maybe something happened during the power outage, when he and Tanner were in the supply room. That was when Amy spilled the tea that Felicia had been standing near Quentin's station when the room went dark. I didn't think she needed to cheat to win, but who knows what people will do to get what they want.

Too bad for Quentin that no one could prove anything was sus. I had to focus on winning more than on what went down in round one.

Quentin still got to come along today, even though he was cut out of group shots. He kept mouthing *wow* and touching plants like he was having a religious experience. I didn't blame him. I was more into libraries than nature, but this place felt immense and peaceful. It made you a tiny part of something older and more beautiful than human problems.

Amy and Dylan seemed to be enjoying themselves, too, though poor Amy had to huff an allergy charm as soon as we got here. She wore a long-sleeved dress to protect her skin, and a cute straw hat with sunscreen spells woven into the brim. We'd all lotioned for safety, but she was definitely the palest of us.

Felicia's hat was more fashionable: white straw with a turquoise ribbon that matched her turquoise-and-yellow shirt and white capris. Big chunky sunglasses hid her eyes. Once again she wore heeled sandals that made her even taller; I thought I would twist my ankle just being near them. She looked like a runway model. A winner.

Charlotte rocked a sleeveless pantsuit and pearls that felt more corporate than nature walk. I hoped that maybe, possibly, I might be able to chat her up and convince her I was a hundred times more awesome than Felicia, but so far no luck. She stuck with her partner, even though neither of them seemed super talky.

I was hyperaware of Leandro standing near me the whole time. Today he wore a cream-colored guayabera embroidered with black and yellow butterflies, which—of course—matched my off-white shirt with black stripes. The universe conspiring.

I really wished I knew more about flirting. I second-guessed everything. Should I touch him more? Where? His arm? Should I smile at him? Point stuff out to him? Act natural and stop worrying about it so much? Was worrying making things worse?

"Hey." Leandro nudged me and pointed with his chin.

It took me a few seconds to see the sculpture that looked almost exactly like a cluster of bananas.

I giggled into my hand. "Oh my god, are you going to be bananaing me for the next two weeks?"

"Absolutely." He grinned. "I'm going to practice pulling them out of random places. My sleeve, your ear—"

"No, do not!" I slapped his arm gently. He rubbed it like I'd hurt him. Exagerado.

Oh, was that flirting? Ay! Shut up, brain.

The tour guide talked about the history of the gardens and the plants in the area. Syd occasionally cracked a joke; I wondered how many of them had been prepped in advance. Being funny all the time must be hard.

Probably for Leandro, too. Huh.

The tour ended at the lake, where we stopped for lunch. Tables had been set up at the far end of the covered area, all super fancy: wooden chairs and white tablecloths, actual glass glasses and nice plates, like a rich couple's wedding. We even had assigned seating. Once we'd all settled, waiters served us baskets of bread and individual meals of mahi mahi, rosemary garlic roasted potatoes, and asparagus. Big step up from yesterday's party platters.

Leandro, who sat next to me, leaned closer. "Are we still filming *Cast Judgment*, or did I time travel back to my Tía Sandra's wedding?"

"I was just thinking the same thing," I said.

"You were at Tía's wedding, too?"

"No jodas! You know what I meant." I smiled anyway. Was this flirting? Wait, we weren't on camera right now, so it didn't matter.

"I hope we get cake. And not the one my tía had."

I swallowed a bite of fish. "Was it one of those party cakes? With the pudding?"

"The soggy ones with the rum?" He made a gagging face. "No, it was dense, too much fondant. Huge white roses all over."

"My cousin Gina would die. She's an event planner, and she has, like, perfect taste."

Leandro used a piece of bread to push fish onto his fork. "So what's your favorite kind of cake?"

"Does it have to be cake cake, or can it be cake adjacent?"

"Either? Both?"

"If it's just regular cake, then chocolate with chocolate frosting. Cake adjacent? Tiramisu. What about you?"

"Chocolate lava cake, for sure."

"Ooh, lava cake. With ice cream." I had a brief cake fantasy as I stared at the wiggly jellyfish sculpture. When was the last time I'd even had cake? One of my million cousins' kids' birthday parties? Most of the time I missed them because they happened on weekends, while I was working.

How depressing was that? I had so much family here in Miami, and I never even saw them. How had my life gotten to this place?

Sitting here suddenly felt weird, like my thoughts were smothering me. I put my fork down and stood up.

"Bio break?" Leandro asked.

"I just . . . need to walk a little."

I couldn't be gone for too long; we'd be doing confessionals after lunch. If I got lost, they'd send a PA search party after me. A map nearby suggested a few options: an orchard, an orchid walk, or even just a path circling the lake. I decided on the butterfly conservatory.

The building had greenhouse vibes: a combination of stone, metal, and glass tall enough for whole trees to grow inside. I had to pass through two sets of doors to get in, the first leading to a foyer-slash-greeting room, where a cheerful lepidopterist explained how I shouldn't touch any plants, and to be careful where I stepped or sat, and to please not try to catch any of the butterflies and moths. No food or drinks allowed, either, which was fine since I hadn't brought any. I didn't even have a wallet, just my crew pass and a huge bucket of anxiety.

The second door had an air curtain, which blew down on my hair as I stepped through. I stood there blinking for I don't know how long, totally in awe. Had it always been this magical in here?

Slim palm trees were scattered among flowering plants, some

arranged in low rows and others between taller bushes and hedges: beds of five-petaled red pentas, bright yellow lantanas and goldenrod and daisy-like tickseed, pink zinnias and cosmos, on and on and on—colors everywhere I looked. Orchids sprouted from the limestone walls, and white aquatic milkweed grew on the shores of streams that fell into a peaceful pool, surrounded by ferns and mossy stones and pond apple trees.

And the butterflies. So many butterflies. I wasn't as familiar with their species as I was with the plants, but I recognized atalas, with their dark iridescent blue-spotted wings, yellow-striped zebra longwings, and of course, monarchs. Fruit feeding stations made of tree stumps with sliced mangos on top attracted some of them, like the bug equivalent of bird feeders. The rest fluttered from plant to plant, resting on flower petals or leaves, dancing in the air like relaxed drunks.

I wandered the stone paths until I came to another of the Everly Bale exhibits. The sculpture was taller than me, made of hundreds of tendrils of glass woven into a shape like a crocus bulb. Some strands were as thin as my hair, others as thick as my wrist, all of them different, vibrant colors, turquoise and magenta and dark orange and buttery yellow. They twined together, sliding past each other like a moving tapestry, shifting into different combinations that had no clear pattern or purpose even as they all seemed to be moving up toward the bulb's tip. Organized chaos. A contradiction.

That made sense, for a glass enchantment. Glass was a superdifficult medium to work magic with. It was composed of all four classical Western elements—earth, fire, water, and air. It was a fluid made solid, fragile yet durable, mutable and immutable.

It reminded me of Leandro. Another contradiction.

Ever since his first video Rosy showed me on her phone, I thought: This guy is ridiculous, with his safety glasses and his curly mustache. He's not only making an ass of himself, he's making it look fun to screw up spells. Irresponsible! Unsafe! Remembering that burst of fire in the studio, so close to his face, still made me shiver.

But there was more to him. He'd brainstormed with me and come up with good ideas. He was organized and thoughtful. His spellwork was carefully planned and precisely executed. He brought me coffee, somehow exactly how I liked it. When lightning had struck, the first thing he'd done was grab me, to keep me safe. None of that seemed to match who he was on his channel. I thought he was shallow as a muddy puddle, and suddenly he was a lake like the one outside, with turtles and birds and jellyfish sculptures and who knew what else below the surface.

And that made me think harder about Gil. We'd been emailing for so long, but all our interactions were words on a screen, emails and comments on blog posts. Maybe I didn't know him as well as I'd thought. Maybe he didn't know me, either. Maybe we'd each built up our own versions of Gil and Penelope and were carrying them around like old pictures on our phones. Not even pictures we had taken; ones we'd found on the internet, that might not even be of us, might be other people who sort of looked like us. I thought of that unhinged email I'd sent him a couple days ago and wanted to melt into the ground to feed the plants.

And me? I'd spent so long behind the store counter as some faceless nobody, fake smiling, fixing problems, letting people bitch at me. Ofelia threw me under the bus whenever it was convenient, even when I did nothing wrong. Some regular customers at least knew my name and a little about me, were friendly with me, but that was still my store self. Likewise when I did spell demonstrations. My friends knew me and liked me for who I was, but I spent so much time being the perfect little retail worker that sometimes it blended into other times and places. Sometimes, even with friends, I tried to be the me I thought they wanted to hang out with. Aside from that outburst in the park when I went "reply guy" as my sister called it, I was usually the chill one, the one who wouldn't bother anyone, wouldn't cause trouble.

And then I went home, alone, to my tiny illegal efficiency, and turned it all off like a light switch. Like taking off my bra at the end of the day and relaxing in a T-shirt. But was I most myself when no one else was around? Or was I an empty chalkboard waiting for someone to write on me?

If I won this competition, I'd have a year in a studio to figure myself out. To find that hopeful, ambitious Penelope who had stood up to her parents and stayed in Miami for college instead of moving away with them. To reconnect with my abuela through her spells now that she was . . . gone.

I sat on a bench and watched the sculpture twist and move. I couldn't decide whether it was hypnotic or freaky. It made my stomach weirdly tense, like I was waiting for some resolution that would never happen. What enchantment kept it going in perpetuity? Did it have to be periodically recast? Was it fed by some energy source? I crouched next to it, checking where it connected to the ground to see if there were roots or—

"Did you drop something?"

I yelped and fell onto my butt. Leandro leaned over me, a dark shadow against the bright glass ceiling, looking down with that half grin of his.

"Sneaking up on people is super rude, bro," I said. "I was checking out the sculpture."

"Trying to figure out how it works?"

"Yeah, what's fueling it."

"Might be something in the soil. Could also be solar?"

True. The glass ceiling let in plenty of light.

He sat down next to me. Hopefully wardrobe had cleaning charms for the dirt we were collecting on our pants. My jeans might hide it, but Leandro was wearing loose khakis.

"You okay?" Leandro asked softly. "Want me to leave?"

Weirdly, I didn't. I shook my head.

"What are you thinking?"

A tiny yellow butterfly landed on an orange milkweed flower across the path from the sculpture. I watched it for a bit, then exhaled loudly.

"I used to come here when I was younger," I said. "With school, and my abuela. I don't have time to anymore, or money, and, like . . . I'm not the same person I was then, either, I guess. But I have a lot of nice memories, and it's still really beautiful."

"It is. I came here, too, growing up."

"You're from here?" Why had I thought he wasn't?

"Yeah." He hesitated, like he wasn't sure how much more he should say. "I've done some demonstrations here, too. For kids on field trips."

More depths to the lake. "On the bus you said you liked casting with kids."

"Kids are great," he said. The more he talked, the more cheerful he got. "Especially the little ones. They're so hyped to see magic, and they love to correct you and tell you what to do. The teenagers sometimes are trying to be cool, you know? I have to work harder to impress them."

"Sounds like you do this a lot."

"Mostly through the charity I'm competing for. Have you ever heard of Alan Kazam's Schools Are Magic?"

"Are they still around?" I asked. "They came to my school in third grade. I used to see commercials on TV, and before movies."

He looked up at the sculpture. "Yeah, they can't afford ads anymore. I need that prize money to keep them going."

"That sucks." I could tell he cared about this a lot. I wanted to win *Cast Judgment* for selfish reasons, and here he was, trying to save a struggling charity.

Now who was the shallow, muddy puddle.

He stared at the shifting glass like he wasn't really seeing it, like he'd gone to a dark place inside his own head again. I didn't like it. I wanted to pull him back out, here, into the butterfly garden with me.

"What kinds of spells do you show the kids?" I asked.

Leandro grinned, and for a second, it was like seeing myself put on my customer service smile.

"Simple, flashy stuff," he said. "Jumping water tricks, basic circle work to make feathers levitate, animating popsicle-stick dolls and robots . . . usually I'll do some silly finale like trying to make a giant indestructible bubble dog, and instead I make enough little bubble puppies for them to chase around and bring back to me."

Okay, that was adorable. "They don't freak out when the puppies pop?"

"I spin a whole story about summoning them from Bubble Land and sending them back. They don't pop, they go home."

"Nice. That must be really fun." Did I sound jealous? Maybe a little.

"You could always volunteer. We provide the spells and reagents, you just have to show up."

"I wish I had time . . ." I sighed and hung my head. "I guess I do have time now that I don't have a job. I should probably focus on getting a new one when this is over, though."

"No way." He poked my arm. "We're going to win, and then you're going to spend a year making awesome stuff, and some Charlotte Sharp–alike is going to hire you."

"Hopefully the universe is listening. My friend Rosy—the one who was at the park with me—always says I need to stop catastrophizing and"—I made a rainbow shape with my hands—"maaanifest."

"Well, the first step to"—he made the same shape—"maaanifesting is to have a goal, so she's not totally wrong. We have a goal: win."

"Right, there are just a lot of question mark steps between step one: manifest and step whatever: win."

He shifted to one butt cheek, pulling a deck of cards out of his pocket. God, dude pockets were so usable.

"Let's try some luck magic," he said.

"Seriously?" Luck spells were sketchy. It was pretty much impossible to tell whether a thing might have gone better or worse without the magic.

The cards flew between Leandro's fingers like a manifestation rainbow. "You're going to pick a card, and if it's the queen of hearts, that means we're going to win."

I squinted at him. "No illusions?"

"No illusions." He leaned closer and dropped his voice. "Honestly, I'm not great at those. My visualization skills aren't strong enough."

"I had a friend in school with aphantasia," I said. "Sometimes they had to do alternate spell lessons." Illusions required really good mental picture-making abilities. You could do a basic copy illusion if you stared hard enough at a picture, but for anything more complex, you had to build it in your mind. Lots of people weren't good at it.

"See? You understand." Leandro fanned the cards out in front of his face, and one of them stuck up a little higher than the rest. He raised his eyebrows a few times as he looked at me over the top of the deck. "Pick a card, then flip it over on three."

I was so not taking that sticky-uppy one. I grabbed a random card from the left side.

His grin didn't change. Did I get the queen?

"One."

A striped butterfly drifted past, oblivious.

"Two."

The sculpture colors shifted and squirmed.

"Three!"

I turned the card around and stared.

The queen of hearts. No way.

"Presto!" Leandro said. "Impressed?"

"How did you do that?" I asked. "Let me see that deck."

"A magician never reveals his—hey!" He fell sideways as I tried to grab the deck out of his hand.

"You used a trick deck!"

Leandro dodged and held the cards up where I couldn't reach them, but he was laughing too hard to really fight me off. I tackled him and used both hands to crawl up his outstretched arm, prying the deck from his fingers. With a triumphant yell, I raised the cards into the air, grinning at him.

And then I realized I was sitting in his lap, and his face was inches from mine.

CHAPTER 11

Penelope

My brain almost never stopped. I'd lie awake at night with my eyes closed and imagine random, pointless things. Spells I couldn't afford to try. Conversations with people I'd never meet. Moments from a million years ago that any normal person would have forgotten. Just a constant background noise, like a fan whirring, a refrigerator humming, traffic zooming.

I stared into Leandro's dark brown eyes, and my thoughts dissolved into a cloud of butterflies that flew down into the pit of my stomach. The garden was already hot, but my skin felt like the sun had noticed me and come in for a closer look.

I had two choices: I could climb off him and make a joke, or . . .

I leaned in, closed my eyes, and . . . our foreheads bonked.

I flinched back, more from surprise than pain. My first time trying to kiss a guy in forever, and of course I'd messed it up.

"Sorry," I said. "Are you—"

Leandro grabbed my face with both hands and kissed me.

Our lips pressed together softly at first, sweetly, his mustache tickling me. He smelled like sweat and apples and lavender and a little pepper. I put my palm on his chest and tilted my head, my mouth opening enough to taste a hint of the chocolatey dessert I must have missed. I wanted more, so I licked my way inside.

One of his hands slid to my neck; the other arm wrapped around my back. He held me tighter than he had in the studio, so I could feel his muscles flexing through his sleeves. I shifted in his lap, trying to get closer, wanting more of my body to touch more of his. Was I rubbing against him like a cat? Maybe. I didn't even know. My hormones, which mostly hibernated, had woken up and gone feral. My fingers dug into the pleats of his guayabera and grabbed fistfuls of linen. I kissed him and kissed him, and he kissed me back. It went on forever and not nearly long enough.

We broke apart to catch our breaths. Leandro looked like I felt, like we'd just stumbled off the teacups ride at the fair and everything was still spinning.

Something moved out of the corner of my eye.

The glass sculpture bloomed, opening to reveal an egg-shaped bubble, milky white and iridescent like an opal. As the light caught it, there seemed to be a shadow inside, like some creature was about to be born. I gasped and waited. Then the tendril-petals closed and went back to writhing as if nothing had happened.

"Wow," I breathed. How many people had missed that because they'd wandered off too soon? How long did it take for the enchantment to go through that state change? Or was it triggered by something environmental?

Oh no. My brain had started up again. Also: I was still in Leandro's lap, his arm around my waist. Also also: I had just kissed Leandro Presto. The day after we had been told to pretend to be into each other.

Apparently we didn't have to pretend very hard.

I stared at the sculpture, blushing. What could I even say to him? What was I supposed to do now?

Kiss him again? I mean, it was an option.

"Penelope," Leandro said.

"Mm-hmm?"

"Do I need to apologize?"

Now I did look at him. His eyebrows scrunched together, and he'd leaned away just enough that I could wriggle out of his arms if I wanted to.

"No," I said. "Do I?"

He smiled softly. "No way."

Well, that was good. Wasn't it?

My brain inhaled deeply and started to spew.

Now every time you look at him for the next two days you're going to think about this kiss. You'll be distracted and make mistakes. And then you'll lose and Leandro's charity will shut down and you'll have to move in with your sister. Or worse, do the drive of shame back to your parents after you said you'd never, ever live with them again when your mother told you not to waste your life studying magic theory when you could major in something useful like your sister. Why can't you be more like your sister? Why do you always have to make everything so hard?

What about Gil? I'd spent months crushing on a guy, and all it had taken was two and a half days of nice-smelling, muscular, curly mustached distraction to make me jump to a new ship? I didn't even know Leandro. His videos were clearly a front, so who was he, really?

"There's steam coming out of your ears," Leandro said. "What are you thinking?"

Oh no, I'd made him feel bad. It wasn't his fault my thought trains were actually thousands of corgis riding around on skateboards until they got distracted and started chasing bubbles.

"Too many things," I said.

He rubbed the back of my neck. "Do you want to talk about it?"

No, I wanted him to kiss me until my thoughts went away again. Instead, I looked him in the eyes and my brain said helpfully: Gil has dark brown eyes, too.

"Later," I said. "Talk later. We should . . . confessionals."

"Right." He rested his forehead on mine. "Are you sure you're okay?"

No, I was shook. Customer service smile: go. "Totally."

Instead of smiling back, Leandro frowned. "That's your fake smile."

"It's real!"

"You don't have to lie to me."

"I'm not lying," I lied.

"Okay." He lifted me off him, giving me a chance to stand before he let go. Then he got up and brushed the dirt off his pants.

I was still holding the deck of cards, the one I was so sure was a trick. Maybe Leandro was, too. Maybe all his shy talk about fan panties was how he got into people's pants. What did I know?

Catastrophizing. Overthinking. I had to stop. If nothing else, we were a team. We wouldn't win if I second-guessed everything and didn't trust him.

Did I trust him? Trust had to start somewhere.

I held out the cards. "Here."

Leandro gave me a sad half smile. "You don't want to check them, after all that?"

"No. It was a good trick. Knowing how it works would ruin the magic."

"Sometimes knowing makes it more impressive."

"That's true. But sometimes . . ." I gestured at the sculpture with its shifting threads. "It's okay to just enjoy something, right? Like a kid. Have fun and not worry about the why and how. Sometimes magic can just be magic."

I had forgotten that at some point, hadn't I?

Leandro's smile slipped into what I was starting to recognize as his stage mode. Maybe that's why he noticed when I did the same thing. He held up the deck and fanned it out, then turned it around so I could see the cards.

All of them were different. He stacked them together again and passed his hand over them, then held the deck out to me. "Check the top card."

I turned it over. The queen of hearts. Magic.

I tried to give the card back, but he pushed my hand away.

"Keep it," Leandro said. "For good luck."

"But then that deck won't have a queen."

"Ah, but it doesn't need one. You're already the queen of my heart, m'lady."

I rolled my eyes. "Is that one of Sam's pickup lines?"

"Nope. That's a Leandro Presto original."

I slipped the card into my back pocket, which was too small, so it stuck halfway out. Hopefully I wouldn't lose it before I could put it in a safer place.

On the walk back to the lake, I rebuilt my calm stone by stone until I was once again Penelope Delmar, spell technician and *Cast Judgment* contestant. I wasn't sure who I'd been for those minutes in the butterfly garden. Maybe the real me.

Or maybe overstressed me. Didn't some people do wild stuff in high-stress situations? Like making out with cute available guys, and how about let's not think about Leandro's hands on me because now I was hot again. Hotter, I mean. It was Miami. Always hot.

Now that I knew what might happen between the two of us, I could be more careful. Pretend to flirt in ways that wouldn't get me all . . . whatever this was. Unlike the sculpture, I didn't need to open up to him and show him my boring center. Nothing to see here, move along.

Or . . .

No "or"! Shut up, brain.

My brain did not shut up. I got hotter. Thankfully we were hustled into hair and makeup as soon as we got back, and then we had separate confessionals instead of paired ones.

I had told Leandro we would talk later, but I still didn't know what I wanted to say, so I didn't look for him when we were dropped at the hotel. He didn't come find me, either, and I didn't see him at dinner, possibly because I grabbed my food and took it to my room for some quiet time.

Except my brain was too loud. I thought about Leandro, and Gil, and kisses, and life. When I finally got to bed, the queen of hearts rested on the nightstand next to me, and we both stared up at the ceiling in the dark.

Quentin and Tanner's station had been cleared out, leaving only the appliances. It probably shouldn't have felt weird, but it did.

The rest of us stood next to our areas, Syd and the judges once again at the front of the room, about to deliver our new brief. We were running an hour behind schedule. Lights were lit, cameras pointed in the appropriate directions, and the thing Leandro told me was called a slate finally clapped, super loud in the space.

Tori had taken me and Leandro aside to tell us we were doing a good job "vibing" as requested, and to see if we could turn it up a little without overdoing it. I didn't know whether we would overdo it, underdo it, or just do it do it—no pun intended. My stomach fizzed every time I thought about our kiss.

And of course we matched. Were we ever not going to match?

Leandro wore yet another long-sleeved button-down shirt someone's abuelo had rocked fifty years ago. This one was white and covered in breakfast items: reddish bacon, buttered toast, cast iron pans with fried eggs inside, red carafes and cups of steaming coffee, random utensils . . . I wondered if it had ever been cool, or if that mystery abuelo had also been a giant nerd.

My apron for the day, courtesy of my sister, was the red of his shirt's carafes. Instead of breakfast stuff, mine was Cuban coffee–themed: gray cafeteras, white cups and saucers, and swirls of sugar and coffee grounds rising out of iron cauldrons. No yellow, so Bruno had tied yellow ribbons around my buns that brushed my neck every time I turned my head.

Maybe I shouldn't be flirty. I already looked unprofessional. Who would hire me if this was what they expected? Meatball hair and silly aprons and fooling around with coworkers.

Still, I'd put that queen of hearts card in my apron pocket for luck. After what had happened in the first round, we would need it.

Syd raised their arms. "Welcome, everyone, to round two of *Cast Judgment*! We're down to four pairs of casters and Spellebrities, and with every elimination, the difficulty of the brief will increase."

Right, because coming up with a whole new lighting spell hadn't been hard.

"You will also be judged more harshly as the rounds progress, so make sure your next effort is twice as dazzling as the last."

So round three would need to be eight times as awesome as the first round? Also, how could Hugh Burbank get harsher? By replacing his blood with acid?

"Remember, every spell you design and cast must be celebration-themed."

Whee. My hormones were certainly celebrating.

"Without further ado, the brief!" Syd then, of course, paused dramatically and looked around at all of us. "What would a party be without extravagant ornamentations? We want you to create a spectacular party decoration or centerpiece that goes through at least two complete transformations. As always, no illusions allowed."

Two transformations? One was hard enough, depending on what enchantments we used . . .

Syd gestured at the LED clock on the wall. This time—no pun intended—it lit up with a giant number sixteen and a bunch of zeroes. "Your time begins . . . now!"

Fifteen fifty-nine and counting down. Even knowing it would be split into two days, it seemed like too much and too little.

I pulled out my notebook and a pencil and leaned against the counter. Leandro joined me, mimicking my pose.

Focus, Penelope.

"Decoration or centerpiece," I muttered, writing, "Two transformations."

"Maybe we start with a theme and back into the theory?" Leandro suggested.

"Makes sense."

We stood there, thinking. His shoulder touched mine. I froze. He shifted a little and we weren't touching anymore. I exhaled.

We were supposed to level up the flirty. Should I lean on him more? Smile? Flutter my eyelashes?

Okay, this was ridiculous. I was going to be normal and stop thinking about it, or I'd never get anything done.

Hah. Me, stop thinking.

"Werewolf?" Leandro said finally.

"Man turning into a wolf? Hmm." I wrote it down, though it didn't sound party-ish. "Maybe something from a story? Lots of transformations in folktales."

"Or magical girl animes?"

I groaned and nudged him with my hip. "Don't start with the body pillows."

Leandro laughed. I tapped the pencil on the paper. Tap, tap.

"Are flowers and butterflies too obvious?" he asked.

Was he teasing me? Reminding me of yesterday? I gave him a quick side-eye. His mouth was too close. I blushed and looked down at the paper again.

"Those definitely transform," I said. "But they're pretty basic. We'd have to make it really cool."

"Like that sculpture."

"Yes! But we can't copy it. We can totally say it inspired us, though."

We started sketching out more ideas: what to make the original piece look like, how the first transformation should work, then the second.

"So many people are late to parties," I said. "We should make it repeating."

"Maybe make the catalyst something that can be re-added?" Leandro suggested.

"Right, like a seed bomb." I wrote down a list of possible tropical flower options based on what we'd seen at the gardens. Some would be tricky, since they were usually propagated with cuttings or offshoots instead of seeds. Maybe a wrapped leaf ball, like a blooming tea?

Leandro stepped away to get our tools ready. I kept sneaking looks at him. Partly I wanted to know what he was doing, but also I kept thinking about yesterday. His eyes. His chest. His mouth. Even with that silly mustache, his mouth was a total fantasy. And I was pretty sure a certain part of him I had sat on was not a pocket banana.

Truly, I had lost my brain. Possibly the butterflies had taken it.

Why couldn't we have kept our damn hands to ourselves? Ah! I didn't need this. I needed to finish this recipe.

Forty-five minutes slipped away. I had ingredients and most of the methods, at least. I just wanted to run a few things by Leandro before finalizing.

And of course he had snuck off, to do a scarf summoning trick for Amy and Jaya, who seemed to find it adorable. I wanted to be mad, but after what he'd said about working with kids, I knew he enjoyed this. Recording a video to release into the wilds of the internet was one thing; seeing the happy faces of the people you were doing magic for was another.

That was—had been—one of the few things I liked about working at Espinosa's. When someone came to me with a question or a spell problem and I was able to answer it or fix it for them, and it made them happy, that made me happy, too.

Maybe I would volunteer to teach kids magic when this was all over. I could use a little joy in my life, even if it didn't pay.

Leandro came back, grinning. "Did you figure everything out already? Or did you leave something for me to do?"

I booped his nose with the pencil's eraser. "Slacker. What do you think about these sigils?"

"Hmm." He stole the pencil and started making his own notes. "We want to link the repetition to the cutting ball, right? Which means at least partially dispelling the original manifestation so it doesn't double or cause a corruption."

"Right," I said, "that's why I added the Klein symbol here." I tapped the squash-shaped figure.

"A coiled ouroboros might be best, though?"

We debated a little longer, settled on a final circle diagram, and off I went to the supply room. I wasn't sure they'd have all the fresh flowers we wanted, and I wasn't wrong, but they had a lot. Then there were the herbs, and the other reagents . . .

Amy passed me, looking lost again. We had a quick chat about where to find bone ash—aisle two—and whether wing feathers or down would work better for manifesting a bird when considering the law of synecdoche—wing feathers for sure, in my opinion. Felicia stomped past, grabbing a bunch of herb jars from the shelf and leaving. By the time I realized she'd taken all the tarragon, which I needed, it was too late.

When I got back, the wall clock said an hour and a half had passed.

No screaming. Nope. I would be calm and cool and—what was Leandro doing at our station with that chalk?

I did not run, because I was pushing a shopping cart. But I definitely power walked, hoping my face didn't look as worried as I felt. Sound guy Liam was probably wondering why my heart was dancing salsa and I was panting like a dog.

Calm. Cool. "How's it going?" I asked.

Leandro looked up at me from the floor and spun the chalk in his hand. "Almost finished with the inner ring sigils. Want to check my spellwork?"

How dare he be adorable, and also, his sigils were perfect, and so were his circles and lines. My heart settled into a cumbia.

Trust him. I had to trust him. I should trust him.

"Good," I said. "All good. Help me with the groceries?"

He stood and bowed. "As you wish, m'lady."

We pulled everything out of the cart and arranged it neatly on the counters and tables. Again, as I always did, I checked each container's expiration date, then opened them one by one to sniff and scan. Rosemary, check. Spearmint, check. Twice-blooming cereus, check.

"You really do that every single time, huh?" Leandro asked. "Even here?"

"Even here," I said. "You never know. You'd be surprised what can slip through quality control."

"Sounds like a story."

"More than one, unfortunately." I'd learned some lessons the hard way, even when I'd tried not to.

After everything was set up, we were still missing the tarragon. I headed for Felicia and Charlotte's station. Okay, Penelope, opportunity to network. Be professional. Friendly smile.

"Hi!" I said.

"Are you lost?" Felicia replied.

Charlotte made a scoffing sound as she carefully positioned a mirror and prism array. Was she irritated? Or laughing?

"I just need some tarragon, please. You took all of it."

"Use something else. We need it."

I kept smiling, even if my jaw was clenched. "I guess we'll figure something out. Thankfully we know enough magic theory to do that, unlike you, apparently."

I decided that was a good exit line and went back to our station. Take that, esprit d'escalier. When I glanced back at Charlotte, she was looking at me with a closemouthed smile.

Hah! Maybe I had impressed her.

"No tarragon?" Leandro asked.

"Nope. We can use something else."

"Anise seed?"

"Or fennel . . ." We wouldn't need it until later, anyway.

Leandro finished the outer circle while I mixed the first set of ingredients, and we dove into casting. Minutes walked; hours ran. We ate lunch while we worked, careful not to spill anything. The judges circled us like sharks waiting for blood to hit the water, but this time when they came to ask us questions, I felt more ready.

At some point around hour six, Felicia came over. "Here's your tarragon," she said, holding out a jar like it was a dead animal.

"Thank you so much," I said sweetly.

"Whatever." She left without looking back.

Leandro watched her hip-swaying, high-heeled walk, and something ugly dug around in my chest. I had no right to feel even slightly jealous. She was pretty, and he could look.

"Do you think her farts are super high-pitched because of the huge stick in her ass?" he asked.

I snort-laughed so hard I had to cover my mouth. The thing in my chest disappeared.

"She has to take it out to poop," I said.

"Does she hold it the whole time, or does she rest it on her lap?"

"That's disgusting. And we probably shouldn't shit-talk the other contestants."

"Shit-talk?" Leandro waggled his eyebrows.

"Pun not intended!"

I opened the tarragon to check it, imagining Felicia waving around a poop-covered stick. Hold on. I wafted the scent of the jar toward me again, then checked the label. Tarragon. Except it wasn't. I shook some of the herb onto the counter, then tasted it to be sure.

"This is thyme," I said.

Leandro tried a pinch, too, then grabbed my wrist and turned the jar so he could read the label. He was touching me. My brain crashed and rebooted.

"Wrong ingredients can cause huge problems in a spell," I said.

"Someone could get hurt," he agreed.

I glared at Felicia, who was either ignoring me on purpose or had no idea what she'd done. Only one way to find out. I took the jar back to her station and held it up.

"What's this?" I demanded.

Felicia looked at me like I'd lost my mind. "I know you're dense, but I assumed you could read labels."

"This isn't tarragon," I said. "It's thyme."

Felicia wasn't dense; she understood what I was implying. She grabbed the jar and checked it, her blue eyes narrowing. But instead of fighting with me, she started going through all her other jars of tarragon. Charlotte joined her a second later.

"Who's in charge of the supply room?" I asked Leandro, who stood quietly next to me.

"I'm not sure." Leandro smoothed his mustache. "Maybe we should grab Syd? Or Tori?"

"Tori, yes." She was important. She'd want to know, either that

Felicia was screwing around or . . . Except I didn't see her. I did see Big Manny, looking grumpy. I walked over to him, waving the jar.

"Yes?" Big Manny asked, watching the jar move.

"This has the wrong ingredient in it," I said.

He blinked. "Are you sure?"

The memory of Ofelia asking me whether I'd messed up the reagents for sparkle-hair guy flashed through my brain. My customer service smile appeared on my face like dark magic, hiding the irritation buzzing in my chest.

"She's sure," Leandro said firmly. "Get Tori."

My irritation fizzled. He'd backed me up. No hesitation. No jokes. He looked angry, actually, which was new.

He trusted me. It shouldn't have felt so good, but it did.

Big Manny walked toward the door, muttering something into his collar mic. He ran into Tori coming in, and they whispered back and forth. Big Manny pointed at me, and Tori's face went all flat again. She gestured us over.

I handed her the container. The other contestants and celebrities were watching us now, and Felicia grimly brought over a jar of sage that apparently wasn't. I tried to stay calm, but inside I was still freaking out. What if Quentin had used a wrong reagent that broke his spell? What if Felicia hadn't done anything after all? Or maybe she had messed with her own stuff to cover her sabotage?

Sabotage. No way. It couldn't be. Could it?

"Shut it down," Tori said into her collar mic. "We have a problem."

CHAPTER 12

Gil

We didn't get to work on our spells for the rest of the day. Tori shut down the production, and a team of quietly freaked-out people invaded the supply area. Big Manny and another burly PA stood guard at the entrance like bouncers, I guess to make sure no one could get in and mess with the auditing or whatever.

Eventually Isaac Knight roared in. His hair looked like he'd been grabbing it, all clumped together and sticking up in different directions. He climbed onto Dylan and Zeke's table, ignoring their disgusted looks.

"Listen up," Isaac said, clapping for attention as if we weren't already staring at him. "I don't know what the fuck is going on here, but if any of you is doing anything you shouldn't be doing, I'm going to sue your ass so hard, your great-grandkids will still be paying the lawyers."

Tori cleared her throat like she wanted to talk, but Isaac pointed at her, then made a fist. Her face went blank.

"I'm told this may just be an 'accident' with our suppliers," Isaac continued, his air quotes audible and sarcastic. "In which case, Frogtail is going to be the one hearing from our lawyers. I don't give a shit who pays, but someone is going to, and it won't be me.

This is fucking with my production schedule. This is fucking with my budget, and I don't need the accountants up my ass more than they already are."

Tori's left eye twitched.

Isaac pointed his fist at the rest of us, snarling like an angry dog. "If any shit-sucking, mud-fucking journalists hear even a whisper about anything that leads to questions about the integrity of this competition, I'll fucking end you. I'll bury you in anonymity until not even your friend's daughter's basement podcast will want to interview you, and you won't be able to get a job that doesn't involve an ugly polo and the words, 'Thank you, come again' repeated eight hundred times an hour."

Tori said, "Isaac, we agreed—"

"Shut up, Victoria," Isaac said without looking at her. "None of you knows anything about any problems here. You don't know anything, nobody around you knows anything, and none of you are going to talk about the nothing you don't know about. Not in public, not in private, not to anyone else on this production, past or present. Zip your lips or I'll zip them for you, capisce?"

He climbed back off his pedestal and stormed out, Tori following with her shoulders near her ears. I felt bad for her. Dealing with Isaac seemed to require selective hearing and a suit of medieval armor.

"Do you think he's serious about the lawyers?" Penelope whispered.

"Probably, but the network decides that stuff," I said. "All he can do is yell." I was pretty sure, anyway. But Penelope seemed to be freaking out, and I didn't want to make her more anxious.

Jaya talked quietly to Amy and rubbed her arm while Amy wiped away tears underneath her glasses. Dylan and Zeke stood stoically, arms crossed. Felicia checked her spell components the same way Penelope had, while Charlotte had cornered Big Manny and was telling him something that made him alternately nod and shake his head. Syd and the judges had left, presumably to go back to their trailers.

"Funny that Isaac thinks the worst he can do is make us work retail," Penelope said. "Clearly he forgot that was literally my job."

"Do you think he's worked retail before?"

"No way. Can you picture him at a store?"

I gave her an angry glare and did my best Isaac voice. "Are you gonna buy that shirt? It's puke green! It's giving 'baby doesn't want to eat his peas, so he threw them at you.' Come on."

Penelope stuck her fist in her mouth and tried not to laugh.

I kept going. "Why don't you buy the black shirt? If you spill something on it, there won't be a stain, just a smell. That's what body spray is for. Hey, where are you going? You didn't buy anything! Fuck you, too!"

"I'm dying," Penelope gasped. "I can't breathe."

I almost made a joke about giving her mouth to mouth, but we were in public. Unfortunately that sent my thoughts spinning off in other directions.

That kiss yesterday. Holy shit. I'd spent all day today playing it cool when I wanted to drag her into an empty office and do it again.

She'd said we should talk later, and we hadn't. Maybe she'd changed her mind and wanted to pretend nothing had happened? I had to know. The only way to find out was to ask.

Except we were stuck here. No privacy. All I could do was not "overdo" flirting and tell bad jokes.

The inventory check took so long, we were eventually hustled back to the hotel. The sun had almost finished setting, high-rises around us casting their long shadows on the roads and shorter buildings. Penelope sat next to me, making her duck-lip thinking face, her leg touching mine. I wasn't sure if she noticed, but I extremely did.

Dinner would be on the pool deck again since the bar-slash-restaurant was open to regular customers at night. I ran up to my room and peeled off my mustache, cleaned my skin, and moisturized. As I rubbed lotion into my upper lip, I wondered if taking my mustache off was the equivalent of someone with boobs taking their bra off at the end of a long day. For me, there was the extra layer of shedding my Leandro persona, going back to being Gil Contreras. Grandpa Fred's rule number four: leave work at work. I'd have to put the mustache back on to go get food, though, so I wouldn't have a naked upper lip for long.

I slumped in my desk chair and stared at a moving picture of a bromeliad hanging on the wall. I needed a plan for The Talk. How would I get Penelope alone? What would I say? Should I just listen? She'd said she didn't want to apologize, and didn't want me to, but what did she want?

What did I want?

Easy. I wanted Penelope. And not just physically, though that was definitely a thing. I wanted to go out with her, to eat cheap takeout on my couch and watch documentaries, to talk about magic theory books and figure out spell recipes together. I wanted a girlfriend, not a fuck buddy.

But wanting it badly enough wouldn't magically solve the logistical issues. Dating as Leandro was out of the question; he was a character. A part of me, yes, but not real. If I dated someone as myself, I'd have to hide the fact that I was also Leandro until I was sure I could trust them, which meant I'd have to lie about a huge part of my life. Secrets were a shitty foundation for a relationship.

And the more Penelope liked Leandro, the more I worried that maybe she didn't like Gil as much as I'd thought. It didn't matter that they were both me, because she didn't know that.

Did her switching teams so easily mean I shouldn't trust her?

What would Grandpa Fred tell me to do? He'd given me the rules I followed, so he'd probably have some good advice for this whole situation. Maybe I could call him on our rest day.

But what would I say to Penelope now?

I put my mustache back on and went upstairs to eat, still lost.

The pool deck was crowded, food tables set up in their usual spot, drinks at the poolside bar, lounge chairs around the pool and regular chairs and tables scattered everywhere else. The sun had set, but it was still hot as balls, even with cooling charms and the breeze coming in from the bay. The views to the sides were blocked by high-rise condo buildings, but that still left the water in front of us, stretching out to the causeway, with its pink and purple neon running the length of the bridge. A few stars twinkled above us, the lights from the beach and downtown reflected in the water.

After Isaac's pissed-off speech, nobody talked about the production shutdown. They went for non-competition topics: movies, TV shows, sports . . . Big Manny and Little Manny were arguing with Penelope about something, which Dylan seemed to find funny. I took my plate of chicken and mashed potatoes and sat next to Penelope, who quickly finished chewing and gestured at me.

"Leandro, back me up," she said. "Best empanadas. Alvaro's, right?"

"No way," Little Manny said. "Castillo de las Frutas."

"I eat those all the time because my friend works there. They're pretty good, not the best."

"I keep telling them, there's this ventana in an office building," Big Manny said. "I forget the name, but it's the best. Good coffee, too."

Penelope swallowed. "Hold up, is it the one in the Trinity building?"

"Yeah, that one! The ventana on the first floor?"

"That's my aunt's ventana!" Penelope smacked Big Manny on the arm, then winced. "Sorry. Okay, you win, though: her empanadas are choice. She never brings any to parties because she's like, 'Oye, por favor, I make them all week, I'm not making them on my day off.'"

I ate quietly. I knew I should make jokes, be more Leandro. Rule number two: stay in character. I'd never had to do it for so long, though. I hadn't realized how tired I would be.

"You okay?" Penelope whispered.

Shit. She noticed. Turn it up, Gil.

I grinned at her. "I'm good. Just thinking about all the nothing that didn't happen today."

Penelope sucked her teeth. "I'm trying not to think about it, because I don't want psychic lawyer ninjas to kidnap me. I'm definitely not thinking about it anywhere near Quentin."

Quentin was talking to Amy, his hands moving like he was building something in the air. Tanner hadn't made an appearance, but neither had any of the other celebrities. I wondered whether they were all hiding in their rooms, or if they'd escaped the lockdown. Maybe they were eating together and hadn't invited me.

Normally the thought of not hanging with the cool kids wouldn't bother me—this wasn't middle school. But I was supposed to network. Mingle. Not with the contestants and PAs, but with the people who could help level up my career.

Then again, Grandpa Fred's rule number six: everyone is important. He always said to act like every person I met was having the worst day of their life, and I had the chance to turn it around. If I started to rank the people around me by how much they could help me, what kind of shitty suck-up would I be?

"Hey," I said. "You're Little Manny, and you're Big Manny, but where's Just Manny?"

Little Manny shrugged, and Big Manny shook his head.

"He's around," Big Manny said.

"Nobody sees Just Manny," Little Manny added. "He's like a, what do you call it? The animals that maybe don't exist?"

"A cryptid?" I asked.

"That. You tell him what he has to do, and he does it, but no one ever sees it happen."

We ate dessert as we plotted ways to trap Just Manny into showing himself. I suggested a cardboard box propped up by a stick with a Cuban sandwich underneath. Penelope thought slipping a magic tracker into a box of stuff for him would be easier and sneakier. We worked our way up to trip wires and mirrors and people doing their best Isaac impersonations pretending Just Manny was in trouble. Little Manny, hilariously, nailed his facial expressions.

The later it got, the harder it was to see myself talking to Penelope about anything private. Maybe that was for the best. Leave it alone until we knew whether we'd be continuing in the competition. We needed to focus on our strats instead of getting distracted.

Penelope stood up and stretched. "It's getting late. We should go."

We?

She tugged my arm. "Come on, we need to adjust our plan for tomorrow."

"Totally." I brushed cake crumbs off my shirt. Classy.

"Don't stay up too late 'adjusting your plan,' you two," Little Manny said, waggling his eyebrows.

"No jodas," Big Manny said, shoving Little Manny halfway off his chair. "What do you care what they do in private?"

"As long as they don't do it with a hot mic. Get it? Hot mic?"

I groaned. Penelope turned bright red. We headed for the elevator, and I was glad I'd reapplied deodorant before I came up for dinner; the heat was bad enough, but now I was sweating bricks.

"Should we . . . go to one of our rooms?" Penelope asked. She didn't sound like she wanted to, but I didn't know whether it was because of what Little Manny had said, or because she was nervous about being alone in a place with a bed. Not that we were going to jump each other's bones, but it would be standing there. Menacingly.

We definitely couldn't go to my room. I couldn't remember whether I'd stashed my mustache stuff.

"How about the business center?" I asked.

"Yeah, okay."

The elevator came and we stepped inside. The doors closed, and I almost had to hold my breath because her smell filled the small space. Rosemary, mint, and something else . . . her deodorant? Jasmine, rose, a hint of vanilla. It was like being back in the gardens, which was not a thing I needed on my mind right now.

Did she really want to talk about our spell, or other stuff?

A year later, the doors opened and we stepped into the lobby. Alina waved at us from behind the front desk as she chatted on the phone. We walked past her, down the hall. Even though the hotel was small, it had a gym with a spa, an arcade-slash-playroom, a library-slash-lounge with books we could borrow, a small movie theater with free popcorn and a soda machine, and a business center with a private casting room that doubled as a small sound booth. Super fancy.

The business center lights came on when we opened the door. Pale green walls, one with five clocks showing different time zones. Desks that matched Alina's, same Key West vibe. Ergonomic leather spinny chairs. Every desk had a computer with monitor, keyboard, and mouse, and a tray with paper and pens and pencils, all covered in the hotel logo. In the corner, an open door led to the casting booth, a soundproofed pentagonal mini-room with a tiny shelf inside. The outside was covered in distressed wood, trying to make it match everything else.

Penelope took one chair; I took another. She grabbed stuff to write with, so I did, too. I wasn't sure whether to be relieved or disappointed that she really did want to work on the spell.

"We have to be super careful tomorrow," she said. "More than usual."

I nodded, spinning the pencil between my fingers. "Maybe today was a supplier issue, but maybe not. After what happened with Quentin . . ."

"We have to be paranoid. No leaving the spell alone. Watch anyone who comes near it."

"Anyone?"

Penelope hesitated. "Maybe not the judges? Or the crew. I don't know why they would want to cause trouble."

I tapped the pencil eraser on the paper. "Could be someone paid them off. Money can make people do bad shit."

"Still, it's most likely one of the contestants."

"You're thinking Felicia."

"Definitely." Penelope put her pencil down and leaned forward. "Amy said she was near Quentin and Tanner's station when the lights went out. And she's the one who gave us the wrong reagent."

"If she did anything, someone's going to catch her. But we can't take any chances. Trust no one except each other."

"Exactly." Penelope blew out a breath. "I'm so glad you get it. I was worried you'd be super chill about this."

Uh, no? "Some things are too serious for chill. Even people like me have some sense. Rules, even."

"Leandro Presto has rules?" she asked, grinning like I'd made a joke. "About what?"

It shouldn't have annoyed me to hear that, but it did. "Nothing. It doesn't matter."

"It matters to you, clearly." Penelope's smile turned to a worried look. "Sorry for laughing. Are the rules like, for life, or your show, or . . . ?"

I stared at the ground, derpy smile back on. "The show, yeah. I don't usually talk about them."

"Oh. No worries. You don't have to tell me."

"I didn't mean it like that. They're not secret, just personal? Stuff like . . ." I mentally went down the list, skipping the ones that said too much. "Leave work at work. Hands off the fans. Everyone is important."

"Those are good rules." Penelope tilted her head. "So you never date fans?"

"Never."

"Not even the ones who don't give you their underwear?"

"No."

"Huh. Okay."

Why did that "okay" make me so tired? I suddenly, desperately wanted her to understand me better, even if it meant a tiny break in character. A little Gil slipping through the Presto.

"Some people just want to hook up with someone sort of famous," I told her. "That feels like they're using me? Even the ones who aren't like that, they don't really know me. They know who I am in my videos, or when I chat online. That's not . . ." Real? True? ". . . the whole me."

Penelope stared like I'd just handed her a tricky spell problem. "But if you don't go out with any of them, how will you get to know each other?"

I opened my arms and shrugged. "I don't know. But I can't risk it."

"Can't, or won't?"

"Won't. I won't take chances on strangers I don't have a reason to trust."

Did I trust Penelope? I thought I did . . .

Her frown smoothed out. "I guess I'm not a fan, so that rule doesn't apply to me anyway."

Did she realize what she'd just said?

And then she did, because her eyes got huge and she turned red as a pitanga. "I mean, not that we're going to—well, we already did, but I won't assume you want to, you know, again. I don't want to make things weird."

"You're not making . . ." I stopped, hearing footsteps coming down the hall. Clacky high-heeled ones. And voices, two women. It sounded like—

"It's Felicia and Charlotte," Penelope whispered. "Quick, hide!"

"What? Why?"

"Shh! Get under the desk!"

That made no sense. I pulled her into the casting booth instead.

The door was heavy, but I managed to close it behind us quickly. We crouched so we couldn't be seen through the small window in the door. There was barely enough room for both of us; my back and right shoulder hit the foam on the side walls, and Penelope's back was pressed against my front, her butt dangerously close to my crotch.

From this angle, with the outside sound muffled, I couldn't tell whether Felicia and Charlotte even came into the room. I started to get up to peek, but Penelope squeezed my arm and looked at me over her shoulder, shaking her head.

"Why are we—" I started to ask.

"Shh!" Penelope whispered, twisting so her mouth was closer to my ear. "They might hear us."

"This booth is soundproof," I whispered back.

"Are you sure?"

I tried to remember what Ed had told me about sound booths, but, well, butt. Distracting. "No."

"Then shh!"

Her scent filled the tiny space quickly, especially since she was practically in my lap. This was worse than the elevator. How long did she want to hide in here?

"Even if it isn't totally soundproof, they won't hear us whispering," I said.

"Can we hear them?"

"No, it works both ways." Hold up. "You wanted to spy on them?"

"Maybe. Yes."

"What if they find us?"

"It's a casting room. We pretend we were doing spell stuff."

Right. With no reagents. I didn't even have chalk.

Penelope took a deep breath, held it, then let it out slowly. Her muscles were so tense, they shook. I had to stop her freak-out, since I didn't know how long we'd be stuck.

I sat down on the chalkboard-painted floor, then made her do the same, nestling her between my knees and wrapping my arms loosely around her upper body. Not totally snuggled up, but close. She gripped my forearms with both hands.

Hmm. There was something else we could pretend to be doing in here.

"Hey, girl," I whispered. "Is your name Chamomile? Because you're a hot tea."

Penelope covered her mouth with one hand. "Oh my god," she whispered through her fingers. "Do not."

"Feel my shirt. It's made of boyfriend material."

She made a sound between a muffled snort and a squeak.

"If you were part of a contract, you would be the fine print."

"Stop!" she whispered, but now she was shaking from trying not to laugh.

I tightened my arms around her. "You must be a great caster, because every time I look at you, everyone else disappears."

That one didn't make her laugh. Probably because I meant it. Ah, Penelope. All the reasons I should keep my distance seemed so unimportant as soon as I was holding her.

I kissed her under her ear. She sucked in a breath. My lips kept going, down her neck to the collar of her shirt. She angled her head, giving me better access, so I trailed more kisses all the way up to her hair, then dropped one on the back of her ear.

I had no idea whether the booth was ventilated, but it was getting hotter inside.

Penelope turned so she could reach my mouth with hers.

Mmm. Our second kiss was as delicious as the first, but sweeter and slower. No film crew to hurry us along, no fake smiles, no producer-mandated creeping. Only her and me in this small, quiet space, finding our rhythm, feeling our way along each other's skin.

I sucked on her bottom lip and she opened for me. Our tongues danced the bachata, the tango, stroking and teasing. My heart raced like I was moving my whole body instead of just my mouth. My glasses bumped her face and I ripped them off, tossing them on the shelf above us without looking. I didn't even worry she might recognize me. The wrong head was doing all my thinking.

I'm not sure which of us got more . . . impatient? But between one kiss and the next, Penelope climbed on top of me. Her arms twined around my neck, and she rode my thighs while I grabbed her ass with one hand. With the other, I skimmed my fingers over her breast; she gave a throaty little hum, so I did it again, and she pushed into my palm.

Too many layers of clothes between me and where I wanted to be. I slid my hand under her shirt, stroking her stomach, moving higher until I hit the bottom of her bra. Would she stop me? She didn't seem in a stopping mood.

I shifted the bra's fabric down and circled her nipple with my thumb. She scooted her hips forward and rolled them, giving my cock a preview of coming attractions. I groaned into her mouth and she did it again. If I hadn't been hard as a rock before, I definitely was now.

And then the lights went out.

Penelope pulled away and froze. I squinted at the total darkness. Had something happened to the power? I didn't hear a storm. Then I realized what it meant and banged my head against the foam-covered wall.

"The motion sensor," I said, in a normal voice. "It turns off the lights if there's no one in the room."

Penelope gave a rusty laugh. "You were right. They never even came inside."

"Maybe they did and left."

"Well, at least we know there's nobody out there. We, um, don't have to keep hiding."

Except I did. I was hiding behind a costume and a name I invented with my friends. I was hiding behind the anonymity of the internet, the distance between emails. I spent most of my time hiding these days, and more and more I realized I was getting really tired of it.

Mood ruined. With my free hand, I groped for the glasses I'd thrown on the shelf and slid them back on, then stood up.

"Do you want to work on the spell?" I asked.

"Maybe we should sleep," she said. "Start fresh in the morning."

I was glad she couldn't see my face, because it was hard enough making my voice sound normal.

"Okay," I said. "Be careful with the—"

A thunk was followed by a naughty word I wouldn't have expected her to use.

"—shelf."

I opened the door and the lights came on, showing a scowling Penelope rubbing the back of her head.

Please stay, I wanted to say. We don't have to do anything but talk. Don't go yet. Not yet.

What came out of my mouth was, "Are you okay? Let me get you some ice for that . . ."

"It's fine," Penelope said, wincing. "I have a hard head."

I reached out to her. "Come here."

She took a step closer, and I rubbed the back of her head gently. "Sana sana, culito de rana," I said. "Si no sana hoy, sana mañana."

A grin cracked Penelope's face. "Seriously? Are you my abuela?"

"I really hope not. I don't kiss my abuela like that."

"Sucio." She smacked my arm, and I pretended it hurt more than it did.

Another terrible Sam line ran through my mind as she walked out: I hated to see her go, but I loved to watch her leave.

I'd have loved it even more if she'd come back.

CHAPTER 13

Gil

Penelope hauled me up to the pool deck for a breakfast-and-planning meeting; no smooches, all business. The Miami sun roasted us even in the shade of the beach umbrellas sticking out of the poolside tables, cooling charms dangling from their spokes, but we had more quiet and privacy than in the restaurant. A few blocks away, Biscayne Boulevard traffic honked and vroomed and screeched; in front of us, the sunlight sparkled on the water so brightly it hurt to look at. I didn't get to spend much time in this area—Sam and Ed and I lived in a part of South Miami rich people were trying super hard to gentrify—so it was nice to have a little of that stereotypical Miami waterfront experience.

When we finally left for the warehouse, we had a checklist and schedule with times listed next to each step in the recipe. She'd even included lunch breaks.

I loved it. I couldn't tell her I loved it, because Leandro wasn't like that, but I wanted to.

Maybe I would tell her I was Gil, sooner instead of later. Maybe my secrets would be safe with her. But dropping that reveal now felt like a huge mistake. If we didn't make it to the next round . . .

We had to make it. She needed the money and the prestige,

and I needed the money for Grandpa Fred's charity. We had to stay focused and sharp, and I was already using up necessary brain space thinking sexy thoughts. Adding my "secret identity" to the mix would be one more catalyst that could blow things up in our faces.

A messier-than-usual Isaac Knight awaited us on the soundstage after we finished with hair and makeup and mic placement. Someone had brought him a box to stand on instead of using Dylan and Zeke's station again. Tori stood next to him like his faux-hawk-wearing shadow.

"Our techs and supply reps have gone through the storeroom," Isaac told us. "You'll be happy to know they didn't find any other 'irregularities' back there." He made air quotes with his fingers. "We still don't know what happened with the two bottles of whatever the fuck—"

"Tarragon and sage," Tori said.

"—but it seems to be a one-off. So don't start thinking your fuckups aren't your fault." Isaac pointed at the clock, which gave us a little under ten hours remaining. "Now we have to hustle so we don't fall behind, which means a long day. Judging comes after, as usual, so if you can do basic math, we're looking at fourteen hours minimum. Suck it up, buttercups. Especially if you're non-union." He got down from his box and stomped off, alternately muttering under his breath and yelling at the top of his lungs.

We went back to our stations, the camera people readied their rigs, and the countdown started counting.

Penelope and I split our duties today. She handled the cauldron, and I was in charge of circle work. Instead of glass, our centerpiece core was made of interwoven vines and stems from the flowers we'd be magically growing with the spell. It wasn't much to look at, just a green wreath about sixteen inches in diameter; once activated, it would get much bigger.

To make that happen, though, I had to layer in a separate enchantment for every type of flower we'd be using. It was pure grunt work, the kind I'd done in labs back in college, but not as much since I'd started the Leandro videos. This competition was forcing me to pull shit out of the depths of my brain that I hadn't thought about in years.

This was what I'd hoped for when I got my PhD, this kind of boundary-pushing, theory-testing spellwork. Regardless of how my parents thought the job market worked, I hadn't expected a cushy tenure-track position, on a team with a huge research budget from multiple major grants, to happen right after I graduated. Still, I'd imagined better than adjuncting, for practically minimum wage if you counted grading time, and then Leandro Presto got big . . .

Four hours passed in a blink. I got up to stretch my aching calves and noticed the judges had arrived. Their call time was later than ours, no doubt. They wandered around, examining things, asking questions. They'd reach us soon enough.

Penelope stretched, too, and gave a little groan as she rubbed the small of her back and rolled her head around. Today she was wearing a black apron with yellow straps, the outline of a pointy hat with "Kiss the Witch" in yellow cursive on the front. I wanted to do just that, but not in front of the cameras, obviously. Had she picked this apron specifically to tease me? Not likely. That's not how she thought.

I walked over and put a hand on Penelope's neck, squeezing gently. "Massage, m'lady?"

Penelope's shoulders went up, but she forced them back down. "I'm getting a cramp, so yes, please. Not too long; we have a schedule."

I'd given Sam and Ed enough rubs to have a decent idea how to manage. I started at the top of her neck, then worked my way down and sideways to her shoulders, then reversed and went back up. By the third repetition, she was practically jelly, and her butt had gotten a little too close to my crotch for decency.

"Good?" I asked.

"Yeah," Penelope said, a little breathy.

"Sweet. Back to work, then." Except I needed a minute to get the tiny brain in my pants under control. Hopefully the cameras wouldn't see anything they shouldn't.

Tori did, though. She gave me a thumbs-up. Ugh.

The judges eventually made it to our station. Hugh dressed like his wardrobe was sponsored by one of the high-end stores in the Design District; Fabienne wore a corporate-chic purple dress and her usual unreadable smile; and Doris was going full abuelita, with pearls and a mint-green sweater covered in pink flowers.

"Tell us about your spell," Fabienne asked, her dark eyes digging into us like awls.

Penelope explained while I looked excited and derpy. It wasn't hard, for a change. The more we worked together, the happier I got.

"Are you certain the naudhiz rune is suited for this particular circle?" Hugh asked.

"In this case," Penelope replied, "we've combined it with kenaz, which should guide the transformation—"

The table we'd been assembling our centerpiece on jolted under my hands. One of the glass jars that held some of our catalyzing solution tipped sideways. Before I could grab it, it fell over and shattered, spilling its contents across the table.

"Oh dear!" Doris said.

Shit, shit. I rushed to grab a towel to clean up the mess. Penelope picked up the centerpiece before the liquid could reach it and disrupt the enchantments I'd spent hours laying.

Tori ran over, looking grim. "What now?"

"An accident," Penelope said, glaring at me.

At me? Hold up. "I didn't—"

"How does this impact your spell?" Tori asked us, her face suggesting it had better not be a problem.

Penelope aimed her fake smile at Tori. "We'll need a minute to figure it out." She moved the wreath to the other end of our station, as far from me as she could get.

Meanwhile, Felicia held Doris by her elbow. "Are you okay?" she asked, in the most syrupy voice I'd heard from her since we met.

"Yes, I'm fine, thank you." Doris patted Felicia's arm.

What the fuck?

Tori hustled the judges away before I could ask Doris what had happened. Had she fallen against the table? Had Felicia pushed her?

Would it matter? Not likely, after Isaac's speech.

Time for damage control. I checked the wall clock. A little under six hours to go. Penelope had started putting the catalyst together yesterday. No way would she have time to brew it up again. Unless . . .

When I finally finished cleaning the mess up, Penelope had retreated to an empty corner of the table with her notebook and was furiously scribbling something.

"We have to shortcut the process," I said. "There's a way that should work, but . . ."

"But?"

"We have to watch it super carefully or it could cause a blowback."

She stopped writing. "You want to use Papin's thaumaturgical pression process. To pressure-cook it."

Of course she'd know. "Yeah. That."

Penelope choked the pencil, her skin losing color. "Have you . . . ever done it?"

"In college, when I had to pull a few all-nighters." The first time, I'd been in a cold sweat, worrying that I'd get caught by a TA and yelled at, or worse, wreck the lab. "Have you?"

"Once." The way she whispered it made me wary.

"I can take lead if—"

"No," she said. "No way. I swore I'd never do it again."

She snapped the pencil in half and stared down at her hand in horror.

"Okay," I said quietly. "I hear you. I'm just not sure how we can re-create that potion without it."

"We can . . . do something else." Penelope laid the broken pencil pieces on the table. "It won't be as elaborate as we'd planned, but . . ."

"It's a risk." I smoothed down my mustache nervously. "We could lose the round like Quentin and Tanner did."

"Well, maybe if you hadn't spilled the potion, we wouldn't have this problem."

Wow. Even after our conversation last night, she still jumped to the worst possible conclusion. That felt fucking great.

I forced a derpy smile as I leaned closer. "We can talk about what really happened later, but for now, we have to keep pretending we like each other and fix this. If you don't want to pressure-cook the spell, I respect that. What's the backup plan?"

"Gassman's one-pot fusion," she said. "It bypasses the separation and purification steps."

"That can't hold both transformations, though."

"So we brew two potions simultaneously, one per transformation."

It could work. Maybe.

"Okay," I said. "What do we need?"

Penelope took a deep breath, grabbed another pencil, and started writing.

We'd been serious and focused before, but we doubled up now. I had planned a couple of jokes and tricks for some of the tiny gaps in the schedule; fuck that, there wasn't time.

I did have to make a bathroom trip to deal with my mustache. The adhesive was supposed to last all day, but it seemed like the edges might have been loosening. Maybe it was just paranoia; maybe I was sweating more than usual. Regardless, I locked the door, cleaned up the mustache sides with an astringent, and added more adhesive, just to be safe.

When I got back, Penelope had rigged everything and was chanting over one of the cauldrons as she dropped in reagents. I started on the other cauldron, refusing to check the time. This would take as long as it took.

Penelope finished her potion first. A gentle puff of magic steamed from it, scented with cinnamon and flowers. It was hard to see the color against the metal background; Penelope ladled a tiny bit into a borosilicate glass container to check it.

Green! Lush, vibrant green. It had worked. Or at least, this was as close to confirmation as we would get until the final casting.

Mine followed about twenty minutes later. Closer to yellow-green because of how we'd split the enchantments, and it smelled more like fresh-cut grass, but it seemed right.

Three hours, twenty-two minutes left.

Now we had to put everything together. The base needed to be soaked in the potions sequentially, and a binding spell cast to combine the separate elements. Then we had to repeat the process with the catalysts Penelope had woven from the same materials as the base.

When Syd yelled, "Ten minutes remaining!" we were in the middle of the last sealing spell. Unlike the first round, we'd be cutting this extremely close.

At the "One minute left!" mark, I considered another run up and down the aisle, waving my arms like a hysterical puppet. I was too tired. And I had a feeling if I asked Penelope about our secret handshake, she'd bite my head off, so I leaned against the table and counted down from sixty. I was going too fast, apparently, because I finished before Syd called time.

They hustled us to our separate greenrooms instead of going straight to judging. We'd been here for a little over eleven hours. None of us felt like socializing; we sat separately and ate like machines. I wondered if Penelope was doing the same.

A half hour later, we were back on the soundstage. Syd and the judges looked disturbingly fresh; maybe their trailers had rejuvenation spells. Hair and makeup did touch-ups, and Liam checked our mics. Isaac yelled at everyone, Tori quietly translating for him. Penelope and I stood at our station, not speaking to each other.

We got our assigned order numbers, and this time we were first. If we did a bad job, then everything else would look great by comparison.

"Our contestants have been through a grueling two days of casting," Syd said. "Now they're ready to present their spectacular party decorations or centerpieces, each of which must go through at least two transformations."

Penelope touched the front pocket of her apron, then put her hand back down. A nervous gesture? Worried that our rushed potions wouldn't work, probably. Me too.

"First to present tonight will be our yellow team, Penelope and Leandro!"

Syd's voice snapped me back to reality. Showtime.

Our spell was small enough that Penelope could carry it alone to the display table. Moment of truth. We stepped back and faced our fates, her on one side, me on the other.

"Tell us about your spell," Fabienne said.

Penelope fake smiled as she gestured at our wreath. "We call it 'Miami Metamorphosis.' Our visit to Tropical Oasis Botanic Gardens, and Everly Bale's sculptures, inspired us to make a centerpiece that transforms from what you see here to a little piece of a tropical paradise."

"That sounds lovely," Doris said. "Why don't you show us how it works?"

Penelope took one of the catalysts from the side of the table. "We wanted to make the spell repeatable, so we put together these propagation balls to trigger the initial transformation. No command word—it just has to be placed inside the circle." She dropped the ball into the wreath and stepped away.

About five seconds later, glowing green tendrils sprouted from the catalyst and wound their way into the circle of woven vines and stems and stalks. They grew and twined together in a bulb shape, similar to the sculpture in the butterfly house, but more organic, all shades of green and brown that luminesced faintly and sent off glittery sparks. Roots stretched down as well, hanging over the edge of the table like a curtain. As the spell progressed, it grew larger until it hit its peak, about five feet tall and four feet in diameter at its widest point.

"Now, the first transformation," Penelope said.

I held my breath. If we'd messed up our potions, nothing would happen.

The bulb glowed with a brighter inner light and unfurled, uncoiling in a series of offshoots that lengthened and spread up and out. The tendrils turned into a leafy canopy, like a poinciana tree made from overlapping plants, now about ten feet in diameter at the top and three at the trunk. It smelled the way it looked, all green garden goodness. Success!

"Second transformation," Penelope said.

This was where it might break down again. I stared at the lush green vines and crossed my fingers.

Buds formed on the vines, slowly getting bigger. Then they started to open, not all at once, but in waves and clusters, each carrying their signature scent. Pale blue plumbago, creamy white jasmine, orange and yellow marigold, pink and white plumeria, red and orange hibiscus . . . Some didn't trigger, but it was still impressive. Hopefully impressive enough for the judges, especially if the reset worked.

They didn't look impressed. Fabienne smiled her secret smile, Doris her kindly one, and Hugh's nostrils flared like he was swallowing a yawn.

"Does this complete your spell?" Syd asked.

"No," Penelope said. This seemed to surprise the judges, especially Hugh, who woke up a little.

"You can examine it now," I said. "Before the last part."

They climbed down from their observation tower and circled

the centerpiece. Doris touched a cluster of jasmine flowers, snapping one off at the stem. It persisted long enough for her to sniff it, then dissolved in a puff of sparkles.

"What happens next?" Hugh asked.

Penelope circled the vine-tree until she found the reset trigger: a light green chrysalis jutting out from a section of the trunk. "If you remove that," she said, pointing at it, "the spell will go back to its initial state, and it can be restarted using another propagation ball."

Fabienne got to it first and pulled it off. We waited. And waited.

Shit. It wasn't going to do the thing. Penelope's smile cracked as she realized it, too.

"I take it this portion isn't functional?" Hugh asked, his green eyes sharp.

"I guess not," I said, making myself sound cheerful. "But hey, two transformations, as ordered!"

With a sigh, Penelope got a spray bottle of salt water as the judges returned to their places. She spritzed the tree, starting near the base, and the whole thing dissolved into a messy fog that sank to the floor, leaving the original wreath and a moist sheen that was almost but not quite a puddle. It gave off a whiff of decay.

"Thank you, casters," Syd said. "Judges, your thoughts?"

Fabienne said, "It's a solid premise and execution. Portable greenery isn't an unprecedented enchantment, but this did make for quite a pretty centerpiece. If the recursion portion had worked, that would have put it a step above typical single-use models."

Time for Doris. "I thought it was absolutely charming. The growth was a joy to watch, and the flowers looked and smelled exactly as they should. The dispersal of removed elements was also lovely."

I gave Hugh my biggest, most Leandro smile. He raised an eyebrow at me as if sensing a challenge.

"As noted, however, this isn't a particularly novel concept," Hugh said. "What would have elevated it above the mundane didn't function. Still, you met the terms of the brief, so it wasn't a total waste."

"Thank you, judges," Penelope and I said in unison. How we both managed to sound chill, I have no idea. Staying in character, I guess.

Dylan and Zeke made another masterpiece: a model of a fancy car, almost as big as me, that transformed into a dinosaur and then into a giant humanoid robot. It looked incredibly realistic, and every part of it was apparently edible, airbrushed chocolate and sugar-spun glass and cake and frosting. If Dylan didn't get hired by some fancy bakery after all this, maybe even by Zeke himself, there was no justice in the world.

Felicia and Charlotte put together a pumpkin that transformed into a carriage, including mice that turned into horses. In a swirl of magic, the whole thing morphed into Cinderella herself, fancy dress and glass slippers and all, dancing with her prince. Then an unseen clock chimed midnight, and they turned back into the pumpkin again, mice sticking out of the top. They'd nailed the recursion, timed instead of conditional.

As my abuelo used to say, "Calabaza, calabaza, cada uno pa su casa"—basically, pumpkin, pumpkin, everybody go home. Except the pumpkin wasn't ours, and we would be the ones going home. I could practically feel Penelope melting next to me.

Me? I imagined having to tell Grandpa Fred that I'd failed him, and the charity. He'd be so damn nice about it. *You win some, you lose some*, he would say. *Everything comes to an end sometime, Bert. We had a good run.*

I barely paid attention to Amy and Jaya, shamefully. I was too busy wallowing. That's why the fire took me by surprise.

A ball of flame burst from the podium where the spells were presented, huge and bright, rippling orange around a blinding yellow core. Sparks shot in various directions, like a firework, hitting the edges of the containment circle etched into the floor.

I shielded Penelope with my body. People screamed; Amy and Jaya backed away; all the camerapeople moved fast, trying to maintain their shots without getting burned. Tori shouted, "Get the extinguisher!" while Dylan tossed a bowl with salt and water at the fire. It sizzled and shrank, smoking like a chimney, but didn't go out. Zeke joined him, taking turns.

Little Manny ran up with a giant cart-mounted canister. He yanked the nozzle and hose off, aimed, and let it rip. White foam sprayed out, coating the fireball until it looked more like the bottom of a snowman. It hovered in the air for a few more heartbeats, then dropped to the podium with a loud thump and rolled to the floor.

The room went dead silent. From outside, Isaac yelled, "What the fuck was that?" loud enough to be heard down the street. Tori whipped out a phone and started typing furiously, then snapped at Rachel to follow her and left.

Penelope shivered, her face pressed against my chest. Her breath came fast, too fast. She was going to pass out if she didn't calm down.

"Hey, shh," I said, stroking her hair. "It's okay. Everyone is okay. Breathe." I kept saying things quietly, whatever popped into my head, in English and Spanish and even random Italian I'd learned in college.

I didn't know if she could hear me, but she turned her face away from the podium and started muttering between deep breaths. The shaking stopped.

I didn't let go of her, though. I held on to Penelope while Rachel led Amy and Jaya out of the soundstage, and one of the PAs poured more salt water all over the charred lump that used to be a spell.

An ugly part of me thought, I guess our pumpkin isn't going home after all.

CHAPTER 14

Penelope

Seeing Leandro spill our potion had hit me like a punch to the gut. Having him suggest using the pressure cooker had stressed me out immensely because of what had happened the first and last time I'd done it.

And then . . . this.

The fire. The screaming—some real, some in my head, in memories that still gave me nightmares. It was a hundred times worse than Leandro's trick in the first round. I'd gone so deep into a panic attack that I thought my heart would explode. I couldn't think, couldn't breathe.

Leandro finally got through to me enough that I could remember the exercises my therapist taught me, back when I had health insurance in college. First, box breathing. Then, listing things I could see, feel, hear, smell, and taste.

At first, it was all Leandro. His ridiculous shirt, with shapes like construction paper cutouts, in black and red and yellow and pale blue. Silky material against my cheek, his arms holding me tightly, like he was afraid I might fall if he let go. He whispered to me that it would be okay, everyone was okay, other stuff I couldn't understand in another language. Italian? I could smell him, apples and lavender and sweat. Adrenaline made my mouth taste sour and sharp, like licking a battery.

The panic drained slowly as a clogged sink. Now I heard Isaac yelling, and people moving around, here on the soundstage and outside. Even though the ceiling in the warehouse was super high, the smell of smoke still lingered. Someone, maybe more than one person, had done a brine and confine—salt water to neutralize the spell, plus the containment circle to hold any other magical blowback. They'd be able to tell whether it was truly inert soon, but meanwhile, this kept everyone safe.

Tori came back through the hallway entrance and clapped; even though I was looking right at her, the sound still made me jump. Leandro hugged me harder.

"We'll film the elimination as soon as the area is secure," Tori said. "Give me shots that don't show the mess on the floor. Upper bodies, faces, whatever."

Cameras were shifted into new places, with Nate moving to the back of the room.

"Mic checks," Tori said. "When I point at you, say 'check, one, two, three,' got it?"

We all got it, and did as we were told. I made myself step away from Leandro, who didn't seem happy to let me go.

Are you okay? he mouthed at me.

I nodded. Total lie.

The judges, who had left to discuss point allocations, came back in with Syd and took up their positions. They very carefully did not look at the mess of Amy and Jaya's spell.

Now that my brain was climbing out of its screaming panic pit, it started yeeting thoughts at me. The biggest one was a single word, all caps, in huge font: SABOTAGE.

This was the second spell that had gone catastrophically wrong. On a typical season of *Cast Judgment*, there might be problems here and there. Contestants were expected to be good at casting after so many rounds of auditions, but nobody was perfect, and magic played by its own rules. Random factors could throw off a spell in unexpected ways.

The celebrities, though? They were all professionals with their own businesses and shows and stuff. They might make mistakes, too, but not like this.

Would the producers have to stop the show and start over? They couldn't just play this off like it was nothing, could they? Even after Isaac's speech this morning, I couldn't believe that. They had to know this was messed up. There were laws about tampering with competitions.

We moved to our places and Syd gave their speech about people winning and people going home. Just like the last round, we all knew what was coming as far as losers went. Only the winner might be a surprise.

Felicia and Charlotte got it this time. I was so sure it would be Dylan and Zeke again, but apparently the judges were more impressed by the degree of transformation in the Cinderella spell. Harder to go from gourd to carriage to moving people and back than it was to shift chocolate and cake to differently shaped chocolate and cake, no matter how good it looked and tasted.

Leandro and I were separated again after a short joint confessional. I didn't know whether they rushed us because our day had already gone too long, or they didn't want us spilling any tea about what had happened. Por qué no los dos? Either way, I barely remembered what I said. Something about how we'd keep learning and upping our game.

On the drive back to the hotel, I tried to organize what I was going to say to Leandro about his potion-spilling shenanigans. Brain fog from the panic attack and not having slept enough made it hard to do more than have a pretend fight with him inside my head—and even that was mostly just me asking him, "How could you?" while he smiled his himbo mustache smile.

It didn't make sense. Yesterday, and in the first round, he'd done silly stuff that looked like his usual *Mage You Look* oopsies, but none of it had actually affected our spells. We'd talked about how important it was for both of us to win. We'd made a plan! A schedule! Why would he intentionally wreck things today?

He wouldn't. Not unless he was a lying liar who lies and I was totally wrong to trust him. Did I believe that? No. So something else must have happened. Which meant I'd been an asshole to him again.

Maybe I should accept that the problem was me. Leandro shifted from flake to focused like he was changing a jacket, but it was my job to compensate. And I didn't even have to! He was doing the work, and I was refusing to meet him halfway when he made reasonable suggestions for how to solve problems. He didn't know why I couldn't use that pressure-cooking method. It probably would have saved our spell, and instead, we'd once again survived because someone else's magic combusted. Literally.

I had to apologize ASAP.

We all climbed out of the van at the hotel, said good night, and separated to our rooms a mimir. I thought about tracking Leandro down, but I was starting to get a forehead ache from working magic for too long on little sleep. Thankfully tomorrow was our rest day. No filming, no field trips, no promo stuff.

That meant I should have plenty of time to make things right with Leandro.

Part of me wanted to avoid him, because apologizing was hard, and so was explaining why I'd freaked out. Another part of me wanted to get it over with, rip off the bandage so we could get back to work—assuming he'd even forgive me, which, this was the second time I was shitty to him, so maybe not.

The rest of me wanted to climb him like a tree, even with his awful mustache. I had dry humped the shit out of him on the floor of that casting booth, and if the lights hadn't gone out, my shirt probably would have come off.

What was I thinking?

I wasn't morally opposed to one-night stands or booty calls or friends with benefits. I'd had random make-outs with near-strangers at college parties twice, dates that had led to sweaty fun times, a couple of boyfriends who hadn't lasted more than the few months it took to get past the new-relationship energy. After I started working six days a week, I was too drained to even think about opening a dating app. If I didn't want to be alone, I'd hang out with friends. If I wanted an orgasm, a vibrator was more likely to get the job done.

Leandro made me want things. He made me want him, specifically. Not that he was deliberately trying to get in my pants—well, maybe he was, but he wasn't playing me or manipulating me. He wasn't leading me on. He'd told me he doesn't date and why, and his reasons made sense.

It must be the stress, and the fact that we were stuck together all day, every day. That was supposed to make people horny, right?

As tired as I was, I lay awake with all these thoughts running around in my head like my aunt's hyper dogs. Finally I managed to make myself relax by remembering I'd be able to talk to my sister tomorrow. Maybe she'd have some wisdom for me.

Sleeping in was amazing! Is a thing I wished I could say.

The hotel room had blackout curtains, so without an alarm yelling at me to get up, I figured I would chill in Club Cama until my body was fully rested. Instead, stress dreams led to cold-sweat awakeness where I was absolutely, positively sure I'd be late for work. Once I remembered I was unemployed and this was my day off, I was too wired to go back to sleep.

I couldn't find Rachel, keeper of the cell phones, so I stole a million tiny waffles from the breakfast bar and stress-ate them with my hands like chips until she made an appearance.

"Remember, you can't talk about the show," Rachel said as she handed me my phone from the magically warded box. "You can check your email and voicemails, talk to your emergency contact, that kind of thing. Absolutely no posting on socials. If you have any questions, let me know."

I had a lot of questions, but none she could answer. I ran back to my room and threw myself on the bed, texting Emelia.

ME: got my phone back for the day

ME: can I call you

ME: say yes or I'll have to day drink

EME: free mimosas what what

> **ME:** I wish
>
> **ME:** just coffee and juice

> **EME:** boo
>
> **EME:** let me go to my car
>
> **EME:** for PRIVACY

I zoned out until my cell started playing Emelia's ringtone. "Eme, ahh! Don't ask me about the show because I can't talk about it."

"What if I just ask yes-or-no questions?"

"No way! I don't want to get jumped by lawyer ninjas."

Emelia snorted. "Lawyer ninjas? Mira que tu hablas mierda. FYI, remember how you forwarded all your calls to me?"

"Yeah?"

"You have gotten so many spam calls! Is that normal? Why do they think you have a car warranty that's going to expire?"

"I don't know! Oh my god, and the ones that are like, 'the IRS is coming for your sooooul'?"

"As if you have any money to give them. Especially now."

Speaking of which . . . "Did Cari find the store keys and take them back?"

Emelia made the humming noise that meant she was stalling. "She found them, but don't get mad."

Oh no. "What happened?"

"Your old-lady neighbor saw her using her lock-gun thing on the door to open it? And she threw like five chancletas at Cari and threatened her with a broom."

Great. "Did my landlady call or text or anything?"

"Nope. But Cari says you owe her for chancla-related emotional distress."

"Whatever she wants," I said, rubbing my face. "What did Ofelia say when she dropped the keys off?"

"Something like, 'She couldn't bring them herself?' And then Cari said, 'What part of "she's in another state" didn't you understand, vieja podrida?' And then Ofelia threatened to call the police, so she vamoosed."

I'd probably never get my last paycheck. Awesome.

"I can hear you catastrophizing. Para. If you can't talk about the show, what can you tell me about?"

I jumped out of bed and started pacing, because I sort of had to talk about the show. But I had to be careful about it.

"I can't tell you who my partner is," I said. "But . . . ah! So like . . . the thing is . . . How do I say this . . ."

"Just say it. I wish I could hit you like a stuck vending machine."

I took a deep breath, then spoke quickly. "My partner is really sweet and hot and I'm sort of hooking up with him?"

Emelia groaned loudly and with maximum vocal fry. I held the phone away from my ear until she stopped.

"Who is he?" she asked. "No, you can't tell me. What happened? Make-outs, obviously. Is it serious? It can't be serious; it's only been a few days."

"Can I talk, or are you just going to answer your own questions?"

"Go. Talk. Proceed."

"Thank you, Your Majesty."

I proceeded, leaving out any details that might let her figure out who Leandro was. I didn't think she watched his videos, but I might have mentioned him at some point, or forwarded something Rosy sent me. I said nothing about his mustache, or his glasses, or his tacky shirts, and everything about how he was cute, and funny, and sweet, except when he was frustrating. I also mentioned the fake flirting, since it seemed both relevant and highly telenovela.

"What about your pen pal crush?" Emelia asked.

"Gil." Big sigh. I dropped into the desk chair and banged my head on the table. "If you had asked me that"—I counted off on my fingers—"five days ago, I would have said he was the only guy I was interested in. But now?"

"Now what?"

"I keep thinking, I've never met him. We haven't talked on the phone. He doesn't even know my name! All we ever did was email each other. Why did that turn me into such a simp?"

"Weren't they pretty personal emails? Flirty, even?"

"Yeah, but, like, he never asked me out. I didn't ask him, either. Doesn't that mean something?"

Emelia made an exaggerated fake-clucking noise.

"I'm not a chicken!" I spun the hotel pen on the desk as I talked. "Okay, maybe we're both chicken. But maybe I built up a thing that wasn't there. Maybe we didn't know each other well enough to catch actual feelings. Maybe I was crushing on an imaginary version of a real guy, which isn't cool."

"That's surprisingly mature, coming from you."

"Thanks." I didn't tell her my mature insight came from Leandro talking about having that exact problem with his fans.

"However!" I could imagine her holding up her finger like she did when she wanted to make a point without being interrupted. "If you're not sure where you stand, the obvious thing to do is ask, instead of sitting around like a sad cartoon donkey while a rain cloud dumps on you."

"You sound like Rosy."

"Sometimes your friend knows what's up. So?"

"So, I emailed him right before they took my phone."

"And?"

"And I got an auto-reply that he wasn't checking emails because he was going out of town."

"What about now?"

"I haven't looked yet."

Emelia clucked again.

"I called you first!"

"Comemierda. Put me on speaker and look!"

I did. A bunch of emails popped up. Random stuff from stores, Jinxd updates, an email from my landlord . . . nothing from Gil. I guess he was serious about not checking while he was out of town? Unless he was trying to find a way to let me down gently and hadn't—

Wait, my landlord?

My brain flushed Gil while I opened that email and skimmed it, then read it again, more slowly, because I couldn't believe what it said.

"Did he email you?" Emelia asked.

"No," I said, my throat tight, "but apparently the rent on my tiny illegal efficiency is going up. By a lot. Or I have to move out."

"Fffff. And you don't have a job."

"I don't have a job."

"So you're fucked."

"I'm extremely fucked."

We sat there in silence.

"Well," Emelia said, "if you're already fucked, you might as well do some fucking, right?"

"Eme! Coño! This is not funny."

"I know, I know, I'm sorry."

I couldn't be mad. That's how she was. I catastrophized, Eme joked. Maybe that's part of why I liked Leandro in spite of myself: he reminded me of her.

"My lease is up in two months," I said. "That might be enough time . . ."

"To get a new job?"

I threw the hotel pen against the wall. It bounced off and landed on the desk, rolling right back to me.

"It doesn't matter," I said. "It's basic math. I can't make enough money to afford this on my own unless I win the competition, or get hired somewhere that pays way more than Espinosa's."

"Take it one step at a time," Emelia said. "Either you're going to win, or you're not. I'm going to assume because you said 'unless I win' that you haven't lost yet."

Oops. I slipped. Well, come at me, lawyer ninjas.

"If you win, problem solved," Emelia continued. "If you lose, you still have at least a month to make a backup plan, right?"

"Yeah, I have to give thirty days' notice."

"So focus on winning. Where you live is a problem for Future Penelope."

She was right. There was that sisterly wisdom I'd called her for.

"Now, as for your boy toys . . ."

Ah! "They're not boys, or toys."

"Do you need permission to fuck?"

"Do I what?!"

"You know, like Cari always says. Do you need permission to do the thing you already want to do?"

Did I? I usually thought a thing to death and then didn't do it until it was too late. The only reason I was on *Cast Judgment* was because Rosy had pushed me into applying. I needed . . . Some way to sort out my feelings, I guess.

"I get it," Emelia said. "You just met this guy. You were told to pretend to like each other, and it stopped being pretend. You're confused. You want a clear solution. I'm not going to tell you what to do, one way or the other. But you overthink everything. Dichotomize."

"Dichotomize" was Emelia code for "reduce to two options." She did it for basically every decision in her life.

"You have a choice between two guys," she continued. "What is your gut telling you? Be honest with yourself."

Be honest? How? One of the things I tended to overthink was my feelings.

"I've known Gil longer," I said. "We like a lot of the same things, and he's smart and nice."

"And new guy?"

"New guy feels like Gil in some ways, different in others. It's like I've known him forever. Like we fit. And then he'll do something that makes me want to shake him, and I'll wonder if I've got it all wrong."

"Are you only into him because he's hot and convenient?"

"No!" I yelped. "Of course not. I have self-control. I don't throw myself at guys just because they're . . ." Oh, shit.

"There you go. Honest feelings. So, dichotomize again. Do you want to have a thing with this guy, or not?"

Did I? What was the worst that could happen? Someone could catch us and think I'm a groupie sleeping my way to fame. I'd already committed to pretend flirting, so what was the difference? I could feel like a loser because he'd played me to get laid, except I didn't really think Leandro was playing me.

That didn't mean I could assume he wanted a relationship. Just like I shouldn't have assumed anything with Gil.

Maybe the real question was: Would I really miss out on a guy who was clearly into me, right now, for a chance with a guy who had never made a move?

"I'm going to talk to him," I said.

"Good," Emelia said. "Now go win so you don't have to sleep in my bathtub."

We said our goodbyes, but I was already gone, plotting my next move.

Step one: find Leandro. Step two: grovel and hope he'd forgive me.

CHAPTER 15

Gil

Knowing I would have trouble sleeping, I had a couple of edibles and one of my emergency meds. By the time I woke up, the clock on the nightstand said it was after eleven. My eyes felt a little gritty, my head a little foggy, but at least I'd gotten more rest than in the past week or so. I'd also successfully avoided all the unhappy thoughts that had started piling up now that I was conscious.

We'd almost lost again. Being saved from elimination by two spell wrecks in a row meant that, unless we got lucky at someone else's expense or we upped our game hugely, we wouldn't make it to the final round.

We absolutely couldn't count on Dylan and Zeke or Felicia and Charlotte fucking up. It was true that magic could be fickle because of its intrinsic reliance on various individual casting conditions, despite some consistently repeatable methods. Anyone could spark a pre-made charm or potion, anyone could learn to craft their own spells based on known theories and practices, but anyone could also make unforeseeable mistakes. Especially with spells created from scratch.

Still, I had my suspicions. They were about my height, super snobby, and could have modeled for a fashion magazine. If I was right, she'd bumped Doris into the table, and that had knocked over Penelope's potion.

It still hurt that Penelope had assumed it was my fault. I'd thought we were vibing—not in the gross Isaac way, but in the good, on-the-same-wavelength way. Maybe that was just wishful thinking. Maybe I wanted to believe she was catching feelings for me, when it was pure lust.

Breakfast was over, so I ordered room service. It was good to be a Spellebrity. I had the hotel attendant leave the food outside, then covered my mustache-free face with my shirt, and yoinked the tray inside. While I chugged coffee and scarfed a thousand mini-waffles and an entire pig's worth of ham, I planned my day.

Step one: check texts, voicemails and emails, including the stuff that had auto-filtered into the "not important" folders. Mostly that was ads, but also anything from an email I hadn't added to my white list.

Step two: text Sam and/or Ed to see how things were going with *Mage You Look* stuff. I doubted anything was on fire, and if it was, they'd probably handled it. There might be good news, though. I sure needed some.

Step three: call Grandpa Fred to see how he was doing and beg him for advice.

Maybe that would be step two.

Grandpa Fred was pretty much the model for my life and career. He'd always talked to me like I was a grown-up, instead of like my ideas and goals needed to be deflated and trashed like old birthday balloons—even when my brilliant plan was to become a dinosaur robot when I grew up. He helped me think through things instead of shutting me down and ordering me to do what I was told. And he never put conditions on his time and attention the way my parents did.

Ugh, my parents. I should call them, too. Step four? I had talked to them before filming started, figuring that would give me a solid week before one or both wondered what I was up to. My dad had his own life, but freaking out was basically my mom's hobby, and she'd use any excuse to indulge.

Step five: talk to Penelope. Hopefully Grandpa Fred would help me figure out what to say to her.

I felt like I'd be breaking character no matter what. Leandro Presto would have no problem accidentally spilling a potion. He would laugh it off and say it had all worked out. After the other night, he might even try to kiss Penelope until she forgot what she was mad about.

But then what? She'd be kissing a character, not a real person. Leandro, not me. And the more that idea dug its claws into my brain, the worse I felt for leading her on. Lying to her.

Sometimes I wished I'd never started being Leandro Presto. The good parts were worth it, but the bad parts . . . The bad parts were tough. As an adjunct professor, I had the same low pay and lack of benefits, the same stress of wondering whether I'd have a job next semester. But at least I could date anyone except my students.

Well, I didn't have students anymore since I'd quit for the show, so no worries there.

Enough. Voicemails and texts, oldest first. Memes from Sam, motivational quotes from Ed. Spam, more spam, the alumni association begging for money I didn't have. Long message from my mom about how if she had an emergency I wouldn't know because I never answer my phone.

Emails next. Sam and Ed were on top of Leandro Presto business, nothing to worry about. My regular email was, as expected, mostly spam and ads. A note from my agent about the direct deposit for my show income—hell yeah. Bills set to autopay. A couple of questions for *Doctor Witch* that I could answer later.

Then I found one from Penelope Delmar. Subject line: Hi this is me from Espinosa's Spell Supplies!

I dropped my phone like it was on fire. It bounced off the bed and hit the floor with a thud, face down. Panic spiked in my veins. Did I break it? As long as I didn't look, it might be okay, or it might not.

Don't be a chicken, Gil. I climbed down and picked it up, turning it over. No cracks. Enchanted phone cases for the win.

I opened the email, my stomach tight.

Dear Gil,

I'm writing this in a hurry I won't be able to check email for a while but I wanted to tell you I got fired from Espinosa's. I don't know what my boss might do if she reads our emails but just in case she sends something weird or rude I wanted you to know it wasn't form me. And you won't be able to email me there anymore.

I realize also that I never actually introduced myself as not my boss because I usually don't do that for work emails. My name is Penelope and this is my personal email if you want to stay in touch about recipes and book suggestions and stuff. Maybe we could hang out sometime. Not for a few weeks because I'm going to be not available but if you don't mind waiting and it's cool with you. No worries if not.

Penelope

Now that I had met her, I could hear it all in her voice. And I could tell she'd written it fast, because it was way more rambling and grammatically questionable than usual. But she told me her name, finally. She asked if we could hang out. She did want to meet me! Our friendship—and maybe more—wasn't totally in my head.

Sam was right: I should have asked her out sooner. And now, here I was, and here she was. Except I was Leandro, not Gil. And she'd sent this before we'd started making out in casting booths.

What did that mean?

I called Grandpa Fred, hoping he was near his phone. Sometimes he left it to charge and wandered off. After a few rings, he picked up.

"Hey, hey, if it isn't little Bert!" Grandpa Fred's voice boomed into my ear. "Aren't you supposed to be incommunicado right now, buddy?"

"Hey, Grandpa, yeah," I said. "I'm still at the hotel. We can talk, I just can't tell you how the contest is going."

"Zip those lips. And before you figure out a slippery way to ask how I'm feeling, I'm fine. My blood sugar got away from me, and your mom made a scene, but the doc isn't worried."

That explained the angry message.

"That's good. I know how Mom can get."

"She started going through my cabinets and fridge and checking the sugar content on every package. I told her if she threw anything out, I'd go to her house and return the favor with every bottle of rosé I found."

I laughed. "You'd mess up your back trying to clear out her wine closet. She buys in bulk."

"For her book clubs and whatnot, I know. It was not an idle threat. But what are you calling me for, huh? You bored or do you have a story?"

In all the months I'd been writing to Penelope, I hadn't said anything to my grandpa. I scooted back against the headboard and crossed my legs in front of me, trying to figure out where to start.

"You know all the rules you gave me about showbiz?" I asked.

"Sure, yeah. I probably made some of them up on the spot, but not from nothing. Why?"

"I'm just wondering what to do about . . . you know, girlfriends?"

"Oh ho ho!" Grandpa Fred made a sound like he'd slapped his leg. "And here I thought you were hiding your love life from me, like it was a dark secret." He paused, but before I could say anything, he added, "So which rule exactly is the problem here? Refresh my memory."

"Rules one and two," I said. "Be someone else and stay in character." I banged my head against the headboard, then filled him in on everything, starting with my first emails to Penelope and ending with an extremely edited version of the last few days, plus the email.

"Ah, so. You had a good thing going with your pen pal, but you never made a move. And now she's interested in Leandro Presto instead of Gilberto Contreras, except they're both you."

"Yeah. Basically. I kept him separate like you said. Rule four: leave work at work. But I have to be on all the time here, so I can't do that. And now . . ."

"Aw, buddy." Grandpa Fred must have sat down in his leather recliner, because I heard it creak and squeak. "You were always such a little lawyer. Not like your dad, though. You wanted rules so you'd know what to do, how to behave so your parents wouldn't go for your neck."

"It didn't help," I said quietly.

"No, it didn't. Your dad wanted to be right, your mom wanted attention, and they fought like cats in a sack. Except you were stuck in the sack with them, trying not to get scratched. But I digress. The thing is, kiddo, you've taken this alter ego thing way too far. I know you enjoy being Leandro Presto, and that's good, but not if you're shutting out every other part of your life."

"But what about that stalker who—"

"The Stalker Incident, as you call it, is not your fault," Grandpa Fred said, his voice hard. "I told you when it happened, you didn't do anything to make her go after you like that. Some people take things the wrong way and run with them, right off a cliff."

Fine. I wasn't going to argue with him. "Nobody ever knew you were Alan Kazam," I said. "Except Mom and Grandma, and your agent, I guess. But you were already with Grandma when that started."

"More people knew than you think. Contract guys, mostly. Their jobs depended on them keeping their mouths shut, though. But apparently I instilled too much healthy fear in you of what might happen if folks knew who you were. Everything is on the internet now: names, addresses, all kinds of crap that used to be harder to find."

"Yeah. And if I tell the wrong person . . ."

"The trouble is, how do you figure out who to trust?"

"Exactly!" I knew he would understand.

"Buddy, what did Alan Kazam always tell kids before every experiment?"

"Safety first?"

"No, dingbat, the other thing."

Ah. Right. "Trust the magic, and the magic will trust you."

"That. At some point, you have to accept that you can't know everything, not about the world, and not about other people. All you can do is your best. You keep an eye out for liars and brown-nosers and folks trying to take advantage. But you can't let worrying about those jerks keep you from ever trusting anybody."

I bent my leg and rested my forehead on my knee. "What if I trust Penelope, and we have a huge fight, and she outs me on socials because she's mad? All it would take is the one time, and everyone would know who Leandro Presto is."

"Cheese and crackers, bud, your parents really did a number on you with all their fighting, huh? Plenty of other couples aren't spiteful shits like they were."

I felt like he'd poured a bucket of cold water on my head. My parents. Of course. As far back as I could remember, they'd constantly argued. One of them would do or say something that pissed the other one off, and they'd scream for a while, then go to separate rooms or leave the house. They talked shit about each other to me all the time, bribed me with food or toys to prove which of them loved me more and was the better parent.

Worst of all, they made me keep secrets. I don't think I'd realized until this moment how hard that was on me. Half the time they'd use those secrets as weapons later, to throw something in the other's face. And when it was me who accidentally slipped up? Not only did I cause that fight, but I'd get punished for it.

Holy shit. No wonder I was a mess.

"Earth to Bert, come in, Bert?"

"Sorry," I said. "I think my brain just broke."

"Well, put it back together. I said, do you really think this girl would do that to you, or is that just your nerves talking?"

Did I think Penelope would do that? She had more of a temper than I'd expected, but it seemed mostly aimed at me when I was pretending to be a fool and she was worried about our spell. Or at Felicia when she was a jerk. I hadn't seen her do or say anything mean otherwise. I'd actually seen her go out of her way to help people and be nice, which fit with what I'd heard from my friend before I even started emailing her.

And hadn't she helped me in the first place when she didn't have to? She could have just said her store didn't have the reagent I needed and been done with it, but she called around for me and found it. And then she'd helped me fix a mistake in one of the recipes on my blog. She didn't get anything out of that for herself, in either case. She never asked me for any money, or favors, or to buy anything from the store. She just . . . helped.

Even when she told me off in front of my fans that night at the park, Penelope seemed mostly worried that I was harming other people—or myself.

No, I had no reason to believe she'd do something to get back at me if I made her angry. She'd probably lecture me about it, if anything. And why did that make me smile?

"Lost you there again, kiddo."

"You're right, Grandpa. Penelope wouldn't do that. She's not like my parents at all. She's pretty great, actually. Smart, and nice, and funny."

"Good-looking?"

"Definitely."

"Then what are you waiting for? An invitation?"

I wasn't going to explain enthusiastic consent to my grandfather. I'd already said enough.

"I need to talk to her," I said.

"That's my boy. You bring her by whenever you're ready, hey? Let me get a look at her."

"I can't promise anything." I didn't know what Penelope wanted yet.

Grandpa Fred made a pssh sound. "I'm not asking for promises, bud. Unlike your dad, I'm not a lawyer trying to strangle you with fine print." He paused, then added, "And while I have you on the line, stop worrying about the charity so much, for god's sake. You're going to give yourself an ulcer. Just have fun and see where this show takes you."

He'd told me that before, and I wanted to listen, I really did. But I knew the charity was important to him. It had been important to Grandma Louisa, too. She'd been an elementary school teacher from when they'd met until she'd retired, and if we lost the charity, it would feel like losing her again.

"Doing my best," I said. "Thanks for the advice, Grandpa."

"Don't just take my word for it," he said. "Listen to yourself, too. You've got a good head on your shoulders when you use it."

I laughed, and we went back and forth about nothing important before we hung up. Talking to him always made me feel better. I hoped it made him feel better, too.

As soon as I finished my to-do list, I was going to find Penelope and drag her back into the casting booth. One way or the other, things needed to be settled between us. Not forever, maybe, but for now.

Groaning internally, I called my mom to get it over with. But at least I had something to look forward to afterward.

By the time I finished with my mom's complaining and Ed's methodical, chronological list of everything he thought I needed to know about, it was past one. I could order room service again, but if there was a group lunch in the restaurant or on the pool deck, that was probably where I'd find Penelope. So I glued my mustache on, slicked back my hair, and got my safety glasses. A dashing superhero, Leandro was not.

The pool deck was indeed the party spot, with people swimming or tanning, taking advantage of the lack of rain. Dylan said Penelope and Amy had left together after eating, that Amy was still upset about her spell; she kept "quietly going to pieces," as Quentin put it. I ate at an appropriately sociable speed while chatting with people, then headed to the first floor, finding Alina at the desk again.

"Do you ever sleep?" I asked her.

"A little every time I blink," Alina replied with a grin. "Can I help you with anything?"

"Maybe. Did Penelope and Amy come through here?"

"They went down the hall, I think to the theater."

I thanked her and headed that way.

The theater room's dark walls looked like stained bamboo interspersed with cloth-covered acoustic panels. The floor was an enchanted purple galaxy print, rolls of film floating between sparkling stars. Rows of plush chairs, with drink holders in armrests that went up and down, sat in front of a giant screen. Along the far wall was one of those fancy choose-your-own-soda machines next to a table with a small glass-sided popcorn popper.

Penelope and Amy looked up from their seats in the front when I came in. Neither of them was eating, but both had drinks. Penelope also had her notebook and a pencil, and looked like she'd been writing something when I interrupted.

"Sorry," I said. "I didn't mean to bother you two. I was just looking for Penelope." I almost added "to talk about the next round," but that seemed cruel.

Amy smiled, her eyes crinkling behind her glasses. "I should probably go . . . do something, instead of feeling sorry for myself. My partner told me to enjoy the hotel amenities."

"Everyone else seems to be swimming," I suggested.

"That does sound nice. And there's a thing in the lounge later." Amy looked at her hands. "I promised I'd play the piano. I've learned the basics of enough popular songs to fake them, and Quentin wants to do karaoke."

Penelope tapped her pencil on the notebook. "Can I talk to Leandro about this?"

Amy's smile disappeared. "Yes. You can. Maybe he'll have some ideas. Not that it will do much good, but I at least want to know, if that makes sense?"

"It does," Penelope assured her. "Go have fun. I'll see you later."

Amy paused in the doorway and smiled at me again. "Do you sing?"

"Not as well as I dance," I said honestly.

That made her laugh, sweet and light. "Maybe you and Penelope can dance tonight, then." And on that line, she left.

Penelope stared at her notebook. Now that her hair and makeup weren't being done by the pros on the set, she looked different—not better or worse, just different. Instead of space buns, she'd pulled her hair back in a ponytail of messy curls, some loose around her face like they'd escaped. I didn't usually notice eye shadow or lipstick unless they were extreme, and if she was wearing any now, she'd made it more natural than obvious.

I had this sense that she'd taken a mask off, a mask someone else had given her, and now I was seeing a more real Penelope. And yet, here I was, with my mask on. But before I spilled my guts to her, I had to be sure there was something serious enough between us to take that step. Her email made me think, made me hope . . . but it hadn't been for Leandro. It had been for Gil.

Only one way to be sure. Here we go.

CHAPTER 16

Gil

I sat in the chair next to Penelope, the armrest between us. Everything I wanted to say fell right out of my head like I'd fumbled a tall stack of files as soon as I was looking into her clear brown eyes.

"What's up with Amy?" I blurted out.

"We were going over what happened with her spell," Penelope explained. "I wanted to take notes while it was still fresh in her mind."

"Why?"

"Because that's two spell disasters in a row. It has to be sabotage."

"Yeah, no, totally. I was only wondering about the notes part."

"Oh." She frowned at her notebook. "I guess . . . I like fixing things. And figuring out how they went wrong. I thought maybe I could do that for Amy, or prove that she didn't mess up. To help her feel a little better, you know?" She took a deep breath and looked at me. "Speaking of mess-ups."

Oh no. My whole body tensed.

"I know this is getting old," Penelope said, "but I'm really sorry. About yesterday."

She was?

"I know you didn't spill that potion on purpose. You wouldn't do that. You didn't deserve to have me bitch at you about it. And the pressure cooker . . ." Penelope slouched down in her seat and looked up at the ceiling. "It doesn't matter. I was an asshole again. I'm sorry. I just wanted to say that up front. And I understand if sorry isn't good enough, especially since this isn't the first time. But I am. Sorry, I mean."

That was a good start, I guess. My hurt feelings weren't gone, but they felt better. Something she said snagged in my brain, though.

"What about the pressure cooker?" I asked.

"It's a story. You don't have to hear it. I don't want it to sound like I'm trying to excuse myself, you know?"

"Do you want to tell me? No pressure." I paused. "Pun not intended."

She snorted a laugh. "I wouldn't have noticed if you hadn't said anything."

"I'm not kitten around right meow," I said solemnly.

Her shoulders dropped an inch, but she fiddled with the straw in her drink, swirling the ice around inside. The plastic lid creaked.

"I always used to help my abuela with her spells when I was little," Penelope said, staring at the blank screen like she was watching a movie of her memories. "She met my abuelo when they were both in college; she was studying magic theory, and he was going to be a doctor."

"Not a curandero?"

"No, he was getting his Doctor en Medicina, though I think in Cuba the program covered some healing magic, too? I'm not sure. Anyway." She sighed. "They fell in love, they graduated, they got married. My aunt was born, and my abuela pretty much became a housewife."

"Pretty much?"

Penelope grinned, a quick flash of teeth. "The wife of a doctor, working? No me diga. She never stopped learning, though, and making spells for people. When they moved here from Cuba with my aunt and my mom, they lived in a one-bedroom apartment in Hialeah, and she supported the family with her magic while my abuelo struggled to get a job. He couldn't be a doctor here unless he did his residency again, and took all his exams, and they couldn't afford it. Eventually he sold cars."

"Wow. That's a big change." And here I'd been complaining about being an adjunct-slash–internet celebrity.

"They made it work." She sipped her drink. "Anyway. My sister and I grew up learning spells from my abuela. There was always a language thing because I was born here, speaking mostly English—both my parents learned young, and we spoke it at home more than Spanish. I sometimes had trouble understanding her directions, or figuring out which reagents she wanted, but she was always super patient with me." Her voice cracked, her eyes watery and her nose turning red.

Quietly, I asked, "When did she die?"

Penelope sniffled. "She isn't dead. She has dementia. For years now. She's there physically, but otherwise she's gone."

God. I could only imagine.

"When I was sixteen," Penelope said, "I was more . . . I don't know, confident? But I procrastinated a lot. I wanted to cast a spell on my own, for my abuela's birthday, but I left it to the last minute. It was a simple soap enchantment. I'd done them so many times . . ."

"You tried to pressure-cook it."

"Yeah." She rubbed her face with one hand. "It probably wouldn't have been so bad if I hadn't mixed up an ingredient. Put in a teaspoon of spearmint instead of bay leaves for the catalyst."

Ouch. "It grew too fast."

"It grew too fast," she agreed. "If I hadn't gone to the bathroom when I did, I would have been in the kitchen when it exploded."

Holy fuck. "You could have died."

"My abuela almost did. She ran into the kitchen to . . . she thought I was still there, and it was burning, smoke everywhere . . . and then something under the sink went up in a huge fireball . . . She was in the hospital for two weeks. Even with healing magic, she needed skin grafts, and her lungs were never the same."

Penelope turned her face away, like she didn't want me to see her cry. She shivered, but didn't make a sound. Nothing like my mom, who went all out with big sobs and dramatic wailing. I moved the armrest up and scooted closer, gently wrapping my arms around her.

This explained so much. Why she triple-checked all our ingredients. Why my little fireball had freaked her out, and Amy's spell explosion had given her a full panic attack. And most importantly, why she was so angry at Leandro Presto for messing up his spells and acting like it was no big deal.

Was I encouraging my fans to do things wrong as a joke, when they might get hurt? I always explained, always showed the correct way, but if Sam was right, most people didn't care about anything but the fuckup.

Shit. Maybe Penelope was right about *Mage You Look*. Maybe something needed to change. Possibly a bigger issue was, would she ever be able to accept me being Leandro if I kept doing what I was doing?

Penelope blew her nose on a napkin and swallowed, her face

splotchy. "Like I said before, I don't want you to feel like this is me trying to make excuses. It's just . . . reasons."

"I get it," I said. "We're both stressed out."

"Are we . . . good?" she asked meekly, looking at the space movie carpet.

"We're good," I assured her.

"Okay. Okay. That's good." She paused, then said, "I also wanted to talk about . . . us?"

My heart sped up like a car in the HOV lane. "Yeah?"

"Yeah. As in, not our team, but our . . . vibe?" She laughed and shook her head. "Why is this so hard?"

"That's what she said?"

Penelope smacked my arm lightly. "I'm just trying to figure out what we're doing here? And the thing is . . ."

When she didn't keep going, I said, "The thing is?"

"The thing is, there's this guy."

My racing heart crashed into a highway wall. "Oh. Okay."

"It's not what you think," she said quickly. "It's . . . This is probably going to sound super ridiculous."

"I'm ridiculous professionally, don't worry." I was worried.

"So. I've been emailing this guy for, like . . . months now?"

Oh my god.

"I've honestly had a huge crush on him the entire time, but I never said anything. And he's been friendly, but he never . . . He's been nice. Possibly flirty, but I'm not sure."

Oh my fucking GOD.

"I emailed him right before we started here, because . . . I don't even want to explain because it's more ridiculous than anything else, but I sort of asked him out?"

My brain had climbed onto the roof of my crashed heart car and was quietly screaming. "So you . . . have a thing for this guy and don't want to keep, um. Doing anything. With me?"

Penelope waved her hands in front of her. "Yeah, no, that's not what I mean! I just wanted to be up front about why my feelings are a mess? And you made me think, when you talked about people not really knowing you . . . maybe I don't know this guy as well as I thought. Maybe I was crushing on a version of him that was only real in my mind."

Everything I had imagined about this conversation seemed like a weird dream now.

"So the thing is," Penelope said.

"The thing is?" I repeated, my mouth dry.

"You're real," she said. "And you're here. And I don't want to miss out on where this could go, with us, because I'm waiting on someone who might not even be who I think he is."

She couldn't know she'd managed to hit me in the exact right spot to ruin me. But I could fix this. I could make it right. All I had to do was confess.

"I have to tell you something," I said.

The door to the theater room opened and Mary, Isaac's assistant, walked in.

"Hi hello!" Mary said. "I hope I'm not interrupting anything."

I couldn't even respond. Neither could Penelope, apparently.

"Awesome great so I've been looking for Leandro because Isaac wants to meet with him right now about something super important." Mary inhaled. "So if you could please follow me out to the car outside you don't need to bring anything except yourself okay great!" She stared at me, her eyes big like a lemur on cocaine.

I found my voice. "We are in the middle of something, actually." Was I growling? I might have growled.

"It's okay," Penelope said, putting her hand on my arm. "We can finish talking later. You should see what Isaac wants."

Isaac could eat my balls. "Are you sure?"

Penelope smiled, and my heart melted. "I'm sure. I'm not going anywhere."

God, I wanted that to be true in so many ways. "Later. For sure."

"For sure, for sure."

Kissing her was not an option yet. Not in front of a random almost-stranger. But soon, I promised myself. Soon, and a lot.

I followed Mary out of the dimly lit theater and out of the hotel, and blinked at the sun shining overhead, impossibly bright. Nothing felt real. I didn't know what Isaac wanted, but it had better be good, and fast, because I had to get back to Penelope and finish what we'd started.

There was no sign of the vulture on the balcony of Isaac's fancy room, possibly because someone—Mary?—had put a spike strip on the wall. I felt spiky myself, but Isaac looked like he'd just finished a massage and facial, or possibly smoked a shitload of weed. He sat on his couch, an arm stretched along the back, one foot up on the clear coffee table. A smile spread across his face as I sat in one of the uncomfortable chairs near him.

"Hey, Leandro, how's it going?" Isaac asked. "Good, great. Listen, I wanted to have a little chat with you about something, mano a mano."

That's not what "mano a mano" meant, but okay. "Sure, yeah, what's up?"

"I'm putting a new show together," he continued. "It's kind of a street magic thing, sort of like what you do already, showing up in random places and grabbing people to do tricks. Very fun stuff."

Okay, that did sound fun.

"We've got a few potential options for talent, keeping an open mind right now, you know, but . . ." He tapped the side of his nose. "I think you're it, guy. I've seen some of the dailies of you doing your thing, and you're smooth. Funny."

"Thanks." He'd said a lot of the same stuff when I was asked to be a Spellebrity. I kept my derpy grin on and nodded along.

"We want you to come in for a screen test. Not today, but soon." Isaac raised his arm and waved it around, and moments later, Mary handed him a bottle of something bright orange. Neither of them offered me anything.

"You know where to find me," I joked. "I can do the test whenever."

"Excellente." He chugged some of the carrot or whatever smoothie and wiped his mouth with the back of his hand. "I don't have to tell you to keep this hush-hush. We're still putting the package together, feeling out money options, you know the drill."

I mimed zipping my lips and locking them, like Grandpa Fred always did.

"My people will call your people, et cetera, et cetera." Isaac pointed at me with the bottle. "Speaking of your people, nice work with your partner. You're really selling the fake-flirting stuff."

I kept my himbo grin going, but inside I flinched. "That's good to hear. We, uh, weren't sure."

"If you do end up with this show," Isaac said, "you'll need to ditch her."

What?

"She's fine for *Cast Judgment*, but she doesn't have the 'it' factor, you know what I'm saying? You have to level up your pussy game. And anyway you're going to want to fly solo for a while." Isaac made an airplane motion with his hand. "Let the press see you with a few different people—the hotter, the better—get them talking about you as much as possible. New week, new flavor."

Bad. This was bad. Assuming Penelope and I—

"We'll cross that bridge when we burn it," Isaac said. "For now, keep doing what you're doing, or should I say, keep doing who you're doing?" He cracked a laugh, and somewhere behind me, Mary cackled like a cartoon hyena.

I guess Isaac was all funned out, because he got up and left the room without even saying goodbye.

That worked for me. I had nothing to say to him, either.

ON THE WAY back to the hotel, I frantically texted Sam and Ed that I needed to talk to them ASAP. I wanted to do a video call from my room, but Sam insisted we should get together in person, which was ridiculous. I'm pretty sure she was having major FOMO and wanted to get close to the fun times. We agreed to meet at the hotel bar for happy hour once they made it through traffic.

Plenty of time for me to get Penelope alone and finally explain everything. Unless . . . Maybe I needed to talk to Sam and Ed first?

The stuff Isaac had said kept repeating in my head, making me second-guess my plans from this morning. Would I really have to go around fake dating random people as part of my image? That sounded awful. When would it end? Would it ever end?

Not that I was rushing to get married—look how my parents turned out. But Grandpa Fred and Grandma Louisa had been happy for so long, and so were my abuelos on my dad's side. I guess I always assumed that would be me one day. A husband. A dad. Backyard birthday parties with croquetas and pastelitos and grocery store cakes. Family vacations to overpriced theme parks. Enchantment lessons in the kitchen.

That was definitely not the future Isaac pictured for me. But what did I really want?

Right now, I wanted to hide in my room and pace. So I did. I took off my mustache and glasses, fixed my hair and changed into normal clothes. Better to have this conversation as me than as Leandro.

Forcing myself to answer emails for another hour might possibly have been a special circle of hell. When Sam finally texted that they were downstairs, I was ready to crawl out of my skin and eat it like a bug.

I used the camera on my phone to make sure the hallway was empty, spy-movie-style, then ran for the stairwell with my head down. It dumped me out on the sidewalk, and I casually walked over to the bar like I was some rando from one of the condo buildings.

Sam and Ed had grabbed a table against the wall and were checking out the menu. Sam wore one of her usual T-shirts—a stylized samurai cutting a film strip into pieces—while Ed had on a pale blue dress shirt and gray tie like he'd just come from a business meeting and left his jacket in the car. I threw myself into an empty chair and put my face in my hands.

"Hello to you, too," Sam said. "I see you've temporarily abandoned your secret identity."

"Shh!" I said. "Please don't start with that."

"Okay, then let's start with why you dragged us all the way out here."

I gaped at her. "You're the one who—"

"Incoming," Ed said.

The waiter arrived to take our orders. I got a beer, Sam got a whiskey sour, Ed got a soda. We decided to share a plate of egg rolls.

"All right." Ed folded his hands and looked at me over the tops of his glasses. "We know you can't talk about certain things due to your NDA, so I assume this isn't related to any of that."

"No, it's totally separate. Well, some of it is."

"Is it good or bad?" Sam asked.

"I'm not sure. It's a secret, though, so cone of silence."

Sam mimed dropping a cone over the table.

"I had a meeting today with"—I dropped my voice—"Isaac Knight. He wants me to do a screen test for a show."

"Fuck yes! What kind of show? Deets!"

"Shh!" I explained briefly. "It's not a sure thing."

"It's still exciting," Ed said. "It means you're doing something right."

"But what about us? Our . . . everything?"

"We can manage it," Ed said. "It's just logistics."

"What he said." Sam wrinkled her nose at me. "There's something else bothering you, though. Spill."

"I don't—"

"Incoming," Ed said. I shut up.

The waiter dropped off our drinks. I sipped my beer as I tried to figure out how to get through this part without making Sam screech like a raptor.

"Maybe we should talk about the rest in your car," I muttered.

Ed raised an eyebrow at Sam, who made a *who, me?* face.

"I'll be cool," Sam said.

"I could get in big trouble," I warned her.

"Come on," Sam whined. "When have I ever told anyone—"

Ed cleared his throat. "Is there a way you can explain without violating your NDA?"

I thought about it. No, nothing would make sense if I tried to be vague. I shook my head.

"Sam will be good," Ed said. Sam nodded. In a way, that made me relax a little. As wild as Sam could be, she hated to disappoint Ed. It was like upsetting your favorite teacher.

I leaned closer. "Penelope is here."

Sam clamped her hands over her mouth to stop her scream. Ed and I both looked at her.

"I'm fine," she said through her fingers. "I'm good. Continue."

"She's my partner."

Sam bit her fist.

"Isaac asked us to pretend to flirt with each other, for drama."

Sam groaned and closed her eyes.

"We've been sort of hooking up for a few days now."

Sam buried her face in Ed's arm.

Ed smirked at me. "I think you broke her."

"It gets worse," I said.

The waiter appeared bearing food gifts. I dipped half an egg roll in spicy plum sauce and stuffed it in my mouth, delaying the inevitable.

"Isaac told me," I said, "that if I ended up on this new show, I'd have to drop Penelope because I need to 'level up my pussy game.' Direct quote."

"What the fuck?" Sam asked. "That's disgusting. He's disgusting."

Ed made a face. "I can see where he's coming from."

"You what?" Sam exclaimed. "What the fuck, Ed!"

"Shh!" I said.

"I'm not saying he's right, or that you should listen to him," Ed said, pushing his glasses up his nose. "But if Gil does end up doing this new thing, how is that going to change his personal life? What is he going to have to compromise for his career?"

"Yes. That. It's not just Penelope. I don't know what's going to happen with her."

"You know what you want to happen," Sam interrupted.

"Yeah. It's more . . . do I want the future where I have my own TV show, but the only dating I ever do is fake? As Leandro? And how long will that go on?"

"It might not be like that," Ed said.

"It might not," I agreed. "And this is just a screen test. It isn't a contract. Lots of shows die before they go anywhere. But I need to figure my shit out, you know? Get my priorities straight so I can set boundaries."

Ed popped shredded carrot garnish into his mouth. "You don't have to rush anything."

"I need to talk to Penelope, though," I said. "Before things go any further with us. I can't keep messing around with her, pretending to be Leandro. I want her to like me, not a character."

Sam took a big gulp of her drink. "So, just curious, what's she like?"

"Here's the wild thing: you met her at the park."

"Angry girl, right?" Sam asked.

"Yeah! She's not actually angry. She's really smart, and fun, and—"

"She's right over there," Sam said.

I turned so fast, I knocked my drink into my lap. Penelope stood near the doorway between the hotel lobby and the restaurant, staring at me like she'd seen a ghost. But she couldn't have figured out . . . could she?

She took one step back, then another, her eyes locked on mine. I stood up, wet beer soaking my jeans. She spun around and ran for the elevator.

"Shit, shit, shit!" I muttered, tripping through the crowded restaurant as I hurried to catch up. Behind me, Sam yelled, "Don't fuck this up!"

Had I, though? Was it already too late?

I bolted through the lobby, past Alina at her desk, my heart pumping faster than my legs. The doors of the elevator were starting to close when I threw myself between them, and they opened again. Penelope stood inside, backed into the corner, hugging herself tightly.

"Hey," I said.

She just stared at me.

I took a deep breath and let it out. "I need to tell you something."

The doors slid shut behind me.

CHAPTER 17

Penelope

I'd imagined meeting Gil so many times, in so many ways, and not a single one of them involved being trapped in an elevator with him after finding out he was Leandro Presto.

Seeing him in the restaurant, at first I had refused to believe the obvious. It had been shocking enough for the guy I'd crushed on for so long to suddenly appear out of nowhere. Then I realized he was sitting with Leandro's crew, talking and drinking and being normal. And then! He did the thing! Where he tried to smooth down his mustache, except he didn't have a mustache, so he just rubbed his upper lip where the mustache should be. I don't think he even realized he was doing it.

I couldn't believe I didn't see it before. But Leandro's hair was almost black and slicked back, instead of dark brown and curly. His big safety glasses hid his eyes, and he had that mustache, and the ridiculous shirts . . . This just proved I didn't know Gil at all. I didn't really know either of them, apparently. Either of him.

How? Why? I had so many questions, so many emotions slithering over each other like snakes in a basket. My mouth struggled to make words happen, so we just stood there in the elevator until it dinged and the doors opened.

Gil was facing me, so he didn't see Quentin coming up the hallway behind him. I jumped to press the button for the third floor, then held the one to close the door. Quentin was far enough that he'd never make it, but near enough that his confused expression made me feel guilty for shutting him out. No way did I want this conversation to be public, though.

"What . . . ?" Gil started to turn, but I grabbed his face.

"Quentin," I explained.

His eyes got big. "Thanks."

"Where's your room?" I asked. I hadn't wanted to go there the other night because it felt too . . . bed having? But I wasn't going to do this in the restaurant, not in front of his friends or anyone else, and I had a feeling that the two of us being seen together might make other people connect the same dots I had.

"First one on the left," he said.

The doors opened. Nobody there. I pushed him out backward and toward what I assumed was his room. He pulled his key card from his back pocket and struggled to get it to work. I'm glad it wasn't just me with those damn things. The "Do Not Disturb" sign hung on the knob, and I had a ridiculous image of a housekeeping person dusting his fake mustaches.

His room was nicer than mine, with an enchanted painting and more space and even a bigger bed. A peek at the bathroom said that was also extra classy, but I wasn't going to explore.

Instead, I stood in front of an overstuffed chair and crossed my arms. "Do you need to tell your friends? Where you went?"

"I'm pretty sure they'll figure it out," Gil mumbled. He'd shoved his hands in his pockets and stood near the wall just past the door, shoulders hunched like he was waiting for me to yell or get violent.

Was I going to yell? Probably not. I sorted through the snake basket of my feelings. Anger was there, yes, but mostly I was . . . sad? Disappointed? Hurt? I'd be lying to myself, though, if I ignored that I was also at least a tiny bit relieved.

Gil was Leandro. In some ways, it made things so much easier; in others, extremely harder. No pun intended.

Okay, smol pun.

"I was going to tell you earlier," Gil said. "It's why I was looking for you. To tell you. But you were with Amy, and then I didn't want to interrupt all the stuff you were saying, and then Mary dragged me off . . ."

And I'd told him it could wait. "Right. Okay." My brain shuffled a whole deck of questions and started pulling random cards. "Did you get my email?"

"This morning. I, um, already knew your name, by the way. My friend who recommended your store told me about you. All good things," he said quickly.

Considering I'd stalked him online, I couldn't really get mad about that, I guess. I mean, I could, but it would make me a hypocrite. "So you knew it was me the whole time here? Since the first day?"

"Yeah. I didn't know at the park, but I knew as soon as I read your bio, before we started filming."

Puzzle pieces started clicking together. "You didn't say anything because nobody knows you're Leandro, except your friends?"

"Only the friends who work on the videos with me. The ones you saw today. And my agent. And my grandpa Fred."

Only four people? Seriously? "Not even your parents?"

He looked away and said softly, "Especially not my parents."

That sounded like a bruise I wasn't going to poke. "How did you even start being Leandro Presto? It seemed like you went viral out of nowhere and then you were all over the place."

"That's pretty much what happened." Gil's shoulders relaxed and he took his hands out of his pockets. "It's kind of a long story. I should, um . . ." He gestured at the beer stain on his pants.

"Yeah, no, for sure."

He pulled folded jeans out of the dresser and took them to the bathroom. "Do you want a drink?" he asked through the door. "My minibar stuff is free, or I can get you something from the vending machine?"

"Wow, celebrities living it up, huh? I don't even have a minibar, just a fridge."

"I mean, I'm not like everyone else here, but I do get some perks." He came back out, crossed the room and opened a door that looked like a regular cabinet. "Options are bottled water, soda, beer, tiny rum, tiny vodka, tiny whiskey, and tiny wine—red or white."

Was it too early for a tiny Cuba libre? Probably. "Caffeine me."

He passed me a soda—regular-sized, thankfully—and opened a beer for himself. We both sat down, me in the comfy seat, him in a wheelie desk chair.

"So. Leandro Presto." Gil took a swig of his beer and sighed. "Flashback to a few years ago. I started my *Doctor Witch* blog when I was getting my PhD. Some of the other people in my cohort, and my professors, thought it was a neat idea and spread it around. So did my roommates, Sam and Ed—my friends who work on *Mage You Look* with me."

"It seems pretty popular," I said. "Your blog, I mean."

He shrugged. "Not compared to Leandro Presto, but at the time, yeah, I was happy about my hundreds of followers. I thought it would make me look good as a faculty candidate, you know? That's not why I did it, but it seemed like it could help."

"I assume it didn't?"

"Not that I know of. It was on my résumé, but nobody ever brought it up in an interview. All anyone cared about were my academic publications and teaching experience and letters of recommendation." He drank again and rested his arm on the desk. "At first, I applied for tenure-track positions all over the country. Anywhere that was hiring for their magical theory program, I tried to shoot my shot. Either they ended up promoting internally, or they went with someone who had already been teaching somewhere else. My faculty advisor tried to help me out, but no luck there, either. I was broke, and it only got worse."

"That sucks a lot," I said.

"Yeah." Gil zoned out, then shook his head and came back. "I started applying for adjunct jobs. I'm not sure why, but a whole bunch of them asked for video auditions. Present-certain-topics-you'd-be-teaching-in-a-class kind of thing."

"Did Sam and Ed help with the videos?" I asked.

"Not at first. I didn't want to bother them, even though they were both film people. I couldn't pay them for their work, which was important to me. Still is." He took a drink. "Anyway. It was hard, harder than just teaching. I'd never had complaints from students on my course evals when I was a TA—aside from, you know, how I gave unfair grades or I wouldn't let them turn stuff in late or whatever. The usual shit. But I like to get interactive, call on people and answer questions and stuff. Talking to a camera was so . . . blah."

"Your videos sucked?"

"So much. I got like one interview. Eventually I told Sam and Ed, and they gave me shit for not asking for help sooner."

I leaned forward in my chair. "And you started pretending to be Leandro Presto. To be more funny and interesting."

"Sort of. Sam said I should loosen up, be less professor and more cool guy." Gil grinned. "I actually did mess up a spell demonstration because I was trying so hard to make jokes. Turned my skin pink, like neon highlighter pink. Sam and Ed totally lost it laughing. I told my grandpa Fred about it, and he reminded me that one of the ways we taught magic through the Alan Kazam volunteer work was by pretending to do things wrong and letting the kids correct us. I think I mentioned before how they love that. It's an old stage magic thing."

"Did you send that video somewhere?"

"Hell no. But we started joking about how pink-skin guy wasn't me, it was my alter ego. Leandro is my middle name, and Presto is, you know, a magic word. Eventually we thought, maybe we could do the thing on purpose and post the videos online? See if we could make some ad revenue from it."

"And then you went viral?"

"Not from those videos, no. It was Sam's idea to post shorter, edited versions on Jinxd, and the seventh one took off. Then people found the other ones and shared those, and within a week we had tens of thousands of followers. We added subscriptions, started doing live stuff and taking requests, and it just . . . kept going from there."

"And now you're a Spellebrity."

Gil laughed. "Yeah. It still doesn't feel real. Maybe because so much of what we're doing is fake."

I winced, thinking of my hair albondigas and wild makeup. Nowhere near as fake as his mustache, but still. And of course, there was our Isaac-mandated flirting . . .

"Is all this why you never asked me out before?" I asked. "Because you didn't want to say anything about *Mage You Look*? Or did you . . . were you not interested in me, like that? When we were just emailing each other?" My face burned getting those words out, but I had to know.

Gil put his drink down and wheeled his chair closer to me. "*Mage You Look* was part of it. You know from our emails that I've been teaching as an adjunct—until this semester, anyway. I quit to do this show, which . . ." He huffed out a breath. "I hope that wasn't a huge mistake."

"Mood," I said.

"Yeah, when you told me you got fired the first night, I was like, 'Cool, being unemployed is one more thing we have in common.'"

"Not for long, hopefully."

"Fingers crossed. So yeah, I could talk about teaching, but I'd have to lie about being Leandro. I'd be randomly unavailable because of filming, and I'd have to hide stuff at my apartment if you ever came over. All kinds of shit."

Leading a double life like that would be exhausting. Probably was exhausting. "You said that was part of it. What's the rest?"

Gil gripped the arms of his chair. "I told you about my hands-off-the-fans rule? A thing happened that made me go hardcore secret identity about Leandro."

I wanted to know, but I wasn't going to ask.

"I never flirted with anyone online, and that didn't change when we started filming stuff live." He hunched over like he was trying to hide inside his own body. "This one woman started showing up whenever we announced a taping on our Jive server. She just lurked at first, then she would talk to me, and I was nice, you know? Rule number six: everyone is important."

Oh, Gil. You and your rules.

"She private messaged me on Jive, asking me personal questions that got more and more uncomfortable. She started bringing me presents. Little things, then more expensive ones. Sam and Ed agreed she was crossing lines, so I asked her to stop."

"She didn't," I said.

"No. It got worse. We banned her from the server, then banned her alts. Somehow she kept finding out when we were filming and showing up, but she stayed far enough away that I didn't want to make a scene by saying anything." He rubbed his face with both hands. "A few weeks before Christmas, she followed me home."

"No!"

"Yeah. She tried to trick the maintenance guy into letting her in our building, but she didn't know our apartment number, or my real name. He told her to leave, she kept lurking, he chased her away with a giant plastic candy cane—"

I couldn't help it. I laughed, then covered my mouth. "I'm so sorry."

"No, it's okay, it was funny. We saw it from Sam's bedroom window. He was swinging it around over his head like a sword, and she screamed and ran to her car. I don't know why that finally did it, but we never saw her again." He chugged more beer and smoothed his nonexistent mustache. "The thing is, I kept thinking, it could have been so much worse. You hear horror stories—almost always about women—and I mean, I'm not saying what happened to me was nothing, but it wasn't *that*. I got lucky. No one was hurt, she went away, and nothing like that has happened again."

And he'd gone overboard with being careful. I could relate.

"So you were worried I might be another stalker?" I asked.

"A little, at first. And it wasn't just you. I stopped dating anyone, period. I was too paranoid. The more I got to know you, and like you, the more my fear . . . changed. What if you were just being friendly? What if I was the stalker this time? You seemed cool, and nice, and I figured if I tried anything, I could screw up what we had." His eyes met mine and my heart sped up. "Plus, if we did start going out, I'd have to lie to you until I was sure I could trust you. That seemed bad, you know?"

"You did lie to me, though," I said quietly.

"I did," he agreed. "I'm sorry. I didn't know all of this would happen. With us, here. I should have kept my hands off you, too, even if you weren't a fan. It wasn't fair to you. Leandro isn't real, and you deserve to . . . to be with a real person, not a character."

My heart already felt like it was trying to thump its way out of my body, but what he said, and the way he said it . . . He'd known who I was this whole time, and he'd kissed me, more than once . . . I wouldn't know unless I asked, but making myself say the words was so hard.

"What do you want?" I asked. "For . . . us?"

"I like you," he said. "A lot. I already liked you when we were just emailing, but now . . ." He half smiled. "I've got felines for you."

I groaned. "A cat pun? Seriously?"

"Leandro isn't all fake. Only mostly."

And I'd fallen for him. Except . . . I'd crushed on Gil first. And they were the same person. So where did that leave me? What did it mean for my feelings?

What did I want?

I stood up. "I think I need a minute. Alone. To think. This is a lot to process."

Gil got up, too, putting his beer on the desk. "Right. Yeah. Totally. Take as much time as you need. I'll be here whenever you're ready to talk. I mean, I'm literally not going anywhere, since we're sort of stuck in here, but—"

"I know," I said. "Are you going to karaoke later?"

"Are you?"

"Yeah."

"Me too, then."

"Okay. I'll see you there."

The door clicked shut behind me. The hallway was empty, quiet except for the hiss of the air conditioner. Everything seemed weird and out of focus, like when I finished reading a great book and suddenly found myself back in the real world, except my insides were rearranged and nothing was the same.

What did I want?

The ice machine whirred and thunked; I nearly dropped the soda I'd forgotten I was holding. I was just standing there like a zombie. Normally I'd be overthinking, catastrophizing, coming up with bizarre worst-case scenarios that led to me jumping out a window and bleeding out in a parking lot. Instead, my head was empty.

I pushed the elevator button. It didn't open right away, so I wandered over to the vending machines to wait. Why even have a drink machine if there were minibars? Variety, I guess. The snack machine had so much weird stuff, too: fancy protein bars and artisanal chips, but also toothbrush kits and earbuds and quick-cast facial illusions and . . . condoms?

The elevator dinged and the doors opened. I walked over and put one foot inside, then stopped.

What did I want?

Gil had lied to me, if only by not telling me the whole truth. He had his reasons, though. Was that enough to justify it? Could I trust him not to lie to me again?

Did I want him, all of him, enough to take the chance either way?

The elevator chimed at me for standing there too long. I took a step, then another. The doors closed. I stared at my reflection in the metal for several breaths.

Then I threw my soda away and went back to the vending machine.

Gil opened his door on the third knock and stared at me with his mouth half-open, like he thought I was a hallucination.

"So I thought about it," I said.

"Oh," he said. "Okay."

"I like you, too. A lot."

Gil smiled. The butterflies in my stomach took off.

"We could talk more, or we could, um . . ."

"Um?"

"I bought this vending machine condom for you."

"Oh," he said, then, "Ohh," his voice suddenly twice as deep.

I threw myself at him and he caught me with both hands, stumbling backward.

We went totally feral.

I wrapped my arms around his neck, standing on my tiptoes to kiss his cheeks, his chin, his mouth. No stubble, no fake mustache, only smooth skin and beer-tinged lips. Our tongues tangoed as he gripped my ass, pulling me up against him until there was no space between us. It wasn't enough. I climbed him, trying not to think about bananas as I ground myself against the growing bulge in his jeans. It wasn't great, honestly; the fabric was too thick and the zipper was uncomfortable. Not a fun pants party.

A giggle fell out of me, and Gil stopped to look at my face.

"What?" he asked.

"We're having a pants party," I said.

His grin turned wicked. "I'll give you a pants party."

I squealed as he spun me around, tossing me onto the bed. He pulled his T-shirt off and threw it on top of the dresser, giving me my first look at the greatest chest I'd ever seen in person. He definitely worked out, though he was more toned than bulky, and he either shaved or was naturally hair-free in most places. I scrambled to get my shirt off, too, but he beat me to it, peeling it over my head and tossing it in the same direction as his. My bra followed a few fumbling seconds later, leaving me bare from the waist up.

He stared at my chest like he'd never seen boobs before. It was kind of sweet, until he licked in between them all the way up to my neck. My eyes closed as one of my hands gripped the back of his head, fingers twining in his dark curls. The other stroked up and down his back, tracing the valley of his spine. He laid a kiss on a spot behind my ear and I shivered. His apple-and-lavender smell was so strong, I wondered if I was hallucinating it.

Settling between my thighs, he cupped my breast, thumb rubbing a slow circle around and across my nipple that sent sparks of pleasure down to my happy place. I tried to wrap my legs around his hips, but my jeans were annoyingly tight. Letting go of him, I unzipped and wiggled, finally getting the damn things low enough to push them off the rest of the way. They almost took my underwear with them, but instead the deeply unsexy beige cotton rolled down awkwardly and stayed halfway down my butt.

Gil apparently didn't notice. He definitely noticed my pants were gone, though, because he followed the leader and lost his, too. The outline of his cock pushing against the fabric of his boxer briefs was . . . wow. I gave it a friendly stroke, which made him groan and start kissing me again.

I lay down on the bed and he climbed on top of me. He alternated teasing one nipple, then the other, with his lips and tongue, while I rubbed my clit as best I could against his shaft. He took over the rubbing with his hand, my body tightening and tingling and rushing toward the orgasm tide that was about to come in. One finger slipped inside me, then another. I rode his palm as he fingered me, until he moved so his thumb was circling my clit and pressing just right and . . . that did it.

I moaned and came hard and fast, shuddering as I dug my nails into his back. Gil kept going through the aftershocks, then kissed me and stood up. I must have made some kind of puppy whine, because he grinned at me.

"Don't worry, we're not done," he said. "Pants party, phase two."

His boxer briefs came off. Was I drooling? Maybe I was drooling. He was incredibly yummy.

He leaned over me, smirking. "There's something in your ear."

"What?"

With a quick hand motion, he made the condom appear as if by magic.

"Bro." I tweaked his nipple, and he yelped, then laughed.

All the card tricks had clearly given him some serious manual dexterity, because he had the condom on while I was still catching my breath. His dark eyes met mine as he nudged the head of his cock near where I wanted him.

"You still want to . . . ?" Gil asked.

"If you do not fuck me right now, I might curse you. And don't you dare make a cat pun."

He kissed me instead and slid inside me. Thank goodness I was so wet, because he filled me right up.

Things got a little blurry after that. His weight pressed me down onto the mattress as he thrust into me, slowly at first, then harder and faster. My ankles twined around his thighs; my hands moved down his back, to the tight muscles of his ass. I think I might have bitten his shoulder? He tasted like sweat and soap and skin, better than every fantasy I'd indulged in for the past few months.

My legs moved higher as I rolled my hips to match his pace. He shifted positions, somehow going even deeper. Between a handful of breaths I was coming again, shuddering, shaking, fireworks exploding behind my closed eyelids along with the pleasure between my legs. Gil went over the edge a few seconds later, stiffening and gripping my thighs and groaning my name as he pumped into me a few final times.

We stayed where we were for a little longer, caught up in the moment. My whole body felt warm and loose and tingly. I smiled up at Gil, and he smiled down at me, and we kissed again, slow and sweet.

"I guess that was worth waiting for," I said finally.

"Yeah," Gil said. "It was."

"Maybe we shouldn't wait so long for the next time, though."

He laughed and slipped out of me, stumbling to the bathroom to take care of the condom. When he got back, he climbed into bed, pulled me into his arms, and kissed the top of my head.

"So you're thinking, what, fifteen minutes?" he asked innocently.

I smacked his arm. "Malo. I only bought one condom."

"Okay, but how many were there in the machine?"

"I didn't count. Just that one cost me five bucks, though. And I had to charge it to my room, so Alina will know what we did."

Gil gave a low whistle. "Maybe I can sneak off to a store . . ."

My turn to laugh. Then we both got quiet.

"What are you thinking?" he asked.

"I'm happy," I said.

"Yeah," he said. "Me too."

Gil gripped me tighter, like he was worried about me slipping away. Whatever was happening with us, I had a feeling it hadn't magically gotten less complicated. For the moment, though, I nuzzled his chest with my cheek and enjoyed just being there. With Gil, who was also Leandro. Life was so weird sometimes.

Cool weird. Good weird.

CHAPTER 18

Gil

I don't think anyone had ever watched me put my mustache on until now. Sam and Ed had seen the before and after, the experimental attempts with different styles and costume ideas, but they'd never stood in the bathroom with me while I applied the adhesive and carefully stuck the fake facial hair to my upper lip. Having Penelope peek at me from the doorway felt strangely intimate, almost more than being balls-deep inside her.

Almost. And I really needed to not think about that right now, because it was distracting as hell.

We were getting ready to hit the karaoke party, which honestly wasn't my scene, but people would wonder what happened if neither of us showed up. After so many days of pretending to pretend to flirt with Penelope on the show, it was going to be hard to keep my hands to myself now that I knew exactly how it felt to have them all over her. My already-decent imagination had acquired new spank bank material, and it was probably going to keep offering me ideas at inappropriate times until my feelings settled.

I smoothed the mustache down and checked for integrity. Looked okay. Tinted gel was next. Slick it back with a comb, wash off the leftover goop, and . . . done. Add safety glasses and look complete.

"It's like you're getting ready for a Halloween party," Penelope said. "Except you have to do it every day."

"Only while we're here," I said. "Usually it's once or twice a week for a few hours."

"Does it bother you?"

The easy lie almost came out: It's fine. No big deal. I'm used to it. I didn't want to lie to Penelope, though. Not anymore, and not about this.

"It kind of does." I looked at her in the mirror, looking at me. "It's one thing to be Leandro for a little while and me the rest of the time. Doing it all day for so long has been stressing me out. What if I slip up? What if I break character?"

Penelope grinned. "What if some girl you like ends up liking the wrong you?"

"I legit wanted to walk into the bay," I said, leaning on the counter. "It was bad enough when you hated me—Leandro, I mean."

"I never hated you. I just . . ."

"You thought he was a flake getting people to do unsafe magic."

"Pretty much. Bad news, bro: you totally broke character with me."

Shit.

"Too competent," Penelope continued. "Too careful. All your accidents were fake, except the spill. I think you reminded me too much of . . . you, I guess. What I knew from emails and blog posts, anyway."

"Well, hopefully I did enough goofy tricks that the editors can make me look appropriately derpy."

Penelope stepped into the bathroom and wrapped her arms

around me from behind. "It'll be okay. And hey, now that I'm in on the secret, we can work together better, right?"

That did cheer me up. Then my second thoughts about what Isaac had said dropped me back into my own personal pity hole.

I hadn't finished talking with Sam and Ed, but they had accepted my text apology for disappearing and my brief "she knows and we're good" explanation. They were both happy for me, which for Ed meant a chill "That's so great, dude" and a smiling sunglasses face emoji, and for Sam meant "FINALLY!!" plus a GIF of two cartoon characters humping doggy-style.

I hadn't talked things out with Penelope, either, but that seemed slightly less necessary now. The major part was done; we could figure out logistics once the competition was over. That's what I told myself, anyway.

We stopped by Penelope's room so she could fix her face, and ran into Dylan. I shot the shit with him in the hallway waiting for her—super-nice dude, worried about his mom back home and his bakery job. I told him I hoped he'd get promoted after this, and he said he hoped he'd beat the rest of us so he could open his own place. Then he could promote himself to boss.

It would be cool if all of us could win, honestly. We all had dreams, and goals, and stuff we'd do with our prizes. Every single person in the competition was hardworking and skilled, and it seemed a waste of talent to send any of us back to where we'd started with nothing to show for it but our accumulated day rates and something to put on our CVs. But it was a contest, and only one team would take the top prize.

The library-slash-lounge had a wall of bookshelves in that same distressed wood as everything else in the hotel. Cozy reading nooks and living-room-like couch-and-table areas took up most of the middle space. Against one wall was a stand-up piano; Amy already sat behind it playing a song I didn't recognize. Quentin had grabbed the guitar from the lobby and was jamming along, nodding and tapping his foot to the rhythm. Nobody was singing yet, but I assumed that was because no one wanted to be first.

Penelope and I sat together on a love seat, chatting with Dylan and a couple of the PAs. Her thigh brushed mine sometimes when she moved, and I had to cross my legs to hide how it affected me. She had changed into a skirt, which, if we were alone, I could just flip up and—

"You okay, man?" Dylan asked. "You got a funny look on your face."

Whoops. "My face always looks funny," I joked. "It's the mustache."

He raised his eyebrows in an *if you say so* expression, then went back to paying attention to the conversation.

Yeah, this was not going to be easy.

Drinks happened, singing happened, and as Amy had requested, Penelope and I danced together. Slower at first, bachata moves, basic steps and turns. I kept it clean, didn't pull her too close with my hand that was on her waist, or let it slide down a little lower like I wanted. She really was a good dancer, and I hoped I wasn't making a fool of myself. Either with the dancing, or with the sappy smiles I couldn't avoid having every time I looked at her.

Then Amy played something faster, somebody whooped and shouted, "Dale!" and Penelope gave me a look that said it was on. She kicked off her shoes and went full pata sucia, and I went with her. We spun, I dipped her, we slipped in and out of each other's arms, and a few times our moves would have been a whole different kind of fun if we'd been naked and somewhere else. Eventually I tapped out to wash off some sweat and get a drink of water, watching as Penelope kept dancing her ass off.

"Hey," Quentin said, nudging my arm. "You should ask her out."

What should I say to that? Pretend nothing was happening?

"Yeah?" That was neutral, right?

"Come on, you two are a perfect pair! We've got bets going on how long it will take for you to hook up."

I couldn't tell him someone had already won the bet. It still felt weird, though, for people to think Leandro was perfect for someone when he wasn't real.

"Penelope deserves better than a hookup," I said.

Quentin's eyes got big, and so did his smile. "Oh? Sounds serious."

Ugh, rule two: don't break character. I pretended my arm hurt. "I hit my funny bone is all. The serious will stop once I can feel my humerus again."

"It's okay to be serious about some things," Quentin said. "Especially some people." And then he wandered toward the piano, accepting a drink from someone as he went.

It might be okay for me to be serious, but not Leandro. I had to keep things up for another week. And then what?

Oh, shit, then what?

Penelope bounced up, eyes shining. "Dance break over, let's go!"

I let her pull me into a turn, and then my body took over as I firmly told my brain to shut up and enjoy this while it lasted.

I STEPPED OUT of the elevator into the lobby, enjoying everyone's reactions when they saw what I was wearing. Some people rolled their eyes or shook their heads, but most of them pointed and laughed, which was the idea.

Little Manny came up to me first. "Bro, that is sick. How did you even find it?"

Sam had gone thrift shop hunting for weeks, eventually ordering my outfit online. "Magic," I said, wiggling my fingers at his eyes.

Today was our third field trip, to a cruise ship docked at the port. We wouldn't actually be sailing anywhere, but we'd get all the perks of being on board: fancy food, unlimited nonalcoholic drinks, live entertainment, and—unless I'd been lied to—a soft-serve ice cream machine. I was going to eat a truly obscene amount of ice cream.

I'd already warned Penelope about it earlier, in my room. She'd laughed and said we could have a contest, because she was sure she could eat more than me. I took that as a challenge, and also a double entendre, and pretty soon she was coming on my mouth.

Mmm. Maybe later we could . . .

"Oh my god, what are you wearing?" Penelope asked.

I turned around and had to stop my tongue from rolling down my chin like one of those old cartoon wolves. Her dress was that dark red with a name like burgundy or oxblood, and the swishy skirt stopped a little past her knees. Her shoulders were bare, her upper arms partly covered with sleeve-like bits that had to be decorative since they weren't holding anything up. The front curved and crossed over her chest down to her waist, which had me looking right at her perfect cleavage.

She had asked me a question. I tried to skip back to earlier in my brain-track, but the stream had frozen.

"You look like you're going to prom," she said. "In the seventies."

I found my Leandro grin somewhere and put it on. "What, you don't like it?"

"It's so . . . yellow. And the frilly shirt is so . . . frilly." She shook her head. "And we match. Again. How?"

"It's honestly a little creepy," Dylan said. He wore a much more normal light brown suit with a blue tie.

My bow tie was maroon, and the lapels of my jacket had maroon stripes along the edges. Not the same color as Penelope's dress, but close.

"Clearly it's fate, m'lady," I said, giving her an elaborate bow. "We were destined to be the best-dressed team this show has ever seen."

"This is the first time they've had teams."

"I said what I said."

Miami weather was its usual wet self, turning the street into a mess of puddles under the gunmetal-gray sky. No party bus to transport us this time, just regular vans with cast and crew piled in. I probably should have gone with the other celebrities, but Penelope was a fridge and I was a magnet. And honestly, I felt way more comfortable with her group than mine.

Sam would probably say that meant I should spend even more time with the stars, so I could get used to it and network. I couldn't bring myself to care right now. I'd have plenty of time to be in their space on the ship.

Traffic to the port hadn't hit rush-hour nightmare yet, but it still took us a while to make it down Biscayne, partly because the rain turned driver brains into mush. As if it wasn't like this every other day. Then we had to sit through a security checkpoint, where dudes with radios and guns checked whatever paperwork Rachel pulled out of her messenger bag. Finally they waved us in and we drove past a line of empty docks and parked ships to the one waiting for us.

I'd never been on a cruise ship before—my parents preferred resorts. The *Argent Siren* towered above the parking lot, white and gray and shiny, easily twenty times as big as our hotel. It had to have thousands of rooms, and I counted ten decks above the silvery bottom part. So many balconies.

We were hustled through an area similar to an airport terminal, across a tunnel and into what felt like a combination hotel and shopping mall. It was two stories high, with a marble tile floor and thick wooden columns leading up to a fake-skylight ceiling. A massive sculpture of a hibiscus flower lit one end of the room, its stamens sending out a slow stream of glowing magic bubbles that drifted across the space, bursting into silvery glitter.

"Ours was cooler," Penelope whispered.

"No, it wasn't," I replied.

"It super was not. Can you imagine having the time to make something like that, though?"

"And the materials. It must have cost a bazillion dollars."

We silently did the math and shook our heads together. In our dreams. Though, if we won, maybe Penelope would have the chance.

Rachel and Little Manny hustled to get all of us in and out of hair and makeup. Since we were all in fancy dress clothes, we got similarly fancied up compared to our usual show looks. I wondered if they'd do a classy version of the anime eyeshadow and double buns they kept giving Penelope. When she got out, though, she looked . . . wow. Sort of a half-up, half-down hairstyle curled down her back with strands on the sides of her face. They'd done sparkles around her eyes in gold, and a bit around her lips, too, which were dark red to match her dress.

I could almost pretend we were on a date, heading to some event together as a couple instead of temporary partners. Then again, my pretend date would involve me wearing a nice suit or tux instead of this yellow nightmare.

"Do I look less waifu?" Penelope asked.

"Totally," I said. In her ear, I whispered, "I'd still use you for a body pillow, though."

She blushed and smacked me, and I grinned.

We were led into a huge dining room, three stories high and full of tables with everything laid out like we were going to eat. Since they'd just done our makeup, I found that hard to believe. The camera crews had positioned themselves in a few places, but we hadn't been miked yet. After we found our assigned seats, Tori clapped to get our attention.

"Meals are going to be brought out," Tori said. "They're not real. Don't touch them. Look excited and hungry." She looked straight at me. "Seriously, do not touch them."

I raised my hands, palms out.

It went like she said. Servers put extremely delicious-looking things in front of us, but they smelled like . . . yuck. Vaseline and hair spray? I didn't pretend to eat anything, but I did do a couple of spinning tricks with my butter knife that Nate caught on camera.

After that, we were scooted into the casino, all dim mood lights and bright, blinking machines chiming and jangling like a toddler band. It smelled like bergamot and tobacco, though I was pretty sure smoking wasn't allowed except in the clearly designated cigar room.

Syd played slots, their face painted in flashes of greens and purples and yellows. Hugh, Dylan, and Zeke sat at a blackjack table for a round. Fabienne and Doris were handed bingo cards with a bunch of spots already marked, and Doris had to pretend she'd won.

Charlotte and Felicia stood at the roulette wheel with piles of chips in front of them. Tori made Felicia lean forward to put chips down several times, and judging by the camera location and the deep cut of her dress, anyone watching later would get an eyeful. Maybe it wasn't as bad as it looked from my angle, but I wasn't optimistic.

Penelope and I were sent to a poker table, and they handed me a deck of cards.

"Do a trick," Tori said, crossing her arms and staring at me.

I tried not to feel like a trained dog as I warmed up with some one-hand single cuts, then multiple cuts, then two-hand shuffles. By the time I'd worked up to table flourishes, she was about to stop me, but I held up my hand.

"One more," I said. Then I boomeranged a card toward the camera and caught it when it came back, winking at the lens.

"Perfect," Tori said. "All right, moving along."

We clapped for acrobats whose enchanted costumes changed colors and moved in counterpoint to their twists and leaps. We sat at a bar and pretended to drink magical cocktails that sent up spirals of smoky images to match their flavors. We banged each other around in bumper cars. Dylan and I took off our jackets and had a rock-wall-climbing race. It was like a speedrun through all the stuff on the ship, though it took at least four hours. Through it all, Penelope and I laughed our asses off, even when it was totally fake — sometimes especially when it was fake, because now we could enjoy how ridiculous that was together.

Finally they led us to one of the smaller restaurants, where actual food awaited us, along with the eliminated contestants, a string quartet, and a bunch of strangers. They were all dressed up, too, in fancy tailored suits and dresses from stores I didn't even glance at when I passed them. Their haircuts looked expensive, and unlike us, they seemed to be using a combination of makeup and glamour for that extra chicness level.

"Who are they?" Penelope asked.

I shrugged. "No clue."

Isaac strolled in, wearing a tuxedo whose fabric twinkled like it was covered in diamonds constantly catching the light. I couldn't decide whether it was tacky or incredible. His hair seemed sculpted, and his beard had been trimmed into a goatee that made him look satanic.

"Hey, everyone," Isaac said, grabbing a glass of champagne from a passing waiter. "It's time for our midpoint mixer, as we like to call it. You all get to rub elbows with important people in the industry, and I get to drink on the company dime."

Some people laughed politely. Tori's face did that statue thing I realized was her version of wincing.

Next to me, Penelope tensed. I squeezed her hand, and she squeezed back. This was a big deal for both of us, potentially. She needed a job, and I needed to raise money for AKSAM. Forget sitting together in a van; this was where the real networking would happen.

"Eat or mingle first?" I asked.

"I don't know," she said. "I'm starving. Will it be more embarrassing if my stomach growls in the middle of a conversation, or if I anxiety-barf on someone?"

"Barf for sure."

"Mingle first, then."

Neither of us moved.

"Should we go together?" I asked. "Or do we not want to seem too . . ."

"Couple-y? Arm candy?"

"Exactly, Jelly Bean."

"Don't start with me, Gummy Bear."

We grinned at each other. Someone cleared their throat and we both jumped.

"Penelope," said Charlotte Sharp. A champagne glass dangled from one hand, but it looked barely touched. "We haven't had much time to chat. Let me introduce you to a couple of people."

Yes! I shook my internal fist at the sky triumphantly. Penelope would probably do the same later, but right now she looked shocked.

"Unless you're busy?" Charlotte asked, raising a perfectly plucked eyebrow at me.

"She's extremely not busy," I said. "I'll catch you later, partner."

I gave her a double thumbs-up as I backed away . . . straight into Tanner.

"Whoa, nelly," Tanner said. "How many have you had already, son?"

"Nada nada, limonada," I replied. "Just trying to do Penelope a solid."

We chatted until he drifted away, and I watched the patterns of the crowd as groups formed and dissolved. I was supposed to be networking, but instead I was, I don't know, vibing? The music was nice, and some of the glamours people wore were interesting; I mentally invented recipes for a few of them as I grabbed appetizers off passing serving trays.

A gray-haired man in a toned-down charcoal suit came up to me. The low lights reflected in his glasses made it hard to see his eyes.

"Mr. Presto," he said. "Happy to catch you alone. Could I persuade you to join me in a more private venue for a quick chat?"

"Sure, Mr. . . . ?"

"Jones," he said. "Robert Jones."

I followed Mr. Jones to a small table with two chairs in the corner of the room. A single flickering candle lit his angular face from below; honestly, it was a little creepy.

"I'll get straight to the point, Mr. Presto," he said, clasping his hands together and leaning forward. "I have an offer I think you'll find lucrative. For your charity, specifically."

"Oh yeah?" I smiled, trying not to seem too eager. "Alan Kazam's Schools Are Magic is a really great organization, and we're always looking for new donor support at whatever level you can manage."

Mr. Jones smiled without showing his teeth. "I'm glad to hear that. I represent an anonymous donor who is interested in offering you a sizable contribution."

"That would be amazing!" Tone it down, Gil. "What are you—or your donor—thinking?"

"We're prepared to hand you a check for fifty thousand dollars tonight."

Did he hear me inhale and forget to let it out? If not, my shocked face probably said it all.

"That's extremely generous," I said. "Thank you so, so much."

"Of course. Anything for the children." Mr. Jones shifted, the candle's flame reflected in his glasses. "There is one small proviso, but I don't think you'll find it particularly objectionable."

For fifty grand, I'd strip off my tux and dance on the table. "Sure, what is it?"

"Given that the show's prize is double what we're offering, I'm sure you understand that we want to ensure our donation goes to a truly needy cause."

"Right." What was he saying?

"If you were to win the competition, you wouldn't need us."

Was he implying . . . "So this only happens if my team loses?"

Jones didn't answer. He just smiled.

This was a bribe. He was trying to bribe me to lose on purpose. Holy shit.

"Who did you say was your donor?" I asked.

"Anonymous. But if you're amenable, I'll hand over this little slip of paper here." He pulled a check out of an inner pocket of his suit jacket and showed it to me. It was made out to the charity, and the amount was what he'd promised.

"If I say I need to think about it?"

"I'm afraid this is a onetime offer. Now or never." He held the check over the candle's flame, high enough for it to be safe, but the threat was clear.

"What if I take that now and win the next round?"

"We'll stop funds. The charity might even be accused of fraud, which would be quite the scandal."

Fucking fucker. "And if I say no?"

"I walk away, and you won't hear from me again." Jones pushed his glasses up his nose. "I cannot promise there won't be other repercussions. Quiet gossip reaching influential ears. Perhaps even bad press. Donors can be fickle."

Blackmail, too, huh? Great. Part of me was scared, but the rest was pissed off. A lot of people busted their asses for the charity, and this douchebag sinvergüenza wanted to wreck it over a TV show competition?

Not to mention that Penelope was counting on me. I'd come into this figuring I wouldn't get far, wouldn't win the grand prize, would take the minimum and be glad. Penelope, though? All that money and a year to cast whatever she wanted? It would change her life.

We still might lose in the next round, but if I took this deal, it would be a guarantee. Clearly someone thought we were a threat, or they wouldn't be trying to bribe me. Probably.

Definite money now, or possible money later? Sell out or stay in? Why did it feel like I was back in the casino, trying to decide whether to put chips down on red or black?

What would Grandpa Fred tell me to do?

"Do you honestly think you have a chance to win?" Jones asked, letting the check drift closer to the candle. "Be reasonable, Mr. Presto. Let's not make this difficult."

Was he reading my mind? Nah. But he did make my choice easier for me.

"I'll take it," I said, holding out my hand.

Mr. Jones passed me the check. "A pleasure doing business with you."

"Oh, we're not." I smiled. "I just wanted to have the check as evidence in case you thought blackmailing me or the charity later would be a good plan."

His smug expression vanished. "Is that so?"

"I mean, I could take this straight to Isaac and see what happens. He's already threatened us with lawyers about thirty times, so I have a feeling he'd freak out and go after you with one of the enchanted ice sculptures."

"It would be your word against mine."

"Does he know you? Are you on the guest list? Will he be able to figure out who your anonymous donor is with a truly basic amount of research? These are all questions you could have asked yourself before you threatened me, but apparently you decided I wasn't smart enough to think it through."

Jones stood. "I believe we're finished here."

"I believe we are. One more thing, though."

"What?"

"Smile, asshole."

Jones turned just in time for the roaming event photographer to snap a picture of us together, with me holding up the check. Busted. I wished I could bottle the salty-ass look on his face to enjoy it again later. Without another word, he disappeared into the crowd.

"Hey," I said to the photog. "If you pass me a copy of that pic, I'll give you a free sub to my channel."

I didn't wait for him to say yes; I had a shithead to catch. Jones scooted around the edges of the party toward the exit. He didn't stop to talk to anyone, but he paused in the doorway, turned, and made a throat-cutting gesture. I followed the direction he was looking.

Unless I was wrong, he'd aimed his signal at a small group by a moving ice sculpture of a ballet dancer going through an elaborate routine. I only recognized three people there: Penelope, Charlotte, and . . . Felicia, who was facing the door.

It could have been a coincidence. After everything else that had happened, I doubted it.

CHAPTER 19

Penelope

The high from spending so much of the mixer with Charlotte kept me floating through the rest of the party, all the way back to the hotel and in the shower and when I was snuggled under the covers in bed. And then, of course, it immediately turned into me overthinking everything I said and did, trying to figure out how badly I'd embarrassed myself.

Knock, knock. Who? Gil? I jumped up to get the door.

Gil, still in Leandro disguise, slipped in and gave me a quick kiss. "We need to talk."

"Okay." He sounded really serious.

He slumped into my desk chair and took off his glasses, rubbing his face. "Shit went down earlier. I didn't want to wait to tell you, just in case."

The next few minutes were a roller coaster of emotions. If I could have found the dude who threatened a charity for kids, I might have done violence in the form of cursed dolls that couldn't be traced back to me.

"You're sure he was looking at Felicia?" I asked.

"Not a hundred percent, but it was either her or Charlotte."

Couldn't be Charlotte. "Fuck."

"Double fuck. We have to be super careful tomorrow."

"Did you get the picture?"

Gil held up his phone. "It's in my email. And I still have the check."

"Felicia is probably going to try something since her minion failed."

Gil grinned. "I love it when you say things like 'her minion failed' like you're some kind of spy."

"You're the one having meetings with shady dudes trying to bribe you! I cannot even with this."

He could have sold me out. His charity needed the money, and we totally might get cut the day after tomorrow. Instead, he told the guy to fuck off and got evidence. Dios mío. And I hadn't even told him . . .

"I might be homeless in two months," I blurted out.

"What?" Gil jumped out of the chair. "Are you serious?"

"My landlord is raising my rent and I don't have a job. I'm seriously fucked. Unless."

"Unless we win. Or Charlotte hires you."

Was I that obvious? "It doesn't have to be Charlotte."

Gil hugged me and kissed my head. "You want it to be, though."

"She's so cool!" I groaned. "But what I'm saying is, thank you for not doing the thing. Not that I would expect you to, but I know how important this all is, and if we don't win, then—"

"Oh, we're going to win. We're going to win so hard, people will beg you to work for them."

"And throw money at Alan Kazam for the kids." I paused, thinking. "But what about you? What do you get from all this?"

"Subscribers, hopefully. Advertisers." His grip tightened, pressing my face against his chest. "Possibly my own show? On TV, not just online."

He didn't sound excited. "Do you want your own show?"

"Who wouldn't? Get rich, get famous, live that fantasy."

I put together everything I knew about Gil, the sweet blogger and pen pal, with what I'd seen of Leandro Presto, happy himbo magic disaster, and came up with a puzzle whose pieces didn't fit. But it was late, and we had to be up early for round three, so I didn't push.

Wrapping my arms around his neck, I went up on my tiptoes and kissed him. Not a sexy kiss, not a *let's get it on* kiss. It was a *things will work out* kiss, a *we're in this together* kiss. An *I see you and you're already enough* kiss.

I don't know if he picked up on any of that, but he kissed me back the same way. When we stopped, he rested his forehead on mine.

"We should get some rest," he said.

"We should."

"We're going to crush it tomorrow."

"Abso-fucking-lutely."

He kissed me again and I walked him to the door, backward, still holding him. I slid my hands down his chest, then pushed him gently away.

One more kiss.

One more.

"Pero, like, for serious," I said. "You need to go."

Gil gave me a wicked grin that was pure Leandro. "Are you sure?"

"No. Yes. Come on, we're not horny teenagers; we can control ourselves for two days."

"Two days," he agreed. "And then, pants party."

A lot could change in two days. We would make sure it changed for the better.

"THREE TEAMS REMAIN," Syd said. "Who will proceed to the final round, and who will magically disappear back onto the beaches of sunny Miami? Time to find out on today's episode of *Cast Judgment*."

They paused for a five count, then kept going. "After last night's fun on one of the ocean's most exciting cruise ships, I'm sure our contestants are ready to continue the celebration theme with our next challenge."

I was ready to sleep more, honestly, but I was also hyped. Nervous, yes, but not in the way I had been for the last two rounds. The difference was Gil. Knowing it was him, knowing I could trust him in ways that I'd been unsure I could trust Leandro, helped me relax. When he clowned around, I'd know it was for the show. When he drew a magic circle, I wouldn't stress over triple-checking it.

I'd still double-check, but that was just normal safety stuff.

I looked at him out of the corner of my eye. His pale blue shirt was covered in sailboats and clouds, with dolphins leaping out of inky waves. Of course he matched my apron, which was a darker blue full of mermaids casting bubbly spells while fish swam around. I guess we both wanted to go with the cruise ship theme.

"Today's brief," Syd said, yoinking my attention back. "The judges would like you to create two dozen party favors. They can be as small or as large as you'd like, as long as they're identical and impressive."

I'd only ever gotten favors at kid parties and weddings. This was going to be great. Not.

"You have two days to envision and enchant your miniature masterpieces of merrymaking. Your time begins . . . now!"

The clock on the wall started counting down from sixteen hours. Eight today, eight tomorrow, unless something went super wrong again. Hopefully the crew would be paying closer attention to everyone out of paranoia. I sure would be.

Spell design first. I pulled out my trusty notebook and pencil, flipping to the next empty page. It was easier now that I had a bookmark.

"Is that the queen of hearts I gave you?" Gil asked.

I blushed. "Yeah. For good luck." I didn't tell him I'd been carrying it around every day since the gardens.

Our first kiss. It would always be special to me, whatever else happened. We couldn't talk about that now, though.

"Penelope—" he started.

"Party favors." I wrote that at the top of the page. "Again, I wish my cousin Gina was available for consultations. Have you ever been to cool parties?"

"Not ones with stuff to take home," he said. "Besides leftover food or beer or, you know, those little bags of candy and toys?"

"My mom hated those."

"The plastic noisemaker things."

"And the clappers."

"So loud," we said together, then grinned.

I glanced at Charlotte, wondering what she and Felicia would be making. Something super sophisticated, probably.

At the party, she'd asked about my background and experience and career goals. It had felt almost like a job interview, or maybe the interview before the interview? I was trying not to get my hopes up.

"Maybe something with bubbles?" Gil suggested. "They had them at my cousin's wedding instead of rice."

I wrote "bubbles" on the page. "We can't do candles, or incense. Potpourri?"

"Soaps?"

"Chocolates?"

We both looked at Dylan and Zeke.

"Not chocolates," we said, again at the same time.

"They'd wipe the floor with us," Gil added.

"Bet." So what else?

Gil kneaded his neck. "Sorry, I'm struggling. It's hard to think of fancy stuff when I don't really do fancy."

"Yeah, same." I tapped the pencil on the table a few times, then stopped. "Why are we trying to do fancy?"

"So we can beat the other fancy people? Be impressive for . . . reasons?"

He meant me. He was trying to make me look good, because he knew I needed to advertise my skills. That had been the whole point of this, from when I first applied because Rosy twisted my arm. To get a better job, to stop working my ass off at Espinosa's for shit pay and shit treatment.

But this wasn't all about me. It was about Gil, too. He needed to look good so his charity would get donors. So he could get more subscribers and advertisers. He had a brand. Why weren't we leaning into that?

"Forget fancy," I said. "What would be fun? What kind of stuff would kids like?"

Gil's eyes got big behind his safety glasses and he grinned like I'd given him a present. Excellent.

"Piñatas," he said.

I wrote that down. "Yes, yes, yes. Ooh, they should like, pop on their own? Maybe in a cloud of glitter? Not real glitter, magic glitter."

"Easier than confetti, probably."

"Okay, but we have to put stuff inside the piñatas."

"Bubbles?"

"Hmm, what could the bubbles do?"

"Animal shapes!"

"Oh, that's good."

Gil leaned on the counter, close enough for me to smell his deodorant, which is what I'd finally figured out gave him that appley goodness. "It's too bad we can't make something that would let kids do their own magic. Nothing big, just something . . . flashy."

"Presto?" I finished.

"Yeah. Presto."

An idea kicked down my brain door. "We totally can. All we need is a closed gather-and-release loop."

"How can we do that twenty-four times, though?"

"We don't. We do it once and let the law of synecdoche do the work for us." I started sketching out my idea on the page, listing potential ingredients and steps.

"Ohh," Gil said. "That's genius. What spell are we going to enchant them with?"

"Dealer's choice. What do you think would be fun? What do kids love to see you do?"

"Fireworks," he said. "Fake ones, obviously."

"Perfect. What do we need for that?"

We jumped into planning with both feet. Recipe, reagents, timing . . . we made our step-by-step plan for both days so fast, it was like we were living in each other's brains. This time, though, we also quietly worked in space for Leandro Presto to do goofy stuff, including an apparent spell oopsie that would come near the end of the night.

I loved it. Everything felt good, and right. The rhythm we'd found in the other rounds beat stronger now.

We even managed to tag-team watching out for sabotage. Nobody got close to our spell without one of us noticing, especially not Felicia. I deployed my full retail *can I help you with something?* smile like a shield on Syd; Gil turned an almost-touch from Doris Twist into an adorable juggling act. Even when I explained what we were doing for the judges, I made sure they were standing several feet away from the casting circle Gil had drawn.

We weren't taking any chances.

By the time we wrapped for the day, both of us were exhausted, but all the piñatas were finished, and the raw materials had been prepped for the surprises inside. We'd even made extras and hidden them in a cabinet, just in case.

Dinner was short and sweet, all of us eating like machines and commiserating in vague terms about the day's struggles. Dylan had gotten a steam burn on his arm while making some kind of jam filling. Leandro had slipped on a piece of chalk and fallen on his back, ending up with flour all over his face—the fall was fake, the flour was real. No accidents for me, but my hands were raw in places from cutting paper for the piñatas. Gil claimed he had a lotion for that in his room, so we went to get it and spent way longer than we should have saying good night.

I slept better than I had in weeks.

BREAKFAST WENT FASTER than dinner. I scarfed eggs and toast while Gil made us both coffee to go. He waggled his eyebrows at me as he stuffed a banana in his pocket. I suggestively bit into a sausage, then realized that was not a sexy thing to do. Whatever, he laughed.

Round three, part two. Caffeinated, skin clear, crops watered, we matched in black, white, and orange today. Halloween apron for me, big flowers and random geometric shapes for him. Seriously, what were people thinking in the '70s?

First, we had to enchant a metric shit-ton of leather cord and a bowl of beads. The supply room had glass, wood, metal, and ceramic options, and we'd gone for the metal ones because they were more durable and would probably hold the enchantment better.

"This is going to work, right?" I asked.

"Law of synecdoche," Gil said, finishing the last line of a rune. "The spell will stay in the cord even after you cut it."

"I swear someone in a video said this was how they did it, but maybe my memory is—"

"The principle is good. It'll be fine. Trust the magic, and the magic will trust you."

Why did that sound familiar . . . "Did you just quote Alan Kazam at me?"

Gil grinned. "He knows what's up. Come on, let's get this done."

We joined hands and chanted, letting our intent and energy pulse into the circle at our feet. Wisps of my hair floated around my face, and tingles went up and down my arms, pooling where my fingers were twined in Gil's. A dim glow filled the runes and other figures, gradually seeping into the center of the diagram, then rising like a heat shimmer. Our chant reached its peak, and the spooled leather cord sucked in all the magic like a vacuum. The light faded, my hair settled, but we kept holding hands as we knelt down to examine our work.

"Feels right," Gil said.

"I think so," I agreed. "Now, the beads."

Those needed a different spell, so we stowed the cord, wiped away the chalk lines, and got ready to start a new circle. We took a quick lunch break first, Gil threatening me with the banana when I was mid-drink. I almost spewed soda out my nose.

"Malo!" I gasped.

"So you don't want my banana?" he asked innocently.

I put my drink down and reached for the bag of powdered chalk we used for the thick outer line of our circle. Dipping a finger in, I swiped some and aimed it menacingly at Gil.

"What are you—" he started to ask.

I drew a line of chalk down his nose. His eyes lit up and he went for the bag, which I tried to keep away from him. We wrestled and he got it away from me, grabbing a pinch and dragging it down the side of my face. Back and forth we went, until we were throwing puffs of chalk at each other as we circled our station, cracking up.

"Having fun, kids?" Syd asked. "Or is this all part of a spell?"

I don't know how I looked, but Gil had chalk smeared and splattered all over his black fake-silk shirt, and his mustache was dusted white like he was trying to make himself look older.

"Very important spell," Gil said.

I sneezed violently.

"Don't let me interrupt you," Syd said, and then they tossed a handful of confetti at both of us.

After I'd cleaned up the mess with a push broom, Gil and I worked on our second circle. This one required more of a mandala-like form, somewhere between Dee's mystic heptagram and Cosmati mosaics, so the beads could be incorporated into the design. It took forever to draw correctly since we had to use sand, in multiple colors. By the time it was done, my thighs burned and my lower back ached super bad.

It worked, though. We enchanted the beads, which seemed to take the magic without any trouble. Then it was time for me to step up. And sit down, thank goodness.

We cut the leather cord into strips, which I laid out in groups, along with five beads each. So many beads. I threaded them onto the leather, then slowly, carefully, wound the multiple cords together to form a single bracelet. Each one had a pair of slipknots so they would be adjustable, with the beads in between.

"Test it?" Gil asked.

I nodded, so nervous I couldn't talk.

Gil slid the bracelet onto my wrist and tightened it. So far, so good. I held my hand out with my palm down and took a deep breath. Then I turned my wrist so my palm faced up and said, "Presto!"

A burst of colored lights, like fireworks, exploded a few inches above my hand with a quiet popping noise. Another followed, then another, one per bead. After the fifth went off, they faded in a shower of sparkles.

"It worked!" I shrieked.

Gil laughed and grabbed my hands, and we jumped up and down like happy kids. I didn't even have to ask if it was secret handshake time. We spun into our dance, going longer than before, adding extra twirls for each of us before we blew it up. And this time, I once again yelled, "Presto!" and let the actual fireworks from the bracelet end the dance.

I wanted to kiss him. I couldn't kiss him. Not on camera. Oh, this fake flirting had gotten so much harder.

We weren't done yet. We still had to finish the bracelets, put them inside their piñata boxes. The judges might not be impressed, might think they were silly or childish. But we loved them, and we'd had fun making them, and that was worth whatever might come next.

The first few were awkward, but I found my rhythm. Gil stuffed them into their piñatas as quickly as I made them, sealing the papier-mâché containers with a quick murmured incantation since they were already primed.

About eight bracelets in, from the other side of the room, a loud crackle of staticky noise was followed by two voices yelling at the same time. One said, "Sugar!" and the other said something that sounded like "farkleberry"? Gil and I raced around the side of our station to see what had happened.

A platter of what looked like tiny radios steamed in the center of an elaborate circle of candles and mirrors. Knowing Dylan and Zeke, the radios were probably edible. They were also making weird hisses and squeals that made me want to stick my fingers in my ears.

Syd marched over, eyebrows jammed together like they were worried. Nate followed, camera rolling.

"Hey, guys," Syd said. "What seems to have happened?"

"It looks like something went wrong with the sonic enchantment," Zeke said. "I dunno, we gotta check some things."

"Will you have time to recast it?" Syd asked.

Dylan's dark skin looked grayish, his lips almost gone because he was pressing them together so hard. Zeke didn't answer, just shrugged.

Felicia had stopped what she was doing to watch the drama. Had she messed with their spell? She didn't look happy, or satisfied, or whatever I might have expected if her evil plans had worked. Instead, she seemed . . . worried? She went back to her work, which involved pouring herbs into small cloth bags I'd watched her sew the day before. I wondered what they did, magically speaking.

Charlotte hadn't even looked up. I wished I could be that focused.

I had to be, because I still had to make a lot of bracelets.

But unlike the other rounds, where spells had collapsed or exploded during the presentation at the end, there was still—I checked the clock—two and a half hours before time was up. My instinct to fix, to help, started a luchador wrestling match with my need to finish our work first.

"You're dying to figure out what went wrong," Gil murmured.

I was. "I shouldn't . . ."

"The person who called every botánica in Miami and Broward to find a reagent for a stranger is going to just let that go, hmm?"

Fine. "Ten minutes. Come and get me if I take longer."

"As mew wish, m'lady."

I'd be back sooner if they didn't want my help. Still, I had to try.

Gil took up a guard spot at the edge of our station as I crossed to where Dylan and Zeke were talking quietly. Fabienne watched me with a raised eyebrow.

"Hey," I said. "Do you guys want a hand?"

"We got it," Zeke said, rubbing his shaved head. The batch of tiny radios squealed as if to disagree.

"Are you sure?" I asked. "I'm pretty good at spell fixes."

Dylan nudged Zeke's shoulder. "She's legit. It's worth a shot."

After a quick look at their recipe, I couldn't see anything wrong. Just like Amy's. Asking whether Felicia had messed with their stuff was pointless; it had to be fixed either way. Unfortunately the music enchantment had been cast into the wet ingredients before the tiny cake radios were assembled, so they'd need an entirely different approach.

"What about candy antennas?" I asked. "You could enchant those and stick them on."

Dylan shook his head. "Not enough time for the spell to cook."

Fire burned under my skin, smoke filled my mouth, and I had to breathe through it all to say, "You could pressure-cook it."

Zeke clapped and pointed at me. "You really are a smartie, you know that? Pressure-cook it. I'll be damned. Haven't had to do a rush job in years."

"It's dangerous," I said.

But he was already off, doing the math and sending Dylan to grab the right pot from the storeroom.

Gil grinned at me when I got back. "I let you go for an extra two minutes. Did you fix it?"

"Maybe." Pressure-cooking wasn't guaranteed to work, but it was their best chance. Just like it had been ours. I'd messed things up for us before, but if this might save Dylan and Zeke's spell, make it a fair contest . . .

I glanced at Felicia, who shook her head at me. Of course she didn't care about fairness. She just wanted to win.

The timer counted down as I knotted one bracelet after another. My hands cramped; Gil massaged them. My neck hurt from bending over the counter for so long; Gil rubbed that, too.

"If your show doesn't work out," I told him, "you could get a job doing those five-minute massages at the mall."

"You think the tips are good?"

"For you, probably."

God, what was I going to do for a job when this was over? At least I was getting paid to be here. That would buy me a little time . . .

except I'd need more money for a deposit on an apartment, unless I could find a roommate . . .

"Worried?" Gil asked.

"Not about this," I said. "Come on, three more to go."

We finished with ten minutes to spare. The piñatas sat on the cutest plates I could find, in bright colors that mostly matched. We all took a break for dinner, only the judges and crew missing from the room. Even Syd stayed to eat and joke with us, telling stories of silly things that had happened in previous seasons of *Cast Judgment*.

Tori stealthed in at some point with Liam, who checked all our mic transmitters and mics. The rest of the crew wandered back and took up their positions, and before the caffeine from my last soda hit my brain, it was judgment time.

Felicia and Charlotte went first. Apparently what I'd assumed were herbs or potpourri was actually specially blended tisanes, lemon and lavender with a color-changing enchantment. Sticking out of the top of each bag was a stirring rod, which could heat or cool the tea depending on which direction you stirred. The temperature changed the tea color. Genius.

Or so I thought. I guess I wasn't fancy enough to know you could already buy this sort of thing in stores—Athame Arts stores in particular—and Hugh Burbank especially wasn't impressed by the enchantments being single-use. Charlotte took the critique well enough, but she and Felicia lost their polite smiles between the presentation pentacle and their station.

Dylan and Zeke were next. I held my breath, wondering how their rushed spell had turned out. The edible radios still hissed and buzzed, but they also played a few notes of what sounded like a tune from an old video game. They joked that it was intentional; the judges were not fooled, since they'd been told what to expect earlier. Still, major points for the delicious rum cake with mango and pineapple inside, and for how uniform they all were.

Finally it was our turn.

"Our spell is called 'Clap and Explode'!" Gil said, with absolutely no chill.

"We made miniature self-destructing piñatas with a surprise inside," I said.

"They don't actually explode, do they?" Hugh asked.

"No, no," I said. "You toss them up in the air and clap, and they'll pop open. If someone can't clap, they can just tear the leaf part off."

"And they're shaped like pineapples because?" Fabienne asked.

Gil grinned. "I like pineapples."

They each grabbed one and looked at each other, as if silently deciding who would try it first. Hugh shrugged and threw his above his head, quickly clapping before it started to fall.

The little papier-mâché pineapple burst like it had been hit with a stick, and the bracelet inside clattered to the ground. I cringed, hoping the metal beads hadn't bent and messed up the enchantment.

"This is what?" Hugh asked, picking it up.

"A charmed bracelet." I explained how it worked, trying not to feel like Hugh's green eyes were lasers putting holes in my head.

Fabienne and Doris both popped their piñatas and got their bracelets. By apparent mutual agreement, they all triggered the spell simultaneously, saying, "Presto!" in unison.

Every single bracelet worked perfectly. Five bursts of fake fireworks faded into showers of glitter. Fabienne even did it again, showing that it repeated.

They grilled us about how we'd made each component, how we'd handled the repeating, how many times we expected the bracelet to trigger before the enchantment wore off, on and on until they had nothing else to ask.

"The piñatas are certainly a solid choice for a party favor," Fabienne said. "I've seen various enchanted versions of the large ones, but I can't think of any in miniature. And you not only have those, but you also went above and beyond with a second spelled item inside instead of, say, simply candy. Well done."

Gil and I smiled at each other. Awesome!

"They're utterly charming," Doris said. "I can envision scores of children happily throwing them in the air and clapping. And as Fabienne said, the piñatas alone were excellent, but the bracelets are inspired."

Two for two! But Hugh was next.

He stared at us in silence for long enough that I had to fight the urge to grab Gil's hand. Fuck it. I did.

"These are exceptional," Hugh said. "You've melded form and function in a way that aligns with the original object, while adding elements of magic and whimsy. The bracelets are also quite the feat, and perfect for the child-centric approach you've taken here. Good work."

I waited for the criticism, and it didn't come. My mind exploded like a piñata. In a daze, I thanked the judges and went back to our station with Gil, still holding his hand.

We waited as the scores were decided. There seemed to be some disagreement, but it was hard to tell what about. Finally they finished and went back to their places. The camerapeople got their cameras ready, Tori retreated to her corner, and Syd took over.

"First," Syd said, "it's my honor to present the winners of this round. They definitely put the party in party favors, and their spells made the judges want to yell, 'Presto'!"

Oh my god. No way.

"This round's winners are . . . Penelope and Leandro!"

Leandro and I high-fived when what I wanted to do was scream and dance. Celebrating too much now would be mean to the other contestants, though.

If we'd won, who was going to be dropped?

"And now," Syd continued. "I'm sorry to say one team will be leaving us today. Both remaining groups did well, but had their troubles. Unfortunately, in the end, the judges decided that a well-executed but less inspired idea met the round's requirements better than a good idea gone wrong."

Oh no.

"Dylan and Zeke, you won't be joining us in the final round." Syd smiled. "But I'll be happy to dispose of the rest of your radio cakes personally."

Dylan smiled, and Zeke shrugged, and that was that. I couldn't believe it.

I knew it wasn't my fault, that I'd done what I could. And it wasn't about me, it was about them. But I couldn't help but wonder: Was this sabotage again? Had someone—had Felicia waited until it was too late for them to fix the spell, then somehow made it go wrong?

And if she had, what would she do to us in the final round?

CHAPTER 20

Penelope

When we got back to the hotel, Quentin grabbed Dylan and towed him to the bar for "commiseration and debrief," as he called it. Amy joined them. I almost went, too, but Gil kept sneakily grabbing my hip and giving me looks I classified as smoldering.

Three seconds after the door to his room closed, we were tearing our clothes off, and also each other's. I got a whiff of myself and decided I needed to shower first, to which Gil said, "Have you seen my shower? We both fit."

He was not wrong. The multiple jets were also enticing.

I did my best to scrub off the day's sweat and dirt quickly, but Gil kept helping me, for a particular definition of helping. I loved looking at his naked body, and with the water painting his skin, he was more delicious than usual.

I kissed his neck, tasting clean skin as I licked my way down. He palmed my breast, kneading it gently, then bent down to flick my nipple with his tongue, electric shocks of pleasure shooting through me. I moaned and pressed against him, my hand slipping down to grab his cock. He was already hard and getting harder. Gripping him tighter at the base, I stroked him and teased the spot underneath that I'd figured out was extra sensitive. He growled. Mmm.

My other fingertips traced the angular shape of his hip, the hard muscle of his thigh. He dipped a finger inside me, then another, as I stroked him harder. His thumb found my clit and caressed it, gently at first, then more firmly as I rode his hand. He sucked my nipple into his mouth and with only the briefest warning, I came, groaning his name as I shuddered and clung to him.

He left the shower just long enough to get a five-dollar vending machine condom. After rolling it on, he pushed me against the marble tiled wall and lifted me onto his hips. He slid his cock inside me, thrusting over and over, gripping my ass while I wrapped my legs around his back. Another orgasm started like a wave rising toward the beach, ready to wash over both of us. I came in a rush of pleasure that spiraled up through my stomach and down to my knees. Gil came right after me, still moving in and out slowly through the aftershocks.

The shower washed away any evidence of our fun. We rinsed off, dried off, and Gil finally got rid of his Leandro mustache. I hadn't even noticed it was there.

We crawled under the sheets of his bed together, still naked. Before I could even start to worry about whether I'd be able to fall asleep, I passed out. It wasn't until four in the morning that I woke up and realized where I was. The walk of shame back to my room didn't feel shameful at all.

It was one of the best days of my life.

THE DESGRAVES STUDIO took up a big corner in The Roads, where old houses were either fancy or falling apart. Condo and office buildings stuck up in random places, towering over the oaks and banyans and gumbo limbo trees in the median. We had to drive through downtown to get there, and what a hot mess of traffic that was. Our van driver got stuck behind the trolley at one point, and started quietly shitting on the hour he was born in Spanish until finally he was able to zip around the bus and move.

The studio itself had a wall around it, with enchantments built right into the bricks and a wrought iron gate that opened automatically. The building was a blend of old and modern, orange tile roof and limestone blocks and ivy on the outside, terrazzo floors inside sparkling with spelled gems, dark red-and-gray walls, and furniture straight out of some industrial glam catalog.

One of Fabienne's employees gave us the tour. He took us through the public gallery space, with current exhibits from two casters in residence along with pieces from previous students and instructors and others. An intricate mosaic by a Cuban-Syrian enchanter shifted as we passed, individual portions turning like gears within gears as ghostly flames danced across the surface. A carved wooden drum played itself, its echoes lingering so that the beats created their own syncopated rhythms and counterpoints, calls and responses. Last year's *Cast Judgment* winner had made tiny terrariums enacting the growth and death cycles of nearly a hundred plants, over and over, beautiful but immensely sad.

Nothing I'd ever made or imagined making could compare to any of this. My abuela's cookbook, the project I'd planned my imaginary residence around, felt super-boring and basic as I stood here. Part of me wanted to give up right then, accept that I would never be this good and just go home. The rest of me wondered if I could level up enough in a year to make something that could possibly sit next to any of these exhibits.

I could almost hear my abuela saying: *Intent and willpower are the most important ingredients, mija.* To which Rosy added: *Maaanifest!*

After the galleries, we went through the studio spaces. There were big group ritual areas with different kinds of basic casting circles inlaid in the floor, and smaller soundproofed rooms covered in chalkboard paint from top to bottom, and lab-kitchen hybrids filled with equipment ranging from ancient-looking cast iron cauldrons to elaborate arrangements of tubes and glassware. There were even multiple "clean rooms" that required ritual cleansing before entering and after finishing.

The stockroom that took up the entire second floor could have fit five Espinosa's inside, maybe more. They also had deals with not only Frogtail, but a bunch of local companies with warehouses all over the city, so almost anything could be delivered within twenty-four hours.

"You're drooling," Gil murmured as the guide explained the organization system.

"How are you not?" I asked.

"I didn't say I wasn't, I just said you were."

I elbowed him gently and he pretended to be mortally wounded. Felicia shushed us like we were children; I stuck my tongue out at her when she turned around.

The third floor held the lecture spaces, which consisted of one big hall plus smaller rooms with different seating configurations. One of the medium rooms, I knew, was about to host a performance by Leandro Presto for a public school field trip. The producers had apparently organized it in advance, because paperwork and red tape; if we hadn't made it to the final round, he still would have done it, but it wouldn't have been recorded and integrated into the last episode. Presumably Charlotte would be doing some charity-related thing, too, but I didn't know what.

"Nervous?" I asked Gil.

"Excited," he confessed. "It's been a while. I love seeing their happy little faces, and getting sticky hugs, and being told how awesome I am."

"That does sound nice." Jealous? Nah, couldn't be me.

"You should be my lovely assistant," Gil said. "We can get you a pair of safety glasses and a mustache, too."

I grabbed his arm. "Okay, but seriously? Could I? No mustache, but do you think I'd be allowed to help?"

"Probably? We can ask Tori, or Rachel, after the tour."

If I hadn't been bouncing before, now I was ready to pinball off the walls. I tried not to get my hopes up, because school stuff usually meant background checks and forms I hadn't signed, but maybe . . .

The tour ended in a small gift shop selling branded shirts and charms and other random stuff I absolutely could not afford. I almost got a fridge magnet because it was one of the cheapest options, but I didn't need a souvenir the way I needed that money in my bank account. Also, I'd already spent my tiny souvenir budget on vending machine condoms because we couldn't risk sneaking out of the hotel to buy them at a store.

Worth it.

We got a quick break right before confessionals. The tour guide stayed nearby to answer questions, so after I gave up on my magnet dreams, I talked to him. His name was Tyler, and he was more than happy to get poetic about how cool the studio was, how nice people were, how everyone encouraged each other, on and on. It sounded amazing, and I told him so.

Felicia had questions, too, but hers were about gallery space allocation, what kinds of events they hosted for residents, who attended those events, how long postresidency the pieces were retained, whether there was an in-house broker to handle sale negotiations and contracts, how rights were handled for spells designed on the premises . . . Super business-focused, and honestly, impressively sharp. I wondered if Charlotte had given her tips on what to ask, or whether she'd come in with that specific business knowledge.

Gil caught me in the hallway right before our team confessional. "Rachel says you can do the thing."

"Sweet!"

"I'll walk you through the spell. It's pretty simple."

The confessionals were in one of the small casting rooms. I let Gil talk about his charity through most of ours; it would pair well with his demonstration for the kids. Tori asked me about my feelings being in the studio, and I didn't have to pretend to be excited.

But then she asked me what I planned to do here if I won, and I totally froze.

"Take your time," Tori said. Her face told me to hurry up.

I swallowed all the words that had gotten stuck in my throat. Gil grabbed my hand and squeezed gently. It helped.

"My abuela, Perla, has dementia," I said quietly. "When she started to get . . . bad . . . she gave me her spellbook, full of recipes she'd collected or come up with herself. She used to . . . She studied magic theory in Cuba, in a time when not many women did, and she didn't get a lot of respect from the other students. She got her degree, and then she got married, and her career . . . She, um, didn't have one."

I could feel my face getting hot from the tears that wanted to come out. I tried to breathe through it.

"She taught my mom and my aunts how to cast, and then she taught my sister and me. I spent so much time in her kitchen, and her garden, and she had a little casting room that was basically just a corner of the garage. We had so much fun together, and I learned so much. I want to . . ." I swallowed again, swiping at the tear that had rolled down my face. "I want to translate her spellbook, and cast all the spells. See how well they work, and maybe experiment with some of my own changes to them. I even thought maybe it would be cool to write about it and publish a recipe book. So other people can try her spells, too."

There was more I could say, maybe even more I wanted to say, but the words wouldn't come out anymore. Just tears.

Gil kept holding my hand, and I knew it was all he could do since we were only supposed to be flirting. I couldn't even look at him. I stared at the floor and wished it would swallow me.

Then he made a little noise, like a frustrated growl, and he pulled me into his arms. I hid my face in his ridiculous orange shirt, with its weird red ink blots, and I sniffled and tried not to get mocos on him.

"Should I stop rolling?" Nate asked.

"No, this is good, keep going," Tori replied.

Gil's arms tightened. "Come the fuck on, Tori."

I pushed away and fumbled for my backpack, pulling out a pack of tissues. Head down, I blew my nose and wiped my eyes.

"Sorry, Penelope," Tori said. I couldn't tell if she was serious. "I thought you were giving us drama for the show. We've got enough for the segment; you can go."

I nodded, struggling with a raw throat as I breathed through my mouth. Gil helped me up and we left the casting room.

"I can't believe she thought you were faking," he grumbled.

"We agreed to fake other stuff," I said quietly. "She probably thinks we're doing a great job with that, so why not this?"

Gil shook his head, lips pressed together like he was keeping what he wanted to say inside.

"Thanks," I told him.

"For what?"

"For having my back." I gave him a watery smile. "I'm going to wash my face so I can get made-up again before it's kid time."

"I'll go prep, then. See you in a few." He gave me a one-armed side hug and left.

Signs directed me to the bathroom, which was the same old-new fancy as the rest of the place. Copper sinks, granite counters, big stalls with actual doors and walls that went all the way to the floor. A pair of padded plastic chairs and a table took up one corner, so I dropped my backpack there while I splashed water on my red eyes and nose.

It took a lot of cold water to get the color and swelling under control, and even then, I had a feeling makeup would be extra necessary for skin tone purposes. Fina might even have to use a charm . . .

The door opened. I flinched and splashed water on my shirt. Great. Was there a hand dryer?

To make my embarrassment complete, Charlotte walked in. Looking perfect, as usual, in a silk shirt and pencil skirt.

"Penelope," she said in her musical voice. "I'm so glad I ran into you. I wanted to have a private chat after the other night."

In the bathroom? "Oh?"

"Your performance in the semifinal round made a decision for me." She sat in one of the chairs, lounging back with her knees together, as if we were in some private club or office instead of the pee room. "I'd like to offer you a position at Athame Arts, in our Miami location."

A job. Oh my god. I was saved! The rest of my life flashed in front of my eyes like a near-death experience, except it involved a real apartment, my student loans finally being paid, and a bank account with four digits in it.

"What position?" I asked. Please don't say sales.

"We can work out the exact details after the show is finished filming," Charlotte said. "I'm willing to be flexible, to ensure you're in a role that you find fulfilling."

"That sounds amazing." Should I ask about money? It had to be more than Espinosa's.

"Our salaries are quite competitive, in case you were wondering."

Could she read my mind?

"I can have a contract for you to review by later tonight if you're interested."

"Yeah. Sure. Thank you."

"There's one small condition," she said. "For your own benefit, of course."

"Oh?"

"If you do win the competition, you'll be stuck here in your residency for a year. I'm afraid the company can't be expected to wait that long for a new hire to start."

Charlotte smiled, baring her teeth in a way that suddenly reminded me of a shark. It was the cold eyes.

"So this offer is only if I lose?" I asked.

"In a manner of speaking."

No, I'm pretty sure that's exactly what she meant. Worse, actually. "You're asking me to lose if I want to work for you."

"I wouldn't dream of saying any such thing," she said patiently. "That would be illegal, not to mention a violation of our respective contracts."

She wouldn't say it, but she would sure as hell imply it. And I needed the money. Whether she knew my life or was just guessing didn't matter. I was sinking, and she was throwing me a boat.

Was there a downside to accepting? If we lost, she wouldn't know whether it was on purpose or not. I'd have a job, and she'd have what she wanted. If we won, she'd tear up the contract and . . . Wait.

"I assume there would be some clause that would cause me problems if I won after signing it?" I asked.

"That would be prudent," Charlotte said. "It wouldn't be quite as you describe; more of a . . . penalty for early termination."

Was that even legal? In Florida, probably. Our labor laws sucked.

"I'll have to think about it," I said.

"I'll have the paperwork brought to your room later," she replied. "I'll need an answer by . . . let's say midnight, Cinderella."

"Okay."

Charlotte stood gracefully and smoothed her skirt. "So good to chat with you again, Penelope. I know you'll make the right choice." She paused near the door. "A word of advice, from one career-minded woman to another."

"Yes?"

"Stop throwing yourself at Leandro. It makes you look desperate, and he's not exactly a winner. You'd be better off trying for Isaac if you want to sleep your way up." With another dead-eyed smile, she walked out.

I stared at my reflection. Apparently, to Charlotte fucking Sharp, I was a sucker. And that comment about Isaac? Gross. Was she wrong, though, about me looking desperate? I'd thought this might happen when we started fake flirting—

A toilet flushed, making me jump and shriek.

A stall door opened and Felicia came out, her lips scrunched together like she'd sucked on a lemon. She silently click-clacked her high heels to the sink and washed her hands, then dried them with the air dryer. I stood there, unable to speak while the motor roared and then died.

Felicia got halfway to the door, stopped, then turned around. Her fists clenched and unclenched like she was fighting herself.

"Watch your back," she said. "Charlotte has been trying to get me to sabotage people since the show started. I told her I wouldn't, and she said I needed to put on my big-girl panties if I wanted to win." Her lips curled up in a sneer. "I said if I wanted underwear tips, I'd ask my personal stylist, not a washed-up CEO trying to avoid a hostile takeover."

A what? "What do you mean, washed-up?"

"Her company is a hot mess. She expanded too fast in the last couple of years, tried to start a few trends that didn't catch on, tried to follow some that were over by the time she got there." More details came spilling out of Felicia, stuff I didn't know about because I didn't follow the right gossip, apparently. All I'd seen was Charlotte's public face, the glam stories and the hype.

Exaggerated. Fake. Word by word, Felicia took a sledgehammer to the statue of Charlotte Sharp I'd put on a pedestal, until it was lying in pieces on the floor of my brain.

"Has she been sabotaging people's spells?" I asked.

Felicia shrugged. "I never saw her do it. I don't think she'd want to get caught. She might have tried to bribe some of the others, though."

"Like me."

"Like you." Felicia looked down her nose at me, which wasn't hard since she was a half foot taller barefoot. "Your clothes say you desperately need money, but if I were you, I wouldn't trust that witch. She'll hug you with one hand so she can stab you in the back with the other."

I grimaced. "Thanks for the tip."

"Whatever. It's your life." With a flip of her hair, Felicia left.

My emotions swirled inside me like hurricane winds. Anger, disappointment, frustration, exhaustion . . . Charlotte was probably the one who'd sent that dude with the check to Gil, too. I had no idea how we could prove it, and did it even matter? Only if they tried something in the final round, I guess.

I'd talk to him as soon as I could. But first, spell time.

I almost decided to duck out of the demonstration. He'd understand. How was I supposed to get up the energy to be fun with kids after the confessional and that little conversation?

No way. I wouldn't let anything or anyone ruin this for me. Not Charlotte, and not Felicia, though unfortunately I had to admit that she had been annoyingly helpful just now. Unless she was lying? But I didn't think so. She didn't get anything out of it. She could have walked out and let me make bad choices, and she would have won the contest for sure. Instead, she'd set me straight.

Ew. I didn't want to feel grateful to her. One good deed didn't change that she was an asshole.

"You're going out there right now," I told my reflection. "You're going to have a good time, and make kids laugh, and teach them magic. Then you're going back to the hotel and fucking a hot guy's brains out. Okay? Okay."

Was I really the same person who'd spent years letting my boss make me feel like a loser? Was this what growing a spine felt like? I stood up straighter and gave myself a high five, because I'm a giant dork, and then I went to get my makeup fixed.

My abuela would have been proud.

THE CHATTERING AND squeals of the kids echoed down the hall as I followed Rachel to one of the lecture rooms, my face and hair repaired. As soon as I stepped inside, I saw Gil kneeling, surrounded by tiny people, kindergartners if I had to guess. He was doing a card trick, and they were totally freaking out . . . Aha! He'd "lost" a card, except it was stuck to the back of his head. Every time he turned around to look for it, the kids saw it and screamed, and he acted more and more confused as he spun in circles like a dog chasing its tail. Finally he pulled the card off and showed it to them, apparently shocked. Then, so smoothly I wasn't sure if it was magic or sleight of hand, he made an identical card appear from behind a little girl's ear. She grabbed his hand and jumped up and down as he grinned at her.

He looked so, so happy. Like he was exactly where he should be, doing what he should be doing. I loved it. I loved . . . him?

Holy shit, did I?

How could I tell the difference between love and lust? Or a hardcore crush? Between something that would keep going and growing, and something that would fizzle out fast like a mediocre enchantment?

I'd known him for months, and yet in some ways I'd only really known him for a week and a half. Less if you didn't count the time I thought he was just Leandro Presto. Logic said that wasn't enough time for real feelings to develop. But since when were feelings logical? Who said you had to know everything about a person before you were allowed to love them?

Didn't we all have mysteries and secrets that lived inside us, and wasn't discovering them part of the joy of a relationship? And even if we went as deep as we could go, found everything there was to find, couldn't we still make new secrets together?

Gil waved me over, saying something to the kids as he pointed in my direction. A dozen faces turned the full force of their sunny smiles on me, and I could almost feel the darkness Charlotte had dragged me into vanishing from their sweet light.

"Miz Belelobe!" a little boy said, yanking on my arm. "Come on, we wanna see the magic!"

"Show us the spell, miss!"

"Mister Leandro said it's animal bubbles!"

"I wanna see a cat!"

"I have a cat!"

"I have a dog, miss. My dog's name is Ginger, and she's white and brown!"

They didn't stop talking the entire time it took me to cross the room. Gil held out his hand, and I took it, and together we faced the excited crowd.

If this wasn't love, I didn't know what else it could be.

CHAPTER 21

Gil

It was raining when we got back to the hotel. Mary, Isaac's assistant, waited for me outside the van under a giant umbrella, wearing a magenta dress and a deranged smile.

"Hey Mr. Presto how are you I'm great thanks," she said in a single breath. "Isaac wants to meet with you right now about the thing he talked to you about okay great!"

Penelope raised her eyebrows. "What thing?"

"I'll tell you later." I'd almost forgotten about it, honestly. So many things had happened since then, and Hollywood stuff seemed to be, as my abuela used to say, mucho ruido y pocas nueces—a lot of talk, but no action.

A black sedan drove me and Mary through the usual slow and shitty traffic to a parking garage off Brickell. It took me a few minutes to realize her dress was spelled to change colors; I thought I was losing it when I looked out the window, then looked back, and it was suddenly orange. Her lipstick had changed to match, too.

A valet opened the door for each of us. Mary led me through a long hallway paneled in enchanted wood to Stefania's Steakhouse. I knew of it because my dad took clients here sometimes, and my mom ate here with friends, hoping to run into him so she could show how happy she was without him. So mature.

The walls were all coppery wood, carved into intricate geometric designs spelled to absorb voices while amplifying the soft classical music coming from hidden speakers. The ceiling was more wood, the floors slate or gray marble. No cloths on the tables, just ingrained patterns that likely held enchantments to repel water and stains. Leather chairs, some with arms, some without, some those high-backed bucket-shaped kind. Instead of chandeliers, rippling curtains of light hovered in the air like brighter versions of the aurora borealis in a uniform yellowish white.

Isaac sat in a bucket chair across from a guy with thick black hair and icy blue eyes who looked about my dad's age, dressed like a TV mafioso. Fancy suit, thick gold chain, big gold watch probably enchanted to do a bunch of random stuff like repel mosquitoes, passively check for illusions, and summon his minions with a gesture. He flashed me his perfectly even white teeth as I sat next to Isaac, who dismissed Mary by flapping his hands at her.

"Leandro Presto," the man said. "A pleasure to meet you in the flesh."

"Likewise, Mr. . . . ?" I asked.

"Ricardo Noboa," he replied. "But you can call me Rick."

Isaac nudged me. "Rick is producing the show I was telling you about, the street magic one."

Yeah, I'd kinda guessed. "Isaac told me a little bit about it. Sounds cool."

"Cool. Yes." Rick raised a finger and a waiter appeared at his elbow. "Get the boy a menu and a drink."

I was twenty-eight years old, but okay.

"What can I bring for you, sir?" the waiter asked as he handed me a spelled piece of parchment—no, vellum. Menu items magically wrote themselves in elaborate cursive on the surface as I watched. None of them had prices.

I wanted water, but this felt like some kind of man test. I rattled off the name of some whiskey I'd seen at my dad's house. Male ritual complete, hopefully.

Rick tapped his glass with a big gold ring on his forefinger. Tap, tap. "I'll get right to it. We're putting together a new show for the network called *Magic in the Streets*, where the talent will walk around doing spells for random people. Sort of like what you do already."

Sort of.

"We think you have a good rapport with people," he continued. "It's one thing to talk at a camera or a studio audience, and it's another to be out there mingling."

"Totally different," I agreed. I wasn't sure I was as good at "mingling" as he needed me to be, but I probably wouldn't literally be running up to strangers.

"We want to bring you in for a screen test, but between you and me, you're at the top of our list." Tap, tap. "Isaac here is producing and showrunning, and he says you've been particularly . . . open-minded about certain requests."

I didn't like his smile. Not the one Isaac gave me, either.

"You and your little spice rack are really selling the vibe," Isaac added. "The high-five dance you came up with is great."

Did he just call Penelope a spice rack? Who does that? "That was both of us, actually," I said.

"No need to be modest. The girl isn't here." Rick brought his glass to his lips and took a swallow.

I swallowed, too, even though my mouth was dry.

"The point is," Isaac said, "you can upgrade from himbo to the smooth-Latin-lover thing."

Memories of his butt dance immediately came back to haunt me.

"It will be good for ratings to have you work your street magic on sexy women, is what Isaac is saying," Rick clarified. He gave me an appraising look. "We'd want to elevate your style. Nicer glasses, more expensive clothing. Less bumbling, more panache. Selling the illusion that if you approach someone on the street, after the cameras stop rolling, there is a potential for intimacy to follow."

"Magic in the streets," Isaac said, "magic in the sheets, know what I mean, eh?"

Wow. So the fake flirting with Penelope was getting upgraded to me going full fake man slut. Awesome. Toss rule number five out the window. Thankfully my drink came, and the waiter wanted to take my order, so I had time to plan my answer as I sipped expensive peat juice.

"I don't normally interact with fans that way," I said. "I try to be . . . respectful."

"We certainly don't want you to do anything objectionable," Rick said, his icy eyes narrowing. "That's how you get lawsuits. You'd simply be playing the same game you are right now, with a larger scope and for a substantially higher pay scale."

Except I wasn't playing, but they didn't know that, and I wasn't going to correct them. I didn't want either of these guys to connect me to Penelope in a personal way.

I froze with the whiskey partway to my mouth, then made myself finish the motion. A terrible thought was digging its way into my brain, a thought I'd managed to avoid since my last conversation with Isaac.

If I took this job, this show, I couldn't be with Penelope.

It was one thing to keep my life and Leandro Presto's stage presence separate when it was just online stuff, occasionally filmed live with fans. Rick wanted me to deliberately blur lines I'd drawn for my own safety and sanity, and do it publicly. And Isaac? He'd straight-up told me to hook up with different famous women to get press attention.

None of that would be fair to Penelope. Even if we were totally honest about it with each other, even if we both knew I was pretending the whole time, it would be a level of gross and fake that neither of us deserved.

The thought of letting her go now made my stomach hurt, along with the whiskey. But this was potentially a huge career opportunity. Was I really considering giving up fame and, more importantly, money, for love?

Was I in love with Penelope?

"I'm sure you have questions for us," Rick said, gesturing with his glass. "Don't be shy. What are you thinking?"

Questions. I'd better ask some normal ones. "Would we be filming here?"

Rick shrugged one shoulder. "We'd likely start in LA, since we have the crew on hand for it. Location shoots in tourist destinations seem reasonable, depending on tax incentives and other considerations. Miami, sure, Vegas, New York, maybe Atlanta or Chicago or Boston."

"Would I still be coming up with my own spells?"

"We have people for that, but you can be involved if you want."

I did want. That was most of what I enjoyed about *Mage You Look*. It definitely sounded like they wouldn't be hiring me for my brains. And speaking of my existing work . . .

"What would the time commitment be?" I asked. "I do still have my channel."

Isaac snorted, and the smile Rick gave me seemed . . . amused? Indulgent?

"You'll make more in a few weeks than you do now in a year," Rick said. "If you want to keep that as your little hobby, that's up to you. You'd have to be sure it doesn't interfere with network commitments, of course, which would include filming as well as publicity work."

"So this would mean a lot of travel, potentially," I said.

"Potentially. You'd want to relocate to LA, for convenience, which would also give you more opportunities for additional work in the area in the future."

If I took this job, Sam and Ed would have to work around my new schedule, whatever that looked like. Which would be especially tough if I wasn't even in Miami anymore. Would they want to move with me? Would *Mage You Look* be over? Probably. It would be too hard to keep it up.

Fuck, everything would change. Whether the show failed or took off, whether I ended up in LA permanently or came back to Miami within months, I'd be busting my life apart and I'd have to deal with whatever pieces were left when it was over.

I told myself to chill. Like Grandpa Fred said, everything in Hollywood was "yes, yes, yes" until it was suddenly "no." This might never happen. But every yes was a step away from where I was now, toward a future that looked nothing like my current normal.

The waiter brought appetizers. I'd gotten fancy smoked bacon, Rick had tuna tartare, and Isaac slurped back a half dozen fresh oysters so quickly it made me sick. He also consumed a truly disgusting number of martinis, which kept appearing and disappearing every few minutes. The staff never hovered or came by to ask us anything, but Isaac would wave his hand and they'd appear like magic.

Not actual magic, just really good customer service. It still felt weird to me, maybe because I was used to other ways. Felt like a metaphor for everything happening right now.

Another question occurred to me as I ate. "You said you're going to run this new show?" I asked Isaac. "What about *Cast Judgment*?"

Isaac sucked an olive off a bamboo toothpick, talking as he chewed. "It's toast. Circling the drain. Ratings are down, and we're replacing Doris Twist next season with someone else. Someone younger. Hotter."

Wow. Just . . . wow.

"Keep all that on the DL, obviously," Isaac added.

I nodded. The only person I'd tell was Penelope, because I told her things now.

Except I hadn't told her about this. There hadn't been a good time, and it had seemed like some potential far-off thing, and now I'd had two meetings about it in a week.

What would she say? What would she tell me to do?

Our entrees came only a few minutes after we finished our first course. None of us had gotten soup or salad, apparently. Filet mignon had sounded appropriately fancy, so that's what I'd ordered. Both Rick and Isaac got steaks, too, though Isaac's came with lobster tails. I didn't want to think about how much this cost. I wasn't paying, anyway. Was I? Oh, shit, I should have asked.

Too late now.

They talked about football and I pretended to care while I ate the best steak I'd ever had. No wonder my dad brought clients here. Bowls of side dishes sat in the middle of the table for sharing, but I wasn't sure I'd be able to fit anything else in my stomach. As it was, my guts were trying to climb out through my belly button from sheer nerves.

Fake smiles. Fake enthusiasm. Fake appreciation for expensive whiskey. Fake, fake, fake. The whole meal was a Leandro Presto performance from start to finish, but it was a Leandro I didn't even like because he let two skeezy dudes think he was one of them.

Was this a preview of life in LA? Did I really want that life?

Could I afford to turn it down?

A waiter brought the dessert menu, but I said I was too stuffed.

"Take something back to the hotel with you," Rick said, all mellow smiles and lazy gestures, like a lion who'd just finished eating a gazelle. "You could give it to your girl, maybe get a little dessert of your own if you play your cards right."

"Yeah, play those cards," Isaac said. "Strip poker, ha!"

Thank god Isaac wasn't staying at the hotel to see us sneaking out of each other's rooms, or he'd probably make worse jokes. As it was, his assumptions made me feel like I needed a shower. And not the sexy kind.

Penelope probably would like a fancy dessert, though. I checked the menu and spotted tiramisu. Perfect.

Mary appeared at the same time as the already-packed dessert, ready to take me back to the hotel. Rick stood, shook my hand, and slapped my shoulder.

"We'll be in touch," he said. "Good luck on the last round. Nice work choosing a kids' charity, by the way. Easy to root for those. Audiences love them."

It wasn't worth explaining anything to him. He wouldn't get it, and he'd probably think I was a loser for actually caring.

Not everyone in the industry was like this, I told myself as I watched the city pass in a blur of tinted-window golden hour traffic, holding the spelled box keeping the tiramisu cool. Part of me wanted to call Sam and Ed again, have another bar meeting, but honestly? The rest of me wanted to forget any of this had happened until the finals were over.

Penelope would want to know where I'd gone. And I wanted to tell her. I just . . . didn't know how. Not when she might tell me to go for it, when it would mean the end of us when we had only just started.

There had to be a solution, and I needed to figure it out fast.

TRAFFIC IN THE hallway outside Penelope's room was as bad as Biscayne. PAs heading up to the pool deck or down to the bar, Liam and Nate talking tech near the ice machine, Amy being dragged to the lounge by Quentin for more piano playing, Dylan quizzing me on what was in the box. Everyone knew the show would be ending soon, so these last couple of days were like the time before school let out for the summer, when people were signing yearbooks and swapping contact info and partying their way out.

Penelope opened her door on the third knock, and I presented the box to her with a flourish and a bow because people were watching.

"Sweets for the sweet, m'lady," I said with a grin that was more fake than real, even though I knew she'd be happy.

"Ooh, what is it?" she asked.

"Open it and find out."

She dragged me inside and closed the door, ignoring a few people whistling in the hallway. After what went down at dinner, it made me deeply uncomfortable. Maybe I should have stayed outside . . .

"Tiramisu! My favorite! Well, one of my favorites. Thank you." Penelope threw her arms around my neck and kissed me. I kissed her back—apparently not enthusiastically enough, because she pulled away.

"Are you okay?" she asked, frowning as she searched my eyes for clues.

"I'm . . . something." Staring over the ledge of my life and feeling like I was about to fall instead of flying.

"I'm something, too, but mine can wait. Tell me what happened with Isaac while I eat? Or—"

"Eat, yes." Where would I even start?

This time, she took the chair at the desk so she could use it as a table, and I sat on the bed, resting my elbows on my thighs. I needed to rip this revelation off like a bandage, even if I knew it would hurt.

I started with a repeat of why I'd come on *Cast Judgment* in the first place: charity money, yes, but also publicity and the hope of new advertisers and subscribers and possible job opportunities. Then I outlined the show offer, leaving out the fake-flirting angle even if it felt like lying by omission. At first, she was excited for me. Money, fame, money, more money . . . She knew how big a deal that was. The more I explained, though, about having to move and travel and possibly give up *Mage You Look*, the less Penelope ate, until she'd totally abandoned her dessert to watch me with a worried expression.

"That does sound like a lot," she said hesitantly. "But it all seems like a good opportunity? For your career?"

"Yeah," I said, smoothing my mustache.

Penelope sat next to me and took my hand. "You do that when you're nervous."

"Do what?"

"Mess with your fake mustache." She laced her fingers through mine. "Do you not . . . want a show? A bigger-deal one, I mean?"

It had sounded cool when Sam and Ed and I talked about it, way back when my agent—Grandpa Fred's agent—had first asked whether I would want to be on *Cast Judgment*. We'd joked about buying Leandro clothes from nicer thrift shops, replacing our busted coffee table with one that had four same-sized legs, having good booze instead of paint thinner that had to be mixed with something to be drinkable. A bigger apartment, new cars, all our student loans paid off. Red carpets, award shows, hiding in bushes from paparazzi.

We'd dreamed, but we hadn't really expected anything to happen. The idea of me getting an actual show offer was on the same level as the Cuban retirement plan: buy lottery tickets and hope for the best.

"Gil?" Penelope asked. "Are you worried about your brand or something else?"

So many something elses.

"Do you think you won't be able to do a good job?" She squeezed my hand. "You're awesome. You can totally hang."

She was being so careful not to say anything about us. Was she trying to be supportive, or did she not think we had a future together? Isaac and Rick definitely wouldn't want Leandro to have a girlfriend tagging along . . . not that she was, technically, since we hadn't talked about it . . .

Leandro couldn't even have a girlfriend! He wasn't real! He'd never take Penelope out to eat, or to see a movie, or to sneak-read books at the store because we couldn't afford to buy them. If someone saw Penelope with Leandro, and then with Gil, they'd either figure out who I was or they'd assume she was cheating on me. With myself. What a fucking mess.

I shook my head and laughed, but it wasn't a real laugh. It was dark and bitter, like day-old coffee grounds left in the cafetera.

"What are you thinking?" Penelope asked. "You sound . . . not good."

I wasn't. Had I said I was on a ledge? More like I'd dug a pit and fallen into it, and I desperately needed a ladder to get out.

I thought back to what I'd told Sam and Ed, about having to decide between the future Isaac wanted for me, where all my dating was fake or secret, or . . . something else. And I knew, finally, without a doubt, that I wanted something else.

I didn't want to have some fake life, with or without Penelope. I wanted her. I wanted us. We couldn't have that with Leandro standing in the way. He was a problem, and I had to fix it.

A sense of clarity settled on me. The fake dating needed to end. If it did, she and I could be together for real. That was the solution I'd been searching for. That's what we had to do.

I let go of her and stood up. "This isn't working. This thing we're doing. It was a mistake. A huge mistake."

Penelope flinched, and her face shut down. "Right. Okay."

She didn't get it. "People already think we're hooking up, and Isaac wants us to keep it up after the show airs, but it's going to be a really big problem for us later." And I wanted a later. I wanted a lot of laters with Penelope. For me, not Leandro.

"So you want us to stop," she said.

"I think it's better if we do, yeah. Before things get worse."

Penelope blinked, over and over, her face turning red. "I didn't think it was going that bad."

"Not yet. But after? We'd have to be so careful, all the time.

Sneaking around. Trying not to get caught, so we wouldn't get dragged on some gossip site."

She swallowed hard. "I guess. It all seemed easier before, when we first started. But you're right. It would be a mess. Especially if you get this show."

"Show or no show, you deserve better." I fell on my knees in front of her, grabbing her hands. "You deserve something real."

"I do," she whispered. "So do you."

I kissed her knuckles, feeling relieved. We still had to figure some things out, but this felt like a good first step. She could be just friends with Leandro, and then we wouldn't have to worry about weirdness later.

Penelope smiled, and I smiled back.

"You should go," she said, her voice raw. "So people don't think, you know . . ."

I extremely had not intended to leave yet, but . . . "Right. Yes. Good idea." It was only for a couple of days. We'd have plenty of time later to be together, in every way I'd imagined and ones I hadn't yet.

"I'll see you tomorrow," I said, standing up, still holding her hands. "You've got your lucky card?"

Penelope nodded.

"Then we can't lose. Don't worry. We've got this, Jelly Bean."

I gave her one last kiss on her cheek, quick and sweet, so I wouldn't be tempted. She walked me to the door without saying another word.

"Wait," I said, my hand on the doorknob. "There was something you wanted to tell me about?"

"Another time," she said. "You've been in here too long already."

True. "Tomorrow, then."

"Sure."

I was halfway to the elevator before I replayed that one word and realized she had sounded sad. Unless I was imagining things? Probably stress getting to me. I couldn't wait for all of this to be over, so we could finally start figuring out our life after *Cast Judgment*. Together.

CHAPTER 22

Penelope

One good thing about being in a hotel was that I could spend an hour in the shower, standing under the hot water while I cried myself into a super bad headache. Then I flopped onto my bed and cried some more, tried to distract myself with TV and failed, and got back up to stare at the thick envelope sitting next to the half-eaten tiramisu on the desk.

Charlotte had come through with the contract. She hadn't brought it herself—some assistant had given it to me, with the reminder that I had to return it before midnight.

Before Gil came back, I'd been completely sure I would turn down Charlotte's offer. Especially after what Felicia had said. I'd intended to tell him about it, to explain how I thought maybe she was the one who'd sent that dude after him with the check, to see what he thought and what we should do to prep for tomorrow.

Now?

It shouldn't matter that he'd ended things, but it did. I'd been so worried about winning when I'd seen Leandro Presto appear in the doorway as my partner on that first morning, but by round three, everything had changed. For a few wonderful days, Gil and I being a team in every way had made me feel awesome, unstoppable.

Dreams of a future with him had turned the intense stress of this competition into something sweet and magical.

And now that spell was broken. I knew how Quentin's busted automaton felt, like I'd been about to hang the moon and instead everything had fallen apart. I was Amy's phoenix egg gone wrong, burned into a pile of ash, never to rise again. My thoughts were the same painful static as Dylan's radios.

I pulled the contract out of the envelope and tried to read it. The words shifted and swam and blurred as if they were enchanted to be illegible, on top of being lawyer ninja language.

What did it even matter? I needed a job, and she was giving me one. This was the whole reason I'd come on the show, and now here I was, getting exactly what I wanted. Charlotte and I wouldn't be driving into the sunset in that imaginary convertible, but at least I wouldn't be hitchhiking down Alligator Alley in the dark.

Rosy would be happy for me. So would Emelia. As long as I didn't tell either of them about Gil, or losing on purpose, or how I almost wished I had never applied for this fucking show in the first place.

Could someone take secrets like this to their grave? Asking for me.

At least Gil would be okay without me dragging him down. What had he said? No sneaking around, no worrying about gossip. He could move to LA and get his own show and be super famous. Live that dream.

I wished I could hate him for dumping me like this, the night before the final round, but I couldn't. All I could do was drop a fresh round of tears onto my already-soaked pillow.

"Suck it up, Penelope Frances Delmar," I told myself. "Do what you have to do."

I washed my splotchy face for the second time in a day and signed the contract.

Quiet knocks at my door woke me up from stress dreams of Ofelia firing me and my mom sending me to live in a dark room in the basement she didn't actually have. I nearly fell out of bed trying to get up too fast, and went to see who it was through the peephole.

Gil.

"Yeah?" I asked, without opening the door.

"Just checking on you," he said. "Breakfast is almost over."

Shit. Of course I overslept, today of all days.

"I'll be right down," I said. Just had to throw some clothes on and go. Fina and Bruno could fix me.

"I'll save you a banana," Gil joked.

How could he be so cheerful? Maybe someone was outside and he was faking it for their benefit. Maybe he was honestly relieved to be done with me.

I felt like I had missed a step and fallen down the stairs.

People were already getting into vans when I finally made it down. Gil waited for me with a travel cup of coffee and a muffin.

"Thanks," I said, taking both. My stomach felt full of rocks, but I bit into the blueberry goodness anyway. Instant regret. Not even sugar and carbs could fix me.

"Nervous?" Gil asked as I tossed the rest in the trash.

"Yeah." Among other things.

Little Manny passed us, did a double take, and backed up. "Whoa, what happened to you two?"

"What do you mean?" Gil asked.

"You don't match."

I looked down, then at Gil. Little Manny was right. For the first time in almost two weeks, we wore completely different colors. I had on a plain button-down black shirt, and he was wearing cream, brown, and red.

Gil's eyes went wide behind his glasses, and his mouth dropped open in a silent *oh*.

"I guess it had to happen eventually," Little Manny said. "Honestly, it was getting weird."

"Yeah, haha," Gil said, fake smiling through the awkwardness.

"It's fine. Wardrobe will fix it. See you guys there." With a wave, Little Manny left us standing there, alone in a sea of people.

I followed him out, drinking my coffee. Maybe I'd get lucky and spill it like I did on day one.

WARDROBE DID, INDEED, make me change. I was issued a red shirt that looked like the fancier version of a SpellMart uniform. The universe had a sense of humor today, clearly.

I hadn't even brought an apron. I'd grabbed my backpack when I rushed out, but I hadn't packed anything. When Rachel finally led us to the soundstage, I had nowhere to put my notebook and pencil, so I dropped them on the table and stood in our usual spot.

Gil kept sneaking looks at me. I ignored them. What did he want? Was he worried that I couldn't keep my shit together?

Yeah, well, so was I. A burst of irritation burned away some of my nerves, then a wave of depression put the fire out. I was going to lose. Gil's charity would have to find money somewhere else. This was a disaster.

It didn't help that Charlotte looked so fucking smug standing next to Felicia. Sinvergüenza.

Syd and the judges took up their positions at the front for the last time, Syd smiling their benevolent hostly smile.

"Welcome, finalists," Syd said. "It's time for the final round of this season of *Cast Judgment*."

We stood like statues. I wondered what would happen if I threw up right on the floor in front of me.

"Fuck me, this isn't a funeral," Syd said. "Did any of you sleep last night or were you all drunk as fucking lords and you woke up hungover?"

Gil laughed uncomfortably. I wished I was drunk now.

"Come on," Tori said, "all of you, clap and act excited." So we did. Gil hooted and whistled. If I smiled any bigger, my face might split open. Fake, fake, fake.

"You're all here," Syd continued, "because you've stuck it out through round after round, making spells that kept the judges from casting judgment on you."

No, we were here because our spells hadn't exploded.

"And now, you'll face the final challenge." Syd paused for effect. "Without further ado, your brief for this round: design a large enchantment that functions as an awe-inspiring, celebration-culminating spectacle. The kind that people will talk about long after they've gone home from the party. You have sixteen hours to produce your masterpieces. Your time starts . . . now!"

I grabbed my pencil and notebook. Gil crowded in next to me, and I tried to shift sideways without being too obvious about it.

"Oh, right," he muttered, and added an extra few inches.

Yeah, dude, remember how you dumped me last night? It was like twelve hours ago.

The only spectacles I could think of right now were the parades and shows I'd seen at theme parks when I was a kid, or on TV for random holidays, or at Calle Ocho. I'd been to a few concerts with big magic, too. I should probably just pick the easiest thing to copy and go for it.

"We already did something with fireworks, sort of," Gil said.

I jumped. Apparently I'd zoned out. I tried to stay present, but it was so hard. "Yeah. We need something different. More creative." Hah. Easy.

"Something fun again, though."

"Right. Fun."

"Maybe something like that bubble spell, but bigger?"

"Sure, sounds good." I wrote that down.

"A giant balloon animal bubble that bursts to become lots of little ones?"

"Okay." I wrote that down, too.

"We could add sound effects, dogs barking maybe."

"Dogs . . . barking . . ."

"And roosters. Like full-on sunrise cockfight noises."

"Uh-huh." My hand moved on autopilot.

Gil grabbed my pencil and ducked his head to look me in the eye. "Penelope, that's an incredibly bad idea."

Was it? I guess it was. I struggled to care. My chest was a hole, and I was tossing in rocks that never hit the bottom.

"What's going on?" Gil whispered. "Do you need more coffee? A banana? A few more minutes to finish waking up?"

"I'm okay," I said.

"You're not."

"I said I'm fine. Come on, we need to figure this out. We don't have time to fuck around."

Gil flinched like I'd slapped him. "Penelope, what is wrong? What happened?"

I almost snapped, *You know what happened! You dumped me right before the finale! Did you develop amnesia between last night and this morning?*

What did he even care? But he clearly did care. A lot. Unless he was faking?

Listen to your gut, my sister whispered in the back of my brain.

My gut said something was off. My gut said, I should have told Gil last night that I didn't want to give up on us. It said I should have fought instead of hiding my feelings behind my fake smile so they wouldn't bother him, wouldn't upset him, wouldn't make him think I was desperate and pathetic and a stalker instead of cool, normal cool, good cool.

I should have told him I did deserve better, that I deserved someone who would care less about how hard it would be to sneak around, and more about not having to sneak in the first place. I deserved someone who was proud to be with me, not someone who treated me like a dirty secret.

Too late. It was over, and I had to focus on getting through this round.

"We can talk about it later," I lied, putting my pencil to the page. "I think the bubbles could work, actually. Remember that big floral enchantment on the cruise ship?"

Gil looked at the clock, then at the paper. He closed his eyes and took a deep breath, in through his mouth, out through his nose. Then he must have decided something, because he checked his posture, shoulders back, and faced me.

"No," he said.

"No bubbles?"

"No, we're not talking later. We're talking now."

"We don't have time."

"We need to make time. I don't want to . . . to pretend everything is okay when it's not, and have it get worse."

"Fine." I put the pencil down and stalked toward the exit. Gil followed. Tori raised an eyebrow at us, and I smiled and shrugged. Nothing to see here—everything's fine.

We went past various crew sitting or standing outside, past cables and boxes and all the accumulated clutter of nearly two weeks of filming. Isaac slumped in his fancy chair, three paper headache charms stuck to his forehead. Liam saw us and mimed turning off the transmitters.

Right, I thought as I flipped the switch, wouldn't want anyone to record this. It would definitely make for a super-dramatic last episode. The opposite of fake flirting: real arguing.

I yanked open the door to the private office we used for confessionals and turned on the soft lights. Gil followed me in, and I closed the door behind him. The two chairs waited next to each other against the far wall; I dragged one of them across the floor so it was farther away and sat in it, crossing my arms.

Gil sat in the other chair, moving slowly, like his bones were tired. He stared at me in silence, and I let him. I couldn't remember the last time I was this upset. Even getting fired, finding out my rent was going impossibly high—those problems felt manageable by comparison. They shouldn't, because they weren't, and yet.

I must love Gil, because nothing less than love could do this to a person. I still loved him, even though he'd dumped me, and it hurt that I couldn't turn that off the way he apparently had.

Gil took off his safety glasses and rubbed his eyes. His mustache was impossible to remove so easily, I knew, but the small gesture made it clear that I was talking to him and not Leandro Presto.

"I'm sorry," he said. "I'm really bad at confrontations, and I know you don't want to do this right now, and we're wasting time when we should be working on our spell, but . . ." He looked everywhere but at me: up at the ceiling, down at the floor, at his hands clenched together between his knees.

"It's fine," I said.

"It's not fine." His voice was quiet, almost too quiet for me to hear. "Every time my mom says, 'it's fine,' what she means is, 'I'm not going to tell you what's wrong until I can use it to hurt you.'"

"I'm not your mom."

"No, you're not. I've never seen you do something to intentionally hurt someone. That's why I don't understand why you won't tell me what's wrong now."

Seriously? What the fuck?

"I'm not trying to push you," he said. "If you tell me to, I'll back off. But I spent a lot of years with my parents refusing to talk to each other except to fight, and I don't want us to be like that."

"What 'us'?" I said, letting my hurt spill into my voice. "You said 'us' would be too hard, and you left me. You said it was over."

Gil's eyes got huge as he jumped out of his chair. "What? I said what?"

I stood up, too. "You said you didn't want to sneak around and end up on gossip sites. You said I deserved better."

"Because you do!" He reached for me and I backed away. He let his hands fall.

"So how can you pretend like you don't know what's wrong? You dumped me! I was so happy, and you . . . I thought we were . . . I thought . . ." Fuck, I was going to cry again. I would not let him see me like this. I could at least keep my dignity.

I yanked the door open and walked out.

"Oh my god, Penelope, no!"

I walked faster, I didn't know which way. Away.

"Penelope! Holy shit, whatever I said, that's not what I meant."

I couldn't breathe. Doors flew past me in a blur. Bathroom. Where was the bathroom?

"Penelope!"

Arms wrapped around me from behind. I struggled. Something hit the ground with a clatter. Gil picked me up and I squealed, kicking the air until he put me back down and let go. Crunch went something under my sneaker.

"Penelope, please," Gil said. "Please, stop. I love . . . I love you!"

I froze. What?

"I love you," he repeated. "I don't want to have to sneak around because I want to be with you all the time. I don't want to fake flirt because I don't want people to think you're cheating on Leandro with me. He isn't real. We are."

Oh . . . Oh!

"I don't know what I said last night, but obviously I totally fucked up. Please . . . please let me fix it? Please?" His voice cracked on the last word, as if he was struggling to keep it together as much as I was.

I turned around. His mouth was half-open, his forehead wrinkled, his eyes . . . his eyes!

"Your glasses," I said. "Where are your glasses?"

We both looked around. I spotted them first, on the floor, where apparently I had stepped on them. They were totally destroyed.

Gil nudged the plastic shards with his shoe. "I don't care. I'm done caring about Leandro Presto. I care about you more."

The hole in my stomach flooded with butterflies that burst up and out, through my heart and my veins and the rest of my body, until it felt like I was floating.

I flew toward Gil, jumping on him so hard I nearly knocked him down. He caught me, and I kissed him, over and over. I kissed him like I needed it to breathe, like our love was a spell we were casting on each other, binding us together with an enchantment that couldn't be broken.

"I love you, too," I whispered.

Behind us, someone started clapping. Shit, we had an audience. I looked over my shoulder as more people joined the applause. Little Manny whistled, and Big Manny grinned, and Liam gave us a double thumbs-up. Even Fina and Bruno were there, smiling, and in Bruno's case, wiping a tear out of the corner of his eye.

Isaac was the only one who looked annoyed. He stalked over to us, glaring at Gil, his forehead charms flopping around.

"What the country-fried fuck are you doing?" Isaac asked. "You're supposed to be pretending to flirt, not acting out the end of your mom's favorite rom-com in front of the crew."

"We aren't acting," Gil said coldly.

"What part of 'level up your pussy game' did you not understand?"

Excuse me?

"Are you seriously going to blow off being the lead on your own show for this . . . mediocre salesgirl?" he continued.

Gil shifted me sideways but didn't let go. "No, I'm blowing it off because you're a piece of shit and I don't want to work with you again."

He what? I was missing something here, and it sounded bad.

A charm fell in front of Isaac's eye and he yanked it off. "You'll be lucky to get a job picking up my dry cleaning by the time I'm through with you. You're done. Finito. Shark food. Now get the fuck out of my sight and back on set."

I would have flipped him off, but he'd already turned around to stomp back to his fancy chair. Unfortunately he was right: we were still in the middle of the round, and time was running out.

"Are we good?" Gil murmured into my ear.

"We're good," I replied.

Except I hadn't told him about the contract. Oh no.

"What, what's wrong? You just tensed up."

"I signed a contract," I said. "With Charlotte's company. I was going to tell you about it, but then you, um, said what you said and I didn't get the chance."

He turned me so he could look at my face directly. "What contract? For a job?"

"Yes. She wanted me to lose the contest on purpose or I get no job, plus some kind of penalty."

"You thought after what happened that we'd lose anyway, so it wouldn't matter?"

"Yeah."

"Shit."

"It's okay." I grinned at him. "I never gave it back to her. It's still in my room, and Charlotte hasn't signed it. I was thinking of ritually burning it on the pool deck tomorrow night, actually. I'm desperate, but there are lines I won't cross."

Gil rubbed my back with one hand. "I know. I trust you."

I should have trusted him, too, but in my defense, he had extremely sounded like he was breaking up with me. I wasn't thinking straight, or I'd have realized something was off sooner.

"I wanted to warn you that she's probably the one behind the sabotage, not Felicia," I said. "I think she paid someone else to do it so her hands would stay clean, but still."

He kissed me. "If she tries anything, we'll make her sorry."

I kissed him back. "We'd better go before Isaac yells more."

"Ugh, fuck that guy."

"Why are you so mad at him?"

Gil shook his head. "I'll tell you later."

My plans for later had involved ice cream and more crying. Now? Okay, maybe still ice cream. But I was done crying.

"Seriously, though," I said. "What about your glasses?"

"I have a backup pair in my bag," Gil said. "Leandro is a mess, but I like to be prepared."

Ah, I did love this man. We were going to rock this round. As soon as we figured out what the hell we were doing.

CHAPTER 23

Gil

Penelope and I had to get our hair and makeup fixed before we were allowed on camera, so by the time we were back at our station, hunched over her notebook, we'd lost a half hour. Felicia and Charlotte were already sorting through their reagents and prepping their equipment; we needed to hurry if we wanted to catch up.

With a last dot on an exclamation point, Penelope put her pencil down. "Perfect. This is going to be awesome."

"Extremely."

Once we started brainstorming for real, Penelope had suggested the best thing we could do for the final spell was celebrate the charity I was competing for. If we lost, it might still impress enough people to get them to open their wallets. Maybe even pull in some new sponsors who wanted to be part of the magic, too.

We were calling it "Making Magic Together": using the base spell I'd cast the night we met, we'd make a top hat that would pop out residual echoes of old stage magic stuff—flowers, cards, rabbits, white doves. There were more cool bits, like fog and sparkle effects and fireworks, but that was the general idea.

"Hopefully Felicia didn't grab all the duskywing butterfly wings they have," Penelope said. "We can substitute crushed amethyst, but then we'd have to change the—"

"Go check first," I said. "We'll adjust if we have to."

"Right. Stop catastrophizing." Penelope smiled softly. "You know, after what happened last night, I almost feel like nothing could be worse? It makes all of this weirdly chill by comparison."

I was still recovering from the adrenaline check of a few minutes ago, but I knew what she meant. This wasn't over, though. Penelope needed the cash prize and the residency, and I needed the charity donation. None of that had changed, even if everything else had.

"We just have to stay focused, and watch out in case of . . ."

I nodded. In case Charlotte or whoever she paid to sabotage the others tried again now. If Felicia was right, and she wasn't doing it herself directly, basically anyone on set was a suspect.

"It's too bad we can't . . ." Hmm, didn't want to say it out loud, so I took the pencil and wrote: "Trap."

Penelope grabbed my arm. "Yes! I used to make charms at the store, for when I had to do casting in the back. I can't believe I didn't think of it before."

"Do you need an extra cauldron, or—"

"Nope." She pulled out another pencil and wrote down a list of ingredients: a jar, a black candle, vinegar, a lemon, paper, and twine.

I raised an eyebrow and wrote, "Freezer spell?"

Penelope nodded.

I'd never heard of those being used in stores. They could be bad news, but I trusted Penelope to know what she was doing. And if anyone deserved to get an ugly shock, it was whoever kept sabotaging stuff.

She left to grab our supplies, while I started setting up our gear.

It was a routine now, and honestly, I loved it. Maybe she'd work with me on *Mage You Look* when this was all over? The thought made me grin.

I paused, crouched in front of the open cabinet with a cauldron in my hands. Thinking about working on the show with Isaac and Rick had given me so much anxiety, even before I'd known the specifics. So had being on *Cast Judgment*, but I'd sucked it up because I'd agreed with Sam and Ed that it was a great opportunity.

Imagining working with Penelope, though? I was totally amped up. I wanted to do it, looked forward to it, instead of being freaked out so much I had to self-medicate. Even the idea of cutting back the explanation tiers like Sam and Ed had suggested? I still thought we shouldn't, but if we did, it wouldn't sting so badly because I would be able to talk things over with Penelope, in ways I couldn't with my friends.

Those conversations—trading ideas and getting into debates and thinking deep thoughts about how magic worked—were why I'd majored in magical theory in the first place, why I started my *Doctor Witch* blog, and why I didn't completely hate being an adjunct even when the work was grueling and demoralizing. *Mage You Look* was so one-sided by comparison. Most of my fans wanted to laugh at me and move on, and even if they wanted to chat for real about magic, I couldn't because I had to pretend to be a clueless fuckup.

With Penelope, I didn't have to pretend. Even if everything in my life stayed the same after this show, having her changed how I felt about it. And that made all the difference.

Failure to launch a career in Hollywood might disappoint my friends, and it would be bad news for my bank account, but there had to be other ways to get ahead that wouldn't make me miserable, right?

Shit, I hoped so. I probably shouldn't have snapped at Isaac, but seriously, fuck that guy.

Penelope got back with all our stuff, and we went through our checks. Everything seemed okay, thankfully.

"Cover me while I make the other thing," she said. "Go full Presto."

"As you wish, m'lady." Resisting the urge to kiss her hand was not easy.

I made a production of setting up our actual spell, pretending to fumble bottles and catching them at the last second, spinning knives and juggling pieces of chalk. Syd came by, and I made random small objects appear from their ears and nose, much to Nate's delight from behind the camera.

Felicia and Charlotte seemed totally into whatever they were doing, though I couldn't identify their reagents from a distance. They had at least two pots boiling and a trio of connected spell circles, which meant some kind of cascading enchantment . . . Interesting.

"All done," Penelope whispered.

Unless I'd been looking for the knotted pieces of twine strategically arranged around our equipment, I probably wouldn't have noticed them. Nice.

Five and a half hours left. Damn, time went fast. We had to hustle.

Even though our station was now booby-trapped, I still kept an eye on anyone who wandered close. Syd again, with Nate; Tori, who positioned us for a few specific shots from the dolly camera; and finally, the judges, who did their usual interrogation and commentary. Slightly nicer this time, because I guess finalists got special treatment. Even Felicia and Charlotte seemed genuinely friendly instead of like a pair of ice queens trying to figure out how to talk to peasants.

The hours passed, and nothing weird happened. Smooth casting all the way. When we wrapped, Penelope added more twine to our fridge and other equipment just in case, and back to the hotel we went.

Alina smiled at Penelope as we walked to the elevator. "You're looking better."

Penelope blushed and gave her a shy smile back. "Yeah. I am. Thanks."

Little Manny leaned on Alina's desk. "You should have seen it. We were all minding our own business, doing our jobs, and—"

"Bro," Big Manny said, wrapping a beefy forearm around Little Manny's mouth. "NDA. What happens on set, stays on set." He winked at me, and I grinned.

Then it hit me. Everyone in the production knew about Penelope and me now. They'd seen me without my safety glasses. We didn't have to hide or pretend anymore, not here. Our secret was out.

"Hey," I said to Penelope. "We should make sure our plans for tomorrow are solid. My room later?"

Penelope's eyes got big. "I thought we were going to, you know," she whispered.

"That was before I told you I loved you in front of almost every single person in this hotel." I waggled my eyebrows at her and she snorted a laugh.

"Tomorrow is a big day," she said. "We need to rest."

I could probably say something about sleeping better with her in my bed, but I didn't want to push. "Okay. Let's get food, then."

Up we went, to the pool deck and the dinner buffet awaiting us. I was so hungry, I could eat ten steaks. As soon as we walked out into the warm night, though, the whistling and applause started again, because we were the current hot goss and nobody here had any chill.

Quentin practically tackled me. "I knew it! I knew the two of you had a thing."

Amy smiled and took Penelope's hands. "I'm so happy for you. You're both so sweet and nice."

"It hasn't even been two weeks," Dylan said, folding his arms and giving me a dad look. "You really serious about our girl?"

"Totally serious," I said solemnly. Then, because I couldn't help it, I added, "Meow and forever."

"Yeah," Penelope said. "It was kitten in the stars."

If the smile on my face got any bigger, my cheeks would break.

Quentin groaned. "You dorks definitely deserve each other."

I certainly hoped so.

MORNING CAME TOO soon and not soon enough. I hadn't wanted something to be over this badly since I'd defended my dissertation.

Today I wore what Sam had called my "winner shirt," which she had forbidden me from using unless I made it to the finals. It was the least wild-colored option in my Leandro Presto wardrobe, just black and white and red, but the design made up for it. Each of the front panels featured an old-timey stage magician with a cape and wand, holding a top hat with a deck of cards flying out of it. The huge collar, side panels and sleeves were covered in tiny card suit symbols, diamonds and spades and clubs and hearts. Perfect for our spell.

Penelope sat at one of the tables in the restaurant, a plate of untouched food in front of her. We saw each other at the same time, and she smiled in what seemed like relief.

"We match," she said when I got to her.

We did. She wore a loose V-neck red shirt covered in white dots and black hearts. Hell yeah. All was right with the world again.

"What about your apron?" I asked.

"You'll see."

We ate, I got Penelope's coffee ready to go, and we waited in the lobby for the van, surrounded by hungover crew. Today would be a long one, because after casting we'd have judging, and then final confessionals. Rain poured down outside, turning the street into a river; I hoped it wasn't an omen, or if it was, that it wasn't for us.

Felicia and Charlotte stood nearby, juntos pero no revueltos, as my dad would say. Together, but not close. Felicia had on her full resting bitch face, while Charlotte kept checking her watch like it would make time pass more quickly.

"I should have realized something was up the first time you made my coffee," Penelope said suddenly.

"Oh?"

"It's perfect. I was like, how did he know?, and I assumed you'd gotten lucky."

Oh. "You told me how you like it in one of our emails."

"I'm surprised you remembered."

I squeezed her knee. "That was one of my failed attempts to set myself up to ask you out. I had this whole elaborate plan, where I'd ask how you liked your coffee, and you'd tell me, and I'd say, 'I know this great place on Coral Way near the Turnpike,' and then bam! Coffee date."

Penelope squinted, thinking. "But all you did was tell me how you liked your coffee and then we started talking about . . . that documentary on weather magic?"

"Yeah, I chickened out. Again."

"So." She nudged me with her knee. "Want to get coffee at that place you like?"

"It's a date." I held up my travel cup and she tapped hers against it.

The van finally came for us all, and we arrived, slightly moist, at the warehouse. Fina did her best on makeup, and Bruno gave me this quietly desperate look and asked whether I would consider a different hairstyle, just for today. I had to turn him down. Rule number two: stay in character.

"But don't you want to look nicer for la novia?" Bruno asked.

"Yeah, but I have to look like this for the cameras," I replied.

"Bueeeno," he said. "Como tú quieras, brother."

Liam, horrified as always by my shirt material, taped the mic on and left to fiddle with dials and buttons. Nate asked if he could maybe have my autograph if it wasn't a bother—it wasn't, and I promised I'd take a selfie with him later, too. Little Manny hugged me, Big Manny gave me a good luck fist bump, and as I was heading back to the greenroom, I ran into an enormously excited Penelope.

"You'll never believe what I found," she said.

"What?"

She held out a walkie-talkie. Okay. Wait, it had a label.

"Is that . . . Just Manny's radio?"

"It is!"

"Should I get a box and a stick?"

She smacked me with it. "Don't be ridiculous. We're going to put it on a table and then hide."

"Do we have time to—"

"Over here."

Penelope dragged me to the last lonely cubicle in what used to be a room full of them. She put the walkie-talkie on the desk, standing up so the antenna was clearly visible, then dragged me behind the fabric-covered metal partition. We waited in silence, occasional bursts of static and voices assuring us that the thing was still there.

It occurred to me that we were alone where no one could see us, and Penelope's back was pressed against my front. Fond memories of a similar position in a casting booth gave certain parts of me ideas.

I kissed her neck. She shivered and gently elbowed me. I slipped my arms around her and kissed her again, and she melted into me with a soft little sigh. I nibbled my way up to her ear—

Footsteps. So quiet I almost missed them. We both froze, waiting.

The scrape of plastic on plastic. Someone had picked up the radio.

Penelope tore out of my arms and jumped out. "Aha!"

The person screamed. I peeked over the top of the wall.

A perfectly normal guy stood there, staring at Penelope like she was loca. Brown hair, brown eyes, like a million people you'd pass in a mall any day.

"Got you, Just Manny," Penelope said smugly.

"You were . . . looking for me?" Just Manny asked, totally confused. "Did you need something?"

"We're good," I told him, hooking my arm through Penelope's and tugging her toward the soundstage.

"Vindication!" Penelope shouted.

"I think the stress has broken your brain."

"Wait until I tell Big Manny and Little Manny."

I looked over my shoulder, intending to apologize, but Just Manny was already gone, disappeared back into whatever dimension he existed in when Penelope wasn't tricking him into revealing himself.

Magic? Nah. People couldn't teleport or turn invisible. Unless . . .

A frantic Rachel herded us with her tablet, because apparently we'd made everyone late. Isaac shouted, "Fuck on your own time!" as we passed, and I ignored him, because I was a mature adult. I did imagine cursing him, though, because I was also occasionally petty.

Felicia and Charlotte once again waited together but not together. Syd and the judges were there already, too, at the front of the room as usual. Syd, thankfully, didn't crack a joke about us. Presumably Tori or Isaac had told them our real relationship was not part of the show.

Since this was the second half of the round, all Syd had to announce was, "Contestants, you have eight hours remaining! We're halfway to the end and the final judgment."

With that, the timer started counting down again, and off we went.

Penelope checked the freezer spell; no change. We moved on to the rest of our checklist: I had to enchant the rabbit and dove components, and she had to finish brewing the potion that would make the environmental effects along with the critters.

I put the reagents at the correct positions in the chalk circle I drew yesterday, checking to be sure none of the lines or sigils were smudged. All good. Yellow candle at one corner, rabbit fur at another, pure spring water at the third, and a dove feather at the fourth. In the center, the coin that would be the catalyst. I sat on the floor and lit the candle. Inhale, focus, exhale. I did that a few more times, until I was sure I was ready, then I channeled my intent into the circle.

The chalk lines lit up, sigils floating just above the floor along with the feather. Energy rippled across the surface of my skin. I muttered the incantation Penelope and I had written together. On the twelfth repetition, the magic got sucked into the coin, which glowed briefly before fading. I hummed a little tune to discharge any extra energy, cleaned up the used reagents, then got up to check on Penelope.

She was stirring the cauldron and murmuring her own spell, so I didn't interrupt. I'd need her for the next circle enchantment, but I could start setting it up.

We kept working like that, side by side and together, for hours. I made her stop to eat lunch; she brought me ice water and some paper towels to wipe up my sweat when I overextended. I rubbed her neck and shoulders when they ached from stirring; she pounded my lower back when it hurt from crouching to draw spell circles on the floor.

Just like this, I thought. This is what I want. The two of us, casting together, bringing each other sandwiches and coffee. Not some big show in LA, not red carpets and flashing cameras. This. Her.

Penelope caught me looking at her and smiled, and I fell in love again. Life was good. It would only get better when we won.

Three hours before presentation time, I was so absorbed in drawing and redrawing a particularly stubborn symbol that the judges surprised me. Legs burning, I stood up and stretched.

"Almost ready?" Hugh asked, his green eyes boring into mine like lasers.

"You know it," I said, spinning the stick of chalk on my open palm with a flourish.

Fabienne gestured at the circle I was working on. "Which portion of the enchantment will this be?"

"Part of the spell involves cards doing tricks in the air, so I'm going to do them myself, and this will basically record my movements."

"Interesting," Hugh said. "What technique are you using to—"

On the other side of the station, a red light flashed. Doris gasped in pain and stumbled backward, holding her left hand with her right.

"Are you okay?" Syd asked, concern on their face as they approached her.

"I'm . . . fine," Doris said. "Just a sudden cramp."

Penelope stepped out from behind the stove, angrier than I'd ever seen her, even when she was yelling at me in the park. "Just a cramp? You were trying to sabotage our spell!"

Syd stared at her, mouth open. Doris shook her head, hazel eyes wide. From across the room, Tori straightened up like a meerkat sensing danger.

"How dare you accuse me of such a thing, young lady!" Doris said. "I've never been so insulted in my life."

Penelope gestured at the freezer. "Let's check on my charm, then, and see if the water changed color."

"What's this about a charm?" Fabienne asked, raising a perfectly shaped eyebrow.

"Penelope made a freezer spell," I explained. "It was designed to go off if someone tried to touch any of our stuff with malicious intent."

Both Hugh and Fabienne looked at Doris, whose pale skin had turned bone white. Tori stalked over, looking grim. Charlotte and Felicia stopped what they were doing, too.

"Malicious intent?" Hugh asked, his voice low and harsh.

Penelope plunked the jar from the freezer onto the counter. The frozen liquid inside had gone from clear to a reddish purple, frost coating the inside of the glass, but the words on the spell paper dangling by a piece of twine from the lid were still legible.

"Doris," Tori said through clenched teeth, her normally statue-calm face twitching. "Tampering with this competition is a federal crime. You know that."

"I've done nothing wrong." Doris crossed her arms. "I will not be subjected to this, this insinuation."

"I'm not insinuating, I'm straight-up saying it," Penelope muttered. "I just don't understand why."

I remembered the conversation I'd heard the first day of filming, confirmed by Isaac at the restaurant. "She's being forced to retire."

Doris glared at me, lips thin.

"It's gotta be revenge, right?" I continued. "She's pissed that she's getting pushed out of the show she helped start, so she's wrecking it on the way out. If she can't be here, no one can."

Penelope shook her head. "Super petty. Wow."

"Pure nonsense," Doris said, but the way Hugh and Fabienne were looking at her, I knew I'd nailed it.

Isaac stormed in like a low-rent Zeus ready to spit lightning. "Now what the fuck is going on in here?"

"Doris has been sabotaging everyone's spells," I said.

"What did I say about talking shit?" Isaac yelled. "Get back to your stations and finish this fucking round."

"No way," Penelope said. "This show has been rigged from the start. If it weren't for Doris, the whole competition might have gone completely differently. Any of the other teams could be here instead."

"Speak for yourself," Felicia grumbled.

Penelope rolled her eyes.

"You can't prove shit," Isaac said.

Unfortunately true. All we could prove was that she'd set off the freezer spell, and even that was our word against hers. Out of the corner of my eye, I noticed Nate quietly filming. There would be evidence of this, at least, assuming the footage wasn't destroyed later.

I said, "I'll bet if you go through all the dailies you might be able to catch her in the act."

Doris made a scoffing noise. Okay, maybe she was too careful for that.

Charlotte spoke up then. "Listen, the round is almost over. Why don't we finish and then figure things out afterward?"

Penelope shook her head. "I won't let our work be judged by someone who was trying to sabotage it. She can't be trusted to be fair."

"What she said," I agreed.

"Then Hugh and Fabienne can judge without Doris," Charlotte said.

I narrowed my eyes at her. "You want to take the chance that your spell hasn't been compromised?"

"Ours is fine," Charlotte insisted.

"How can you be sure?" Penelope asked. "I bet you bribed Doris the way you tried to bribe me."

"And me," I added. "Maybe Doris hadn't even planned to risk sabotage until she knew there was an extra check in it for her."

Charlotte glared at us both. "I never did any such thing, and if you even hint it in public, I'll bury you in lawsuits."

"That's what I said!" Isaac yelled.

"I knew this would come down to lawyer ninjas," Penelope muttered.

"It's okay," I said. "My dad is the best lawyer ninja around."

Isaac growled, grabbed the freezer spell off our table, and threw it. The container shattered against the wall, spraying glass and colored ice all over the decorative arcane symbols and the floor.

"Fuck this and fuck you!" he shouted. "I have a date with enough tequila to put a horse in a coma, so get back to your stations and finish this round." He gave all of us double middle fingers and then stomped back out.

"Places, everyone. We'll start up again in ten." Tori smoothly delivered a few more orders, then stepped outside with her phone glued to her ear. Probably calling someone higher up to off-load the whole problem now that it was, as my dad used to say, above her pay grade.

Penelope stared at the glass-and-ice mess. "Is there a rule about the showrunner wrecking a contestant's stuff?"

I grinned at her. "What does Leandro Presto know about rules?"

She snorted, then busted out laughing. "Oh my god, this round really did end on a spectacle, didn't it?"

"I liked ours yesterday better," I whispered in her ear.

Penelope blushed and bumped me with her hip. I put an arm around her shoulders. No matter what happened with the show now that it had all gone to shit, at least we had each other, and that was pretty magical.

CHAPTER 24

Penelope

Our spell was missing something.

Whatever Doris had planned to sabotage, she hadn't managed to do it, thankfully, so Gil and I were still on schedule. But as he finished the circle for his card tricks, I had this nagging feeling . . . or maybe it was more that I didn't have the same sense of everything being right that I'd had in round three.

I spun my pencil on the table and tried to figure it out. Was I nervous? Overthinking? Catastrophizing? Did I need more caffeine, or less?

Felicia and Charlotte were arguing at their station, if I was reading their ice-queen expressions right. Both covered their mics with their hands instead of turning them off.

Syd and the judges, minus Doris, watched from one corner, while Rachel stood in another. Tori followed Nate and his camera like they were tied together with a rope. No one was taking chances now, I guess. I still couldn't believe they were making us finish this when it had clearly been rigged, but I wasn't a lawyer ninja, so what did I know.

"You okay?" Gil asked.

I yelped and spun the pencil right off the table.

He caught it. "What's going on in that big brain of yours?"

Felica cut the air with one hand, while Charlotte shook her head so hard I thought it would pop off.

"I think our spell needs something," I said. "I don't know what."

Gil leaned on the table, looking up at me sideways. "Conversation hearts?"

I clicked my tongue at him. "No."

"Jellyfish?"

"No."

"Kittens?"

"No!"

"You're right, it would be hard to keep them from going after the bunnies and birds."

I bumped him with my hip. "I'm serious."

"Me too! Look, so serious." He narrowed his eyes and made a duck face at me.

I laughed and made the same face back. He crossed his eyes, so I stuck out my tongue.

Later, he mouthed, waggling his eyebrows.

Felicia put her hand up in front of Charlotte's face, palm out, then walked toward the exit. She paused at the edge of the warding circle, glancing over her shoulder at . . . me? With a sigh so deep her whole body got into it, she headed for our station.

"Incoming," Gil said.

Hands opening and closing like she wanted to punch something, Felicia clacked to a stop. "Penelope," she said through clenched teeth, "can I talk to you?"

"Okay." What could she want? Gil made big eyes at me and I shrugged.

We headed for the supply area, moving halfway into a row with drawers of hardware and various kinds of wood. Felicia slowly got a grip on whatever was upsetting her until only the ice queen was left, then switched off her mic. I did the same.

"You owe me," she said. "For telling you about Charlotte."

I blinked at her, not sure what to say.

"She's going to ruin our spell," Felicia continued. "She wants to mix rose hip oil with garlic in our catalyst."

"That won't work," I said. "They'll cancel each other out."

"That's what I told her!" Felicia threw her hands in the air, pacing in a tight circle. "She won't listen to me. She's a stubborn asshole who thinks she knows everything."

Memories flickered through my mind, of Past Penelope wanting to work with Charlotte so badly and freaking out about being stuck with Leandro Presto. I grinned, unable to stop myself.

"Laugh," Felicia said. "Go on. Get it out of your system. Then tell me how to fix this."

Now I knew why she'd led with me owing her.

"What is the garlic supposed to do?" I asked.

"Just a potency enhancer."

"Are you going to be stirring or mashing the reagents together?"

"Yes, stirring."

I stared at the meticulously labeled containers of nails and screws and bolts, thinking. My abuela had used garlic all the time, so she'd drilled me on what worked and what didn't in her calm, firm voice.

"Using a stainless steel spoon or pestle on the garlic should neutralize it," I said. "You could also try adding some tomato juice or cinnamon, if they won't react with something else in the spell, or use lemon as an enhancer instead."

"Stainless steel, tomato juice, cinnamon, lemon," Felicia repeated to herself. She started to walk away.

"How do you know I'm not lying?" I asked her back.

Felicia gave a short laugh. "Are you kidding? You've been helping out every single team since you got here, even though it could have made you lose. I don't think you could give me bad advice if you tried."

Ouch, but fair. "If you know that, you should know you didn't have to tell me I owed you anything. I would have just helped you because you asked."

"Really?" Her tone said now she thought I was lying.

Was I? She'd been a total asshole to me and everyone else here from day one. No one would have blamed me if I sabotaged her as soon as I had the chance, or told her to go fry ice. But my abuela taught me better than that. Magic knowledge was meant to be shared, to help people, not to get revenge or hurt anyone.

"Really," I said firmly.

Felicia shook her head and left me standing in the aisle, wondering whether I'd made a mistake. Gil probably wouldn't think so. Neither would my abuela; she would have wanted me to win fairly, which meant everyone's spells should have a chance to work and shine.

My abuela. That's what was missing from our spell! I'd been so focused on Gil's charity that I hadn't put anything of myself in this. Too late now.

Or was it? I thought through our concept and presentation, our recipe and reagents and processes, as I walked back to our station. By the time I got there, I'd sketched out a plan that I thought might work, and I immediately started making notes.

Gil booped me on the nose. "What is this?"

"Making our spell more awesome." I talked him through it, his eyes getting bigger behind his safety glasses.

"That's a lot. Are you sure we can do all this in time?" he asked.

My hands shook, and my pulse sped up. I swallowed spit and made myself say, "We're going to pressure-cook it."

"Whoa, hey, are you sure?" He put his hands on my shoulders. "I don't want you doing anything that makes you uncomfortable."

This whole competition made me uncomfortable. I'd let Rosy talk me into it because she said I knew more about magic than half the people who usually competed; then I'd cosplayed as confident until even the producers were fooled; and then, to top it all off, I'd agreed to fake flirt with my derpy partner. No part of this had ever been comfortable for me.

But that was the point. I'd been stuck in my crappy job for so long, I'd believed it was the best I could do. I'd believed that my parents, especially my mom, were right about me being a failure with delusional aspirations. That I'd never be as good as my sister. I'd let myself get comfortable in my life, except it wasn't comfort, it was avoiding new ways I could fail and feel worse about myself.

I needed to be uncomfortable. To try harder. To take risks like . . . Leandro Presto. Okay, so those were fake, but still! It was the attitude that mattered.

You can't let one accident stop you from casting forever, mi vida.

I hadn't, and it wouldn't stop me now. No matter how much I wanted to throw up.

"We're doing this," I said firmly. "We'll show those two who the real jokers are."

Gil smirked. "It's us, right?"

"Yeah, but in a cool way."

"Cool weird."

"Exactly."

We reworked what we had to, tweaked our schedule, and I

ran back to the supply room for the extra stuff we'd need. Meanwhile, Gil set up the equipment that would let us pressure-cook—"thaumaturgical pression" was the official name for it, and the exact process varied depending on the spell. In this case, I'd need not only a complex magic circle, but also an array of mirrors and prisms and gemstones.

Also, I'd have to keep from completely freaking out.

Gil hustled to do twice as much stuff, while I crawled around on my hands and knees with tempera paint made from tea rose petals, a compass, and measuring tape. I barely noticed Nate creeping past me when I struggled to get the angle of a mirror right, or the camera on the crane dipping down to get a closer look at my reagent placement. I was so in the zone that even Gil's chanting was a background buzz, and the occasional bursts of magical energy from him and Felicia and Charlotte slid across my senses like warm breezes on a sunny day.

Finally everything was ready. I stared down at one of the most complex circles I'd ever created, and my stomach tried to crawl up my throat. My heart sped up, fast as a hummingbird's, so loud I wondered if Liam could hear it through my mic. If this worked . . . It would work. It had to work. I wasn't a teenager anymore; I knew what I was doing, and nothing distracted me from my focus and intent.

And I had Gil. He stood inside his own circle with his arms open, a crackle of blue lightning gathering between his palms. It formed a sphere that he carefully placed on top of the coin we were layering all the enchantments into. With a rush of energy and a gentle pop, the lightning vanished into the metal. He exhaled, then looked over his shoulder at me with a *did you see that?* grin.

I grinned back. I saw it. I saw him. All of him—inside and out, serious and goofy, real and fake. I couldn't wait to keep seeing more when this was over. My panic didn't go away, but it drained a little, enough that I could breathe instead of drowning.

"Let's go, Presto," I told him.

"Anything for you, m'lady!" He practically bounced over to my area, rubbing his hands together to discharge the last of his spell's energies.

"Behold." I gestured at my work. He walked around it, checking symbols and mirrors and prisms and pieces of hematite. I waited nervously for him to approve or adjust it.

He gave me two thumbs up. "Want me to measure just in case?"

"Measure twice, cast once." I knew he'd do it anyway, but he had to himbo.

"As you wish." He spent a few minutes crab-walking or on his hands and knees. I tried to check out his butt; unfortunately it was hidden under his shirt, and his pants were too baggy. Well, I'd grab it later.

I remembered Quentin telling me Leandro was checking out my butt almost two weeks ago. How the turntables had, uh, turned.

"Looks good to me," Gil said finally. "Last chance to go with the original plan."

The urge to barf came back and all my veins filled with burning ice, but I shook my head. "In it to win it. Anyway, we have luck on our side." I showed him the queen of hearts card I kept tucked in my apron pocket.

"Your Majesty," he said, bowing. "We won't fail you." Gently, he pulled the card closer and kissed it, looking up at me as he did. I felt that promise all the way to my bones.

He handed me the coin and took the athame I'd sterilized. With one last surge of nerves, we stepped inside the circle's outer ring.

I put the coin in its spot at the center of the circle, then backed up and slipped my hand into Gil's. It took me longer than usual to center myself; years of panic attacks from fires and any associations with pressure-cooking weren't going to magically disappear. But Gil squeezed my hand, and I listened to his breaths, matched mine with his, inhaling and exhaling in a steady rhythm until I was calm enough to keep going.

We started to chant, a simple couplet: "As I will it, so shall you be. Take your shape from my memory." Magical energy rose, hovering around us like a heat shimmer. After nine repetitions, I held out my hand, and Gil carefully nicked the tip of my ring finger—connected to my heart line. Together we knelt down, and I squeezed a drop of my blood onto the coin.

Light blazed through the lines of the circle, starting at the center and moving outward until all my painted lines and symbols glowed as brightly as fluorescent lights. As we stood, the light reached the hematite array, then the prisms, then finally the mirrors. So much energy filled the space, it was like standing in a sauna with a wet blanket dropped onto my head. Heat, pressure, but also a feeling almost like being drunk, lightheaded and spinning and ready to dance until my feet were dirty.

I closed my eyes and pictured my abuela. It was embarrassing how difficult it was, how long it had been since I'd seen her—I didn't want to, didn't want to remember her sitting near-comatose in a recliner with a blanket up to her chin, staring at nothing. Instead, I thought back to my childhood, before the fire and the burns, before old age swallowed her like quicksand. I imagined her dancing in the kitchen, a spoon in her hand, salsa playing on the radio. Her eyes closed, shoulders bobbing, hips swaying, feet shuffling. The high-waisted pants that had gone out of style years earlier, the short-sleeved button-down shirt covered in a tiny floral print. Her short brown hair pushed back from her pale face by an elastic hair band.

More than that, I remembered how she felt, who she was. Strong and capable, smart and funny, patient and cheerful, even when things went wrong. The heart of the house, the one who cleaned my scrapes and pulled out my splinters and hugged away my tears. The one who insisted I could do and be anything I wanted if I believed hard enough.

Today, I believed as hard as I could.

The coin glowed, brighter than the rest of the circle, so bright I could see its shape through my closed eyelids. The smell of anise and cumin filled my nose, so strong I could taste it. After I don't know how many heartbeats, all the energy inside the circle swirled toward the center like a whirlpool. A heavy wind scraped across my skin, pulling on my clothes. If my hair had been loose, it would be blowing sideways. Gil held my hand, grounded me, kept my fears from letting the magic get out of control. The spell would be fine as long as we stayed strong and anchored in our focus and intention.

We would. We could do anything together.

My ears popped as the last of the energy was sucked into the coin. For a few seconds, I couldn't breathe, like all the air in the circle was gone, too. I opened one eye, then the other, blinking away the afterimages of all the bright lights.

"Presto," Gil whispered.

I laughed. My body shook and my legs turned to jelly, adrenaline crash mixing with magic energy drain. Down I went, sitting on the floor. Gil went with me, still holding my hand. I don't know how long we stayed there, leaning against each other, wrung out like wet towels.

"Is your butt starting to hurt?" Gil asked.

"Little bit," I said.

"We should probably get up, then."

"Probably."

We didn't get up. I looked at the countdown timer and groaned. Gil helped me stand.

"Time to finish the rest of this spell and win," I said.

We high-fived and got back to work.

THE JUDGES, INCLUDING Doris, took up their usual positions as Syd gave their speech about it being the final round, celebration theme, amazing espectaculo and so on. Jokes were involved; I laughed on cue. We were all doing a great job pretending the whole sabotage thing hadn't happened, that this was all normal show stuff. I'd stuck on my customer service smile, Gil was full Leandro himbo face, and Team Ice Queen looked all sophisticated and untouchable.

It was nearly midnight. Gil and I had chugged double espressos to keep from yawning nonstop, even though we were also both wired from nerves. Fina and Bruno had retouched our hair and makeup. I couldn't smell myself, but I doubted it was pretty. I heroically did not sniff my armpits to find out.

The coin flip decided we were presenting first. Part of me was happy to get it out of the way; part of me wished I could see Felicia and Charlotte's spell before ours so I could manage my expectations. The rest of me wanted to run laps around the block screaming until I passed out.

Gil rubbed his thumb along the side of my hand. I was squeezing him tight enough to make my fingers numb, so I relaxed my grip.

"Penelope and Leandro," Syd said, "please demonstrate your spell for the judges."

Showtime.

Gil carried the top hat, while I carried the coin. The top hat went on a small table, open side up; the coin burned a hole in my hand, figuratively speaking.

"Tell us about your spell," Syd said.

"We call it 'Making Magic Together,'" I said. "It honors the charity Leandro is competing for, and my abuela, my grandmother."

Syd waved their hand. "Amaze us."

I patted the queen of hearts card in my pocket for one last bit of luck, kissed the coin, then dropped it into the hat and stepped back outside the containment circle. Gil immediately grabbed my hand again and we leaned on each other, holding our breaths.

Mist poured out of the hat, giving the area a cool, mystical vibe. Sparkles twinkled like sequins catching the light, except there was no light—until there was. A single bright spotlight shone on the hat, which seemed to float in all the fog.

A pair of white gloves rose out of the hat and spread out like the hands of an invisible magician. They picked up the hat and showed there was nothing inside, then reached in and pulled out a ghostly white rabbit. The cutie hopped around the table a few times before suddenly hopping in two different directions simultaneously, splitting into two rabbits. This repeated until two dozen bunnies leaped off the table in waves and bounced around in the mist.

The gloves once again showed the hat was empty. This time, they pulled out a white dove, which cooed quietly. It took off flying and flapped around, then started dividing like the rabbits, until a dozen doves hovered and made lazy circles above the fog.

Now the gloves made a bouquet of flowers appear from nowhere. They tossed the bouquet onto the floor in front of the table, and the flowers spread into a lush green carpet covered in wildflower blooms in varying shapes and colors. The rabbits started to nibble at the flowers . . . which burst into a flock of butterflies that drifted around as a bright, fluttering cloud before landing on different flowers, their wings opening and closing gently.

Now the gloves began to arc a deck of cards back and forth between them. After a few impressive shuffling cuts and passes, the gloves spread the cards across the table in front of the hat, face down, then flipped them all over in a fluid motion without touching them.

The various heart cards slid forward and floated into the air, then one by one they drifted across the area, dropping pearly pink hearts like snowflakes. The diamonds emerged next, and those shot up and burst into fireworks. Strands of shimmering color rained down on the doves, staining their white feathers, then the rabbits' fur. The rest of the cards reformed into a single stack, then arced across the flowery field as a rainbow disappearing into the mist at both ends. The animals scampered and flew into the rainbow and vanished, leaving the landscape empty.

I swallowed nervously. Now we'd find out whether the pressure-cooked portion worked. What if it didn't? What if I'd failed again?

As if sensing my tension, Gil leaned closer and whispered, on the quietest breath, "Believe."

Faint strains of music echoed throughout the room, some song pulled from the closet of my mind. A spiral of mist rose from the floor and formed into a ghostly figure. My abuela, just as I remembered her. She danced through the flowers, one arm across her stomach, the other bent with her hand raised. Her eyes were closed, and she smiled like she knew the secrets of the universe.

The gloves reached for my abuela's hand, spun her around once, then helped her climb misty steps to the top of the table. She put a foot inside the top hat and began to shrink and dissipate into mist, like a genie going back into its bottle.

I didn't even realize I was crying until Gil's hand brushed tears off my cheek.

With a flourish, the gloves threw the hat toward the flowers and grass and rainbow, where it landed opening-up on the floor. Everything turned misty, dissolving and drifting into the air like bubbles in champagne, only colorful and glittering and glowing faintly. The fog slowly disappeared into the hat like my abuela had, until the only things left were the gloves, the hat, and the spotlight.

The gloves picked up the hat, then swept it forward as if an invisible magician had bowed. It angled up as if being placed on the magician's head at a jaunty angle. The gloves and hat spun in a quick clockwise circle, and in a burst of sparks, vanished into thin air. The spotlight remained for another moment, then went dark, turned off by some unseen, ghostly stagehand.

Total silence. I swallowed, hoping my hearing hadn't been affected by the magic.

"Does this complete your spell?" Syd asked finally.

"Yes," I croaked. We'd done it. Everything had worked, exactly as we'd intended.

"Presto!" Gil said. He grabbed both my hands and pulled me into our dance, his eyes serious even though his mouth was laughing.

I laughed, too. This was nothing like our first dances, awkward and fake when we were still stumbling and figuring each other out. It wasn't like the one when we nailed our bracelet spell, after I'd found out who Gil was and everything had seemed to finally click. Now, all our layers were peeled back, all our secrets and fears exposed, all our hopes shared, our future waiting for us no matter what happened now. It felt like another promise, and I promised, too, spinning in his arms and exploding away from him at the end, then coming back for a hug that was probably inappropriate.

I didn't care. I loved him, and he loved me, and in that moment, our love was more important than the show or winning.

The judges started their questions about our intentions and methods. Hugh's eyebrows went all the way up when he heard we'd pressure-cooked the part with my abuela at the last minute; I wasn't sure whether he was impressed or just shocked. As late as it was, they didn't cut any of it short, though Doris was quieter than usual. I wondered if she'd been told to back off to try to make things seem fair.

Finally they finished and went to the corner to talk. Gil wrapped his arm around my shoulder. I snuggled against his side. We waited. We were way past chihuahuas for nervousness comparisons. We'd gone out the other side of nervous and into calm.

A million years or probably like ten minutes later, the judges came back.

"This was a nice homage to a vaudevillian-style magic show," Fabienne said. "Certainly the kind of celebratory spectacle we were hoping for, with a number of different casting skills represented. I would have liked a more cohesive sense of a narrative rather than simply movement from one element to the next."

Not totally nice, but not too bad?

Doris sounded like she was reciting something she'd been told to say. "A lovely performative spell. I especially enjoyed the portion at the end where you incorporated your memories of your grandmother as the magician's assistant, Penelope. Well done."

Yeah, I'll bet she liked seeing an old woman being happy when she was such a miserable prune. I wondered if she would go to jail after all this.

If Hugh's eyes could shoot lasers, Gil and I would both be little piles of ash the way he was staring at us. Finally he said, "It was certainly representative of both your aesthetics and backgrounds, and incorporated some fine technical work, including a risky method that paid off. But I agree that overall it wanted a better flow between components, and a more cogent incorporation of your pressure-cooked portion into the whole."

Gil and I thanked them all. He retrieved the hat and we went back to our station. I felt deflated as an old balloon, or maybe like our piñatas after they'd exploded.

Now we had to see how our work compared to Felicia and Charlotte's. Would we win because the other team once again suffered a failure? Possibly, given Felicia's fight with Charlotte over the reagents. But I'd told her how to fix it, and if that worked, it would be all about whether they'd done a better job than us.

Their spell container was a crystal lattice arrangement that suggested some kind of fractal emanation. Charlotte explained that it was going to produce a winter wonderland, blah blah blah—guess the ice queens decided to go all the way with their vibe.

As soon as the spell started, I knew we were going to lose.

It was everything ours wasn't. Beautiful, graceful, an expanding piece of magic that started with a perfectly rendered snowfall. Ice trees and flowers sprouted from the snow-blanketed ground; icicles dripped down to hang from glistening branches, tinkling in a chilly breeze. The tinkling became sleigh bells, and then a tiny sleigh pulled by bunnies drove through, a pair of blue fairies inside. There was a whole fairy dance, with ice-skating and snowflake crafting and so many other things I could barely keep track of. Everything felt choreographed, fluid, one thing leading to the next, and when it all finally disappeared back into the lattice, all I could do was marvel at how far I had to go if I ever wanted to truly compete at this level.

Maybe I was wrong. Maybe I was overreacting. The judges' comments on our spell were fresh in my brain, and it seemed like none of them applied to Felicia and Charlotte's spell. Gil had my shoulder in a tight grip, and I was holding on to his waist like I'd fall over if I didn't. I probably would; it was late, and I was totally wiped.

Fabienne balanced praise and criticism. Doris loved their spell. Hugh . . . also balanced praise and criticism, surprising me. He thought it was "somewhat derivative and emotionally cold."

Little Manny brought us snacks to keep us alive through the last part of filming. He whispered that Isaac had already left, because I guess he had more important things to do than his job. Just like Ofelia used to, and wow, it still felt strange for that chapter of my life to be over.

This one would be, too, any minute now.

As if I'd summoned them with that thought, the judges finished their point arguing and let Rachel know they were ready to film. Tori started calling out orders, still calm. Liam rechecked our mics and Nate gave us a double thumbs-up.

This was it.

I squeezed Gil hard enough for his bones to creak.

Syd rocked back and forth on their feet, grinning. "I haven't been this excited for a finale since I got obsessed with that K-drama *The King's Personal Guard*. Have you seen it?"

I shook my head, and so did Gil. Charlotte glared at them instead of responding. To my immense shock, Felicia said, "It was good, but *Petals on a Cold Wind* had a better ending."

"That one was a slow burn to a bonfire, wasn't it?" Syd agreed. They bantered about their favorites as Gil and I traded looks.

"Who knew she had a heart at all?" Gil whispered.

"Only for K-drama, apparently," I replied.

Tori waved a pen at us. "Places, people. Penelope, Leandro, let's take the hugging down a notch. Give me confident, apprehensive, smiling, whatever feels right."

Hugging Gil felt right, but I settled for hand-holding. We could hug later.

Syd sipped some lemon water, shook themself like a wet dog, then stared into the camera. The slate clacked.

"Our judges," Syd said, "have cast their final judgment of this competition on our remaining teams. Felicia and Charlotte, Penelope and Leandro, it's been amazing to have you all here with us and to see your fabulous spells. No matter what happens now, I know you all have spectacular magical futures ahead of you."

I smiled. I had job and apartment hunting ahead of me, but maybe with Gil helping, it wouldn't be so bad.

"This was a difficult decision for the judges."

Was it, though?

"They considered the teams' performances not only in this round, but in all the prior rounds as well."

Ouch. We'd barely managed to keep from being cut in every other round, it felt like, and probably would have lost sooner if not for the sabotage. The points couldn't possibly even out for us.

Well, at least our piñatas were awesome.

"Without further ado, the winner of our Spellebrity edition of *Cast Judgment* is . . ." Syd paused, making eye contact with all of us individually. I had a death grip on Gil's hand. My lungs stopped working. Could someone die from suspense? Literally? I would be the first if Syd didn't—

"Felicia and Charlotte! Congratulations, ladies."

Apparently I did still have air in my lungs, because it all left in a big whoosh. I'd known we probably wouldn't win, but I guess I'd still had some tiny hope that maybe . . . But no. It was over. The judges clustered around the winners, shaking hands and smiling. They couldn't hear my dreams crashing to the floor.

Gil pulled me into a hug, and we stood there for I don't know how long. Tori would probably make us do something in a minute, join the celebratory cluster or whatever, but until that happened, I enjoyed how safe and comforting it felt to be held.

And then Gil said, "I know your abuela would be so proud of you right now."

You know what? She would. She really, really would. She would have been proud of me just for being on the show in the first place. She would have called everyone whose number she kept in her little phone book, pages of handwritten names, to gossip about me. She would have told the neighbors, the people in her knitting club, the checkout person at the grocery store. She would have bragged anytime she could find a way to insert it into a conversation.

But honestly, she had been proud that I worked as a spell technician. She'd been proud that I studied magical theory in college. Even when I'd burned down her fucking kitchen, she'd been proud that I had tried to do something difficult. How had I memory-holed all of that? How had I gotten so sucked into feeling like a failure that I'd ignored everything I'd ever done right?

"Your grandfather must be so proud of you, too," I told him.

Gil grinned. "He is, actually. And . . ." He leaned in to whisper in my ear. "He can't wait to meet you."

My face went up in flames. He'd already talked to his grandfather about me? Before I could ask, Syd came up to us, smiling in that slightly embarrassed way that said they knew this was awkward for us.

"Penelope and Leandro, you were amazing," Syd said gently, laying a hand on my shoulder.

"Yeah," I said. "We were. We are."

"We will be," Gil said.

"Presto," I agreed.

We'd won each other, I thought as I hugged him. That was all the magic we needed.

CHAPTER 25

Penelope

I checked that my pigtails were even, slipped on my safety glasses and pointy black hat, then left the bathroom and walked down the hallway. A frazzled-looking teacher passed me going the other way, holding the hand of a kindergartner doing the universally recognizable potty dance. I'd wait a few extra minutes to start so they had time to get back.

As soon as I stepped into the lecture room, a dozen excited kids mobbed me with questions.

"What spell are we doing, miss?"

"Can I be your helper, miss?"

"Miss, do you know what my favorite animal is? It's a koala!"

I smiled and listened and hugged and finally made my way to the table where my reagents waited. Tyler, event coordinator extraordinaire, waved at me from the corner as he chatted with one of the field trip chaperones. I gave him a thumbs-up so he'd know I was ready to start, and he politely disentangled himself from his convo to join me.

"Welcome to the Desgraves Studio, everyone!" Tyler said, waiting for the noise level to drop as teachers hushed the kids and made them sit down. "We're so excited to have you with us for a special spell presentation from our resident witch, the Fantastic Frances!"

He clapped, the others joined in, and I curtseyed in the way I'd practiced that made my poofy sequined skirt do a sparkly ripple effect.

"Are you all ready to cast some magic spells?" I asked, opening my arms to the sides.

"Yeah!" the kids shouted back.

I'd done the bubble spell from the Alan Kazam kit enough times now that I had the steps memorized, but I still wrote them on the board—as drawings in this case, since reading was still a developing skill for five- and six-year-olds. I'd found that it helped them during the parts when I pretended to get mixed up; it was easier for them to correct me by pointing at the picture.

Even though Gil and I lost, our time on *Cast Judgment* weirdly ended up helping me out in the way I hoped: I'd gotten a job. Fabienne Desgraves hired me to work in her stockroom, doing more or less exactly what I'd done at Espinosa's. All the stars lined up perfectly; the show had done all the background check stuff, I already lived in Miami, I had years of experience, and she'd apparently caught me helping the other contestants—including Felicia—which impressed her. She'd also decided she liked what she called "the Title I angle," which she hadn't pursued before; now Tyler was bringing in more school field trips for spell demonstrations using the Alan Kazam Schools Are Magic lessons, starring me or Leandro Presto, or both of us together. Gil and I sometimes did birthday parties and other events at the studio, too.

I hadn't had so much fun in years. Past Penelope with all her sad donkey moping was long gone, and she could stay that way. Not that I had stopped being careful, obviously, but I could be careful and fun at the same time.

I also got to work on my abuela's spellbook, finally. Fabienne let me use the casting rooms at the studio whenever they weren't already booked. I'd gotten through only a few spells so far, but it was more than I'd managed to do in the years I'd worked at Espinosa's, so it was already a win.

"Hmm," I said, looking around the room. "Does anyone know where I put my magic bubble wand?"

"Your hat!" the kids screamed.

"My what? Where?"

"Your HAT!"

I made a show of taking off my hat and looking at it. "Are you sure? I don't see it."

"It's inside!"

My eyes big, I started digging around in the hat. I pulled out a dozen colorful silk handkerchiefs knotted together, a toy bunny, a whoopie cushion—they loved the fart noises—and then finally my star-shaped bubble wand.

"You were right!" I exclaimed. "Thank you so much. I would never have found it without you."

After I finished dispelling the last of the bubble animals and took a bow, I stayed to talk to the kids and adults. I did a few more little spells to entertain them, then said my goodbyes with the Alan Kazam signature line, "Trust the magic, and the magic will trust you," and went back to the bathroom to change. My outfit today was a little dressier than usual, and Tyler winked at me when I got back out.

"Date night?" he asked.

"You know it," I said.

"Where's Loverdork taking you this time?"

"It's a surprise."

I loved when Gil surprised me. Last week we went to an author Q&A for a book we'd read together; the week before that was a movie night at the library, and before that it was a free belly dancing class. Once we'd even gone to a sidewalk chalk magic party with Rosy and Sam and Ed, and spent two hours casting silly spells and drawing random stuff and smearing chalk all over each other while laughing our asses off.

Life was so good, I couldn't believe it sometimes.

Gil was picking me up today, but normally after work I'd go home. My new apartment was close to his—a studio instead of an efficiency, with an actual wall to separate the living room and kitchen from my bedroom. I'd had to borrow money from my sister to afford the down payment, but I was paying her back. Slowly. Totally worth it to have privacy for when we wanted some screaming-each-other's-names time, as Rosy called it, though we were still quiet because I didn't want my neighbors to hate me.

He had a key to my place, and a toothbrush there, and some spare clothes. When his lease was up, we were thinking maybe, possibly, he'd move in until we could upgrade to something bigger . . . but that was months away, and a lot could change.

For one thing, we were both stuck in the middle of arbitration with the *Cast Judgment* people. They'd ended up canceling the season, possibly even the show, and totally buried the whole federal-crime thing somehow—must be nice to have expensive corporate lawyers—but they couldn't get away with doing literally nothing for us when the whole competition had gone to shit. They owed us big fat checks, for sure. Like, so big.

And it wasn't just us, it was the charities they'd promised money and publicity to. Doris might have sabotaged spells in every round because she was salty about getting fired, and Charlotte might have been the one to pay her for it, but proving any of that was hard. Gil and I had the best case of anyone thanks to the bribe check and freezer charm, plus Gil's dad was a total shark of a lawyer, telling us what to do and say at every step.

Yeah, I'd met his parents, though he hadn't met mine yet. His dad was a typical macho Cuban guy, living in a ridiculously expensive condo in Coral Gables with his latest novela-hot girlfriend. His mom was a total drama queen; she offered me a glass of wine as soon as I walked in and then drank half a bottle before dinner was ready, complaining about random stuff the whole time.

I understood why he avoided them, and he understood why I barely talked to mine. Some scars kept hurting long after they'd healed.

His grandpa Fred was great, though. Alan Kazam! So cool. He loved to talk about magic stuff as much as Gil did, plus he was full of awesome stories.

My phone buzzed. Gil, texting that he was outside. I grabbed my purse and ran out, waving goodbye to Tati in the gift shop. She pointed at my dress and gave me two thumbs up as I passed.

Still hot, still sunny, typical Miami at six o'clock. Gil parked on the side street a little ways up, next to someone's driveway. He saw me coming and got out, and if I hadn't been wearing heels, I probably would have run so I could hug him faster. He was wearing a dark red button-down shirt with the sleeves rolled up, and black pants, and he'd combed his hair but left it in messy curls, just how I liked it.

He pulled me in for a kiss, his hands around my waist while mine reached up to his neck. Mmm. Kissing him was like reading my favorite book and watching my favorite movie and casting my favorite spell all rolled into one. Magic, every time.

"We match," he murmured against my mouth.

We didn't always, and that was okay. It was nice when it happened, though, and it did happen a lot. Today I was wearing a black dress with dark red lace over the top. Perfect.

"So where are we going?" I asked.

He put his finger against his lips and grinned. "Let's go and you'll find out."

We went. Rush-hour traffic sucked, but it wasn't so bad when you had someone awesome to talk to and weren't stressed about getting somewhere on time. I told him about my day, he told me about his—college students were way less adorable than kindergartners, but such was the life of an adjunct. He'd gotten hired back for the semester, though the pay was a giant fart noise. Between that and his *Mage You Look* money, two unstable jobs made one decent living.

We talked about his next spell request, mango-flavored snow, and how to make it go wrong without ending up with a huge sticky mess. I hadn't known it before, but he also recorded how-to videos that used to only be released to certain subscribers; after the competition comemierdería, he talked it over with his friends, who had wanted to stop doing them. Now they got released along with the oopsie-doodle version, which had the surprise side effect of bringing in new subscribers happy to see a more serious side of Leandro Presto. Who knew anyone wanted that?

Besides me, I guess. But I'd liked his serious side first.

"Are we going to the beach?" I asked when he got into the lane for the exit.

"Maybe," he said, grinning.

We parked at a garage on Collins and started walking. I wished I'd worn better shoes, but such was the price of fashion. After a few blocks, Gil stopped in front of a neon-signed building that looked vaguely familiar. Oh!

"Is this the bar we went to the first night of the show?" I asked.

"It is. I got the deets from Little Manny. Come on."

The place was full of people tonight, but otherwise it was how I remembered. Same huge mirrored wall of booze, same big stage surrounded by lights, where someone was setting up for a show. Gil kept one arm around my waist as he led me through the crowd to the bar and got us both drinks. I sipped my mudslide and snuggled up on him, mellow and happy and wondering what else he had planned.

"Oh, selfie," I said, pulling my phone out.

We held up our drinks and made duck faces, then took a nice smiling one. I posted both to the private Jive server we'd made for us and the other contestants from the show—except Felicia, who'd ignored the invite. Quentin almost immediately reacted with a heart-eyes emoji and asked, "Where are you? What are you drinking?" I told him, he awwed, and I put my phone away to focus on cuddling.

Since our season didn't air, none of us had gotten any of that magical exposure we'd been promised as a perk of the show, but we'd done okay. I got a dream job, obviously. Amy had almost finished recording a solo album of piano songs she hoped she could license for commercials and stuff, plus one of her recipes would be appearing in a spellbook Jaya was releasing at the end of the year. Quentin had started a side hustle making cute magical automatons, and was quietly working with Tanner to sell them through the Spell Rehab store in Chicago and online. Zeke was mentoring

Dylan through the process of setting up his own magical baking business, though he had to start smaller than he would have if he'd gotten the prize money. Felicia, according to some light internet detective work, was still designing stuff and selling houses, but she had gotten engaged to her personal assistant, who I assumed loves sarcasm and K-dramas and being stepped on by statuesque blondes.

Our dreams hadn't died, they'd just changed. Así es la vida, as my abuela always said.

Since I hadn't eaten, I got tipsy fast, which made the show even better. We were seeing an illusionist-singer who called herself Belle Nocturne—nobody famous, but hey, that was Miami. Full of talented people trying to catch a break.

She was really good. Started slow: changing her own appearance, creating mirror images of herself mimicking her movements, then dancing independently and even singing backup. By a few songs in, the entire stage was changing as she sang, and even parts of the room, becoming dark bedrooms and neon-bright city streets, moonlit castle ruins and caves filled with gemstones and luminescent moss, complete with sounds and smells and the feel of each place on our skin. Gil held me the whole time, sometimes swaying with me, sometimes resting his chin on my shoulder. Finally she sang a capella standing on an ocean of stars with the Milky Way overhead, and it was so beautiful I had tears coming down my face when she finished.

I fished some tissues out of my purse and blotted the mess, hoping my mascara hadn't run. "Wow, that was great."

"Right?" Gil said. "Can't see the illusions on video, but I heard a song of hers online and thought you'd like it."

"I did. Thank you. Super great surprise." I couldn't wait to tell the people at work.

Gil nuzzled my ear and ran his hand up and down my hip. "So, I was planning to take you to this gyro place Ed recommended, or . . ."

"Or?"

"We could go home early, order a pizza, and get to dessert faster."

I grinned at him. "Sir, are you offering me a pocket banana? Perhaps attempting to put out a vibe?"

"I certainly am. Are you picking it up?"

Instead of answering, I turned around in his arms and kissed him. He gave a cute little growl and grabbed my butt, pulling me indecently close.

"I'll get the tab," he said.

We made out in the car long enough to get both of us extremely ready for dessert. Traffic leaving the beach wasn't as bad, but I still had to get my car from the studio. By the time we made it to my apartment, I was nearly feral and coming up with ideas for rapid clothing removal spells.

I parked in my assigned spot while Gil circled the lot, looking for an empty space. Maybe I could be waiting for him naked on the couch? He'd given me a fun surprise, so it was only fair. I jogged up the stairs to the second floor as fast as high heels would let me, power walked toward my front door, and . . . stopped when I realized someone was sitting cross-legged on my "Casa del Carajo" doormat.

It was Emelia. I hadn't seen my sister in over a year because we lived in different states and were both so busy working, even though we texted almost every day. Her brown hair was straighter than mine, her eyes closer to hazel, her skin a shade lighter like our mom's, but anyone who saw us together would know we were related. Especially when we started talking.

Right now, she looked like shit. Her hair was greasy, the bags under her eyes were industrial-sized, and her clothes were wrinkled like she'd slept in them. Two huge suitcases leaned against the wall next to the door.

"Eme?" I said. "Oh my god, what happened?"

Emelia smiled up at me. "Not much. I lost my job and broke up with my boyfriend. Can I sleep in your bathtub?"

Acknowledgments

A writer may do the work of putting actual words on pages, but the process of writing a book is so much more than that. My humble and heartfelt thanks to:

Eric, my husband, for all the cups of coffee and dinners and loads of laundry that enable me to engage in my Thoreau-like existence in our house in the woods. I love you with or without the mustache. Anyway, here's Wonderwall.

My agent, Quressa Robinson, for her patience and hustle and ability to pivot when I do.

My editor, Madelyn Blaney, for helping me make this book the best version of itself with her insightful guidance, and Tessa Woodward for suggesting that we try my secondary world fantasy novel as contemporary instead. It worked!

My mother, Nayra, for care packages and cat memes and weather reports, and my sister, Laura, for correct opinions and snappy comebacks and funny gifs.

Jay, for being the spark that lit this fire, and for being with me from the first draft with its masks and intrigues, to this one with its different masks and intrigues. What a love square this turned out to be, cat puns and all. And I finally climbed Space Smut Mountain! Please clap.

Matthew, Rick, and Amalia, for helping me stay closer to fine, even when this is not normal.

Clint, Clarissa, Tina Marie, Chelle, Drew, Edward, Nicole, Adam, Joe, and all the other folks who hang out with me when the kids are (not) asleep, thanks for the writer rants and nostalgia dives and general support. Don't encourage the banana, or we'll end up in Pun Hell!

Mur, my coeditor in fictional crimes, for all the commiserations and for making me ride that pig.

My Isle of Write friends, for continuing to celebrate secret yays and corralling brain weasels when needed.

My Strange Friends, for all the adventures in our shared imaginary worlds as well as this real one.

My various virtual writing communities, for the coworking and conversations that help me keep my butt in my chair and get the writing done.

My dad and stepmom and siblings and stepsiblings on the left coast, for the encouragement and for always believing my work would make amazing movies or TV shows. Some day!

My family-in-law and extended families, for all the continuous love and support.

My many other colleagues and friends and family, near and far, for being a rising tide lifting all boats instead of crabs in a bucket.

And as always, my readers, past, present, and future. Thank you for allowing me to keep making these fantastic worlds for my characters to play in. Trust the magic, and the magic will trust you!

About the Author

LIA AMADOR is a Miami flower transplanted in Georgia with her husband and kids. When she isn't writing kissing books, she's typically juggling too many other duties as assigned. She also writes science fiction and fantasy stories as Valerie Valdes. Find her online at liaamador.com and valerievaldes.com.